POINT

OF

BALANCE

POINT

OF

BALANCE

A THRILLER

J.G. JURADO

Translated by Martin Michael Roberts

ATRIA BOOKS

New York   London   Toronto   Sydney   New Delhi

ATRIA BOOKS

An Imprint of Simon & Schuster, Inc.
1230 Avenue of the Americas
New York, NY 10020

First Atria Books hardcover edition August 2015
Originally published in Spain in 2014 by Editorial Planeta

ATRIA B O O K S and colophon are trademarks of Simon & Schuster, Inc.

For information about special discounts for bulk purchases, please contact Simon & Schuster Special Sales at 1-866-506-1949 or business@simonandschuster.com.

The Simon & Schuster Speakers Bureau can bring authors to your live event. For more information or to book an event, contact the Simon & Schuster Speakers Bureau at 1-866-248-3049 or visit our website at www.simonspeakers.com.

Interior design by Kyoko Watanabe

Manufactured in the United States of America

10 9 8 7 6 5 4 3 2 1

Library of Congress CiP data is available.

ISBN 978-1-4767-6698-0
ISBN 978-1-4767-6700-0 (ebook)

For Andrea and Javier

POINT
OF
BALANCE

Dr. Evans's Diary

You all think you know me. You're wrong.

You've all seen my face countless times. From when my driver's license photo first appeared on television, when the police began their manhunt, right up to the very moment the jury found me guilty, watched live by hundreds of millions of viewers. I'm a household name everywhere. The whole wide world has an opinion on what I did. I don't give a damn about condemnation or praise.

I have been on death row now for one thousand, eight hundred and twenty-three days, eleven hours and twelve minutes. I've spent almost every waking second of that time pondering the chain of events that brought me here. I would not do a single thing differently.

Except maybe for what I said to Kate.

I am no saint, no martyr, no terrorist, no madman and no murderer. The names you think you may call me are all wrong.

I am a father. That's my story.

63 HOURS BEFORE THE OPERATION

1

It all began with Jamaal Carter. If I hadn't saved him, things might have been very different.

When the pager beeped I rubbed my eyes in anger. It had roused me and I had woken up in a foul mood. Of course, the surroundings didn't help. The surgeons' on-call room on the second floor reeked of sweat, feet and sex. Residents are always hornier than a two-peckered billy goat. I wouldn't be at all surprised if a couple of them had been banging away in the top bunk while I snored.

I am a sound sleeper. Rachel always used to tease me and say it would take a crane to get me up. That simply doesn't apply to the pager: the damned gizmo always succeeds in waking me up on the second beep.

That comes of being a resident for seven years. If you didn't answer the pager the first time, the chief resident would tear you a new one. And if you couldn't find a window in which to grab a bit of shut-eye during the thirty-six hours you were on call, then you didn't last the distance, either. So we surgeons got into the knack of instantly falling asleep while we nurtured a Pavlovian response to the sound of a pager. I had been a staff doctor for four years now and my turns of duty had since been halved, but the conditioning remained.

I grappled under my pillow until I found the gadget. The number

342 flashed up on the LED screen, the Neurosurgery extension. I checked my watch and got really pissed. There were just twenty-three minutes left until the end of my shift, and the morning had been hectic, owing to a traffic accident that began in Dupont Circle and ended up on the operating table. I had spent three hours piecing back together a British cultural attaché's skull. The guy hadn't even been here two days and had found out the hard way that you exit a stateside roundabout the other way around, compared to London.

The nurses knew I was taking a nap, so if someone had paged me it had to be serious. I called 342, but it was busy, so I decided to hurry over and see what was the matter. I splashed some water on my face at the sink in the back but left the light off. Lately I had avoided mirrors like the plague.

I went out into the corridor. It was twenty to six and the sun was already setting behind the treetops in Rock Creek Park. The light shone through giant panes of glass, creating orangey oblongs across the floor. The year before I would have enjoyed the view, even as I ran to the elevator. But now I didn't look up from the floor. The man I had turned into did not admire the scenery.

In the elevator I almost bumped into Jerry Gonzales, a male nurse on my team who was wheeling a gurney. I cracked a shy smile and greeted him with a nod. He was a stocky guy and had to move over to let me in. If there's one thing two straight men hate, it's bumping into each other in an elevator, especially when they haven't showered for many an hour, which we hadn't.

"Hey, Doc Evans, thanks for the book you lent me the other day. I have it in my locker. I'll give it right back to you."

"That's okay, Jerry, you can keep it," I said with a dismissive wave of my hand. "I don't read much anymore."

There was an awkward silence. Time was, we would have busted each other's chops or swapped wisecracks. But that was before.

I could almost hear him bite back the words on the tip of his tongue. Good. I can't stand sympathy.

"You got that gangbanger?" he said at last.

"That why they paged me?"

"They had a shootout down at Barry Farm. It's been on the news for hours," he said, pointing to his ear, which always had an earphone stuck in it. "Seven dead and a bunch of wounded. A turf war."

"So why didn't they take them to MedStar?"

Jerry shrugged his shoulders and stepped out of my way.

I came out of the elevator on the fourth floor, for the neurosurgery unit. St. Clement's is a small, private and extremely expensive hospital. Even most people who live in Washington have never heard of it. Nestling on the south side of Rock Creek Park, near the Taft Bridge, it's a very swanky place. Its client base lives in Kalorama, mainly foreigners and senior embassy officials—people with no health insurance whose governments grudgingly pony up for the humongous bills. The area is not at all accessible and you likely won't have come across St. Clement's, either, on your way through the neighborhood. You don't find that massive Victorian redbrick building unless you really want to.

To my dismay, the hospital's mission was not to support public service, either. The shareholders liked to keep costs low and revenues high. But fortunately, in common with all US hospitals, it was required by law to treat any emergency case that landed on its doorstep. This is how I crossed paths with Jamaal Carter.

He was in the middle of the corridor, outside the nurses' station. A police officer and two paramedics were standing by, their uniforms dripping with blood. His bodily fluids had daubed dark, ominous stains on the reflective patches. The paramedics were shaken and spoke in hushed tones. Considering what they had to cope with in their line of work, some very bad shit must have been going down.

One of the emergency interns hovered next to the gurney, with a suitably earnest look on her face. She must have been new; I didn't know her.

"Are you the neurosurgeon?" she asked when she saw me roll up.

"No, I'm the plumber, but they lent me this cute white coat so's my overalls don't get dirty."

She looked all flustered, so I winked to let her know it was a joke. She tittered nervously. It's always good to lighten up with the new kids. The residents usually treat them like some dog shit they've stepped in, so a scrap of humanity is manna from heaven.

She pointed to the kid on the gurney.

"His BP's one hundred over sixty, pulse rate's eighty-nine. He's stable, but there's a very nasty T-Five–level gunshot wound."

I leaned over him. The gangbanger lay facedown. He wore sagging pants and a blue Washington Wizards jacket. Somebody had cut it open with scissors to treat a light injury to his right arm, which was covered in tattoos. The other arm was handcuffed to the gurney.

Most of the jacket's back was missing. Right where the team's emblem should have been, someone had ripped out a wide expanse of cloth. In its place was an exit wound, which was seeping blood. The bullet had lodged against his spine, between the shoulder blades. His readings were stable, his life was not in danger, but the injury could well have damaged his nervous system.

The gangbanger groaned a little and I crouched to look at his face. He had delicate features and was doped up. I brushed his cheek to attract his attention.

"Dude, what's your name?"

I had to repeat the question several times before I could get him to answer me.

"Jamaal. Jamaal Carter."

"Hey, Jamaal, we can fix you up, but you need to work with me, okay? Can you wiggle your toes there for me?"

I took off his big-ticket Nike shoes, which would have been shiny white before the shootout but were now a dirty crimson. His toes would not move. I dug a pen tip into the middle of the sole of one of his feet.

"Can you feel that?"

He shook his head, very scared. If that kid had turned sixteen, then I was a monkey's uncle. Greenhorns in gangs were getting greener.

Jerk, jerk, jerk, I thought to myself.

"What's this kid doing here?" I yelled at the senior nurse, who had just put down the phone and walked out of the station to come my way. She was wringing her hands.

"They've rerouted him to us from George Washington. They're up to their necks and MedStar is, too. Dr.—"

"I don't mean that. I mean why the hell isn't he in surgery? We have to remove that bullet right now," I said, pushing the gurney.

She stood in front of me, blocking my way. I didn't bother trying to shove. It wasn't worth my while tussling with the senior nurse, above all one who outweighed me by sixty pounds. When she sat behind the counter, she gave the impression she was wearing it.

"I'm sorry to have paged you, Dr. Evans, but I've spoken to the medical director and she hasn't approved the operation."

"What are you talking about, Margo? Dr. Wong is at a congress in Alabama!"

"I called to see if there had been any developments since I paged you," she said with a guilty look, and shook her head. "When she heard about the gang . . . about the patient, she said he should be stabilized in keeping with the law. Now we're waiting for some public hospital to okay a referral so we can reroute him there."

I took a deep breath and ground my teeth. It was all very well for the medical director to rattle off orders from the seclusion of her suite in a five-star hotel. But out there in the real world was a kid who would be foisted onto an overburdened public hospital, where he'd be lucky to get treatment from an overworked resident and would face a high-risk operation with little chance of success. If they booted that kid out of St. Clement's, it was dollars to doughnuts he'd never walk again.

"Okay, Margo. I'll call Dr. Wong," I said as I reached for my cell phone. "You got anything to tell me?" I asked the paramedics while I waited for the call to go through.

"The slug ricocheted off a wall before it hit him; that's why he's still alive," one of them said, shaking his head. "If only it had gone a couple of inches to the right, we'd be talking about a graze here, but . . ."

But his hard luck is now our hard luck, I thought.

I raised a finger and drew away from the paramedics. My boss had picked up the call.

"Don't even think about it, Evans."

"How are the martinis going down, boss?"

"You are not to operate."

"Stephanie, he's just a kid and he needs help."

"Help which will cost ninety thousand bucks that no one can pay us back."

"Boss . . ."

"Evans, we're already way over our pro bono budget for the year—mainly because of you—and it's only October. I'm sorry, but the answer's no."

"He'll be paralyzed," was all I could find to say. As if she didn't know.

"He should have thought of that before he joined a gang."

Let nobody get on Medical Director Wong's case for those words. True, she's a heartless bitch, but she's also an outstanding surgeon. Her duty was to look out for the hospital's interests, which is precisely what she was doing. And as for her prejudices against gang-bangers, well, we doctors are like that.

We rationalize.

We make tough decisions based on the facts and the resources at our disposal. So there's just one kidney available? We give it to the youngest patient, even though he's a few places back on the waiting list. You smoke two packs a day despite those great big warning labels they come with? Well, don't expect us to shed any tears if you come to us with lung cancer. You drink like a fish? When you show us your cirrhosis, we'll probably crack jokes about pâté. Behind your back, of course.

Am I that way, too?

Good question, and one with no easy answer.

I'm not a fiend, I'm a human being the same as you. It so happens I spend so much time seeing bad things happen to good people for no reason that if something bad does happen to somebody for some apparent reason, then I put the blame on them. It's the human brain's instinct for self-preservation. I do my best and try not to take it personally. The Bible thumpers and politically correct will say that's inhumane, but believe me, that's how we provide the best possible service.

Now and again, however, a patient turns up who has a peculiar effect on you. They smell strongly of an aftershave that reminds you of your adoptive father, talk with a lilt, have a certain mannerism, or frightened little eyes, as Jamaal did.

And all those bulwarks you have striven to think of as indestructible are breached as easily as tissue paper. And you do what you never ought to.

You get involved.

"Stephanie, please . . . What do you want me to do?"

"I'll tell you what. You sit out the eleven minutes until your day is done and go straight home. Then someone else will have to deal with it."

There was something in her voice, something odd I didn't get the gist of. I squeezed the bridge of my nose hard, trying to get to the bottom of it.

Eleven minutes.

Then I saw what my boss had insinuated. As the top-ranking surgeon on site, for the next eleven minutes the legal liability for the boy's fate was mine. All mine.

"Dr. Wong, I have to run. The patient's condition has deteriorated. I fear for his life. I must operate to remove the bullet."

"I'm sorry to hear that, Evans," she said curtly as she hung up.

I barked a few terse commands and the paramedics leaped aside. The nurses whisked the patient into surgery. I still needed an anesthesiologist, but there wasn't a single one in that hospital who could say no to me.

Not after what happened to Rachel.

After I scrubbed up for the operation, I made one last call.

"Svetlana, we have a situation. I won't be home for dinner."

"Very good, Dr. Evans," she answered in her mechanical Slavic tones. "I'll put your daughter to bed. Do you want me to tell her?"

I had promised to read Julia a bedtime story that night. A promise I had broken more often than I cared to remember.

I sighed. "No, go get her."

I heard Svetlana call for my daughter, trying to make herself heard above the din from the TV.

"Hi, Daddy! Will you be home soon? There's chicken for dinner!"

"Hi, honey. I can't make it. This boy's in a bad way, and only Daddy can help him, see?"

"Uh-huh."

The ensuing silence was fraught with all the guilt a seven-year-old girl can make you feel. Cold, clammy and unpleasant.

"What's on TV?" I asked to try to cheer her up.

"*SpongeBob SquarePants.* It's the one where Plankton says he doesn't want to steal the Krabby Patty formula anymore and opens a toy store."

"And Mr. Krabs won't stop till he talks him into stealing it again. I love that one."

"Mommy liked it, too."

I took a few seconds to answer. There was a lump in my throat and I didn't want her to notice.

"I'll tuck you in as soon as I'm back. But now I need you to be good, for the team's sake."

Julia sighed, to make it clear she wasn't buying this one.

"Will you kiss me good night? Even if I'm asleep?"

"I promise," I said. Then I invoked our battle cry, the one Rachel had made up. "Team Evans?"

"Yay team," she replied, but with little conviction.

"I love you, Julia," was the last thing I said to her before I went into surgery.

She hung up. No comment.

It was eleven thirty at night. I was staggering across the parking lot and dog tired after a long operation when my cell phone rang again. It was my boss.

"How'd it go?"

Her speech was slurred and I could tell the minibar tab would be hefty. Dr. Wong probably wouldn't expense it to the hospital but cover it herself, in cash. All of us surgeons drink, and the older we get, the more we drink. It helps you sleep and stops your hands from shaking. But what we never, ever do is own up to it in public. Unless you've got nothing to lose, that is, as with me now.

"Well, there's one gangbanger who'll be back prowling the Anacostia streets in three to five years' time. Or less with good behavior," I said, fishing in my pockets for my car keys.

"I'll have to notify the board. There have been complaints about your lavish use of resources, Evans. I hope your forthcoming report can justify the decision to operate."

Exhausted as I was, I got that in one.

"Don't you worry, boss. The report will be word-perfect," I said, my words laden with sarcasm. "It'll be the Victor Hugo of medical literature. I won't give them any excuse to fire me."

Stephanie chuckled.

"If you pull off Friday's op, you'll be untouchable. Forever. You can be med director in any hospital you care to name," she said enviously.

I was thankful she didn't mention the other eventuality. That would be equally clear-cut.

"Come off it. It'll be to the credit of the whole neurosurgery unit."

She chuckled again, a bit too loudly. She was officially drunk.

"I have two ex-husbands who used to lie better than you, Evans. Now, you go home and rest up. Tomorrow you have an appointment with the Patient."

"No worries, boss. I can handle it."

"How old are you, Evans? Thirty-six?"

"Thirty-eight."

"Boy, at this rate, you won't see forty."

I hung up and turned the ignition key. The Lexus's familiar roar boomed under the hood, and I smiled for the first time that day. The first time in many days, actually. Before the week was out, things would finally begin to look positive for us, which they hadn't done since Rachel died. I would have a better job and get a life. Quality time with Julia.

Untouchable. I liked that.

Inside an hour, I would find out how wrong I could be.

2

When I opened the front door, I was met by an eerie silence.

It was almost midnight, but even so it wasn't the kind of silence you expect from a residential neighborhood. We lived on Dale Drive, in Silver Spring. A toehold inside the Beltway, but inside it all the same. It was a thirties house, clad in gray stone. You might have seen some exterior shots of it in the *National Enquirer* or one of those repulsive muckraking blogs. One of them had even gotten hold of some indoor snaps off the Realtors' website, the ones Rachel and I had bought it from. Julia was due any minute when we closed the deal, and Rachel was still painting a huge smiling bear on the nursery wall when her water broke. We raced to the hospital, our elation mingled with fear.

Despite the steep price tag, on both of our incomes we could well afford it. This was shortly before the real estate bubble burst. Then after she left us, keeping hold of it became harder and harder. Rachel had a life insurance policy whose beneficiary was Julia, but needless to say the insurers wouldn't pay out a red cent. We simply received an exquisitely formal letter, which went to town on the "willfulness" of Rachel's decision, and copied out clause 13.7 of the contract in its entirety. I still recall the disgust I felt as I crumpled it up and threw it away. An attorney who had read about the case in the local newspaper showed up one day and said we could sue, but I sent him packing. The idea disgusted me, although we could have done with the money.

It wasn't simply the mortgage; there was also Julia. The working hours of a neurosurgeon who has to put in overtime to pay the bills are not exactly regular. I had to find home help. First there came a Brazilian woman, who vanished into thin air one fine day, a month ago. The next few days I had a nightmare roster and poor Julia had to spend several evenings in the nurses' station, coloring in the black-and-white diagrams in old anatomy books she had found in my consulting room. She did a good job on the kidneys, turning them into cute, hunchbacked Mr. Potato Heads.

Despite all the people out of work, my postings on Craigslist and DC Nanny drew not a single e-mail reply. Then two weeks ago Svetlana's résumé landed in my inbox, and I thought our lucky number had come up. Not only was she great at looking after Julia, but she cooked up a storm, too. She spread big dollops of goose fat over everything, as they do in her native Belgrade, so I had put on a couple of pounds. Whenever I came home, however late, there would always be an excellent meal ready for me. Except that night.

That night there was just silence.

I dumped my medical case on one of the kitchen chairs and took an apple from the fruit bowl to keep the wolf away from the door. While I nibbled at it, I saw a Dora the Explorer coloring book on the table, with a half-finished picture of Boots in it. It struck me as curious that Julia had gone to bed and not finished it. She always made a point of finishing her drawings, partly to put off her bedtime, but it was also out of character for her to leave a job half-done. Maybe she was still upset because I hadn't been home for dinner.

I closed the book and a red crayon rolled off the cover and fell to the floor. I stooped to pick it up and felt a sudden pain in my fingertips. I pulled my hand away and saw I had cut myself—a couple of droplets of blood trickled down my index finger.

I cursed under my breath, got up, went to the sink and held my finger under the tap for a couple of minutes. It is hard to get across to anyone who hasn't devoted half their life to medicine what a neurosurgeon feels for his hands, but the word that comes closest is *worship*.

I obsess over them, and a terrible panic seizes me whenever I have the slightest domestic mishap, until I assess the damage. You know that minor heart attack you have when your boss or wife says, "We need to talk"? Well, it's kind of like that.

That's why I keep Hibiclens, gauze and Band-Aids in a kitchen cabinet, in the bathrooms, in the garage, and in the glove compartment in the car. I prefer to be on the safe side.

When I had slapped on enough antiseptic to sterilize a Dumpster, I kneeled under the table again. This time I pulled back the chair and looked before I fumbled. Stuck between the table leg and the wall was a sliver of pottery. Warily I plucked it out and saw it was part of a Dora mug. The young explorer was headless and the evil fox Swiper loitered behind a bush with a creepy grin.

Julia's mother had bought that mug for her. It was her favorite.

I hope she didn't see it break, or she'll have cried herself to bits, poor baby, I thought.

I threw the shard away and went straight upstairs. I wanted to kiss her there and then, even wake her up if I had to. We had chanced upon that little mug in a Bed, Bath & Beyond, and I didn't think about it very often. But the sudden sight of it in pieces, less than two weeks away from the first anniversary of Rachel's death, brought it all back. It had been a Saturday, and Rachel and I both had our day off from the hospital. The three of us went to the mall for a sofa, and the deal was our daughter would pick it. She bounced on each and every one before she decided none was soft enough, nor had enough elephants on the upholstery. We came away with nothing more than that mug and a thick brown mustache Julia got from drinking hot chocolate. She refused to wipe it off and gave us mustachioed frowns in the rearview mirror all the way home.

A terrible sense of loss overcame me.

Just then I needed a hug as badly as Julia must have when the mug had smashed. I opened the door to her bedroom, which was oddly dark. Julia always slept with a nightlight on. I scrabbled for the switch and a warm, pink light banished the darkness.

The bed was empty.

That was most unusual. Maybe Julia hadn't been able to sleep and had asked to bunk with Svetlana, but if so the least the nanny could have done was leave a note.

And why the hell was the bed made up? Hadn't Svetlana so much as tried to put her to bed?

Upset at this singular breach of discipline on Svetlana's part, I went back downstairs. She had her quarters there, on the other side of the kitchen, a spacious bedroom with a small living area that overlooked the backyard.

I knocked softly on the door, but there was no reply. I gently opened the door, and found the room empty.

It wasn't so much that nobody was there, but that any sign that anyone had lived there at all had disappeared completely. The sheets and pillowcases were all gone, as were the rugs and bath towels. There were no toiletries, and no clothes in the closets. A strong smell of bleach lingered on each and every surface.

The butterflies I had felt in my stomach since I had gotten home now cut loose.

"Julia!" I bawled. "Julia, baby!"

I ran through the house, switched on all the lights and called out for my daughter. I ground my teeth so hard my gums began to ache after a couple of minutes and the blood was pounding in my temples, as if a fork were beating egg whites in my skull.

Stop, I thought, although the voice inside my head belonged to Dr. Colbert, the man who first showed me how to handle a scalpel under pressure. *Keep a cool head. Solve your problems one at a time. Decide on a course of action.*

First get hold of Svetlana.

Call her cell phone.

I had her number saved on my favorites list. I dialed, but it just went to voice mail.

Where could they be at this time of night?

I made a mental list of all the places they might have gone to as I paced frantically up and down the living room. Svetlana ran errands in Rachel's old Prius, but it was still in the garage and the engine was cold. That certainly narrowed things down. Maybe she had gone to a neighbor's house, but if so why hadn't she left a note or called? And most important, why were none of the nanny's belongings in her room?

There was nothing for it but to call for help: the police, the FBI, the National Guard, or the goddamned Avengers. I wanted my daughter back, and I wanted her now.

I dialed 911.

It was busy.

Busy? How the hell can 911 be busy?

I paused for a second and tried to collect my thoughts. I didn't even know what to say to them. What was it they told you to do in those leaflets they hand out at shopping malls and Parent-Teacher Association meetings? To think of the clothes she had on. What could Julia be wearing?

Nothing seemed to be missing from Julia's room, not even her shoes. It all appeared neat and tidy. The pajamas Julia had worn yesterday, the yellow ones with SpongeBob SquarePants's face on them, were not under her pillow or in the laundry basket. She normally wore them for two or three days, then put them in to wash. She always changed into her pajamas before dinner.

And then what? Had Svetlana packed up her things, scrubbed the place with bleach and walked out the door with a little girl in her jammies? Her own possessions would have filled a couple of boxes. She couldn't have taken all of it.

Somebody must have picked them up while I was stuck in the operating theater, removing a bullet from Jamaal Carter's spine.

It's my fault. Damn it, I should have been here for them, for my family.

I dialed 911 again.

It was still busy.

I held the phone away from my ear and examined it, bewildered. That was impossible, but I didn't stop to consider it, because a thought instantly occurred to me.

If someone snatched them away, then why are there no signs of a struggle, apart from a broken mug?

That thought dried up my throat. Svetlana must have had it all worked out. Maybe she had kidnapped Julia for money. For heaven's sake, I had trusted that woman! I had taken her into my home!

Think. What do you know about her?

She was from Belgrade. She was twenty-four. She was an English philology major and wanted to get a doctorate in the United States. She had a letter of recommendation from her professors at the University of Novi Sad. She had moved here to enroll in her new course and needed money to get by in such a costly place as DC.

She was short, thin and frail. She was switched on, but there was a sad air about her. She had hit it off with Julia from the get-go, and they had always gotten along like a house on fire. After all, Svetlana had also lost her mother when she was about the same age as Julia had been when Rachel left us. It had happened during the war in Bosnia, but she didn't tell Julia that. She revealed it to me in our first interview.

She had given me the number for her doctoral adviser in Georgetown. A man with an affable voice, who had assured me Svetlana was a trustworthy student.

It had all seemed trustworthy, and I desperately needed her, so I gave her the job. She didn't even have a cell phone. She had to get one so we could keep in touch. She never phoned home, nor did she have any friends in Washington. She spent her days off shut up in her room, always with her nose in a book. I had never seen her breathe a word to anybody apart from . . .

Apart from a week ago.

A crazy notion began to take root in my head. I grabbed the car keys.

I had to check this out before I tried calling the cops again.

3

Rachel's father and I never did get along.

When she and I were dating, he never went out of his way to be friendly. He would smile and say hello, shake my hand and take it back quicker than a congressman pocketing your last dollar. But the sideways glances he darted at me, when he thought I couldn't see him, would have melted my chrome-vanadium forceps.

"You're imagining it, honey," Rachel whispered to me when she crept out of her room and into mine. "He's simply a grump who wants the best for his daughters."

"I'm going to be a fucking neurosurgeon, Rachel. What more does he want?"

"His whole life he's watched out for his little girls. You wait until you're a father and have a young stud strutting around your house with a weapon of this caliber," she said as she reached under the covers.

Truth is, the Robson family were close-knit. Rachel was the oldest sister, the sensible one. She had an orderly, straightforward mind, was studying to be an anesthesiologist and always scolded her kid sister, Kate, for all the crazy shit she dreamed up. Aura, the happy-go-lucky and talkative mother, would make corn bread while she gossiped about the neighbors. And then there was Jim, the father figure, a Virginian through and through, one who was still seasick from the voyage on the *Mayflower*. He would sip his beer on the porch, irritated by the tall, dark young resident who claimed to be his daughter's boyfriend.

"What news from the North?" he would always say.

"Well, you know, Jim, they do say there's fifty stars on the flag now."

He never laughed at my feeble attempts at a joke, and matters didn't improve much after the wedding. But we both made an effort and normally gatherings at the Robsons' were homey, although they made me feel uneasy. It wasn't all Jim's fault, mind you. I felt I didn't quite fit in. To be honest, I've never been too big on all this family business.

I'm an orphan and I never knew my birth parents. Up to the age of nine I had lived in one foster home after another, where the other kids weren't siblings but rivals you fought with for food and anything else you could get your hands on. Then a couple from Pottstown, Pennsylvania, adopted me. He was a country doctor, and she his nurse and assistant. They died in a car crash when I was in my second year at medical school, before I met Rachel, so I became an orphan twice over. The crash made me flunk the whole year. Sorrow had always loomed large in my life, but for years it seemed to be well inside the closet. It leaped right out again the day my parents died, and mauled away with its sharp black claws. Only Rachel had kept it at bay after that.

Now that she's gone, Julia and her family are all I've got.

So for fifteen years I've made the hour and a half's drive to Fredericksburg every third Sunday, as well as for birthdays, Thanksgiving, Christmas and the Fourth of July. Although the way the Lexus was barreling along that night, I would make it in half the time.

I don't remember what speed I was doing, but I was so full of adrenaline that I nearly got myself killed at the Falmouth exit. I had turned off there hundreds of times but was driving so fast that night I missed it. I jammed on the brakes, left half the tires on the blacktop, and reversed the car right in the middle of I-95. I don't know what the hell I was thinking. Luckily it was past one a.m. and I was on a four-lane freeway, otherwise such recklessness could have cost me dearly. A colossal truck hove into view. Its headlights dazzled in my mirror while its horn blared louder and louder. We were about to crash but the driver slowed down in time to switch lanes. His front bumper almost clipped my rear one and my little sports car might have been a leaf, the way the draft from twenty tons of truck shook it.

I pulled up on the shoulder between I-95 and exit 133, and struggled to collect myself. That was no way to behave and it would not help Julia at all. It had been a close call.

And all because of a stupid hunch.

A couple of weeks before, my in-laws had dropped in to see Julia. Jim owned a small chain of well-known hardware stores, Robson Hardware Repair. You may have heard the slogan: "Do it yourself and you'll get the best workman." Both hardware and the slogan suited good ol' Jim to a T, because he's as hard as nails. There were five or six stores in the chain, but none to the north of Arlington. Jim never strayed across the Potomac unless he had an appointment in the District, which he did that day.

Aura had made her usual entrance, about as subtle as a brass bell falling down the stairs. Twice.

"Juliaaaaa! Where is my little honey pie?"

Julia sprinted and slid the last stretch along the polished floor in her socks. She threw her arms around her grandmother's neck and smothered her with kisses.

"Grandma! Come up to my room, I want to show you something!" she said as she took the old lady's hand and pulled her along.

I said hi to Jim and offered him something to drink, knowing full well he'd decline. He never touched a drop when he was driving. He sat on the sofa and sneered at the fixtures. Rachel had gone in for modern furniture, with clean lines, which did not go down well with her hidebound father.

"Julia's shot up. We haven't seen her in more than a month."

"I've had a lot on my plate," I said by way of an excuse, a little put out.

I admit that since Rachel died the visits had petered out, but it also riled me that we were always the ones who had to make the trip. It was no farther from Fredericksburg to Silver Spring than from Silver Spring to Fredericksburg. But I didn't say so, to be polite. And because I was still in awe of the old buzzard, damn it.

"That's my point, Dave. You work too hard."

That was out of line from someone who'd spent a lifetime traipsing from one of his stores to another and knew by heart what he had in stock, down to the last screw.

"What are you driving at, Jim?"

"It does Julia no good for you to work so hard."

I wasn't about to dignify that with an answer, so I shrugged my shoulders and stared at him. He stared right back.

"I just sold up, Dave."

That took me completely by surprise. Jim had always bragged that when death came calling it would find him behind the counter. I could always picture him scowling at the Grim Reaper's scythe blade and selling him a Bester-brand whetstone.

"But, Jim, those stores, they're your life."

He squirmed and crossed his arms.

"Ever since Rachel's death, I haven't had my mind on the job. I can think only that life is short, and there's more to it than fussing over Allen keys."

Those had been Rachel's very words at dinner, once, between the mashed potatoes and the turkey.

"The Ace Hardware guys have been trying to buy me out for years, as you know," he went on. "Today I sat down with them and we made a deal. They haven't paid me all they would have five or six years ago. Times are hard. Still, I've got more than enough to see me through. I'm sixty-three and I've worked like a dog for half a century. I deserve to enjoy life and take care of the things I love and cherish."

"Ain't that the truth, Jim. You've done the right thing. Good job."

The old guy nodded his head. Maybe he was drumming up the courage for what he really wanted to say. Finally he spat it out, true to form, right between the eyes.

"You don't get it, David. I want Julia to come live with us."

I glared at him, dumbfounded, and made a ridiculous sound, somewhere between a hoot and a snort.

"You've got to be kidding."

But there wasn't a trace of humor in Jim Robson's eyes.

"It'll come as a relief to you. I'll be doing you a favor. And it's what's best for my granddaughter."

"Are you suggesting I'd let go of my own daughter, Jim?" I said, trying to take it all in as I got madder and madder.

"Washington is no place for a girl. They'll turn her into one of those robots in uniform. She'd be better off in a good small-town public school."

That rankled. Rachel and I had searched high and low for the best school for Julia from the very moment we knew she was on the way. We had chosen one that put art and feeling good before competitive edge. They had twelve applications chasing every place at that school. We had waited in endless lines and called in favors from everybody we knew until we got her in. And now this busybody comes along and tells us we've got it all wrong.

"Julia goes to Maret. It's one of the best schools in the country, where they don't wear a uniform, by the way. And I certainly don't think it's for you to tell me how to bring up my daughter."

"Think about it. That way she'll have somebody waiting for her when she comes in from school, someone to take care of her. She'll eat proper food, good home cooking. Julia's all skin and bone."

I got up and stomped around the table to face him. He stood right up.

"Listen, Jim. Out of respect for you and Rachel's memory, I'll pretend we never had this conversation," I said with a wave of my hand, as if I were brushing off a fly. "You're the girl's grandfather; that's all. You're welcome in this house anytime. But I beg you, if you want it to stay that way, then don't you ever come out with such crap again."

I backed off and he sat down.

"You'll be sorry for this, David," he said through gritted teeth, somewhat humiliated. I let that go because I wanted to put the whole stupid business behind us.

"I'd better go and see how Julia's doing," I said, and shot upstairs.

When I came back down, I was surprised to see Jim gone from the living room. I went into the kitchen and found him there, whispering in Svetlana's ear. She nodded, very straight-faced. When they noticed me, they drew apart, startled.

There was a guilty expression on my father-in-law's face.

Back then I had thought no more of it. Jim's veiled threat seemed no more than the typical outburst of a man used to always being in the right and getting his own way. I also took Jim's talking to Svetlana as his trying to show who was boss after I'd hurt his pride. I imagined him lecturing her on what to feed his granddaughter, or on the quality of Virginia tomatoes—which are great, I must say.

But when I had arrived home an hour before and couldn't find Julia, and figured Svetlana could not have moved out by herself, the threat suddenly became very real, and that word in the nanny's ear had taken on conspiratorial proportions.

As I took the last bend in the road to the Robson home, my mind was churning over the same questions I had been asking all the way there.

Would Jim have dared to take away his granddaughter? How had he talked Svetlana into it? Had he offered her money? I didn't know what Ace Hardware had paid him, but I believe years before Rachel had mentioned an offer in the millions. Even if they had settled on the low side, Jim could still afford to put a young foreigner through grad school. For sure, Jim was as stubborn as they came, but would he go to such lengths to get his way?

He couldn't be that stupid, I thought. *He must see that he'll never get away with it. Does he really think I'll turn the other way while he takes my daughter?*

I finally drew up outside the house and parked on the stony slope that led to the garage on the edge of the farm, a place that has been in the Robson family for four generations. They had been poor all that time—Rachel was the first Robson to get into college—but nobody could top them for pride.

A soft rain was falling, which did nothing to settle my nerves. As I approached, I saw the light above the front porch was out. They usually left it on all night, as well as a pair of lights downstairs. My in-laws thought this climate-change talk was something Al Gore had made up to sell books.

I walked up the front steps in two strides and had the knocker in my hand when the door abruptly opened. There was Jim, in a checkered bathrobe. He looked me up and down, and then let me in. He didn't seem surprised to see me.

"Come in and keep quiet. They're both asleep, upstairs."

I felt intensely relieved to hear that. It swiftly took a load off my mind and I could breathe deeply for the first time in hours. I saw he had only one slipper on, and his footfalls sounded off-kilter as he padded along. I was still angry, but the sight of my father-in-law's bare, skinny calves was dismal enough to dismiss any thoughts of quarreling.

I followed on his cracked and parched heels to the study, where he would wind down at night and take in some TV while he had a beer, before he turned in. But that night Jack Daniel's had stood in for Bud in the starting lineup, and to all appearances, Tennessee's finest was on fire.

The other difference was even more worrying. The TV was switched off and there was a big silver picture frame on Jim's easy chair. It was plain the old man had been poring over it. I knew only too well that frame didn't belong in Jim's study, but on the mantelpiece.

He picked it up as he sat down and poured himself another finger of Jack.

"She seemed so full of life, David. And so happy."

He lifted up the photo to show me, but he didn't need to. I knew every bit of that picture, because for nights on end I had sat up with it in my hands, too, and drunk myself stupid gaping at it, like the old man. We had that much in common.

It was a photo of our wedding. Rachel was holding a bridal bouquet by the church door, while we gazed into each other's eyes. I hadn't seen in her face the happiness Jim spoke of, at least not an overdone or mawkish happiness. What I saw was the full knowledge she had found her soul mate. But then I hadn't simply seen the photo; I had been on the receiving end of that look.

"She surely was, Jim. I think she was happy the whole time we were together."

He tilted his head to one side and hesitated. Perhaps he was mulling this over. His skin was bone dry and his cheeks obscured by spider veins. He stared at the bottom of his glass, seeking the answer there. And then he knocked the drink back in one.

"Yes. Yes, I think you're right."

He helped himself to more. He waved the bottle at me, but I shook my head and he didn't insist. Someone had to keep a clear head around there. Besides, I was worn through and too jumpy to hit the bottle. I longed to pick up Julia and split but couldn't do that without talking to him, and furthermore it would break my heart to drag her out of bed that late. I greatly feared I would have to stay the night.

"She was so sweet. Like a love song. *Oh sweet Rachel, oh my darling dear . . .*" He hummed for a while, getting drunker by the minute and slurring his words. "She never got mad. She was so even tempered."

"You think she would have approved of this?"

"She didn't mind her dad having a drink now and then. No, sir."

"I don't mean that, Jim. Where's Svetlana?"

He looked up at me, slowly, with wide staring eyes.

"In your lousy house, I guess. Is Julia here? You bring her?"

I didn't have to stop and guess whether he was lying. His stupe-faction was overwhelmingly real, and with that a wave of confusion washed over me. I felt dizzy and had to hold on to the armrest.

"Of course you didn't. You never do. You're too busy saving other people's lives, Dave," he said, almost in a murmur.

I hardly listened to him. His words were daggers that stabbed me in the guts, but there were more important issues. I breathed deep and tried to get a word in.

"Jim—"

"Everybody's life is important, except your wife's. That right, Dave?"

"Jim, when I got here—"

"The fancy brain surgeon, the star of the future, and you didn't see it coming, did you, big shot? You didn't see it, didn't see it coming."

"Jim!"

"What!?"

"Jim, you said they were upstairs. Who's 'they'?"

He stopped and seemed at a loss for a moment. His ears appeared to have caught merely a faint echo of my question, but at last it found its way through the boozy haze.

"What are you talking about? Why, my wife. And Kate, who else? She's on leave. Come to see her folks. Good girl, Kate. She knows where her heart is."

By then he was mumbling so badly I almost missed the last bit, which sounded more akin to *wherrahardiz*, but I didn't care, because the hunch that had driven me there had melted away. It had all been a big, bad misunderstanding. Julia had been missing for hours and no one was out searching for her. To make matters worse, I was there, sixty miles from home, when I should have been talking to the police to get them to hunt down Svetlana and whoever she was in league with. All of a sudden, fear and anxiety floored me again.

I stood up and grabbed my cell phone. I dialed 911 and pressed it to my ear.

It was busy.

That was bizarre. The emergency number could never be busy. A sneaking feeling gripped my throat, an idea I could dimly remember, a cry from afar I could faintly hear.

Something was amiss, and not only with Julia.

"Listen, Jim . . . I need to use your phone."

The old-timer shook his head and wobbled to his feet.

"Don't you go calling now. I want to talk to you!"

"It's an emergency. I have to—"

That second my cell phone buzzed to show I had a text. I clocked the screen immediately, thinking it might be Svetlana, but it wasn't. The caller ID was vacant. It didn't even say "Unknown." It was blank.

GET OUT OF THERE, DAVE.

I unlocked the phone and opened the inbox to see who had sent it, but the text I had received a moment ago was nowhere to be seen. The latest one was from a colleague, at the hospital.

"What do you mean, an emergency, David? Emergencies have always come before your family, for you. Yes, everything's more important to you, Mr. High-and-Mighty Surgeon, yessir. A piece of shit, that's what you are."

I started at the insult and was about to answer when the message tone buzzed again.

SAY NO MORE. TELL HIM NOTHING ABOUT JULIA.

"Jim, if you shut up a minute and let me ex—"

"How dare you tell me to shut up in my own home! She was sick, you son of a bitch. Sick, all the time, under your nose. Right under your goddamned, smart-assed Yankee nose."

I didn't answer. I was too stunned by everything taking place around me to mind my father-in-law's words. I suppose this was the only way his sort could cry for help, but in that moment all the hatred and resentment he flung at me simply bounced off and rebounded on him, making no impact. Except it made him even angrier.

"Answer me, damn you!" he said while he shook his fist at me, his face flushed with anger and drink.

I dodged him as best I could and shifted to one side. He stumbled, fell forward and knocked over a side table next to his easy chair. The tray with the whiskey and shot glasses fell on the floor to the sound of breaking glass.

The message tone buzzed again.

GO HOME, DAVE.

YOU'RE EXPECTED.

I marched to the doorway, the feeling of unease ballooning inside me. Nothing around me made sense, and I couldn't find my way in the dark. In my haste I had banged my hip on a piece of furniture. I felt a sharp pain in my side as I pulled the front door open. The rain was pouring down now and had turned the front steps into a slide. I tripped again, and this time slithered to my knees on the sodden lawn.

All the skill God put in your hands, he took away from your feet, Dave.

Rachel's dulcet voice came back to me as I got to my feet, my pants covered in mud. I used to hate it when she made fun of my clumsiness. She would have howled to high heaven to see me climb into the Lexus in such a mess.

I would have traded in all the cars in the world to hear her taunt me, just once more.

"Come back, you!" Jim bellowed from the doorway.

I could scarcely see to put the key in the lock. The goddamned battery in the remote was busted, and I could never remember to get it fixed. The outside light came on unexpectedly, so I got the key in place. I turned it, thankfully, then ducked when I saw my father-in-law's whiskey bottle fly my way. It bashed the bodywork and shattered into a thousand pieces, leaving an ugly dent behind.

Then a fourth text landed, which made my flesh creep. I clambered into the car and fired her up. With no time to reverse back to the road, I turned across the lawn. Jim ran down the steps and thumped the hood.

"Run, run! That's all you can do!"

The sight of the old man threatening me with his bony fist popped up in my rearview mirror, but I paid no heed because all I could think of was Julia and the text I had just received.

NO COPS.

4

I don't remember much about the drive home.

I know I was in a total panic, such as I had never been in before and don't think I'll ever be in again. Bewilderment and foreboding had overcome me, so I drove on autopilot, lost in my thoughts. New questions piled on top of the ones that had nagged at me on the way over, and they unsettled me far more. Terrible visions of whose hands Julia might be in crossed my mind in an endless and troubling stream.

"Just let her be okay. Please, please," I said over and over, to try to cast out those visions.

I wonder who I was pleading with. I guess with a God I don't believe in, and one I've turned to so often for help. Just two cells down from where I write these words, there's an inmate who says there are no atheists on death row.

It's easy to see why.

When I got to Dale Drive I didn't even bother to put the car in the garage. I left it in the driveway, open and with the keys in place. I dashed into the house in a beat. I stood breathless in the hallway, more because of tension than the rush, in a complete muddle and covering the mat in mud, until a new text lit up.

GO TO THE BASEMENT.

The doorway was between the hall and the kitchen, papered in the same pattern as the rest of the wall. I had to pull hard because it always jams a bit.

I went down the stairs very slowly. The steps creaked underfoot because the wood was very old, probably the same wood the house was originally made from. We never had the time or money to change them, and we didn't go down there often, anyway. Something hit me in the face, halfway down. It was the pull chain. I tugged it and a yellowy light filled the basement, casting long shadows and illuminating gloomy nooks, where before there had only been a pall of darkness.

I went on down, aware that hours before, when I had looked for Julia, I had barely stuck my head through the basement door, hollered and closed it again, but had failed to go down. Shivers ran down my spine. Perhaps I had made a fatal mistake.

When I reached the bottom of the stairs, the light blinked twice, went out and left me in the dark. There was a box of lightbulbs on a shelf at the back, but I couldn't grope my way through the cavernous basement in the dark without breaking a leg. I decided to run the app that turns my phone into a flashlight.

"Julia?" I called out, in a bid to calm myself. I didn't know what I expected to find, but I was scared, very scared. Not only for my daughter, but because I have a deep-seated fear of the dark. The faint light beam from the phone did little to allay that fear.

I got close to the metal shelving where we kept electrical supplies and other seldom-used clutter. I met with an obstacle. It was Rachel's bike, which was flat on the ground. I thought that strange, because nobody had ridden it in more than a year, and it should have been on its rack by the wall. There were some boxes behind the bike, so I couldn't hop over it. I had to go around and skirt the boiler instead.

What I saw then took my breath away.

She was there.

Neither blood nor death has ever fazed me. I would even say they have come to draw me in a way others would deem unhealthy.

The clearest memory I have of that attraction goes back to when I was eleven. It was summer 1989 and the kids on our block were scuttling back and forth in their bat masks and T-shirts, in the belief it was really cool to be a crime-fighting orphan superhero. I could have told them a thing or two about having no parents, but I was minding my own business.

Dr. Roger Evans, my adoptive father, felt strongly about interacting with other kids, and that afternoon he came into the backyard to share them.

"David, why don't you go out to pl—?"

He broke off midsentence, most surprised.

I was squatting on the ground. A dead cat lay at my feet, one that had belonged to Mrs. Palandri, who lived at end of the block. I had a stick in my hand and was busy hauling out a good length of the poor creature's large intestine with it.

The doctor appeared neither horrified nor appalled. Merely surprised.

Someone else in his situation—myself included, had it been Julia—might have yelled, acted on gut instinct, whatever. But not Doc Evans. He was a patient man whose greatest pleasure consisted of getting himself over to Nalgansett Creek with a fishing pole and sitting still hour after hour.

I had had occasion to try his patience to the limit after I had moved into his home two years before. At first it didn't work out. I broke stuff, valuable heirlooms. I wouldn't eat. I cussed.

Doc Evans simply waited. A few weeks later, he went up to my room and said:

"You've behaved as badly as can be and we haven't thrown you out. We'll never do that. Now, don't you think you've tried us enough?"

His voice carried that selfsame tone of wisdom and boundless patience when he asked me:

"Did you kill it?"

I shook my head and stood up.

"It was that way already when I got here."

"And what are you doing with that stick?"

"I wanted to see its insides. I want to see how they work."

He stared at me for a while, his arms folded. Nowadays that answer would have earned me a couple of years' counseling and stacks of little pink pills. Things were different in those days, but he was a smart guy, anyway. He knew no good would come of kids who tore the wings off flies or stove cats' heads in with rocks. I think he was searching for something perverse or unhinged in my interest in the cat, but he didn't find it. The more I think of it, the more convinced I am that that stare was a pivotal moment in my life. The way I turned out had a lot to do with that gaze.

He finally made his mind up to believe me. He lowered himself next to the animal, examined it and looked around. Our backyard had a wire fence around it with more holes than the Clippers' defense. And behind our house was a wood. Not big, but a thick one.

"That will have been a fox or a coyote. Give me the stick."

I did so, but what came next surprised me. Instead of burying the poor thing, as I thought he would, he put it on the garage table. He spread out some garbage bags and old newspapers and then had me fetch his doctor's bag. It was big and made of worn leather, had his initials engraved on it and weighed a ton. I had a hard time lifting it up to the table. From it he extracted a scalpel and forceps.

"To harm a living thing is wrong, but this was an accident. It's sad, but we can learn from it." He hesitated, then went on. "You still want to see an animal from the inside?"

I nodded.

"Then we have to do this properly," he said as he rolled up his sleeves. His arms were dark, tanned and hairy, while his hands were large and skillful.

I sat next to him while he dissected the animal. He did so in the way he did everything in life: slowly, gently and respectfully. He briefly explained what the internal organs were, what they were for and what happened if any of them went wrong.

Today they don't do dissections in high school, not even on frogs, as they did in my day. In less capable hands than the ones I was in, it can be a traumatic experience. Even many years later, kids shudder to recall the smells and sounds of dissection.

I simply remember the smell of Old Spice and Doc Evans's deep, dry voice. That afternoon he won me over. I began to call him Daddy and he set me on my way to becoming a doctor.

Twenty-six years later, as I beheld Svetlana Nikolić's body, I remembered the day my father had taught me to fear neither blood nor death. I took a deep breath and tried to take in what I saw.

The nanny was bundled up in a thick, see-through plastic sheet. Only her bare feet stuck out from under it. She was clad in a blue sweat suit such as she often wore around the house, although it looked much darker, almost black, through the gruesome wrapping. Her head jutted from the top end, at an unnatural angle. You didn't need to be a brain surgeon to tell her neck had been broken. It was an instant and almost painless execution, but one that required brute strength, a lot more than it seems in the movies. Even for a skinny Serbian college girl.

The worst thing was her eyes.

Whoever had done it hadn't troubled to close her eyelids. On the contrary, her eyes stared straight ahead and accusingly reflected the flashlight. They were at precisely the right angle, which was weird. Anyone who approached that shelving would have to come round the bike and meet those eyes.

Whoever had killed Svetlana was a very sick son of a bitch, and he had Julia.

Then the phone pinged again. In the pitch-dark cellar those three cheery chimes were doleful, a beast howling in the depths of a cave.

I THINK YOU'RE READY TO MEET ME, DAVE.

5

I screeched to a halt by the curb outside the Marblestone Diner. I tore out of the car berserk, ready to beat up whoever might be inside. I would beat my daughter's whereabouts out of him.

I didn't make it around the corner before someone grabbed me from behind and rammed me against the wall. The rough, faded concrete felt cold against my cheek. But not as cold as the steel somebody jabbed in the back of my head.

"You have been invited to a *very* civilized meeting, doctor," said a voice with a strong eastern European accent. "Your host begs you to keep your composure."

I tried to turn around, but the arm pinning me to the wall was too strong to brook any disagreement.

"We can stay as long as it takes to cool our temper, doctor."

I felt the anger that had bottled up inside me die down, stifled by fear.

"That'll do," I said.

"Zen I will let you go. Don't turn around. Walk inside and behave."

The weight on my back was gone and I edged away from the wall. I could sense them, two shadowy figures I had spied out of the corner of my eye when they assaulted me. They didn't seem to follow me to the doorway, but I obeyed them anyway. They had made it clear that this was no time for heroics.

I didn't spot him on my way in. The diner is L-shaped and he was sitting at the back table, engrossed in his iPad. But when he looked up and our eyes met, I felt as if the breath had been knocked out of me.

Ten minutes before I had been staring into Svetlana Nikolić's lifeless face. But believe me, those cadaver eyes were more alive than the two cold, bright blue stones that stalked me from the back of the joint.

He got up as I came close and held out his hand. I made no move to shake it, but the stranger deflected the snub by turning his gesture into an elegant flourish, pointing to the bench in front of him.

"Please take a seat, Dave. I trust you didn't have too much trouble finding your way."

The text had copied some directions off Google Maps, but I didn't need them. I knew the Marblestone well. It was close to home and I would swing by every morning to grab coffee before I dropped Julia off at school. Juanita, the waitress on the graveyard shift, always served me. She walked across, notepad in hand, surprised to see me there at two a.m.

"Hi, Dr. Evans. You up early or working late?"

I looked at her in amazement. So normal, so indifferent. I didn't get it. Could she possibly not see something was wrong? No, indeed not. I wanted to make a sign, to appeal for help, but the stranger wouldn't take his eyes off me.

I tried to act normal.

"It's been a long day, Juanita. I'll have coffee, if you don't mind."

"No one comes here midweek at this time, especially on a night like this," she said, pointing behind her with a pen. The place was empty, apart from us. "Anything to eat?"

I shook my head. Now that she couldn't help me, I just wanted her to go away as quickly as possible. The man and I weighed each other up in silence.

He was young, closer to thirty than me. He had blond, curly hair and pale, smooth skin. His features might have been chiseled out of marble, and you could have cracked nuts on his jaw. He was decked out in a gray woolen three-piece suit by Field, no tie. The way it hugged his shoulders, it looked made to measure and must have set him back three or four thousand bucks.

I can't say I'm really into clothes—that had been Rachel's department, and was now sorely neglected—but I am a neurosurgeon in a private clinic. I spend my days surrounded by snobs who chat about such things. I am fond of watches, although I can't afford much in that way. And I knew the limited-edition Audemars Piguet on that man's wrist cost more than half a million dollars. It wasn't a showy watch. The expense came with the handmade inside, which had more than three hundred moving parts. But its titanium case and foreign brand name would go unnoticed by anyone who didn't know what a doodad like that was worth, which was the whole idea.

Juanita brought coffee and gave my companion a smile, which he returned, revealing a row of nuclear-white teeth. He reminded me of that Scottish actor who plays Obi Wan in the new *Star Wars* movies.

"*Gracias, señorita linda,*"* he said in Spanish.

Juanita blushed at the compliment and slipped behind the counter. The man followed her with his eyes until she was back in place, and fitted the iPad's headphones over his ears.

"The coffee here is excellent, don't you think?" he said, raising his own cup.

His posh accent and appearance, straight out of the pages of *Town & Country*, were unyielding. I could not believe this was the man who had killed Svetlana and sent those texts. I was perplexed but also mad as can be. I balled up my fists under the table.

"Who are you? Did my father-in-law send you?" I said, knowing how absurd the words sounded before they were out of my mouth.

"The hardware dealer? Don't make me laugh, Dave."

---

* *Thank you, gorgeous.*

There wasn't a shred of laughter in his corpselike eyes.

"Tell me where my daughter is, or I'll call the cops this second," I said, raising my voice despite myself.

He leaned over the table slightly and frowned.

"Dave, if you raise your voice once more, I'll have no choice but to give our hostess the same treatment I gave Svetlana," he said, nodding toward the counter. "We'll have to leave here and resume this conversation in a cramped car, rather than this warm, roomy diner, out of the rain. We'll all lose out, especially Juanita's children. Do I make myself clear?"

He said his piece in a cut-glass tone as devoid of feeling as that of a waiter reciting the day's specials. That ice-cold poise was hideous.

For a second I was lost for words, my throat constricting.

"Well, what do you say?"

"I won't raise my voice."

He smiled. It wasn't a real smile. There was no light in it, no feeling. His face muscles merely rearranged themselves. Very different from the deceptive and perfectly contrived rictus he had given Juanita. More authentic, too.

"That's more like it, Dave. You may call me Mr. White."

His hand reached across the table again, and this time I had no choice but to shake it. It was strong and cold to the touch.

"What do you want from me? Money? I don't have much, but it's all yours. Just tell me where Julia is."

"Dave, Dave, Dave. Do I look like I'm short of cash?"

"No, I guess not."

"And even so . . . You want to fob me off with a few bucks, like the conscience money you drop into that homeless guy's jar on Kalorama Circle, when you step down from your Lexus?"

I was frozen stiff. Occasionally, we went to a shopping mall where a panhandler in a 76ers cap would bum around with a sign that said "War Vett." I often gave him change, because I liked him.

"You know nothing about me," I said, offended.

"You are in error, Dave. I know all about you, more than you do yourself. I know your every trait, your every feature. You are the orphan who made it. The whiz kid with the Johns Hopkins scholarship. 'A natural talent for medicine,' the *Pottstown Gazette* said. You've come a long way since you were a newspaper boy in small-town Pennsylvania, haven't you?"

I held my tongue and quietly stirred the coffee I had no intention of drinking. My stomach was churning like a volcano.

"You are the doting but somewhat absent father. The good neighbor. The grieving widower."

"Knock it off," I whispered.

"The surgeon with the golden hands. The wisecracking colleague. Your St. Clement's buddies used to call you Wiseass Dave until you returned from your long break after the business over Rachel. Now they call you Spooky Dave, you know. Not to your face, evidently. They whisper it in the locker rooms and by the water cooler. Some anesthesiologists swap shifts when they see they have a long operation with you lined up. It gives them the jitters."

I knew it, sure. Or at least I suspected. But it is one thing to have an inkling, quite another to hear it from a total stranger who has just kidnapped your daughter. His metallic voice struck home, every word he said a blow to my solar plexus. Stripped of answers, powerless to speak and with no chance to respond with violence, I was putty in that maniac's hands.

"Besides, it's quite to be expected," he went on. "You haven't exactly been the life and the soul of the party since Rachel killed herself, have you?"

"You leave my wife out of this, asshole," I grunted.

"Don't try and tell me you're ashamed now. It was such a sweet way to end it all. And those words she wrote you in her farewell letter"—he adopted a repellent falsetto—"'My darling David. We will be together always. Hold on to each of my smiles, and remember me this way . . .'"

I could take no more and banged my hand on the table, rattling the cups and the cutlery. Even Juanita flashed us a quizzical look, but dived back into her gossip magazine. Luckily she was too far off to hear us.

White gave her the once-over out of the corner of his eye and then leaned toward me.

"You won't make me repeat my earlier warning, will you, Dave?"

I ignored him. I was too busy crying. I turned to face the wall and hide my tears. I stayed that way for a few minutes.

No one but I knew what was in that note. Rachel had not left it by her body but had mailed it to me the same day she went away. I guess she didn't want the police or anybody else to read those words, which came right from the heart. She had left another run-of-the-mill note to explain why she'd done it, and that was it. I hadn't told a living soul about the letter and kept it at home, under lock and key in my study. To hear those words from that slug's mouth was sacrilege. I felt so used, naked and helpless, that for a few minutes I went to pieces.

When I pulled myself back together, I wiped my tears with the back of my hand and garnered the strength to face him. He smiled, and now the smile was for real.

I knew because it frightened the shit out of me.

"You win, White, you goddamned wacko son of a bitch. So you know it all. You call the shots."

"Now you're catching on, Dave."

"What do you want?"

"It's very simple. If your next patient leaves the operating table alive, you will never see your daughter again."

I gawked at him, petrified. Now it all fell into place. Why this White character, who looked to be made of money, had set up such a well-oiled and well-timed plan. He didn't want Julia or to take what little money we had. But the ransom was monstrous, unthinkable. The price was the life of the man I was due to operate on in two days' time.

To save my daughter, I had to kill the president of the United States.

6

"So that's it. You're a terrorist."

White shook his head and clicked his tongue, as though he found the term distasteful.

"That would require an ideology and beliefs, Dave, of which I am bereft. No, my friend, I'm an outsourcer, although that doesn't exactly fit the bill, either."

His eyes shone and he waved his hands about to stress each word. Everyone likes to talk shop. For the vain, self-centered White, it must have been sheer torture that he couldn't shout about his feats from the rooftops.

"Let us say I am a specialist in social engineering. A client comes to me with a problem, and I fix it."

"B-but . . . ," I stammered. "I'm not a murderer. Go look for a soldier, a mercenary, or someone who knows about weapons."

"The cracked lone gunman is so 1960s . . . It's a tired old trick and we've used it too often. No, Dave, that is not my style. Any two-bit hoodlum with three bullets and telescopic sights could set up that kind of hack job. I mean to say, it would turn out badly. In all likelihood with the gunman shackled to a chair and bleating out— shall we say—unseemly remarks about his employers' identities. And let's not even talk about tanking stock markets, social unrest, rising international tension . . . Our country is already in a bad way. A new scandal would tear it asunder. We're patriots and we can't have that, now, can we, Dave?"

"No, of course not," I replied automatically.

He leaned forward and lowered his voice to a whisper. At that moment, the strains of Joan Baez's "Hush Little Baby" faded away and her "Battle Hymn of the Republic" struck up. I cannot tell whether that was happenstance or whether White had set it up, as he had everything else in the whole sordid affair, down to the last detail.

"Nevertheless, my dear doctor, death by natural causes would be perfectly acceptable. The great man checks into the hospital Friday, in complete secrecy. No one knows about his life-threatening illness. He receives the best treatment but dies on the operating table. A brave, tall and dark neurosurgeon faces the cameras. He's a self-made man, an all-American hero, an example to us all. He breaks the news with tears in his eyes, and the country weeps with him. The vice president takes the oath of office, also in tears, that very night, so help me God. The nation is in mourning Saturday, then Sunday the newspapers are full of praise for the new commander in chief, whom 47.3 percent of the population couldn't have named two days earlier. By the time Wall Street opens on Monday, everything is back on track. Factories belch smoke, moms take their kids to school and bake apple pie. The free world is safe. God bless America."

He clutched his chest in an affected imitation of the Pledge of Allegiance. In that diner, decorated 1950s style in red, white and blue, his patter sounded unreal and demented, but nonetheless entirely plausible. I felt sick to my stomach and gulped as I took in the enormity of the mess I was mixed up in.

"You're crazy, White," I muttered.

"You surmise most incorrectly," he said, narrowing his eyes. "I am in fact a thoroughly rational and well-balanced person, who is fully cognizant of the outcome of his actions, and the costs and benefits entailed therein. Are you, Dave?"

He stared at me long and hard, while he slowly massaged his temples, to gauge the impact of his threat.

Every fiber in my body was screaming to get the hell out of there and away from that psycho. But I couldn't.

"What do you want me to do? I can't kill him just like that!" I said in an effort to defend myself, to gain time, to explain how impossible it was to do as he wanted. "It won't be so easy. There'll be eyes everywhere, watching my every move. At least two other neurosurgeons will be with me, as well as an anesthesiologist and two nurses. There'll be cameras recording everything, and half the Secret Service peeping from behind the operating lights."

"Details, details," he said, stretching out his hands, palms upward; seemingly these were petty concerns. "Leave that to me. I'll tell you how Thursday night. I'm sure it will be to your liking."

He spoke with overpowering certainty. He knew he had me by the balls. But like the cornered animal I was, I tried to lash out.

"Damn it, White, you can't ask me to kill a human being. I am sworn never to harm anybody. I'm a doctor, for Chrissakes."

He sighed, as if taking pains to be reasonable.

"See here, Dave. I'm a very patient man, believe me. I appreciate your qualms in this matter. I would rather have taken a different approach, offered you a chunk of money and counted on your willing participation, as I have with other collaborators. It hasn't been so simple with you. You're straight. Your career's at stake and you're compromising the moral strictures by which you have lived your whole life. That I can respect. Nevertheless, allow me to remind you of something."

He drew the iPad closer. It was on the tabletop, in an upmarket Louis Vuitton case. He raised the cover and shielded his hands as he typed for a moment. A couple of seconds later, he lowered the cover and turned the contraption around.

On display was a black rectangle that took up three-quarters of the screen. Underneath were three rows of gray blobs with no visible labels. That was it.

I couldn't see why he wanted to show me all that. I gave him a baffled look.

"Oh, by all means. Let there be light."

He tapped three of the blobs in quick succession and the black rectangle swiftly turned white. I blinked as my eyes adjusted to the brightness. So did the lens on the other side of the screen. And then I got the picture.

It was a webcast, showing some sort of room, hewn out of solid ground. A few untreated wooden props kept the whole shaky construction from caving in. The walls oozed dampness and shone with a sickly glow under the blindingly bright lights. The picture, in HD, displayed every painful detail.

The dugout was small. It must have measured a scant five feet tall by ten feet wide. How come I worked that out so quickly?

Because I know how tall my daughter is.

Groveling in the middle of the pit was Julia. She had her Sponge-Bob SquarePants pajamas on, with the dark blue pants and the garish yellow top many parents have come to hate. Only the yellow was spattered with dirt, and what looked suspiciously akin to dried blood. She was barefoot, apart from a lone sock on her right foot.

She cradled her knees with one hand while using the other to try to shield her eyes from the harsh glare cast by the halogen lamps. Her gorgeous blond hair was matted and sweaty. Tears streaked from her little blue eyes and made runnels in her dirt-encrusted cheeks. The lights had woken her up and she was dazed, helpless and frightened out of her wits. She opened her mouth but no sound came from it.

"Well now, it seems the feed is muted. Allow me, please," he said in a voice as toneless as that of a RadioShack attendant showing a customer a plasma TV.

He gave the iPad another two taps.

The piercing shriek that came from the speakers tore me apart. It was a halting, confused cry. The volume was very low, but an ice pick couldn't have split my eardrums more.

I clenched my fists.

"You're a smart man, doctor," White said, reading in my eyes what I had in mind. "Don't do anything foolish."

Slowly, I unwound my fists. They were the sole part of my body that wasn't as taut as a guitar string.

"The cubbyhole is underground, in a hermetically sealed room. Six oxygen tanks provide the air supply," White went on. "They hold twenty-one thousand, three hundred forty-five liters in all. At five liters a minute, that's exactly enough for a girl of her weight to breathe until six p.m. on Friday."

"Does . . . does she have food?"

"Dave, please. What do you take me for, a monster?" he said, crestfallen. To all appearances my query had deeply hurt him. "Her heat, hydration, food and hygiene needs have all been taken care of. She'll be a mite uncomfortable, unfortunately, but she'll be fine. Until the deadline, that is. After that, her well-being depends wholly and entirely on you."

"You do realize what it is you are asking me to do?"

"Naturally, Dave. My employer expects me to perform a neat, quality job for him."

"Then he'll discard the tools."

"No. That would be most unwise. After the demise of our commander in chief, you will be in the limelight and you wouldn't be able to justify the girl's absence for long. Julia will be home by the weekend and then we shall forget each other's existence."

I didn't believe that for one second but kept my thoughts to myself.

"I still don't understand how you expect me to pull this off," I said, shaking my head.

"Leave the details to me, Dave. You keep up appearances and don't let your feelings show. Regain your, er, well-known sense of humor. Now go home and have a think about our talk. You'll receive instructions in due course."

I lifted a finger to call Juanita. She dropped the check on the table.

"You weren't his first choice. Your patient's, that is," he said when she went away. "But you were mine."

I stood up to leave.

"Why me?"

He appeared to be confounded. I don't think he saw that one coming.

"You could have picked anyone else," I continued. "An anesthesiologist, a nurse. Why me?"

He seemed to muse on the question for an instant, studying his perfectly manicured nails at the end of his long, delicate fingers.

Surgeon's hands, I thought.

"Oh, because you know, Dave," he said airily. "You know death comes to us all and it is acceptable. And because you also know how hard it is to live with the guilt of not having gone the extra mile. What's unacceptable is remorse, a bitter cup we drink from day after day."

I think I ground my teeth and winced after that last barb. I knew that if I stayed there under his icy gaze, I would burst into tears again, and I didn't want to give that vermin the satisfaction of belittling me once more.

I made my way toward the door, but his voice halted me.

"Haven't you forgotten something?"

"Like what?"

I turned back to him, slowly. White smiled and proffered the note Juanita had just brought.

"Pick up the tab, will you, Dave? And don't forget the tip."

7

Here on death row there's a guy four cells down, name of Snow, who plays solitaire all day long. He says that winning is all about getting the right cards. If he deals himself a poor hand, he shuffles the deck and starts again. Outwardly, he has all the time in the world. He doesn't. Snow has six weeks to go, so before long we'll see him walk down the row.

This overarching wish to start again, to clear away the cards life has dealt you, is a treacherous and woeful feeling. We have all felt it sometime, although it is never keener, nor more devastating or lethal, than when it is fed by guilt and self-reproach. Then it is enough to drive somebody crazy. Little wonder that most everyone in this place ends up clinically nuts.

There is no wiping the slate clean.

The night I came back from that first meeting with White and lugged myself upstairs, up to Julia's room, I was almost catatonic. I felt numb, like you do after the dentist leaves half your face frozen.

I don't remember stepping on top of the white stool Julia used to get her clothes down from the hangers. But I must have, because at some stage I found myself grasping a heavy-duty, sealed plastic bag of the kind used to store clothes in out of season. I took an old and worn college sweatshirt out of it, held it to my face and breathed in. It still smelled of Rachel, that smell of deodorant mixed with flower-scented soap and scrubbed skin she left behind every time she put something on.

It was then that it sank in I would never see her again. There would be no more tea in the kitchen before bedtime, no more walks under the trees or knowing winks beside the operating table. The dawning realization ushered in a feeling of closure. All those months of maudlin and guilty grief, which had turned me into a bad-tempered recluse and workaholic, ended right there.

Because I understood.

Rachel Evans, née Rachel Robson, got the results of her magnetic resonance imaging scan forty-eight hours before she took her life. She had been having splitting headaches for days, but played them down, and I had taken little notice. Don't go judging me for that. I've been at it for a while now, and much more scathingly than you. In my defense, I will say that no one is blinder to his own family's health problems than a doctor. The response to any of your wife's or children's symptoms is to give them a Tylenol and tell them to take an afternoon nap.

Rachel was a woman with a high pain threshold who never complained and gave birth to Julia with no more chemical assistance than a couple of Diet Cokes. So when she found herself gobbling down a jar of painkillers a day, she was worried sick. Or at least that's what a colleague in Neurosurgery told me. She had consulted them on the sly and they scanned her while I, wholly unaware, had taken Julia to a school play. While I watched our little girl dance in a raccoon outfit, they told Rachel she had glioblastoma multiforme, grade 4. The most malignant and, sadly, also the most common type of brain cancer. More than half of cerebral tumors are GBM, a ruthless killer for which there is little or no known cure.

"How long have I got?" Rachel asked the neurologist as the tears welled up in her eyes.

"Without treatment, six or seven weeks. Unfortunately it has branched and I'm afraid it will spread quickly. In a few days it'll reach the area that controls speech."

She understood in a flash. Not only was she a great doctor, but she had also taken part in enough neurosurgery operations to know what lay in store for her. How she would lose her faculties piecemeal until she ceased to be everything she was. And how on the way she would suffer dreadfully and make her family suffer all the more.

"Maybe David . . . ," the neurologist ventured.

"No."

"But, Rachel . . . He's achieved results with—"

"No! You won't tell David a thing. Promise me. You'll keep it under wraps until Monday. This weekend's our anniversary and I don't want anything to spoil the party."

The way they told it later, shamefaced, when they came clean, they had fallen for Rachel's story and kept their mouths shut. The same way an anesthesiologist she worked with swallowed another yarn a couple of days later.

"I've got this terrible migraine and am ready to drop. Can you fit me up with a drip? The neuro has prescribed me a mild analgesic every five hours, but I don't feel like waiting around that long. And you know how I hate needles."

He looked at her suspiciously.

"Can't your husband do it at home?"

"David and I won't overlap there, his shift's about to start," she lied.

So Rachel left the hospital with a drip in her left arm and headed for the Four Seasons, where the evening before she had booked a room with a view. She took an envelope out of her purse, with a handwritten letter in it, and carefully laid it on the bedside table. She scheduled an e-mail to be sent three hours later, to tell the police where to find her.

Then from the bedstead she hung a cocktail of propofol, fentanyl and Anectine she had secretly prepared in the hospital and mainlined it with the drip kindly inserted by her colleague. Then she sank into a sweet sleep from which she would never wake up.

In hindsight, Rachel's planning was flawless. That morning she had mailed me her farewell letter, the one I had never spoken about to anybody. Then she had phoned the school to say Julia would be taking the day off, took her out to play in the park and then to eat pizza, ice cream and other junk that was off-limits midweek.

I have often asked Julia about that day. What Rachel said to her, whether she hugged her or said anything out of the ordinary. But Julia remembers very little. It's weird how pure, unadulterated happiness leaves no trace in our hearts, but the murky waters of sadness blight everything. Our little girl simply remembers that Rachel told her she loved her and would be with her always.

"Mommy smelled like strawberries."

When I got home from work, my wife was supposedly about to go on duty. It was usual on such days to steal a couple of kisses between one of us coming and the other going, so it took me by surprise to see her standing barefoot and waiting for me in the front yard.

"What's up?" I asked, giving her an inquiring look.

"I want to feel the grass between my toes."

"You'll be late for work, you slacker," I objected, not knowing she'd already called in sick.

"There's not much going on today. Let's have some tea."

We sat in cozy silence for a bit. When she finally got going, she gave me a big hug and a lingering kiss.

"I love you so much, Dr. Evans."

"And I love you too, Dr. Evans."

As she stepped toward the car, I yelled, "Don't forget to pick up doughnuts on your way back." She stopped and smiled over her shoulder, her medium-length hair wafting in the breeze. I would like to think her determination faltered then, albeit following such a humdrum request. Or maybe I'm merely kidding myself, to assuage the nagging thought that my final good-bye to her was so corny.

"I love you," she said back. "Give Julia a big hug for me."

I waved as she drove off, and that was the last I saw of her alive.

When a burly cop with a bushy mustache knocked on the door, I hadn't the faintest idea anything was up. His long, hard stare could have cracked mirrors, but I was oblivious at the time. I could only nod, stone-faced, while he told me how a maid had found Rachel when she went to turn down the bed.

"There must be some mistake," I answered.

"Who is it, Daddy?" Julia said from the top of the stairs.

"Go back to bed, honey," I shouted. "It's a man who's got the wrong house."

"I'm afraid there's no mistake, sir. Do you have any idea why she would do such a thing?"

"There must be some mistake," I repeated. I felt my legs buckle and the cop sounded miles away.

"In her letter she said she was ill. Were you aware of her condition, doctor?"

"She . . . she . . . couldn't abide pain."

"Was there anything in her behavior to suggest she was thinking of suicide?"

I remember that I fell to my knees, unable to reply. Denial, shock and a sense of failure held back the answers we both sought.

Answers which only now, as I hugged her old sweatshirt in our kidnapped daughter's room, did I finally understand.

Rachel and I were unique in the world. No one else had what we had, and no one ever would. Ours was a special love, a one-off. All we had spoken about, all the wisdom we had meant to hand down together to our daughter, all the mistakes our parents had made that we would never make with Julia . . . All that had gone up in smoke. She had taken a pain-free way out, to relieve our pain as best she could.

It took untold strength, courage and unfailing love to make that decision. Very few would dare to do the best for their loved ones in that way, regardless of the cost or consequences.

What if Rachel could see me now, see how I'd lost our daughter? What would Rachel want me to do to get her back?

Team Evans. Yay!

The sound of the three of us, chanting our family battle cry, rang through my mind. Two decades devoted to medicine, the childhood dream of a boy who wanted to follow in his adoptive father's footsteps and be a doctor, my very conscience. It all disintegrated, as quickly as a sandcastle swept away by a strong wave.

If Rachel's sacrifice had taught me anything, it was that the welfare of those you love comes before all else. If I had to forgo my integrity, my ethics, every single thing I stood for, I was ready. I would play White's game, but I wouldn't be putty in his hands. I could play games too.

"Have it your way, you goddamned son of a bitch. I'll do it," I muttered in an empty room, in an empty house, in the dead of night.

And a few seconds later came a text that made my hair stand on end.

YES, I KNOW.

53 HOURS BEFORE
THE OPERATION

Somewhere in Columbia Heights

White sat back in his chair and allowed himself a slow, smug smile. The leather upholstery hissed quietly as his skin slid over it. All his clothes were carefully folded on a classy ebony stand. The silvery glow from the screens lent an unearthly sheen to his totally naked body, which sparkled here and there with drops of sweat that dotted his skin.

It was hot.

He stood up and walked to the kitchen, his barefoot steps echoing off the empty walls. The small apartment was unfurnished apart from a foam mattress in a corner and a huge flat table with eight twenty-seven-inch screens mounted on steel supports screwed into the woodwork. In a high-turnover neighborhood full of postgrad students and yuppies starting out on the career ladder, the dapper Mr. White was quite unremarkable.

He opened the fridge and a flurry of ice-cold air gave him goose bumps. Each of the five shelves was stocked with bottles of Hawaiian Punch. A flavor for every tray: Fruit Juicy Red, Wild Purple Smash, Lemon Berry Squeeze, Polar Blast and Island Citrus Guava. He went over the names in a low voice, a quiet mantra, until he opted for the first one. He picked up a cold bottle and promptly replaced it with another of the same flavor he had fetched from the cupboard. A completely full fridge consumes less energy than a half-full one. White always considered the environment.

He went back to his seat and to eyeballing the screens, which relayed pictures of the Evanses' home. The cameras had been carefully concealed, although the aim wasn't that Dr. Evans shouldn't know they were there.

Quite the opposite.

He tapped a few keys on the laptop that controlled the whole shebang. Every screen showed Julia's burrow, six minutes previously. The audio feed amplified the slow, heavy breathing and the doctor's whisper murmured like a gust of wind.

"Have it your way, you goddamned son of a bitch. I'll do it."

The text message tone boomed out of the loudspeakers. White hit the space bar and zoomed in. Evans's face showed up on all eight monitors, at the precise moment he read the text. His tense expression, his eyes like dinner plates.

That's it, Dave. Now you can see the extent of my power. There is no escape, *White thought as he swigged the punch.*

He looked longingly at the gritty mascot, the unmistakable Punchy. Political correctness had stripped him of all his character. It was way funnier back in the eighties, when the character used to ask his victims whether they'd like some punch, then let fly with a good wallop. Whenever he saw the ads, sitting on the white Persian rug in his parents' living room, White would laugh out loud.

His had been a happy childhood. That of a spoiled only child, like all New York investment bankers' children. He had seen more of the servants than his blood relatives, but that was no problem. Nobody had smacked him, abused him or given him major trauma.

White was just the way he was.

He was born that way, and there was nothing to be done. He knew that clearly when he was eight, in the park where the au pair took him every afternoon. A little girl fell awkwardly from one of the slides, landed on her left arm and broke it. The end of the fractured bone poked out through her skin and was covered in blood. She howled in pain and stood up. Most of the kids clinched their arms in sympathy.

White didn't.

That day he understood he was a unique and self-reliant being. Human beings have leaky boundaries. They feel other people's pain, see their emotions affected by those of others. They live their lives connected to the rest by a sort of emotional grapevine.

White was unburdened by that flaw.

His total lack of empathy put him a cut above the rest. He could read others' feelings and interpret them, without those feelings sullying him. That evolutionary step forward was most practical.

Learning how to make use of this knowledge had been a long hard road. White took years to find out that every human being has a boundary between the comfort zone of their hopes and fears, and the quicksand of their wishes and needs. To achieve a total surrender of the will, you had to push them out of the former without sinking them into the latter.

Up to the tipping point.

Everyone had a different personality type. For somebody such as Dr. Evans, violence was no more than a back-page story in the Post, *something that did not impinge on the confines of his world. At bottom, human nature is the denial of death, and a committed doctor is the epitome of that denial.*

To get a subject with such strong convictions to resort to violence, you had to burn his bridges, one by one. Steadily, until you forced him to embrace the contradiction between his beliefs and reality. By plotting a road map with pinpoint precision. With someone more unthinking and not as straight as Evans, he would have cut the response time.

White's cell phone vibrated on the tabletop. Just like David's, it was a very exclusive model. It had been modified using state-of-the-art technology, and its signal was protected by a 128-bit encryption key. He didn't bother to see who was calling. Only one person in the world had his number: his employer.

"It's under way."

The voice at the other end of the line mumbled a few words in response. White barely listened to him. His eyes were still glued to the monitors.

He pressed a key to bring the picture back to real time. It looked like the doc was asleep.

White frowned, bemused. He'd never seen him do such a thing; cling to that sweatshirt that way. He thoughtfully stroked his earlobe and jotted something down on his iPad.

Tomorrow would be a most interesting day.

8

When I got to the hospital the morning after, my mind was racing.

Soon after I received White's terrifying text, I had fallen asleep. I was pooped. Discovering they had bugged my house with microphones and God knows what else sent shivers down my spine. But after a thirty-six-hour shift and all the emotional rushes that followed, I was too worn down to do a thing about it.

I was painfully aware when I woke up. As I showered and got dressed, I felt my privacy had been invaded; I felt a pair of dark and dirty eyes spying on me from every corner. I was never much into spy movies or TV shows, but Rachel used to love them. I tried to remember what I had learned from watching *Homeland* and *Person of Interest*, although I'd had only half my mind on them, with the other half buried in a novel or the *Journal of Neurosurgery*. All I remembered seemed like kids' stuff or hackneyed.

I understood all too well why White had sent the text right when he did. He wanted to make it obvious he was eavesdropping on my every whisper. But that morning I had to go to work. He had made it abundantly clear I was to keep to my regular routine and do nothing at all to draw attention to myself. I was sure he had tapped my home phone and cell. But would he have tapped the hospital phones too? I kind of doubted that. An attendant told me once there were more than nine hundred lines in the building. White couldn't possibly tap them all. Unless he had hacked into the exchange and screened calls to particular numbers, such as 911 or the FBI. Damn, I didn't even know whether such a thing was possible.

At that very moment my cell rang. The caller ID was blank.

It was him.

"Good morning, Dave. You'd better get a move on, there's bumper-to-bumper traffic on Sixteenth."

"Thanks for the traffic update," I said in a tone which belied my words.

"Stop looking at that lamp. There's no camera there." I jumped back from it and turned my head every which way.

"Neither is there one on that picture, nor that wall, Dave. Or maybe there is. That's none of your business. You will not search for cameras or bugs. Should you find one by chance, you will leave it be. We don't want to lose touch, do we?"

"Guess not," I mumbled, swallowing my humiliation.

"Now you have to call Julia's school and tell them she's sick and won't be back until Monday. Go on, I'm waiting."

I obeyed, using the landline. When I picked up my cell again, White was humming a tune I couldn't make out.

"Good job, Dave. Just one more thing. You'll be spending a lot of time in a huge building full of telephones, computers and all kinds of other items that are perilous for your daughter. You will be tempted to use them to cry for help. Don't be. You may not think so, but I am watching. Continually. In more ways than you can comprehend."

The message chimes sounded. I pulled the phone away from my ear. A text had now landed with a photo. When I opened it I saw my daughter imprisoned in that filthy pit. She had her eyes shut and her arms were wrapped around her knees, her head resting on them. She was trying to sleep.

"If you don't play ball, Dave, this will be the last picture you see of her. Don't forget."

He hung up without giving me a chance to reply. I looked at the photo for a second longer, but it evaporated in the blink of an eye.

I looked for it like crazy in my inbox and the photo gallery, but it had been deleted from both. That shithead had total control over my phone, a point he made in a text I got that very moment.

TIME FOR WORK.

Cussing again, I got into my car and tried to think.

A half hour later, as I went down to the changing room, my mind was boiling over.

I tried to weigh all my options, but some things I had worked out. First, White was full of it. He couldn't watch me every second, the less so in as big a place as that. Second, I had to get in touch with someone. Third, if I, or whoever I got in touch with, took one wrong step, Julia was dead.

Because I had seen his face, they would likely kill me too. Although if I lost Julia, I cared little what they might do to me.

I went to my locker, but instead of grabbing my own white coat and scrub set, I walked to the storeroom and took out some of the worn gear that smelled of cheap bleach, which the residents wear.

All of us surgeons are alpha personality types. Men and women in this job all fight to be top dog, the best there is. We spend our whole day in pissing contests and the same goes for how we dress in surgery. Believe it or not, they make overpriced monogrammed scrubs and caps in the most outrageous colors imaginable. That's how we set ourselves apart from the residents, nurses, staff physicians and others. We're on top, and we like to rub it in.

I didn't have to operate that day, but I did need to be sure I was carrying no gadget White could have bugged. I completely stripped off, then put on some scrubs and a white coat that was generic and unlabeled. I didn't take my stethoscope or anything else that was mine.

The last decision to make was whether or not to take my cell and pager.

Fortunately I was late, so there was almost nobody in the changing room, but for a while I froze solid, just staring at those gizmos like a man possessed. I was never apart from them and got into a flap whenever the batteries were flat or the charger light showed red. But at that moment those objects were evil itself to me.

To leave the cell in my locker meant losing contact with White. I knew he had meddled with it somehow, and I needed to be rid of it. But to break off might rile him and he could harm Julia in some way by taking it out on her.

And not only that. Right now that little four-ounce device was my one link to my daughter. I put it in my pocket and closed my locker door.

The metallic clang echoed around the deserted changing room as I made my way out.

Unfortunately, I was getting nowhere and the work was piling up. I had skipped breakfast, although stress and nerves had taken hold of my guts and I couldn't have eaten a thing.

Nonetheless, I couldn't let any of my feelings show. White had made that very clear: I had to smile. His weren't the only eyes that would be on me over the next few days.

I got into the elevator and ran into someone from admin, a great big, chipper guy I got along well with. Straight off I could see in his eyes the first signs of rejection everyone has had since Rachel's suicide.

"How the hell are you, Mike?"

"Well, doc, fighting off the anorexia, as you can see," he said, patting his massive belly.

I laughed. "Seems you got that bitch under control."

Mike laughed with me, surprised to see me joking again.

"Be seeing you," I said as I walked out.

"Bet you'll see me first," he quipped, and kept on laughing even after the elevator doors were shut.

I took a couple of steps away from the elevator and had to stop for a second. The lights, the bustle, the phones ringing, the chairs and gurneys wheeling along the passageway, the nurses gossiping in the corner, the chief resident herding the kids from room to room, the smell of disinfectant. All the hustle around me, everything that went to make up the chaos I called home, was alien to me now.

I felt far removed, light-years away from all those jerks who didn't get what I was going through. If they found out Julia had been kidnapped, they'd merely mutter, "Oh my God, how terrible," shake their heads and go home to kiss their family and think it could never happen to them. It was exactly what they did when Rachel died. At most they would avoid me for a few months, a normal reaction in case my bad luck rubbed off on them. We hospital folk are very superstitious, and surgeons more than anyone.

A nurse ambled past me and said hello with a big smile, which I returned by ordering my face muscles to move.

The chasm between that woman's carefree happiness and my torment made me despair.

I got a grip on myself and went to the nurses' station.

"What's up?"

"They called from Stockholm, something about a Nobel Prize they want to give you," said Sandra, who was head of the day shift.

"Tell them I'll pass. They'd give it to anyone these days."

Sandra laughed. She was also surprised I had joked back. I felt a bit guilty. There has always been a covert class war between doctors and nurses. They believe they do all the work, while we take all the credit and give all the orders. We . . . Well, we can be quite despicable. I had always tried to avoid that attitude, but I realized that with my bad mood in the last few months, that good intention had receded and I had made everyone's life around me a misery.

Although anxiety was now back in the driver's seat.

"I'm off to my consulting room to prepare my rounds. I'm running really late."

"Doctor, wait. We need to talk." She rooted around under the counter and placed between us the folder with the surgery schedule in it for the next few days.

I tilted toward her and did a double take when I saw the name

Sandra had underlined. A name I did not need to raise too many questions.

"It's to do with R. Wade. We have his medical records and billing details. His file is all in order, except for his Social Security number. I ran a check on it and got an error message. And the phone number they gave us always goes to voice mail."

Small wonder nobody answered. R. Wade, male, born August 4, 1961, in Des Moines, Iowa, did not exist. The Secret Service had provided the phone and Social Security number. The operating theater was booked up for the whole of Friday morning, and the other one on that floor had a software review lined up which would never take place. No more than three people in the whole building knew the patient's identity: the hospital manager, my boss and me. I had sweated blood over that, in a place where there are no secrets. But that was nothing compared to the fun and games we would have in the next forty-eight hours.

At all costs we had to avoid anyone knowing who would be operated on there. Because if one single person found out, she would eventually tell her husband, who would blab to his best buddy, who would tell his wife and tweet it . . . The operation could be canceled or rescheduled, which would mean curtains for Julia.

"Sure, they must have gotten a digit wrong," I said, trying to make light of it. "Fill in the admission date with the one you've got, and we'll change it later."

"But, doctor, this is very irregular. And if the HMO gets to hear of it . . ."

"Believe me, Sandra, this patient does not have cash-flow problems."

She looked at me, surprised, but said nothing. We were suddenly aware of how close we were to each other and I backed off. She clutched at her hair, embarrassed, and backed off, too.

"I'm afraid I have to get this straight, doctor. You've been on this case from the start, haven't you? Couldn't you—"

I didn't have the patience or the energy to deal with this situation properly.

"Well, if it's so important, take it up with Meyer—the hospital manager. He was the one who recommended him, damn it!"

She turned around, discomforted. Spooky Dave was back.

I ran off and locked myself in my consulting room, and felt bad that I had treated her that way, but I needed to be alone for a few minutes to relax.

I collapsed into my chair. That sort of overreaction would not help to keep the Patient's identity secret. The morning couldn't have gotten off to a worse start, and it would get miles worse yet.

9

I couldn't skulk in my cave for too long. I had to go see my patients. I wasn't down to be with the residents that day—thank God for small mercies—but I couldn't shirk the rounds. I had already reached a decision: I would seek out a cell phone and wangle a way to call the one person in the world who could help me.

The problem was whether she'd be up for it.

At about ten thirty, an hour later than usual, I had mustered enough presence of mind to emerge. At noon I had an unavoidable appointment, so I couldn't delay matters another minute.

I began with Mr. Melanson, a retired lawyer on his fifth wife. His aneurysm must have been because of her, a blonde whose body ought to have scored on the Richter scale. If being hot were against the law, that woman would have had a SWAT team on her tail constantly. For now, a pair of residents, an attendant and another patient's husband were buzzing around her by the coffee machine.

"Good morning, Roger."

"What's she up to?" he blurted at me. He looked strangely younger with the post-op bandage covering up his bald pate.

"She's hitting on a bunch of juvenile delinquents by the coffee machine."

"Damn, and with me stuck here. When the hell are you going to let me go?"

Not five days ago, Melanson had been in my operating theater, with an aneurysm in the Sylvian fissure which literally blew up in my face when I tried to close it off. That old bruiser's blood had spattered my mask, glasses and apron while I cursed and went through hell to perform an arterial bypass and save his life. Had I not operated in time, that skinny, lively old man with mischievous eyes would now be a plant pot, taking his meals through a straw and dumping them in a diaper.

"That aneurysm was about to kill you. Hit the brakes a little. What's the hurry?"

While I checked his readings, I stole a sideways glance at his bedside table. I needed to get hold of a cell without anyone knowing. I would have to borrow one temporarily. And Melanson's was nowhere to be seen.

"I feel like finding me a new Mrs. Melanson, doc. That one's past her sell-by date."

"That'll be number six! Haven't you had enough?"

"Number seven, really. There was a two-day fling in Vegas that was never on record. Well, as long as they keep signing the watertight prenups, then bring 'em on."

I couldn't help laughing out loud.

"I see you're in fine fettle, Roger. So barring surprises we'll discharge you the day after tomorrow. But only if you promise to put off the search for a month or two."

"I promise," he said, then crossed his heart. "But make no mistake, if she finds me, I'm not accountable."

I came across the soon-to-be ex–Mrs. Melanson in the doorway. She simply mumbled a "Hi" while she eyed her phone to check out the gossip on Facebook. I must have flashed her bedroom eyes because she got the wrong idea about where my look was aimed and gave her neckline a snide tug.

I shook my head as I stepped into the passageway.

The next three on my list were very simple cases whom I would discharge that same week. But relatives and friends accompanied them all, and there was no chance to purloin a cell phone. Under my breath I cursed the jobless rate, which was giving people all that time on their hands, as I turned the corner and entered the Warton Memorial suite.

They had remodeled the specialist neurosurgery wing in 2010 thanks to an endowment from Josephine Warton, an agoraphobic and very reclusive multimillionaire, whose sole purpose had been to keep herself apart from the other millionaires when she had treatment for her epileptic fits. In practice the unit comprised a single room with a reception area furnished in execrable taste, and a small nurses' station that was nearly always deserted: a super-exclusive area in an exclusive hospital.

It would have a very eminent occupant on Friday. Ironically, that morning a patient with an entirely different background was recovering in the Warton Memorial suite: poor Jamaal Carter.

Medical Director Wong had given the order to accommodate him there to keep him and his sidekicks, a motley group of teenagers with no particular academic inclinations, away from the paying patients.

They were gangbangers, in other words.

There were four of them, lounging on sofas in the lobby, with their feet up on a cheesy pink marble table with a brass stand. Behind them, a portrait of Warton—whose will had stipulated that the rich bitch should always preside over the room—frowned in stark disapproval. That prim old biddy, a close devotee of Ayn Rand, would have turned in her grave to see us treat Jamaal Carter pro bono in her suite. I wasn't freaking out though. The hospital had cleared $128 million the year before. We could afford it. Respecting the codicil in that witch's bequest was not a priority for me. All the staff were slaves to her, as it were, so every time I saw that portrait I felt like driving to the cemetery, breaking into the Warton vault and cracking her skull with her own tibia.

Three of the four gangbangers got up when I strode in and began to talk all at once.

"It's about time a doctor came to see Jamaal. What kind of joint you all running here, dude?"

"Hey, doc. If there's any problem with the green, you let me know, right?"

"Tell Jamaal we're right here. That cop there won't let us past."

The speaker pointed to a well-worn officer who lolled in a chair behind a copy of the *Post* while he guarded the entrance to the Warton suite. Seeing the lawman there made my stomach turn. Every ounce of me wanted to run over, grab him by the uniform and beg for his help. I was fighting against that feeling when I got a text: THINK CAREFULLY.

I bunched my fists inside my coat pockets and tried to hear myself think above the gang's chatter. How could White know what was happening? He could not possibly have planted cameras or bugs there. The Secret Service had discreetly screened the place the week before, and would do so again the day after.

That confirmed what I had suspected since the night before: the son of a bitch was using my cell mike to spy on me. As long as I had it on me, he could hear everything that was said around me. And he had probably wired the camera, too. That put a wrench in the works.

On the spur of the moment, I stared at one of those kids, the one who had hadn't moved when I came in.

"What's up with you, pal?"

He looked wasted, was boring holes in the marble with his eyes, and his lower lip trembled.

"Ain't nothing wrong with T-Bone, doc," one of them butted in. "You get in there and take care of Jamaal."

I guessed the kid was off his head on crack—how wrong I could be—and went into the suite, painfully aware the clock was ticking and I hadn't gotten what I needed. I greeted the cop, who grunted as I went past. He didn't raise his eyes from the sports page.

I had allotted four minutes but they turned into twenty owing to Mama Carter, the most persistently grateful human being I've ever met.

"Good morning," I said on my way in. "I'm Dr. Evans."

"Is that you!" shouted a lady in the visitor's chair at the bedside. "Did you mend my little boy? Hallelujah! The Lord guided your hands to save Jamaal, praised be sweet Jesus."

She ran over and began to kiss my hands, making me feel terribly uncomfortable. She must have been five feet tall and weighed one hundred eighty, and she had a face as sweet as pie. She was the perfect grandmother, apart from the slobbering kisses.

"Pray with me, give the good Lord thanks for granting you this gift to heal," she insisted.

I have often come up against this attitude. Lots of patients thank Jesus for saving them on the operating table and get lawyered up when things go wrong. We doctors could live without the thanks if the suits were also addressed to Jesus.

"I will, Mrs. . . ."

"I'm Mama Carter. Jamaal's grandmother. My daughter's dead. She's sitting at Jesus's right hand, and every night she has corn bread and pork chops with him. That was her favorite food and the girl was truly a saint. Now she watches over us all and has sent you to heal my little boy."

I succeeded in walking around her and to Jamaal's bed. Dressed in no more than hospital PJs, he looked much smaller and slighter. He had angled his childlike face toward the window, like a dove gaping at unattainable freedom. He turned to face me as I approached. He had one foot cuffed to the bed frame, which jingled faintly. His grandmother hurried to cover him with a sheet. The futility of that move tore my heart out.

"How you doing, kid?"

He contemplated me with his big brown eyes and shrugged. His face crumpled in pain.

"You shouldn't move your arms. You know you had a bullet in your back?"

"Yes, the nurses told me, and the cops that came by this morning. I don't remember a lot about last night, but I remember you, talking to me. You remove the bullet?"

"Look hard at my finger and follow it with your eyes. Attaboy. Your toes . . . Good. Yes, it was me who operated on you. You came within a hair of spending the rest of your life in a wheelchair. You should think hard about that before you hang out with those guys out there."

"They're my blood brothers," he said, bristling. That would have sounded real tough, except that he let out a squeak.

"Um, well, I don't see how they've shed much blood."

"Jamaal wants to thank you. Don't you, Jamaal?" Mama Carter jumped in.

The kid nodded and looked away.

"They'll transfer him to MedStar tomorrow," I told the old lady.

"Can't he stay here?"

"I'm afraid not, ma'am. We need the room."

Mrs. Carter would surely have gone into shock had she known who they wanted the bed for.

"I like it here," she said, pointing at the mahogany paneling on the walls and the Tiffany lamps. "I have some of my pension saved up. Couldn't you—"

Some screams spared me the hassle of breaking the bad news to Mrs. Carter that a single night in the Warton Memorial Suite cost $27,500. The door burst open and the cop popped his head in, looking flustered.

"Doctor, you'd better come here. Something's terribly wrong."

I ran across to the door. Three of the gangbangers surrounded the fourth, the kid who didn't stand up when I came in. He was sprawled on the floor, fighting for breath.

"Get back, get back for Chrissakes!"

His pulse was so weak I could hardly find it. That kid's life hung by a thread. *Damn*, I thought. *Just what I need right now.*

"You," I said, and pointed at the cop. "Go to that door and holler 'Code Blue' as loud as you can."

"I have to stay on guard—"

"Haul your ass, for Pete's sake! That kid's going nowhere."

I gave him no choice and wheeled around to tend to the kid.

I saw he had blood on his hands. I opened his coat to uncover a baseball shirt that was completely wet through.

"What's up with him?" I yelled as I pulled his clothing aside.

"Er . . . He was okay. T-Bone was—"

"Your friend's gonna die, pal. You'd better wise up."

Underneath his shirt, a dressing hurriedly made from clothes torn into strips and duct tape had turned into an unmitigated disaster. That mess couldn't have stanched a scratch from a blackberry bush. I squeezed as hard as I could to try to buy the kid some vital seconds.

"Was it a gunshot?"

"He . . . got poked up," a voice behind me stammered.

"What?"

"A stab wound," the cop explained.

"We didn't say nothing, to keep him out of trouble. We thought he'd make it!"

The Code Blue team showed up just then, dragging a resus trolley with one hell of a ruckus and shoving the gangbangers out of the way. They were three, two men and a woman, the toughest mofos in the hospital. Our best resuscitation team, used to laughing in the face of death. They had steely arms and an iron will. To see them kneel beside me was a massive relief.

"Stab wound to the thoracic cavity, entry only. Pulse below minimum. Been losing blood for hours."

"Fucking prick. Monica, the epinephrine!"

I was about to step back and leave T-Bone in better hands than mine when, between a muddle of knees, I glimpsed a cell phone on the carpet. I slipped it into my coat pocket.

I turned around to see whether anybody had noticed what I'd just done, but they all seemed to have their hands full. The cop looked on, aghast, and radioed for backup, obviously to question the other gang members, now that they had abruptly become witnesses to attempted homicide and who knew what else. Loyalty contended with prudence, then the latter won out and they brazenly headed off down the hospital corridor, followed by the old cop. I was taking no bets on who would reach the elevator first.

I spied the clock on the cell. It was 11:53.

I hardly had time. I ran down to the changing room while I hurriedly wiped away the bloodstains I still had on my fingers with a piece of gauze I'd grabbed from the resus trolley and got undressed.

I left my cell and pager in the locker and stepped into the shower with the gangbanger's phone. It was a prepaid model and must have been a couple of years old. I silently prayed it had enough balance for a call.

I held my breath and dialed the person who held my daughter's one hope in her hands.

Kate

Kate Robson raised an eyebrow when she saw an unknown number come up on-screen. Very few people had her number and they were all stored in her BlackBerry's memory.

She pushed the reject-call button, leaned back in the porch rocking chair, and dug back into the novel she was reading. It was a nice day on the farm, and she didn't feel like wasting it on some goddamned telemarketer.

Like all Secret Service officers, Special Agent Robson never turned the thing off. She was so used to having her days off interrupted after nine years in the service that she didn't bat an eyelid when it happened. While on call, officers had to put up with brutal hours. Consequently in her family albums there was a host of empty chairs in pictures of birthday parties, graduations and other big events.

Kate hadn't known how hard the job would be when she applied to join the Secret Service as she was about to start her third year at Georgetown law school. It had been a patriotic urge that had driven her to fill in the forms a week after the 9/11 attacks. She thought little more of it for months and had almost forgotten about the matter until she received a call from a supervisor asking her to come to an interview.

She went through the long admission process without getting her hopes up, but as the months went by she became more enthused by the idea, precisely because it was so difficult to get in. If there was one way to make Kate Robson relish a challenge, it was to underline its difficulty.

Finally, after an endless broadside of urine tests, lie-detector sessions, and fitness and shooting trials, Kate got a call shortly before graduation day.

"You have been admitted to the Secret Service, Robson."

"May I graduate before I enlist? I'm not one to leave things half done."

"I'll put you down for the Federal Law Enforcement Center in September. Don't make me regret it," was the supervisor's terse answer before he hung up.

The ink on Kate's law degree was barely dry before she hit the road in late August 2003 and went to the Criminal Investigators Training Program, the basic training program for all federal law enforcement officers. It was an eleven-hour drive to Glynco, Georgia, and the whole way she was never rid of accusatory looks in the mirror from her father, who had dreamed of a future for his younger daughter as a lawyer and had forced her to enroll in a program she never really liked.

"Look at your sister on an anesthesiologist's wage up in the big city. Do you really want to waste your life working for Uncle Sam?"

Kate didn't argue. It would have been a waste of breath. She had long since given up as lost the ongoing battle over good-looking, wonderful, perfect old Rachel.

She preferred to drown her sorrows in whiskey that night.

Kate simply blew her parents a kiss and drove on.

Fourteen weeks there and another eighteen on the SATP, the special agents Secret Service training program. Eight physically and mentally strenuous months, topped off by a well-attended ceremony and a pittance for a wage. But that was the least of it. The real bonus was wearing a shield that only three hundred other women in the United States were entitled to. She felt like one in a million. And she was.

The BlackBerry rang again and Kate goggled at it, mystified. The morning was too perfect, and she needed to relax.

She stretched out, and her willowy legs glowed under the sun. She had a hard, wiry body, maybe a little below the ideal weight for someone as tall and with as demanding a job as hers. Her mother shook her head every time she saw her and tried to fill her up with prodigious amounts of meatloaf and stuffed tomatoes. Kate would guiltily try to burn it all off jogging along the stony, overgrown lanes around the Robson farm. The air was so clean and fresh there it wiped away all her woes. She could never get enough of filling her lungs with the smell of Virginia.

She had had precious little occasion to fill them those past nine years. They had assigned her to the Cleveland office when she finished her training, where her duties were above all to fight forgery and fraud. Although the public at large picture the Secret Service as presidential bodyguards, in reality a large part of their job is to crack down on monetary fraud. Cyber scams, printing phony bills, identity theft . . . That was officer Robson's stock in trade, and after arresting her twentieth bartender on charges of cloning a client's credit card, she began to wonder whether she had made the right choice by taking her life and career in that direction.

Then her transfer to Boston came through and Kate was eventually assigned to protecting government personnel, beginning with the Treasury. At first her assignments were few and far between, but little by little her professionalism and unbreakable toughness won her superiors' respect. Officials liked to find themselves in the care of Special Agent Robson, who was as tall as a model and whose powerful figure commanded respect. With her hair pulled in a bun as tight as her lips, she was mystery personified.

It was a mask she liked to cultivate. Her male colleagues indulged in excesses denied to women. A spare tire, one drink too many after a twenty-hour day, a bit of company—paid or otherwise—sneaking into the hotel room . . . Such luxuries were forbidden to female officers, who were under double scrutiny.

"Hey, Robson, I hear you chicks have to pee every three-quarters of an hour. What you gonna do if Obama shows up when you hit the head?"

"He won't show. He's too busy boning your mother, douchebag."

That was the usual banter on the training course and for the first few months. She never gave the slightest sign it bothered her, although she often cried herself to sleep and soaked her pillows in tears of rage and frustration. But then word spread that Robson's shooting scores were 100 out of 100.

Bullets are gender neutral.

And at last, after seven years' hard slog, they had assigned her to the Washington office, to form part of the First Lady's security detail. The pride and the adrenaline rush made up for the step-change in stress and fatigue. Every time the First Lady approached the security barriers to press the flesh, Kate strained to scan every face in the crowd. From behind protective mirror shades her eyes examined every stance, every gesture, in search of somebody who did not fit in, for something awry. Some loose, thick clothing on a day that was too hot. A face that was too happy or too sad. Those hands in pockets . . . Always on a knife edge between ensuring she wasn't so overzealous she gave Renaissance (the First Lady's code name) a bad rep and the mission to protect her above all else.

She stood up and began to flex her leg muscles, bend her knees back and forth. She wore a pink T-shirt with a unicorn and rainbow on it, a throwback to her high school days that had been the butt of many jokes when her Secret Service buddies had seen her in it.

The cell rang again.

Kate cussed and broke off her warm-up. Three times in four minutes. Damn, she'd have to tell that jerk he had the wrong number, to stop him from bugging her.

Her annoyance turned to surprise when she heard the voice on the other end of the line. He was the last person she'd expected to call.

"Kate, it's me."

"David? Why are you calling me on this number?" she asked coldly.

Why are you calling me, period. That's the real question, she thought.

"I have no time for explanations. I need your help, Kate. Julia needs you."

10

They were waiting for me two blocks from the hospital and their eyes shot daggers through me as they leaned on a black sedan. There were two of them, respectively dressed in blue and gray. They must have had a photo of me because when Gray Suit saw me, he hurried me up by jabbing his finger at his wrist.

"Nice watch. Is it new?"

"You're late," he grunted.

"Sorry. Patient almost died on me."

After I had called Kate and showered, I put on a clean coat and scrubs. When I went to pick up the cell from my locker, the screen blinked twice and went out. I tried to switch it on again, but the button didn't respond.

"Couldn't you have worn something less conspicuous?" one of them said, and pointed to my clothes.

I shrugged my shoulders.

"That's what sucks about saving lives, officer. There's often some blood spilled."

They swapped glances, plainly pissed off. They had orders to make a discreet pickup, on a quiet street, and the subject turns up looking like a Christmas tree. I'd have felt sorry for them, had I not been frightened to death and scared shitless.

"Okay, get in," they said, opening the back door. "I think I've got something in the trunk. And for the love of Mike, get that coat off."

Gray Suit took the wheel. Blue Suit tossed me a marines sweat suit and sat beside me. He didn't seem too worried over the small matter of my wearing no underwear, and I didn't give it much thought myself. I was still obsessed with the way my iPhone had turned itself off. It wasn't the battery, which was almost fully charged. I was sure White was behind it, but why? Had he by chance found out about my call to Kate? And if so, then had I sentenced my daughter to death with my decision?

The questions tortured me, a rabid animal devouring my lungs. It must have shown, because Blue Suit glowered at me and took off his shades.

"Everything okay, doc?"

Those dark eyes pierced me like red-hot needles, seeking out my secrets and turning my soul to rubble. Or that's the way it seemed to my anxious and guilty conscience. I had to restrain myself and put on a brave face. The last thing I needed was for those Secret Service gorillas to tell their superiors the man who was to operate on the big chief was behaving off-the-wall.

"Sure. It's simply that I'm still trying to digest last night's dinner. Too many jalapeños. Might be good if you open a window, officers," I said, hiding behind verbal diarrhea as I always do when I'm flustered.

You must understand that in my early childhood, I was surrounded by all kinds of bullies. I always thought a gush of hot air would work as a distraction, like ink for a squid. I have an ugly F-shaped scar on my shoulder to prove I was wrong, and a couple of false teeth. Good old Dr. Evans Sr. had to go without a lot of beer to pay for those implants when he adopted me.

Blue Suit nodded slowly, not convinced.

"Doctor, I now have to ask you to do something uncomfortable."

I peered at him in surprise.

"You don't often hear that from a Secret Service agent. Sounds more like my proctologist."

"I need you to lie down on the car floor, for security reasons. The way to the meeting place is classified, and you do not have clearance to know its location."

"I already know where the White House is, officer. It's that big place on Pennsylvania Avenue."

"Doc, we ain't going to the White House."

"I don't care where we're headed. You will not lay me on the floor like a goddamned mat."

The driver pulled the car over and Blue Suit moved from the backseat to the front. They did not repeat the order, they merely sat there and waited. To them, I wasn't there.

Although pride made my blood boil, I had little wiggle room to argue in. I had arranged to see Kate at four at St. Clement's and could not be late. So I reluctantly hunkered down on the floor and the car started off again.

I wondered whether it was very far to the secret location. And if so, what if I were late for my meeting with Kate? Would I dare call her again and put Julia at risk?

I was getting more and more uneasy and decided to put such thoughts out of my mind as there was nothing I could do about it just then. I tried to think myself back to calmness by calling to mind the first time I had met my patient three weeks before, with no idea of the can of worms I was getting myself into . . .

11

If only I had given the little man in the bow tie a more modest answer . . . That was another of the key turning points in my life, but I was too full of adrenaline at the time to notice. I had just come from a complicated operation to remove a lipoma the size of a golf ball and was relishing one of those moments swollen with godhead we neurosurgeons sometimes have and don't talk about. You walk on sunshine along the corridors on your way to give the relatives the good news, an almighty being with the gift of life. Two things alone kept me going after Rachel's death: love of Julia and that fleeting and awesome feeling of power. Now that it's all over, I must confess with shame that I nurtured the latter more than the former. Another entry on my list of regrets.

I had finished talking to the family and was about ready to take a slide when the little man in the bow tie knocked on my consulting-room door. He had wizened skin, tortoiseshell glasses astride a hook nose and an unmistakable professorial air.

"Dr. Evans, may I have a word? I don't have an appointment."

He gave me a business card with a university logo , which I am not at liberty to disclose. I invited him to sit down and we had a little polite chitchat before he could bring himself to get down to brass tacks.

"I would like you to take a quick look at this MRI scan, if you would be so kind," he said, and opened an expensive leather briefcase to hand me a dog-eared envelope.

I withdrew four large transparencies and put them on the viewbox. I frowned at the sight of the lumpy gray blotch in which I recognized the shape of my oldest and worst enemy.

"Frontoparietal glioblastoma multiforme. A real son of a bitch, it would appear. What's its growth rate?"

"Check the dates. The four were taken two days apart."

I carefully ordered them by the numbers under the name.

"Who's the patient?"

"The husband of a former student of mine. A brilliant and exceptional woman."

"And the physician?"

"I would rather not say. You see, she needs a second opinion and was unable to come to speak to you."

I studied the scan for a good while. She needed a second opinion, all right. She wanted somebody to tell her it was all a mistake, that the cancer that was going to kill her husband was no more than a screwup by the machine, or that it was being reabsorbed, or there was some experimental treatment in Switzerland that would kiss it and make it better.

But there were no screwups, no reabsorption and no miracle cures. It was thank you and good night.

"Well, whoever this R. Wade may be, he is lucky, if you can call it that. The growth doesn't appear to be especially quick. Unfortunately the good news ends there. He'll likely lose his speech faculty within a couple of months. And he'll be dead inside a year."

The little man calmly wiped his glasses on a silk handkerchief that matched his bow tie. In all likelihood, he had already heard this many times before. He folded the handkerchief very carefully and tucked it into his lapel pocket. He blinked shortsightedly a couple of times, put on his glasses and looked me in the eye.

"Would you operate on him?"

And that is where I blew it.

"Of course. Although it will be high-risk and the results far from spectacular. I couldn't buy him much time."

"What about the speech faculty?"

"I believe, and this is no more than a conditional estimate, that the part of the tumor located between the Wernicke's and Broca's areas can be removed."

"Conditional upon?"

"Upon seeing the patient, studying his symptoms and following proper procedure. I understand you want to do a friend a favor, but this is no way to go about it."

He calmly nodded in agreement. It was what he'd expected to hear.

"Thank you very much, Dr. Evans. You have been most kind."

The morning after, my boss called me into her office. My consulting room is usually spick-and-span, a habit my adoptive father inculcated in me by example and many a night without dinner. Stephanie's desk was a jungle of papers, medical magazines and job reports. She sat barricaded behind that mound of paper and rattled her teeth with a pen.

"We're off to see Meyer," she said, standing up as soon as she saw me.

"The prince of darkness? What in heaven's name is going on here, Stephanie?"

"You tell me."

I had to trot to keep pace with her on the way to the elevator. Although she has short legs, my boss moved them at great speed when she was angry, and just then she was seething. She had no clue what was up, and if there's one thing my boss hated, it was being out of the loop.

We went up to the floor, the one with carpets, rubber plants, patchouli air freshener and Kenny G's sax as mood music. I seldom went there but always asked myself the same question: how could anybody stand working for more than a couple of hours under that combination without going mental? The plain answer is: they can't. All hospital execs are deranged and devote every living minute to making our work more efficient and prices more competitive. By "efficient" I mean cheap, and by "competitive," obscenely exorbitant.

Meyer's secretary ushered us in, and he was waiting for us behind a mahogany desk big enough to play tennis on. Robert Meyer was the classic product of an Ivy League MBA program, full of himself and of bright ideas that went down great in the annual report but bombed in the operating theater. You want to know when health care went to hell in a handbasket in this country? When they took doctors out of management and put bean counters such as Meyer in charge. Ask yourselves why an MRI scan costs one quarter in France of what it does in the home of the brave.

"Dr. Wong, Dr. Evans. Please come in. David, I believe you've already met . . ."

Beside him was the little man in the bow tie, who shook my hand shyly. After the introductions, the visitor explained which patient he represented.

"He wants you to operate on him, David."

They all gawked at me: Stephanie in perplexity and with envy verging on hatred, Meyer with towering greed, mentally calculating how much he would milk out of that tremendous stroke of luck, and the little man in calm expectation.

I felt faint. Luckily I was sitting down, or I might have fallen over somewhat unprofessionally.

"Why me?"

"He will tell you everything. Naturally the whole process entails some inconvenient security and confidentiality measures."

"We will gladly embrace them," Meyer hastened to say. "Right, David?"

I can tell when I'm being given an order and was too shocked to quibble.

"Of course."

"Well said. Dr. Evans is our big star."

He bared an enormous row of teeth and slapped me on the back, twice, perfectly camouflaging the fact we cannot stand each other. He thought I was a loose cannon and a bleeding heart. I think I've made my thoughts clear.

"So could you see him today?"

"Is he . . . is he here?" I asked stupidly.

The little man in the bow tie grinned at my innocence.

"As I have said, Dr. Evans, there will be certain extraordinary measures."

An hour later I entered the White House by the servants' entrance for the first time.

It is a strange and unreal feeling to have the world's most important man ask you for help, and all the more so when you have to slink in to avoid prying eyes, like a thief in the night.

"All the journalists are in the press conference, but just in case, we will take you along a slightly unorthodox route," the agent beside me said.

We crossed a courtyard and a well-lit service corridor. Then another courtyard flooded with the smell of good cooking and the noise of food being prepared, up to a room with palms planted in big alabaster pots. We had crossed paths on the way with some of the maintenance staff and uniformed guards, but nobody else.

"Wait a minute," the agent said.

He popped his head through one side door, then another. Finally we went along a gigantic corridor fitted with wall-to-wall gold-trimmed red carpets. We passed by a door with a brass plate inlaid with black letters saying "Doctor's Office," although we didn't stop there, but at the following door.

"This is the Map Room," the man said curtly. "We'll wait here."

Although the room was full of chairs, I remained standing in the middle. The agent stood by the door, legs astride, his bull neck pointing skyward. The strong silent pose I had seen in a thousand movies, and I wondered whether he was simply imitating the way he thought an agent was meant to stand or whether it came naturally.

I was tempted to ask but kept quiet. Before Rachel died I used to try to raise a smile out of those I met. A joke, a funny story, a wisecrack. She would see me make an effort with waiters, receptionists and cab drivers, and award points depending on the scale of difficulty and attainment. Believe me, that was a high-stakes game in Washington. I know nowhere else in the world where people have turned rudeness into an art form.

Rachel would have given me top score for that agent. But she was no longer with us and I had lost the will to play, so all I did was shoot the breeze. My surroundings overwhelmed me. Wood, silver, satin. Everything about the place was designed to overawe visitors.

My hosts overawed me for a long while, at the end of which a bald, broad-shouldered sixtysomething man with firm callused hands entered the room.

"Captain Hastings, chief of the White House medical staff. This way, Dr. Evans."

I followed him through the adjoining door and into a small lobby with two doors. The first led to two consulting rooms which the doctor showed off to me. In the second one, which was next to his office, an old chart with a diagram of the heart and lungs in vertical section that was hung up over a stretcher caught my eye, and I walked across to examine it.

"You like it?" Hastings said in a friendly voice.

"There was one exactly like it in my father's consulting room. I know, because it had the same typo on the subclavian vein."

Hastings smiled and rapped the mistake twice with a long bony finger.

"A memento of happier days. More straightforward and more humane."

I nodded. I liked that guy. He reminded me very much of the old Dr. Evans. Right then I missed him dearly.

"What's your specialty, Captain?"

"Internal medicine. It's been an essential job requirement for years."

"Are you in the army?"

"Navy. Each of the five services provides a doctor to the eighteen acres."

Seeing my puzzled look, he hastened to add:

"It's the term of endearment we use for the complex," he said, pointing all around him. "Come, let's make ourselves comfortable."

"Are you in sole charge of this?" I asked, surprised to see the place so empty.

"Not at all. I have ordered the rest of the staff to take part in an emergency drill this morning. I wanted you and me to talk alone."

"Anyone would think you were all ashamed of me, Dr. Hastings."

We sat in a large but chock-full office. A mahogany desk wedged between bookcases with heaps of books took up the middle of the room, lit up by the daylight pouring in from the Rose Garden. But a smiling skeleton hanging from an old hat rack stole the show.

"That's Fritz. We go way back, to the days when I started off. I won him playing poker with a medical orderly in Pearl Harbor, who in turn had won him off his boss in Korea. He swore blind it was the remains of a Nazi killed in Berlin at the end of the war."

"And you believe that?"

"He's too short."

"They also had short Nazis. At least one of them," I said, raising my right arm in an unmistakable imitation.

Hastings pulled a sly smile.

"Well, that would be poetic justice. Adolf's bones hanging from a hat rack in the White House!"

We both had a good laugh.

"I'm glad you have a sense of humor, Dr. Evans. It's a trait we greatly appreciate in the service, despite everything they say. Without it, a job like this would never get done."

"A lot of burning the midnight oil, I guess."

"And then some. When I tell people what I do the first thing I hear are sighs of envy. People think it's all parties, travel and power. But the reality is much harsher. We live for and by this administration, Dr. Evans. We go with the patient to the asshole of the world, Shitistan, and make sure he sleeps, drinks bottled water, that the heat doesn't get the better of him in the middle of the day's fourth speech. And all in eighteen-hour shifts, sorting out all the migraines and sprained ankles that can befall the rogues' gallery of political staff and journalists. And always, always, we fear the inevitable, the moment when somebody in the crowd will stand up, revolver in hand, and make our worst nightmares come true."

"Inevitable, you say?"

"Among the Secret Service there's an old saying about assassinating the president: it's not 'if' but 'when.'"

"Jeez, they won't be getting any medals for optimism."

"It's their way of preparing for the worst. So far we've been lucky. Remember the grenade they threw at the last guy?"

I nodded. The Texan was at a rally and the device landed at the foot of his podium but did not go off.

"Well, that's one of dozens of threats dealt with every day that we don't talk about, as long as they're kept hush-hush," Hastings added, his face drawn. "Luck will run out sooner or later. We live on borrowed time and merely struggle to ensure it doesn't happen on our watch."

There was an awkward silence. We both had to broach the topic, but Hastings couldn't bring himself to do it, so I made the first move.

"Why am I here?"

"You're here against my better judgment, Dr. Evans," the medic said, looking me in the eyes with an expression that mixed distaste with apology. "The president's health care has always been the services' prerogative. If it were up to me, the chief surgeon at the National Military Medical Center in Bethesda would treat the patient."

"I've heard about him. He's a great doctor. He's operated on several celebrities. Why isn't he sitting in this chair?"

Hastings leaned over the desk and lowered his voice to a hoarse whisper.

"Because the First Lady played the same trick she played on you on many others as well. She sent a flunky with the MRI scans to prevent the patient's status from overshadowing the diagnosis."

I wasn't too surprised; after all, the little man in the bow tie had warned me.

"Even the service doctors?"

"She took it up with them first. They all gave the patient up as lost. They said the risk was too great to operate."

"I . . ." I hesitated. "Was I the only one who said it was feasible?"

Hastings shook his head and rustled the papers on his desk before answering.

"No. There were others."

"Then . . . Why me?"

The medic left that unanswered, because at that moment the door opened and Hastings sprang to his feet. Not so much a jack-in-the-box as a self-pitching tent.

I turned to the door and also stood up. Although I've never been a dresser, I found myself instinctively buttoning up my jacket and folding down my coattails.

"Well, it's a pleasure to meet you, Dr. Evans."

There he was, elegantly shaking my hand. Tall—an inch or two taller than I, and I'm pretty big—charismatic, steeped in authority. I was so used to seeing him on TV that I had the automatic feeling we'd known each other all our lives. Or maybe that was an evolutionary advantage some people had, their ability to imbue a feeling of instant familiarity and closeness to undermine your defenses.

"The pleasure's mine, sir."

I moved forward to greet him, somewhat nonplussed by the presidential aura, and got a warm, strong, vigorous handshake. He was in shirtsleeves, rolled up to the middle of his forearms, his red tie slightly askew, and his face was weary.

"Doc, can you get me a Tylenol?"

Hastings obediently removed himself from the consulting room and the Secret Service agent took two steps forward, never taking his eyes off me. The president turned to him and said:

"That's okay, Ralph. Go to the relaxation area."

"Sir, the visitor has not been security cleared. The special agent in charge has ordered me to—"

"Ralph."

He gave the first order with a friendly smile, the second in a steely tone. It left no doubt. That was true power, and it didn't come merely from the office but from within the person holding it. It inspired a little fear mingled with a feeling that I wouldn't call envy, although it comes close.

The agent bowed his head and left the clinic.

When the door was shut the president sank into the chair I had been sitting in a minute before and massaged his temples. The wrinkles drew huge deadwood trees in his habitually serene face.

"Here, sir," said Hastings, who was back with the painkillers and a cone paper cup. The president took the pills, then squashed the cup. He closed his eyes again and leaned his head back for more than a minute before he turned to us once again.

"I'm sorry," he said. He seemed angry with himself for that show of weakness.

"How many are you taking a day?"

"Six or seven."

"Are the headaches nonstop, or do they come and go?"

"They come and go. When they come, they are intense but don't last long. I had no pain at all yesterday, but the day before was excruciating."

"Were you prone to headaches before?"

"Not particularly. I tend to get them the day after I've had less than five hours' sleep, but not as bad as these."

"Was that the first symptom?"

"A splitting headache. It seemed like the worst ever back then. I was wrong."

I nodded in understanding. The words *the worst headache ever* should be taken as a matter of course by every husband, wife, child and sibling to mean "let's book an appointment with the neurologist." I've lost count of how often patients have come to me too late because they've smothered a telltale headache with painkillers for a few months. Chugging down a jar of eighty Tylenols a week should tip anyone off, although amazingly the idiots prefer to ignore it. Not so amazingly, they die.

"When was that?"

"Four weeks ago," Hastings said. "We had the first MRI scan that same night."

"Where? Don't tell me you've got an MRI scanner here . . ."

The president and Hastings eyed each other hesitantly. The former vaguely shook his head.

"We cannot comment on the specifics, doctor. We didn't go to Bethesda for obvious reasons. It would have been much more difficult to contain a leak."

They stayed silent. Hastings produced the envelope with the scans and gave it to me. I sought the latest and held it up to the light. The soft, golden light shining through the curtains afforded the black-and-white death sentence a snug, dreamy appearance.

"Who did them, then?"

"I did myself," Hastings said.

"Only a handful of people are aware of the situation, all with the highest security clearance, except for your bosses, Dr. Evans. And it must stay that way."

"I hear you, sir. Have there been any other symptoms apart from headaches? Vomiting, impaired vision?"

"I can see fine and I have not been sick."

That was normal. Every patient was a world unto themselves and a tumor which in some triggered the vomit reflex, blindness or splitting headaches hadn't the slightest effect on others. In a neurosurgeon's career, you learn something basic: take nothing for granted. You learn that from seeing one weird thing after another. I once treated a woman at noon who had been shot through the head in a robbery and was back home eating with her family the day after. The bullet entered between her eyes and exited the rear of her skull, no damage done. But that's another story and I was all out of being shocked. What alarmed me was the possibility the US president was in the dark.

"How much have they told you about the problem, sir?" I asked with a glance at Hastings.

"I've given the president a summary briefing," the medic said while staring at the toes of his shoes. "He has declined to treat this other than in the utmost secrecy. There are other complications of a political nature which—"

"Hastings," the other man cut him off.

The poor captain zipped up so fast I feared he had bitten his tongue.

"Mr. President," I barged in. "Glioblastoma multiforme is an irregular tumor. It is not like a ball, compact and smooth, but an octopus. It's a self-replicating alien inside your head. It recruits blood from all the vessels it comes across and advances relentlessly. There is no way to make it recede significantly through treatment without seriously hampering your body and your performance in office."

"But there is surgery, Dr. Evans."

I shook my head.

"You're going to die. Real soon, and there is nothing I or anyone else can do to alter that. All I can do is turn the 'real soon' into 'soon.'"

He nodded.

"I am well aware of that."

"I can operate on the tumor. I can eliminate a good part of it, enough to delay the inevitable and buy you a few months."

"Then do it."

"I could also kill you. The tumor has reached the arcuate fasciculus, on the border between the Wernicke's and Broca's areas. It'll be a long and complicated operation, at least seven to nine hours. And it's a high-stakes game when we get there. A tiny slip and I turn you into a cabbage."

"That has all been spelled out to me, doctor. And it is also something which will come to pass anyway."

"If I don't operate, inside two or three months you will lose the ability to understand and verbalize concepts. Or the ability to speak. Or both at the same time."

"And if I do go under the knife, I may lose both in no time. Before then."

"Exactly."

A dense and unpleasant silence descended. The president leaned forward, his head in his hands, and gazed at the floor with his shoulders hunched and his back bent. Until a few weeks ago he was indestructible, a king among men. Now he was forced to confront his mortality like the next guy, with the added burden imposed by the demands of his throne.

"I'll do it."

I closed my eyes, overwhelmed for a second, and breathed deep before I answered.

"All right. When?"

"How long do I need to recover?"

"Nine or ten days' hospitalization, if all goes well."

"That time frame is unacceptable."

"You tell God that," I said slowly.

He went quiet again for a good while. I could almost hear him going over his schedule, thinking ahead of his rivals' moves. What to do and say. How to spin it. And all without aides, from memory. He was sitting in front of me, with his elbows on his knees, his hands cupping his forehead, his head inches from mine. Seen from above, it had an odd shape, slightly oblong with close-cropped, prematurely gray hair. For me it was easy to ignore his scalp, the skin and bone, which were mere hindrances in the problem's way. For a second, I saw myself prizing apart the structure's casing and sectioning the dura mater to expose the three pounds of brain tissue that made the most important decisions in this country, and a raft of others besides. In the middle of those three pounds of jellylike matter, a couple of unfettered ounces were waging a war with no quarter and just one possible winner.

"I can't for three weeks," the president said. "There are unavoidable commitments. Is that doable?"

"Yes, sir. Although I must tell you that by then the symptoms will most likely have worsened. There is some medication that can help," I said, jotting something down on a scrap of paper and handing it to Hastings.

"Very good," he said when he read it. "I'll entrust myself to take timely steps to book an operating theater at Bethesda in the name of an anonymous patient."

I gasped in disbelief when I heard that.

"I beg your pardon, but I will not operate at Bethesda," I said with a shake of the head.

"It's a flagship hospital. And it has the best equipment, as well as being able to guarantee the privacy of—"

"Please don't go on," I said. "I know the objective arguments, but first answer me this. Why me and not one of the others who said yes?"

"You have operated on two hundred and thirty-four glioblastomas in the past four years," the president said. "Of which sixty-one affected the speech area. Thirty-nine of them recovered without any problems."

"That data's confidential," I said, nettled. "You had no right to—"

"You have the second-best average in the country, doctor. Your college professors said you have natural talent and in your residency—" Hastings began.

I raised two fingers, definitely mad.

"I left two patients paralyzed in that same period due to complications with the brain stem. Another eleven glioblastomas came out as cabbages. Do they not count?" I objected.

"What's your point, doctor?" the president said coldly.

"This is an inherently difficult operation. It is not purely about my ability, nor is it enough to quote my tumor ranking. As it happens, I'm not a slugger for the Yankees. I'll need luck, luck and concentration, and if I operate in a theater that is not my own, with a team that is not my own, then I'll be tense. And that will affect the outcome."

"Doctor, I am sure there's a way you can adapt—" Hastings said.

"No there is not, Captain. It's the president of the United States, for God's sake. You're heaping on my shoulders the biggest responsibility a surgeon can have. I won't take it lightly."

I turned to the president.

"Don't think I'm asking you to be operated on in my own hospital to massage my ego or overcome an inferiority complex, or for the hell of it. I am doing so because otherwise I'll be scared shitless. You understand?"

He chewed on this for a few seconds and I wished with all my heart he'd say no. The situation was too complicated and I had to think of Julia. The risk it would turn out badly was so great, the odds of screwing up so stratospheric, that the chances of successfully completing that operation struck me as ridiculous. "I hear you. But I cannot accept an operation in an elite hospital. Not I, who have fought so hard for quality public health care. Public opinion would run riot for months," he replied, and I sighed with relief.

He'd given me the excuse I needed.

"Then we had better let matters rest there."

The three of us rose to our feet. I shook the president's hand in farewell and Hastings saw me out of the consulting room.

"I'm sorry about all that," I told him in the broad, red-carpeted corridor of power.

"Don't worry. I understand your reasons, and in your shoes I'd have done the same."

Hastings was wrong, naturally. He was a calm, kindly man, as sturdy and loyal as a shire horse. If the president said jump, he'd be in the air before the word was out of the chief's mouth. Somebody with that kind of personality could never be a neurosurgeon, so his understanding was as empty as it was well intentioned.

"Will you see me out or must I wait for somebody?"

"Actually, Dr. Evans, before you go I would like to introduce you to someone very special."

We went back to the Map Room, and there she was.

Seated on the edge of a velvet sofa with her legs crossed at the ankles, she was so engrossed in typing on her iPad she didn't hear Hastings's polite knocks on the door. She raised her eyes when we entered and rose to greet me. Her bearing was even more impressive in person, with an aristocratic air, but there was also a warmth in her voice that belied her expression.

"Good afternoon, Dr. Evans."

I mumbled a polite response, but she appeared not to hear it as she turned to quiz Hastings:

"How was it?"

The medic quietly cleared his throat and dithered over how to break the news.

"Well, you see, the president will not give way on the hospital, while Dr. Evans wants it to be done at St. Clement's."

"May I ask why?"

I replied, "For a solid medical reason: I need to be in my element. And political reasons don't count in this game."

"Dr. Evans, if I got my husband to change his mind, would you operate?"

"To tell the truth, ma'am, I wonder if I'm not in over my head here."

She smiled, a sad and spontaneous smile, a genuine smile.

"We're all in over our heads here, doctor. I cried all through the first night I spent in this house, out of happiness and fear. I know what it is to shoulder a heavier burden than you can bear."

"There are people who have the mettle for this job, ma'am."

"Thank you for putting it so politely."

She paused for a second, looked over my shoulder and was either digging into her memory or choosing her words carefully.

"You know why we picked the neurosurgeon the way we did,

Dr. Evans? When Bill Clinton had his knee operation years ago, there was literally a line of surgeons stretching outside the operating theater door. They all wanted to say they had operated on the president, and each one stuck his oar into the operation. They did not see beyond the office. We"—and her lips trembled a little at using the pronoun—"don't do that."

"Power and influence were used to choose the best available, ma'am. I don't see much difference in what you suggest."

"No, doctor. Judging by raw numbers, we could have chosen Alvin Hockstetter. I believe you know him well."

I shuddered to hear the name of my old chief resident at the Johns Hopkins. That man still unnerved me even though I hadn't seen him in more than five years. It was an obvious ploy, and we all knew it, but it was one I couldn't help falling for.

"You also showed him the scans?"

The First Lady nodded.

"And he was willing to operate," she added.

Damned right he was. Alvin Hockstetter was the most arrogant and pretentious pig I had ever met. He was also a self-promoting genius who chose his patients, whom he saw as no more than a bundle of cells, with infinite care. Hockstetter did not believe in the soul and thought disease was no more than a touch on the tiller of life.

He had a point. In biological terms, cancer is not an error, but one of the manifold ways in which nature clears the decks to make way for those next in line.

In human terms, that damned son of a bitch was the same enemy that had killed my wife.

"Ma'am, tell me why I'm here, then."

"One of the Secret Service agents assigned to me accidentally overheard a conversation with the man who visited you in your consulting room. Your name came up and she told me she knew you."

That stunned me. She could mean only one person, but we hadn't spoken in months. Both she and my father-in-law blamed me for what had happened.

"Kate Robson? But—"

"Agent Robson is an admirable woman. When she said you were related, I asked her what kind of doctor you were. She said she didn't know, but you were a good person, which is all I needed to know."

That show of quiet humility was a lesson in itself. The excuses with which I had masked my fears were finished. There was only one thing left to say.

"Me too, ma'am. I will operate on your husband."

12

I couldn't say how long I spent on the floor of that car. My legs ached from squashing them against the front seat, and my coccyx was wrecked.

Gray Suit and Blue Suit were the world's most boring chauffeurs. They didn't even put on any music, I guess so that I'd lose track of the time. They asked for my cell, checked it was off and kept it in the glove box.

"We'll give it back to you when we drop you off at the hospital."

After a long while—I'd say between three-quarters of an hour and an hour, but that's only a guess—I felt my legs cramp up and a clammy feeling of anxiety washed through me as the car came off the freeway and drove for a few minutes along back roads. Then we took a dirt road, which hurt my behind all the more. I don't know whether there was a single pothole the sedan did not drive over, but if so it wasn't for lack of trying by Gray Suit. I swear that asshole sought them out, every last one.

The wheels scraped the gravel, painfully jarring my bones and teeth. Then the car slowed down a bit and we were back on a tarmac road. After a few seconds, daylight had gone and the car came to a halt.

"You may get up, doctor. Apologies for the inconvenience," Blue Suit said unconvincingly.

I grabbed the front seat as best I could and managed to pull myself upright. My limbs were stiff and my senses dull. We were in complete darkness, with no other light than that shed by the dashboard, and in a strange place. It was akin to a garage, but the walls were too close together.

Several lights abruptly came on and dazzled us in a bluish glow, and I clasped my eyes with my hands. A long metallic click rang out, echoing for a few seconds deep inside my ears, then the whole car began to move.

We were in an elevator. No buttons or signs, just slabs of naked steel. The journey took a couple of minutes, which I spent rubbing my calves to bring back the circulation. When we stopped, the wall in front of the car slowly rose to reveal a cramped garage. There was room for twenty cars, although the spaces, marked out with red lines painted on a shiny gray floor, were all empty.

Gray Suit parked in the spot closest to the one door in the garage. They both got out of the car and I followed suit.

"This way, doctor."

The door opened as we approached and we entered a short passageway that led to another elevator, which had no control panel either. After a brief descent, we emerged in the middle of a rather untidy rectangular room. There were boxes and papers everywhere, also what looked like the remains of office furniture. The place was lit up by wall-mounted lamps that cast blurred triangles of light interspersed with patches of darkness. A somewhat objectionable dank and dusty smell hung in the air.

"Where the hell are we?"

Gray Suit shrugged.

"Tread carefully, doctor. This part's fairly neglected."

We took a route that cut through the mess like a knife. At the other end of the room were several doors and another elevator. I was rooted to the spot, mouth agape, when I passed in front of one of the doors. Inside was a dusty replica of the Oval Office, a perfect imitation, exactly as I'd seen it a thousand times on TV. Even the window behind the desk faked daylight so convincingly I began to doubt we were deep underground.

A cough from my merry companions returned me to reality and we took one last elevator down. It opened up into a passageway lined by glass walls, with several rooms that had the appearance of hospital wards running off it. At the end were consulting rooms, separated by medium-height steel panels. In one of them, with the door open and on the phone, was the president. I wondered how his cell could have coverage down there, although the very existence of that place raised enough questions.

I was about to enter the consulting room when the door closed, or at least that's how it appeared at first. In fact somebody had blocked my way. He was very big and seemed to buy his clothes two sizes too small. Hell, the world seemed two sizes too small for him.

"Dr. Evans, I'm Special Agent McKenna, head of the president's detail."

He didn't offer his hand.

Me neither.

We stared each other down for a few seconds and luxuriated in the mutual ill will that now and again—fortunately seldom—arises between two total strangers. He had close-cropped hair and a neat goatee around his mouth. His skull shone under the lights and ex–navy SEAL was written all over him.

I nodded slowly.

"My pleasure."

"You have been invited to these premises at the president's express wish. Everything about them is top secret and your discretion is requested. I am sure we can rely on your silence."

If only you knew.

"Officer, doctor–patient confidentiality—"

"Yeah, I know the spiel," he interrupted me.

"Then I don't know why you asked."

Spite flashed in McKenna's eyes, while his perfectly trimmed goatee cracked into an expression of annoyance and disgust.

"You're right there, doctor. Maybe I should begin to trust my own insight a bit more."

I had seen too many *National Geographic* documentaries to take that alpha male crap, particularly from a guy whose jacket still stank of minestrone.

"Have you finished pissing on my leg or can I go see my patient?"

A light grunt told me what a mistake I had made. Bullies are normally put out when you don't let them intimidate you, basically because they're one-trick ponies. When the one and only trick they know fails them, they're up the creek. But McKenna was nobody's fool, and my refusal to cringe merely got his back up. He flexed his arms and his suit strained to contain the muscular overbooking inside it.

I swallowed hard but stood my ground.

If it had been a bar, that bully would have wiped the floor with me. But his master's voice interrupted our tryst.

"Doctor, come in, please!"

The agent stood aside, stone-faced again.

"See you tomorrow, doc," McKenna whispered to me on my way past him. "I'll look forward to it."

I had no time to wonder what the hell he meant, because the president was already walking toward the door to greet me.

"I hope our meeting here doesn't bother you. I think you will find everything to your satisfaction."

I omitted mentioning my knees still hurt from the journey.

"Where on earth are we, sir?"

"My predecessor had all this built. The terrorist alert back then was sky-high, and there were signs a dirty bomb might go off in Washington. This place was devised to shelter the president and his cabinet in case of such an attack. Complete hospital installations, food and water supplies . . ."

"They've kind of forgotten about it, haven't they?" I said, wiping my finger on a dusty counter.

The president shrugged his shoulders.

"There is an end to our funds, doctor. When I took over the administration I had to choose, and this place was not a priority. There are others like it. The main thing is that we have this," he said, pointing behind him.

I couldn't fail to notice the gigantic metal tube that took up half the room. It was an MRI scanner. A German model, one of the best, six or seven million dollars' worth. A little old, maybe eight or nine years. It may not have had the latest software updates, but that was a minor hitch. The human brain has not evolved much these past two thousand centuries, so a couple of years wouldn't make a big difference to the scan.

I asked the president to undress.

"I know the drill, no metallic objects, I have no hairpins and I don't need a blanket, thanks," he said nervously, trying to crack a joke.

An absurd, strange feeling came over me when he tiptoed behind a little screen. As I switched on the machine I could hear him carefully folding up his clothes on the other side.

Every step I took in this business drew me farther away from the everyday medical world, the terrain in which I had learned to move and where everything was under my control. I had an almost physical feeling of being part of a movie.

In this screenplay, however, at least for the man in front of me and the gorillas outside, I was the bad guy. If they had the faintest idea of what was afoot, they wouldn't care in the least about my motives. They would pinion me to the ground and handcuff me. And Julia would die.

I could not allow that.

When my patient emerged from behind the screen, clad in hospital PJs, I looked him up and down in surprise. Physically he had improved somewhat, doubtless thanks to having scaled back his activities in the past two weeks. I knew he had seldom set foot outside the Oval Office and one columnist had even wondered why he was under White House arrest. Usually, second-term presidents woke up one morning to discover they had a big plane ready and waiting, and made the most of it. Nevertheless, at that time of year, when he should have been hard at it, the president had cut his public appearances down to the bare minimum.

He looked better and had even put on a bit of weight. He caught me watching him and patted his paunch.

"I know, my wife remarked on it yesterday. She hadn't seen my waistline expand for some time."

I nodded politely.

"Lie back, sir."

He climbed onto the machine's long tray and flinched when his bare legs touched the cold surface.

"Sure you don't want the blanket?"

He shook his head.

"No, but I would appreciate some earplugs. I never could stand loud noises."

On a nearby table there was a box of wax plugs, which I handed to my patient.

"Try to keep as still as possible," I said, and went into the small glass cubicle which housed the machine's control panel.

For the thirty-eight long minutes it took the machine to do its job, the darkest thoughts mired my mind. I felt trapped, a rat in a dark hole, and the animosity I bore toward the man who had put me in the impossible position of having to kill my patient shifted bit by bit. While the huge cylinders inside the machine excited the billions of hydrogen atoms within the president's brain to capture a perfect image of the tissue, I felt resentment swell inside me. Boxed in that cubicle, dozens of yards underground and with no room to move, I felt ensnared.

Claustrophobic.

I have always felt scared in situations from which there is no escape. I guess that comes of being a product of the system. I would tremble every time the Social Services woman firmly hauled me off by the scruff of the neck and took me to a new foster home. There I was, locked in with strangers who did not want me, but for the government check that came every month they kept me. They were the same old people, wherever they were. The same old sullen, vacant expressions, the same old pizza stains on the guy's shirt, the same old nicotine-yellow fingers on her. The same old lost orphans crowding the passageways. As soon as I moved in, I would stay in the rooms closest to the door if it was too cold to go out. I hate the rain. I hate walls. I hate people deciding for me.

When my adoptive parents took me to their home, I wreaked havoc. Just in case. They had the limitless patience to understand and force me to make the second-bravest decision of my life. They made me love them.

The bravest—and the best—decision was to marry Rachel. With quickie divorces these days, that may seem a trifle, but I'm not one to go back on my word once I've given it. For a commitment-phobe, that was a big deal.

Now I could not forget that some years earlier I had taken an oath never to do any harm to others.

Just then a half-formed image on the screen made me frown. It was not good.

When the tray buzzed out, my patient stood up and began to rub his arms and legs to get back the warmth and movement.

"Damn, that was a drag."

I nodded slowly. I wanted to get this over with but still had to give him the bad news, something I did not fancy. But if anybody was used to reading that kind of thing in people's faces, it was him.

"It's grown, right?"

"The growth rate has increased, sir. This is not good at all."

He was quiet for an instant.

"It's not so terrible, is it? After all, there's only a few hours to go before the operation."

"The more tumorous tissue there is in your brain, the harder it will be for me to remove it, sir. That raises the chances it will spread. Or that in the process I make you into a USDA Grade A cabbage."

He burst into one of his nasal laughs, the one heard in multitudinous speeches. But the gloomy half-smile he gave me was new, a side of the president precious few got to see.

He got up and went behind the screen. A few seconds later he came back with a pack of Marlboros and a lighter.

"You smoke?"

"No. And according to your chief of staff, you quit six months ago."

"I'm afraid in that respect we haven't been too straight with the voters," he said as he lit up and sat on the stretcher.

I was tempted to tell him this was no place to smoke, but it was his goddamned bunker. I had given him news that would entitle anyone to have a smoke.

"A lying politician. Why am I not surprised?"

"Why do you hate politicians?"

"I don't hate them. I'm just not wild about the fact they exist."

He puckered his lips, amused by the situation. People didn't usually speak to him that way.

"You don't like me, doctor?"

"Actually, I voted for the other guy."

Hell, it wasn't true. But you can't let them see that.

"Doctor, I know you're angry about all this. I mean, me dragging you out here, and because we are not going through regular channels. I can tell you we've had to break the rules dozens of times in recent years. I'm sure you know, or you can guess. Lately everything gets out on Twitter. Damn, even when we went after Osama there was some guy tweeting about it."

"I don't really follow Twitter, sir. Although I know Justin Bieber has more followers than you do."

He laughed and choked on the smoke he was breathing out. He gave a couple of quick, nervous coughs.

"Before, I thought this shit would kill me. But that won't be the case."

"Probably not."

He stubbed out the cigarette on an old newspaper covering the desk in the consulting room.

"Doctor, I'm sorry. I know you think I should have had the operation a couple of weeks ago, and this could all have been done otherwise. Believe me, that isn't so."

But it is so, dumbass. If you had gone ahead then, White wouldn't have kidnapped my daughter, I thought.

Instead of speaking out, however, I smiled dumbly.

"I'm not in politics for personal glory but to do the right thing," he went on. "We've achieved a great deal so far, but there's still a lot more to do. The Kyle-Brogan tax bill, for example. If we pass it, we'll roll back the power of the one percent in the country."

I wagged my head. Everybody had heard of the Kyle-Brogan bill those last few months. Everybody had their opinion about it, although the *Post* said the draft ran to eight hundred pages and doubted anyone had read it through. It would be a major achievement if it were passed, and make that administration go down in history. But as a doctor I had to raise a very different question.

"And is that worth your life, sir?"

"Good question. It's one I asked my wife the day you and I met at the White House. She—"

His voice quavered and he broke off to contain his emotion.

I am used to patients opening up and pouring their hearts out in the consulting room. They all end up doing so, sooner or later, even the strongest or shyest. Because they need to believe in me, in themselves, in their own chances. They all have stories to tell, something to say, and seeing death up close hastens that need.

My hand, however, won't be any the steadier because they need to live. Nor is it for me to judge, and I do not have the power to change things.

The president forced himself to continue after a while. "She . . . She spent a long time staring out the window without answering. After a while she turned around and looked at me, right here."

He pointed to his eyes with two fingers.

"She spoke in a calm, collected voice. She said if I really could make a difference, leave the world a better place for our daughters' daughters, then it would be worth the risk. That's why I'm taking these—"

I raised my hand, and he stopped in bewilderment.

"Hold it, sir. Do you realize you repeated yourself?"

"No, I did not," he said with a squint.

"Yes, you did, sir. Repeat after me: 'My daughters have a little lamb.'"

He took a while to answer.

"My daughters daughters have a little lamb."

"Are you aware you repeated yourself just now?"

"No," he said. There was terror in his eyes.

"Say *daughters*, please."

"Daughters daughters."

"Now split the word into syllables, please."

"Daugh. Ters," he said, taking a massive break between the syllables.

"All together, now."

"Daughters daughters. Please, no more, doctor. It's humiliating."

A burst of compassion flushed away the resentment I'd been feeling, and for a moment I was ashamed. I had pushed my patient too far.

"Has this happened before, sir?"

The president shook his head, hard. But then he ended with a nod.

"What does it mean?"

"That the tumor's eating into your speech area, sir. In a few days you will lose the ability to speak."

I felt a squeeze on my forearm. When I looked down I found the most powerful man in the world's big, strong hand clinging to me for dear life. And behind the mask of dignity he maintained despite everything, fear blazed like a bonfire.

"Save me, doctor. Please. I have so much left to do."

13

When the Secret Service agents dropped me off on Kalorama's blue-blooded paving stones, I blinked in wonderment at the normality. On the surface, nothing had happened; it had all been a bad dream.

But it hadn't been. My ass still stung from the journeys on the car floor; the sleeve of my white coat was still creased from the president's viselike grip.

And Julia was still in the power of a heartless psychopath.

Thinking of White, I took the phone out of my pocket, but there was no need. The screen was lit up, and my heart missed a beat when I saw it. The boring, default blue wallpaper was gone. Instead there was an image I'd deleted two months before because it was too painful to look at. The one with Julia and Rachel sharing strawberry ice cream. There was more of it on Julia's T-shirt than in the cone.

I was shaken up for a moment. That lousy shit could play around with my memories and feelings as if they were chess pieces on a board. He hadn't even had to send me one of his texts but had still grabbed me by the throat with that picture. He was reminding me what was at stake. Like I could stop thinking about it.

I forced my eyes away from Julia's impish grin and Rachel pretending to be annoyed, and saw the time on the phone.

It was four. I would be late for my appointment.

I felt limp; the tiredness had caught up with me. I had eaten and drunk very little in the past twenty-four hours, and a couple of hours' fitful sleep didn't help matters. If I carried on in that state I would run the risk of making a fatal slip, and I could not allow that just then. I wavered between hurrying to my appointment and grabbing a bite to eat, then finally sacrificed a few minutes to drop by my office.

Even though my stomach was rumbling, there was a far more important reason to be late: I needed an alibi. My phone, that infernal device, could not go where I was headed, or White would find me out in a second. I put the gadget on my desk while I peeled a couple of twenties out of my billfold. I affected nonchalance as I leaned through the doorway and shouted to the colleague next door that I was off to get something to eat and did she want anything from the snack bar? I hoped my forgetfulness would appear natural as I left the phone behind, shut the door and hot-footed it to the elevator.

"Dr. Evans!" said Carla, the head nurse on the evening shift. "Dr. Wong has repeatedly called looking for you. And Meyer."

"I'm famished. I haven't got time for this shit now," I said without turning around.

I could tell without looking she was agog. Carla was a queen bee. One who, when people went to the dining area to heat up what they'd cooked at home, would stare at the one whose plate smelled bad to her, chide them nice and easy, and reduce them to tears. No one ever questioned her.

I disliked Carla, so I tried to treat her with the extreme courtesy I reserve for obnoxious people. My overstepping the mark took her completely unawares, and for a split second her puzzlement made me feel a bit better. It was a momentary and mean relief, which was immediately reversed as I took the elevator down to the sad and lonely snack bar. I wasn't exactly following White's orders to be polite and fly below the radar. Even worse, my boss would chew me out for going AWOL for so long, skipping my rounds with the students and God knows what else.

The sight of the food displayed under the cold fluorescent light was no help. I never ate in the snack bar if I could help it, like most of the St. Clement's staff. That organic residue floating in grease was anything but edible. The one good thing about having a snack bar in a top-notch hospital was that if you had a heart attack after pigging out on the stuff, the coronary unit was just around the corner.

I was doddering and half starved, so I quickly bought a stack of energy bars and a Coke—nothing cooked there, no way—and paid the bored cashier. I smiled at her, trying in part to make amends for my bad temper before with the head nurse, but got nothing in return. No thought seemed to stir behind her bland face.

I didn't use the elevator. The ones on that side of the building went down only if you had a key I did not possess. Instead, I took the stairs right by the newsstand and hurriedly gobbled down one of the granola bars. The sugar flooded my bloodstream and gave me an energy rush I knew I would need. I was very late, so I went headlong down the four flights of stairs, a dumb idea in those stupid hospital clogs. Not a month went by without a colleague winding up in the emergency room after falling downstairs while reading case notes or heedlessly gawking at a cell phone. The edges on those granite steps were worn and chipped after a century and a half of use. The nonslip strips the hospital management insisted on laying down never stayed put but came unstuck and bunched up, making them into sticky traps that caused more accidents than they prevented.

St. Clement's resembles an old Victorian lady. All prim and proper on the outside, with her pretty ivy sprawling over her red brick and plate-glass windows. But on the inside she's an old slut, full of quirks, problems and secrets. The most unspeakable things go on in the subbasement, closed off from the stairs by a door which should be locked but never is. The manager before Meyer was the last to bother enforcing that rule, that I know of. He had a lock fitted and informed all personnel that only cleaners and morgue staff had access. The lock appeared the morning after with a hole drilled through it, which is apt if we consider the use the horny interns make of the dark passages and discreet nooks in the subbasement.

That manager, a devout Methodist, called for a locksmith and sent around a memo reproaching the vandal who had destroyed hospital property. In his note, he insisted that personnel should behave properly and "refrain from using less-frequented areas of the hospital for untoward purposes, unworthy of the decorum becoming our profession and this venerable institution." The lock was forced the next day, and the day after, and the day after that. The vandal took a creative turn on the twenty-first night by bringing along a circular saw to cut out a big piece around the lock itself. To everybody's relief—except the locksmith's—the manager abandoned his efforts to keep staff from their nighttime release.

Nobody had bothered to fix the hole in the door. The gaping wooden breach had darkened over time but still had splintered edges, as I found out the hard way when I shoved it with all of my strength. I rubbed my forearm where I had grazed the skin, looked around and tried to remember the way. The morgue was to the right, on the best-known side of the dimly lit maze. Straight ahead were the laundry and the hazardous materials disposal area, a sinister place covered in biological warning signs, which you would have to be crazy to enter. And way beyond on the left were the generators and the boiler room. The graybeards say that through there is the entrance to a second and far bigger subbasement, which has been locked up for eons. If that's true, I don't even want to imagine what horrors may lurk down there. Rats thrive on that floor despite the tons of poison the janitors dump on every corner. If you stand still for a few minutes in the middle of a passageway, you'll hear them squealing and scurrying about in the gaps between the walls and the steamy pipes. But at that moment all I was able to hear was my own panting as I ran along the passages. I took two wrong turns at an intersection but found my way again.

I got to the boiler room door with my tongue hanging out and a stitch in my side. While I tried to get my breath back, with my hands on my knees, I heard a voice behind me.

"You're late, David."

There was Kate, in a leather jacket and jeans. She was leaning against the wall, her arms folded. She stared at me with her dark, deep, sharp eyes. A mare's eyes in a cat's face: eyes that see too much. The strong, straight jaw jutted out at me. She was worn out and pissed, to mention merely what was on the surface. The wellspring of feelings that had simmered since Rachel's death, and even beforehand, was too complicated. I knew it, and she knew I knew it, which made everything even knottier and all the more wearing. We had kept our distance since then, and she had seen Julia only on the few occasions we met at my in-laws' place. That also hurt, because they thought the world of each other. They were equally unbridled, affectionate and carefree.

"I'm sorry, Kate. Really I am," I said, with a lump in my throat—due in part to the rush and in part to the shit storm that was about to erupt.

She nodded slowly, thinking I meant for turning up late. Nothing farther from the truth.

"Well, David? What the hell is so important you have to drag me all the way from Virginia?"

I took a deep breath and braced myself for her reaction.

Because as soon as I opened my mouth, I would ruin her life.

14

"Julia's been kidnapped."

Kate's astonishment was palpable. She stepped away from the wall and toward me.

"What are you talking about? You sure?"

"Completely," I said, staring at her. I wanted to pick my words carefully.

"When?"

"Last night, between nine and eleven."

"Damn it, and you haven't told the cops yet? The FBI has to get moving as soon as possible, David!" She took her cell from her pocket and began to dial. "I have a friend there—"

I grabbed her arm to stop her.

"No, Kate. They've told me not to."

"That's what they always say, damn it. If it were up to them . . . Shit, we have to get on the horn right now."

"I can't, Kate."

She pulled away from me and clicked on the phone again. There was a note of distress in her voice I had never heard before, and the words fled from her mouth in despair.

"The first few hours are crucial! And you have to gather together all the cash you can. They told you yet how much they want?"

"They don't want money, Kate. And you can't tell anybody."

"There's no coverage down here." She hoisted the phone up and shook it, that useless gesture we all make to try to increase the size of the magic bars on the screen that connect us to the rest of the world. "We have to go up and call as soon as possible."

"I know there's no coverage, Kate. That's why I've brought you down here, where nobody can see or hear us."

She stopped waving her phone around and turned her head toward me, very slowly. She narrowed her eyes and at that moment I realized how unbelievably paranoid I sounded and how suspicious my acts had been in the last few hours.

"David, is this true? Has something happened to Julia, something you want to tell me?"

I would not be the first overwrought widower to lose his head and do something awful, something drastic and unforgivable. Many manic-depressives take their families with them.

"No, Kate, it's just that . . ."

"David, where's Julia?"

I took a few seconds to answer. And when I did it was in the worst possible way.

"I . . . this is all my fault, Kate. I hope you can forgive me," I said, reaching out to her.

Kate reached out, too, but instead of taking my hand she twisted my wrist and followed through to turn me around and flatten my face against the wall. She was seven inches shorter and forty pounds lighter than me, but she subdued me in the space of a second. I didn't try to turn around because I wanted to convince her I hadn't flipped, although it would make no difference what I tried. She had my arm in a lock and could dislocate my shoulder with a slight push.

"Tell me where she is or I swear to God I'll break your arm. I mean it."

She forced my arm and I gasped in pain.

"They've snatched her, Kate. Let me go, for fuck's sake! We won't help her this way!"

We stood still for a never-ending second. I could hear the rats bustling inches from my face and the waste gurgling in the drainpipes. The wall smelled of whitewash and damp.

Finally she let me go and backed away a little.

"Turn around."

I obeyed, rubbing my shoulder and head where they had touched the wall. She stood very close, examining my face and scrutinizing it for signs that I was lying. She was too near, and, strange as it may seem, that made me feel more uncomfortable than the hammer lock she had held me in before. My mouth had gummed up and I had acid breath, so I tried to breathe through my nose until she backed off altogether.

"I'm sorry, David. Guess I overdid things."

"You believe me now?"

Kate put her hands on her hips and kept her eyes on me.

"I believe Julia's gone and it wasn't you. But I think there's something you're not telling me, David."

"I'll tell you on one condition. I want you to hear me out. If afterwards you still want to call the Feds, I won't stop you."

She thought it over for a second and nodded.

"Shoot."

So I did.

I began with Jamaal Carter's operation. I told her how I had come home to an empty house. And how there was a strong smell of bleach in Svetlana's room.

"They've done that to wipe away any sign of her. Any trace of DNA, or blood if there was a struggle."

"No, there wasn't. She's dead."

"She hadn't been in your house long, had she? She must have been in cahoots with the kidnappers."

I nodded and explained how I had driven like hell to Kate's folks' place in Falmouth, how I had crossed swords with Jim and he'd come after my car in the rain.

"He had a cold this morning and was out of sorts. I should have known it was your fault. You're the only one I know who can get him that worked up."

"That's what Rachel always said."

There was a gravelike silence and Kate turned away.

"Tell me about that text you got."

"It summoned me to meet somebody at a diner I drop in to every day. And there he was."

I paused and gulped. I was about to tell somebody his name for the first time. Everything I had told Kate had already broken the ground rules he had laid out. But somehow, to say his name aloud seemed like the real sin, even in the depths of the St. Clement's subbasement.

"Mr. White."

I described him in full detail, him and his henchmen. Or at least what I remembered about them, which wasn't much. But it seemed what I knew about the head honcho didn't amount to much, either.

"His appearance is too common, David. Unless he's got a police record, without a photo or real name, the description's no use. Why the hell did he want to meet you face-to-face? That is not the usual way."

I talked to her about the conversation with White. His refined and cold-blooded voice. His sharklike eyes and contained expression. The iPad with which he monitored the coop where they were holding Julia.

"And after he showed it to me . . . he told me what they wanted."

Kate, who listened carefully with her head to one side, tapping her foot on the floor, stopped dead. Her eyes were wide open and there was terror in them.

"David . . . What have they asked you for, David?"

I told her.

"No."

She stepped back into the passageway.

"Kate."

"No," she repeated, and shook her head. "I have to inform the head of my detail. We have to put the president out of harm's way this second."

"You can't, Kate. If you do, they'll kill Julia."

"David, I'm a Secret Service agent! There's a plot to assassinate the president, for God's sake! And I've got the freakin' assassin right in front of me!"

"She's your niece, Kate. She's only seven."

She stood stock still for a couple of seconds. Then she took a deep breath, turned her back on me, bent over and puked on the floor out of sheer tension. She leaned her arm against the wall and retched a few times while the vomit splattered the instep on her heeled leather boots.

I watched her from afar while I tried to get hold of myself, and felt the sorrow and rage that afflicted her. I couldn't console her, although I wanted to come close and hug her, body and soul, but it would have been counterproductive. One of the first things I learned as a doctor is that there are many more ways to hinder people than help them. Sad and cynical as it sounds, there's less chance of screwing up if you do nothing.

Despite that, and because I'm a jerk, I put my hand on her shoulder. Kate shook herself loose, roughly, then I stepped back. Just as well I did.

A deep sympathy for her bowled me over. I know precisely what it's like to hear something that turns your world upside down. Your heart misses a beat, because your body reacts before your mind. But the world doesn't stop simply because your heart does; after a second or so it carries on beating and the information reaches your brain. If you're smart—which Kate was, and then some—then what you're told becomes a jolt of electricity that lights up a bulb in your head. The light unveils a dark room full of nightmares, a room which has always been there but you never dared go in. You will no longer lead your life in the comfortable living room where you used to put your feet up before a crackling fire. No, your life will now run its course in a slimy, gloomy cell. And there are more shadows behind the walls, shadows you dare not name.

Nothing will be the same again, which is unacceptable.

So you deny it. You assail the information every which way. If it is undeniable, your mind searches for ways to keep you in the living room, out of the dismal cell. Why do you think they always give news of fatal accidents in person? You'd be amazed how often a cop has to stop someone from shooting themselves seconds after telling them their wife or husband won't be coming home that night, or any other.

When you know there's no choice, when you know the new reality won't budge, your body reacts again, a second time. Kate's did so by bending over and throwing up. When she straightened up, she banged on the pipes a few times, made them ring in an echo of her own frustration, and then cussed until she'd gotten enough anger out of her system to be able to talk.

Then she leaned against the wall and faced me, in tears.

"Damn you, Dave. Damn you for making me choose."

Mr. White checked the time in the top right-hand corner of his main monitor and scowled. Dr. Evans had already been gone more than forty minutes, something that totally bucked his normal behavior. Obviously, the whole situation he was immersed in was completely abnormal, but David's personality pattern predicted that in a crisis he would stick even more closely to his routine.

The personality patterns White used to manipulate his subjects consisted of a set of tables and flow charts. After a preliminary study, the subject's patterns were configured using the full range of personality types.

Those tools were infallible. He didn't get them from a psychology manual or anyone else. He had set them up himself after years of study, of direct observation, and above all with a callous, surgical understanding of human nature. If White had shown his results to the scientific community, they would have hailed him as a genius. At least until somebody asked what methods he had used to reach his conclusions, or what use he put them to.

His total lack of scruples had allowed him to experiment on live subjects. Life upon life had been destroyed in the construction of those diagrams. For White, they were his main reason for living. He lived to modify, tweak and expand them. He had begun to chart personality patterns in the psychology department at Stanford. The classes bored him;

the professors spoke too slowly for him. He had done most of the reading for his degree requirements before he finished his freshman year. He showed his tutor a draft of his first pattern at the start of his sophomore year. He had identified the personality traits of a concrete individual, as well as the factors or triggers that would lead said individual to commit a specific act.

"Emotions are changes which prepare the individual for action," he told the professor. "If we stir the right emotions in the individual, we can steer his acts from the outside. By remote control, so to speak."

The professor had gaped at him in horror. He shredded the sheets White had shown him and really lashed out at him.

"Psychology is not about aberrations of that sort. It is the study of human experience to improve it, not to subject others! This is absurd, useless and barbaric!"

White did not listen to the end. He walked out and left him with the words in his mouth. He had already foreseen that reaction. And much else.

Eleven days later, the professor—a jolly and kind family man, a lover of wine and poetry—killed himself in his living room, in front of his wife and three children. The detectives on the case were stumped: the death made no sense at all. The man had no debts, no drug or gambling problems. They searched for lovers and dirty laundry, without success. Finally they shelved the case, to the vexation of family and friends.

White smiled. He had foreseen that, too. The personality type he had taken to the office was the professor's own. He had spent the following days exploiting the man's weaknesses until he drove him to his death. He wasn't altogether satisfied, though. He had estimated he could make the professor commit suicide inside a week. The delay was doubtless down to small errors in the subject's personality pattern, defects that could be fixed over time. New specimens would be needed for that.

College had nothing to offer him now. He dropped out and traveled around Europe and Asia, to build up his library of personalities and develop his system to control them, to take the most unexpected people to extremes. An Italian bishop, an NGO volunteer in Bombay, a Danish cloistered nun, a Vietnamese grade school teacher. A Basque terrorist, a Corsican drug runner, a Swedish underground bookie, the madam of the most exclusive brothel in Moscow. They had all been his unwitting subjects, and they had all died by their own hand, or that of others, after they had committed horrendous deeds.

But that would not suffice for White. He wanted to plot the complete map of human will. Not simply to have the definitive remote control, as he justified it to himself. Deep down in the process was a secret yearning to know what made him tick himself. He was a monster, and he knew it. And like all monsters he was prey to his own private loneliness. If he could hold sway over other people's emotions and empathy, perhaps he could understand the things that were missing, the huge void in his own heart, which he could fill only with vanity, by notching up one hit after another.

But for that he needed money. White's parents had at first given way over his "sabbaticals" in Europe, although in the end they got fed up and cut him off. So White had had no option but to hawk his peculiar wares among people even less scrupulous than himself.

His first client was a capo in the Neapolitan Camorra who had been eagerly seeking a certain writer who had published a book about his clan's doings. White told him to slap a million euros on the table, for which he would hand him the writer's head. The mobster had laughed, because plenty before White had tried to track down the writer and failed. But as he had nothing to lose, he agreed.

Six weeks later, a uniformed cop entered a bleak restaurant in Naples's dire Scampia neighborhood. He was carrying a blue Samsonite wheelie bag. He went to the back of the joint, where two enormous gorillas stood in his path. He addressed the fat, bald man behind them, who was eating ravioli with fried sage leaves by candlelight.

"Your American friend has entrusted me to give you this. The padlock code is one-six-one," said the cop, who couldn't help but show his fear.

The mobster waved the cop away. One of the gorillas opened the case and lifted its contents into the flickering light. The capo wrinkled his nose at the smell but tucked back into his ravioli, wolfing it down.

The day after, a numbered account in the Cayman Islands, belonging to a company whose sole shareholder was Mr. White, received a tax-free transfer of a million euros.

He congratulated himself on the operation. He would have preferred to approach the writer and persuade him to give himself up. That would have been a real achievement. But he was still working at his craft, so he had had to resort to taking on two bodyguards and a legal secretary, all of whom were inexorably burned up in the process.

But for all that, White was happy. He had found a way to meld his passion with satisfying his material needs. For the first two years he had to nose out clients, but as time went by and results came in, they ended up waiting in line for his discreet, costly but very effective services. He was sought after not only by criminals but also by the shadiest branches of intelligence agencies across the world. White took extreme care with the latter and always kept a triple firewall between the client and himself. Many of the straw men he sent into the field were tortured and bumped off in his clients' fruitless efforts to uncover a contractor's identity.

White cared little about that. His sole concern was to be able to pick and choose his contracts, depending on whether they allowed him to enhance his diagrams and hone his tools.

He had come to make those tools infallible . . . until now.

White opened the iPad app that controlled his sound system and played his favorite tune, the one he listened to time and again, compulsively, while he plotted his subjects' patterns—Leonard Cohen's "The Future." The singer's warm, hoarse and silky voice boomed out from the speakers.

White hummed quietly as he switched from the app to the photo album and clicked on the David Evans file. It held more than a thousand snaps, all taken between the day he had agreed to operate on the president and that very morning. White cracked a devious smile when he noticed that some had even picked up the Secret Service detectives who had tailed David to make sure he was kosher. If only they knew.

He checked out the last photo taken, a screengrab from a camera planted in an electric socket in the kitchen. In it David thoughtfully gazed at the empty booster seat before him, the chair in which he sat his daughter every morning. Everything had gone according to plan until then. He had had to break contact for the time David spent with the target, but that, although irksome, was inevitable. All tracking systems were up and running again.

But there was nothing to track. The neurosurgeon had left his cell on his office desk and had now been absent for forty-seven minutes.

The pattern indicated he wouldn't normally be gone that long. The pattern indicated he would never be without his cell.

Unquestionably, those were normal acts, in another person, in another situation. But not in this one, not with David. The pattern said not, and the pattern was always right.

"Was I wrong about you, David? Will we have to play hardball?"

He glanced at the screen that monitored the inside of the cubbyhole where they were holding Julia Evans. The girl was sitting down, rocking back and forth, her eyes glued to a spot on the wall in front of her.

"You need control, David. Control and stimulus."

White reached for his phone and called one of his minions.

"It's me. I have a creeping suspicion something is up. I need you to go to the snack bar and cast an eye on our doctor friend."

15

We let a couple of minutes go by in silence to allow Kate to cool down. I made no apologies, no excuses, for involving her, nor did I bemoan the unfairness of what life had thrown at us. Even if, at whatever price, we managed to save Julia, everything had already gone to pot. I would be expelled by the Board of Physicians and Kate from the Secret Service. If we didn't land ourselves in jail. We had conspired to commit the felony of concealment, which in Kate's case would also entail high treason.

And nevertheless, to feel sorry about it was no use. White had happened to us, like a cancer or a storm on the high seas. To think, *Why me?*—top of the self-pity charts—was ludicrous. Kate could accuse me all she wanted, but I had no choice. And neither did she.

We had to protect Julia above all else.

When Kate had collected herself enough to look me in the face again, something had changed inside her. It was a subtle change and I wouldn't have caught on had I not been expecting it. But it was there, hidden behind her eyes, although I couldn't put a finger on what it was exactly just yet.

Nor did I have time. Kate began to talk in a cold, professional voice. Once she had processed what she was letting herself in for, the part of her brain set aside for such matters took over. She asked me for dates, places, details. She made no note of what I said, because there could be no record of what I told her. She merely committed it all to memory.

"David, I want you to understand something," she told me. "I have received basic training as a federal agent, specifically for the Secret Service, but I have no experience in dealing with kidnappings."

"Don't call on anybody else, Kate. Promise me."

"That's the problem, David. I'm all alone. This will not end well."

"You have a better idea? You trust anybody enough to tell them the score without the whole of Washington knowing within the hour?"

She studied the toes of her shoes and sought the answer we had both known to begin with.

"No. This is too big. Whoever unmasks it will be made. And Julia will simply be a footnote in their report. I can't count on anybody."

"I can help you," I broke in.

"No, you can't. You're the girl's father, you have no training, and if they see me near you they'll suspect in a jiffy. We cannot rule out that one of them is watching you."

"Not only that. They have done something to my phone. They listen in on my calls, and I think they can even hear what I'm saying. And they can send me texts from screen alerts."

"A remote operator must have overridden the handset." She nodded thoughtfully. "That way the kidnappers don't need to plant a homing device, listening gear and security cameras on the subject. Your iPhone does all that for them. They must have the hands-free mike, the camera and the GPS chip permanently activated. Shit, they don't even have to bother fitting batteries. The guy they're spying on kindly recharges the battery every night."

"Now that you mention it, lately my battery's been running down a lot sooner."

"Because of all the apps they run without you knowing. Cocksuckers . . ."

"That tell you anything about them?"

Kate bit her lips, worried.

"For starters, that they're very good. And they really know their shit. You say your cell switched off before the agents picked you up?"

"It didn't go out in a normal way. The screen went all weird on me."

"I don't know how they did it, but I do know why. A set of electronic countermeasures surrounds the president. Some are public knowledge, such as the frequency hoppers which stop anyone from setting off a bomb by remote control when the presidential motorcade drives by. And others are classified, including a gadget which scans a room for surveillance devices. That's why they switched off the cell, because otherwise we'd have been wise to them."

"So there is something screwy about it."

"If I could lay my hands on that phone and take it to my buddies at Computer Crime, we'd know far more about these guys in a matter of hours. Hacking into that sort of device is very hard work. Only a few people in the world are up to such a job, and it can't be done without leaving a trace. But taking your cell with me is out of the question. Unless . . ."

"What?"

"It would be useful for me to know if you lost sight of your phone for some length of time recently, if you've had it serviced or something."

I thought back for a moment, racking my brains.

"About a couple of weeks ago, I woke up one morning and my phone would not switch on. I called Apple and they sent me a new one that day. I restored it from backup and thought no more of it."

"They didn't tamper with your phone, then. You remember the messenger?"

"No, because . . ." I slapped my thigh in frustration when I realized I'd been duped. "It was Svetlana who signed for the package."

"Cool it, David."

"What do you mean, cool it? I gave that woman a home! I left my daughter in her care, for God's sake!"

"It's not as if you ever paid much attention to what went on in your own home, did you?" she said, unable to hold back.

The gibe jolted me. There, it was out. The conversation we had never had but was always brewing between us. All she had wanted to say—and I had ducked—floated in the five feet of dingy passageway in which we were ensconced, a slashing and forbidding, black-winged bird. It preyed on the underbelly of the words, and gorged on my guilt and remorse. We had to face up to it, sooner or later. But this was not the time.

"Go on, blame me for that too, why don't you, if it makes you feel better? But sarcasm won't bring your sister back. Or Svetlana. They killed one of their own, needlessly. Ruthlessly. What won't they do to my daughter, who's in their way?"

Kate huffed and turned aside. Finally she opted to change the subject.

"This morning, when you woke up . . . Did you go down to the basement?"

I shook my head. "To see if the body was still there? No, I didn't have the balls," I admitted, ashamed.

"There's no way they'll have left the corpse down there. If they took that much trouble to clean her room, it was for a reason."

"The nanny's the one link to White."

"Exactly. So they weren't about to gift us a whole body. By trying so hard to eliminate clues, they've marked out the trail for us."

"Via Svetlana?"

"I need to follow her tracks. At some stage they'll lead us to White or his mob."

"How will you go about that?"

"I have to go to your house, David."

My heart leaped when I heard that. The almost sleepless night I had spent agonizing over what my next move would be, how to get Julia back without committing murder, had left its mark. After I got White's text in which he made it plain he'd heard me whisper, I was scared of my own shadow at home. I was sure they had planted cameras and God knows what else in there, and that way they could tell if I so much as farted.

"Kate, there are cameras in my house. White made me double sure of that when he called this morning. He could see me, and if you walk in he'll know we've spoken. And Julia will be dead."

"Think about it, David. We have exactly two leads that can take us to White. The phone's too risky. All we have left is to ferret out some clue about Svetlana in your house."

"It's very dicey," I said, refusing to yield, although I knew she was right.

"It's the only way. I'll have to get in somehow. But you're right about one thing: we can't see each other again until this is over."

"And how do we keep in touch?"

"Not by using that disposable cell you pilfered from the gang-banger, no way. You'll have to take my personal one," she said, fiddling with a somewhat outdated BlackBerry. "I've muted it and disabled the vibration, although the screen still lights up when somebody calls. You'll have to take good care with this so White doesn't catch wind of it. Hide it well and check it now and then."

"What'll you use to call me?"

"I'll buy another cell this evening," she said, and handed me the BlackBerry. When I took it, she clamped her hand on my wrist and burrowed her eyes into me.

"One more thing, David. Out of respect for my sister's memory and because I love Julia heart and soul, I'll help you bring her home again. But let me make something very clear. I don't know what'll go down between now and Friday, but one thing's for sure. Come what may, I won't let White blackmail you. If we don't have Julia back by the deadline, I'll make a call and they'll pull you from the operation. Got that?"

Her voice was cold, glassy and as sharp as an icy dagger in the ribs. I wanted to argue, appeal to kin and our shared responsibility

for my daughter. But I knew I had already asked her to go way beyond the call of duty. And right then I needed to gain time, above
all. So all I said was:

"Roger."

Then she relaxed her grip and I felt terribly uneasy, because at last
I had pinpointed the change I had seen in Kate's eyes.

I was no longer a relative who had let her down.

Now I was a suspect.

16

Kate decamped down the passageway. I gave her a three-minute start, to avoid anyone seeing and linking her to me. When I climbed the flight of stairs, something caught my attention at the other end of the hospital entrance hall. A short, stocky man was standing by the doorway. Big hands, shiny shaven skull, big loose jacket. One with bags of space so they can't tell you're packing heat.

I quickly hid behind a corner of the newsstand. It was silly, a gut reaction. I couldn't be sure. I had seen him only by night, out of the corner of my eye. But I knew. Somehow I knew.

It was the gunman with the foreign accent who'd pinned me against the wall outside the Marblestone Diner the night before. And now there he was, with one eye on the deserted snack bar and the other on the entrance, blocking my way to the elevators. He had a bunch of flowers for camouflage, as if he were visiting a patient. But his attitude told a different story.

You've taken too long, numbnuts, I thought. *And White has sent him to keep tabs on you. Did you really think he'd be content to watch you with the camera phone alone, with all that's at stake?*

I thrust myself against the glass shelving beside the newsstand, trying to blend in with the covers of the *Globe, People* and the *National Enquirer,* not knowing my picture would be splashed on all of them in a week. The glass afforded scant cover. If the hoodlum took so much as two steps toward me, he'd see me and my demeanor would give the game away. I couldn't even fall back on pretending I'd found a quiet corner to make a call, because my cell was supposed to be on my desk.

Will he have seen Kate? Will he know who she is? They have to know. If they've been spying on me for a while, they've simply got to know. They must have seen photos of her. If they know she's here, it's all over for Julia. If they suspect I haven't gone out to eat . . .

He turned his head my way and I slipped away from the corner, scared stiff, feeling small and ridiculous, hiding in my own hospital. Suddenly, I was not a neurosurgeon, I was not six foot three. I was eight years old again, and was cowering in a kitchen cabinet, waiting for the urchins with whom I shared my umpteenth foster home to find something better to do than beat on the new kid. Three decades have gone by and I can still recall the rough and worn touch of that cabinet bought at a garage sale, the smell of varnish slapped on by the owners, the sound of my pullover snagging on the wood while the bullies heaved at my foot to drag me out of my hidey-hole.

That old fear and the emotion I was feeling behind the newsstand were basically the same. Yet the cause was entirely different, because I was no longer afraid for myself, but for Julia. In time, parenthood means transforming fear for yourself into dread of losing someone you love. And for that reason I could not fail.

Think, think, think!

Then one of the cleaners came along and I had an idea.

She was five or six yards away from me. She might as well have been in Texas. Impossible to approach without giving myself away. I tried to wave at her, but she didn't see me, wrapped up as she was in rearranging the dust with her broom.

"Psst, here!" I whispered, to no avail.

I've seen her before, she's been at the hospital for years. I've bumped into her a thousand times. What's her name? What in hell is her name? I couldn't read her ID tag from where I was. But I'd heard her talk to her workmates in the elevator. *Marcela, or Laura, a Hispanic name* . . .

"Amalia," I said, remembering in a flash. "Amalia!"

She turned around and came up to me, wheeling her cleaning trolley. A big one with a trash barrel in the middle.

"It's Amelia, doctor. How can I help?" she said with a friendly smile.

"I have a problem I can't explain," I said as I dipped my hand in my pocket for the money left over from lunch. One of the twenties and a couple of singles. I put them in her hand, all scrunched up, but did not move away from the glass shelves. She looked at me askance. "Listen, Amelia, I am about to do something that'll seem real weird. I'm merely asking you to please forget everything you see, okay?"

Amelia shrugged but put the money in her pocket.

"You'd be surprised at the things I've seen here, doctor."

I stuck my head out enough to check the thug wasn't looking our way, and only then did I dare to step toward Amelia. To her consternation I bent over and began to ransack the garbage bag.

"I take that back. I ain't never seen this before."

I took no notice, as I was too busy delving into the contents of the hospital's ground-floor wastepaper baskets. I pushed aside copies of the *Post*, oozing cans and sticky wrappers until I found what I was looking for.

A Starbucks takeout bag.

It was all creased and one side of it was wet with what I trusted was coffee, but if I held it next to me it wouldn't show. I went back to the newsstand and opened it. There was an empty cup and a half-chewed doughnut. I took out the doughnut and placed it in my mouth, holding it between my teeth without actually biting it.

"Good Lord, baby. They pay you that bad these days? I'll give you back your twenty bucks, if you like."

I shook my head and winked at her. I tried to appear cute, but with someone else's doughnut in my mouth it was more the leer of a man unhinged. Amelia rolled her eyes and pushed her trolley away.

I crept to the middle of the hallway and tried to keep to the edge of the bandit's peripheral vision. From where he stood, he could keep a perfect eye on the entrance, so he would not think I'd come in off the street. But it was a big hospital. He might think I'd used the emergency room exit, although nobody who worked there would go right around the building to leave. But he couldn't know that, unless they had somebody else on watch, or at least that is what I hoped.

It was then he saw me.

I feigned aplomb. I toddled toward the elevators and held the bag with the green mermaid pointing his way, a protective shield. Then I realized what a stupid figure I cut with the doughnut between my teeth, so I was forced to take a good bite. The edge I bit still had some saliva on it from its previous owner. There was something stuck underneath it, maybe a piece of napkin or the receipt.

I repeated to myself what I had learned at medical school about stomach acids and how good they were at destroying germs, while I glossed over all I knew about herpes, mononucleosis and meningitis. I forced myself to swallow the mouthful while I slipped into the elevator with my back to the goon.

"Hey, David," Sharon Kendall, one of the anesthesiologists I usually operated with, greeted me. She was heading the same way, reading a case sheet. "You in surgery today? I haven't seen you on the list."

"Nope, not till Friday. Boss is giving me a break."

"Lucky you. I've got three today, but luckily they're no sweat. And my day off is tomorrow. I'll take the kids to the movies."

"On a Thursday?"

"I don't care if they sleep a couple of hours less. If they don't stop giving me shit over taking them to see the new Pixar flick, I'll kill myself." Then she realized what she'd said and lifted her hand to her mouth. "Oh, I'm so sorry, David, I didn't mean . . ."

"That's okay."

"It's simply a figure of speech."

"No worries."

The elevator came, ejected a dozen people, and we both went into it. I turned around, more worried about the bonehead in the leather jacket than Dr. Kendall's faux pas. I realized she had taken my curt answers as proof that I was offended, but I could do little about that. I was too busy trying to make out that chrome dome between the shoulders of everyone who had gotten out of the elevator. I kept looking while the doors closed, but it was no use.

He had bolted.

17

When I got back, all hell broke loose.

First the chief nurse burst into my office in righteous indignation, wielding her precious clipboard. She meant business. She tore off the top sheet and dunked it on my desk in revenge before she ambled out, real uppity. It was a copy of the bit in hospital regs about pagers, with a couple of lines highlighted. The ones that stipulated senior medical staff—me, in other words—had "the duty to have the pager on their person at all times during working hours," and logically, "to reply to all beeps."

Then it dawned on me that I'd left the pager in my locker, something that had never transpired in all my years at the hospital. With all the hoopla over Kate's call and the trip to see the Patient, I had made a stupid mistake.

I went for my cell. There were no missed calls, but when I held it, it began to ring. There was no caller ID, which told me who I had the dubious pleasure of talking to. The same sense of foreboding engulfed me whenever I spoke to him, but it was now multiplied by the uncertainty over my meeting with Kate.

I picked up.

"Hello, Dave. Were the doughnuts good?"

"What do you want, White?"

"I want to know if the doughnuts were good, Dave. Answer me."

There was a pause.

"Yes, they were good."

"They must be really great doughnuts, Dave. And the coffee must be magic. What's your Starbucks favorite, Dave?"

I really hate Starbucks coffee, but Rachel loved it, so I mentioned hers.

"Mocha Frappuccino, double double."

"Not a bad call, not bad at all, Dave. Want to know what is a bad call?"

His voice had turned into a cold, steely hiss that made my hair stand on end.

"Go on," I forced myself to say.

"A bad call is to vacate the hospital while leaving your cell on your desk. It could have been stolen, and that would have been most inconvenient."

"Listen, I needed some air, I'm—"

"You're a smart guy, Dave. Right?"

"I don't know what this has to do with—"

"You're somebody who can put two and two together."

There was another pause. I decided to quit trying to explain. The more I explained, the phonier I would sound.

"I guess."

"So you know something's up with your phone. That's normal, Dave. I can't blame you for being a smart guy. But if you got too smart, then I could blame you. Only you wouldn't be the one to pay. You do understand, don't you?"

"I do."

"Good. Now I want you to answer a question. I want you to answer it truthfully. If you lie to me, I'll know right away. Okay?"

Deep inside, in some corner of me, something snapped. The sound was almost imperceptible, a glass wrapped in cloth and stamped on. That phrase, exactly that phrase, was the one I said to Julia when she had been naughty. A juice carton spilled in the playroom; an Angry Birds doll smuggled inside her backpack when toys aren't allowed in school; dirty socks under the bed. Small stuff, all for the greater good of building trust and bonding when she'd 'fessed up.

You manipulative son of a bitch, I thought, but said:

"You're the main man around here, White."

"Have you spoken to anybody, Dave? About your, er, situation?"

My daughter's a terrible liar. She gets it from me. Whenever you confront her with the truth, her lips unfailingly stretch into a smile, which turns into a kicking fit when she knows she's been caught out. Rachel always got me. When she asked whether I'd taken out the trash, or paid the gas bill, or bought another of those stupid scratch cards in which I sometimes indulged myself at the 7-Eleven. She looked into my eyes with a half-smile that invariably made me smile, too. She was so good at it that she made me laugh even when I was innocent, something which infuriated me.

"No, I have not."

"Dave, it would be so understandable. Seriously. You walk to the snack bar to get some air. On the way you meet a buddy who's happy to lend his cell for you to make a quick call. Or maybe it was in the line for coffee, a soccer mom making eyes at your doctor's coat. Maybe, just maybe, you were tempted to call the police. But that would be stupid; you don't know anybody and you know that if you involved the police, they'd show up in their oh-so-subtle ties, like masters of disguise. So no, you wouldn't do that."

"I spoke to an underpaid and very ill-mannered barista when I ordered coffee and doughnuts, and spent a while thinking things over, White. No more."

My voice sounded firm, although I felt my left hand tremble when I spoke. He couldn't see me, I knew he couldn't see me, but even so I stuck my hand in my coat pocket and grabbed my thigh until it steadied.

"No, you wouldn't call the police. But maybe, just maybe, you'd be tempted to call your sister-in-law. To tip her off. That would be stupid. Because if something were to crop up, something last-minute . . . Well, that would be bad. And we don't want that."

"Of course not."

"But sure, I could forgive you if you told me the truth. We have time to work it out, I promise. So, one last time, Dave. Have you spoken to Agent Robson?"

A shiver ran down my spine. If I lied and White caught me, if he knew something I didn't, if I had overlooked something . . . it would all be over. And if I told the truth, Kate was toast. They'd find and kill her.

But Julia would be safe.

For a moment I felt tempted to make a clean breast of it, double-cross Kate and buy my daughter a few more precious hours. White's invisible and all-powerful eyes saw everywhere. And he had promised to forgive. I simply had to tell the truth.

That's how good the creep was.

"No, I haven't spoken to Kate. As far as I know, she's at her folks' place."

There was silence again, and on it went. I bit the inside of my cheek until I could taste the blood filling up my mouth. Finally White spoke again.

"Game on, doctor."

And he hung up.

I sank into the chair and quivered with the stress and humiliation I had had to endure. My back was in knots, and I felt I couldn't take any more upsets. I gently laid my cell down on my desk and gaped at it, a deer in the headlights. White had not found me out, although I got precious little consolation from that, if any.

As I tried to mollify myself, I wondered whether I should play catch-up with Kate, warn her White suspected she was in on it, but right away I realized I couldn't phone her till she gave me her new number. I could call her work phone, but she had warned me against that. Now we had to be wary not only of the kidnappers, but also of the Secret Service. In those first few hours, we naively thought it would all work out. That we would be free of the nightmare.

I had scarcely gotten my pulse back to normal when my office phone rang. I picked it up automatically, glad to be able to dive back into my work for a few seconds.

"Neurosurgery, Evans speaking."

"Wong here. Where the hell have you been all afternoon?"

"Treating the Patient, boss."

"With your cell turned off and without answering your pager . . . Damn, Evans."

"Orders from the escort," I lied, at least in part. "And you can believe that where they took me, even the pager wouldn't have worked."

"Okay, makes no difference now. I'm in Meyer's office. I need you to come straight up."

There was something very unsettling in Dr. Wong's tone of voice.

"What's up, Steph? Something wrong?"

"Just get your ass here, Evans."

I had no option but to take the elevator to the top floor. By this time, nearly all the lights up there were out and the offices shut. The execs don't go in for working late; fat chance. The Muzak was turned off and the deep-pile carpet swallowed my footsteps, giving me the impression I was floating down the deserted corridor.

When I got to the door at the end, I went in without knocking, something that really pissed Meyer off. A churlish show of rebellion which had only a slight effect, now that the manager's secretary had left for the day.

On the other side of the door, Meyer and Wong looked at me like thunder. My boss was sitting with her arms and legs crossed. Meyer's jacket was off, his sleeves rolled up past his elbows. He was stretched out in his chair, his hands behind his head. Big sweat stains darkened his bespoke shirt.

"What have you done, Evans?" my boss said.

"I don't know what you're talking about."

"He doesn't know. He says he doesn't know," Meyer exclaimed, and stared at the ceiling.

"The White House called," Wong said. Then she stopped, as though she couldn't bear to go on.

"What did they say?"

My boss spoke some more, barely opening her lips.

"You screwed up, David. You won't be doing the op."

Instantly, I felt the ground give way under my feet, and I was plunging into a bottomless pit. I was still standing on the carpet but inside I was falling down and flailing my arms to try to grab a handhold.

And then the text landed.

BAD PLAY, DAVE.

Kate

She could only just see the roof from where she was.

The afternoon was fading and a portentous leaden sky glowered over the Evans house. The tightly packed clouds loomed and held their breath.

Special Agent Kate Robson aped them, breathing very slowly and trying to concentrate. She hadn't staked out a house for three years, and when she did she'd had a partner and at least a couple of units' backup from the local force. They always maintained constant radio contact with headquarters, and above all, when they moved in they made damned sure the suspects knew exactly who was hammering on their door.

Since she had begun to guard the First Lady, she had boned up on every scenario in which she could be involved while on duty, by making use of maps, photographs and prior on-site inspections. In the most complex cases they would stage virtual dry runs using powerful software that mocked up each last detail of the sites they were to visit, and they had at least three backup routes. The program even perfectly displayed the insides of buildings, based on blueprints and photos taken by agents on recon weeks before the event.

Kate had never operated this way, with so much left to chance and so few aces up her sleeve. And, what was worse, with her niece's life at stake.

She began to make a mental list of the things she couldn't do but got bogged down. Everything she could think of was out of the question. She had no team or time to set up an undercover action, she couldn't approach the house directly because she didn't know whether the cameras were also aimed outward, she couldn't tell whether somebody else was watching from a distance . . . She would sooner make a list of what she actually could do.

Her first trump card was that she knew the house. Although she hadn't come by for months, she could find her way around the place blindfolded. Getting in would be relatively simple. To do so without being seen was another matter.

A car drove past and Kate instinctively hunched up in her seat until she realized such a move would make her look more suspicious than sitting still. She drove a black Ford Taurus belonging to the Secret Service fleet, in which she was due to go back to work the day after. The agents used them almost routinely as private cars at the end of their shifts, one of the job's few perks. The "almost" included one tiny detail: no one outside the service could get in the car. Those were strict Secret Service rules, which in effect meant that if you had family, you had to buy yourself another ride.

That was not the case with Kate, for whom "starting a family" was a fuzzy item in her life plan. An unreachable goal, something she longed for but could not see herself pulling off. Like climbing Everest or winning the state lottery.

The spotless Taurus proved the point. If she climbed into her father's Dodge Ram, screws strewn on the carpet got stuck in the soles of her boots. When you rode in Rachel's Prius you could tell without looking you'd have to shake the crumbs loose from the pleats in your pants, because Julia was not exactly a stickler for cleanliness.

Life taints you. Families cramp your style.

She grabbed the disposable Nokia phone she had just bought at T-Mobile, a few blocks away, and plugged it into the cigarette lighter with a cable that had set her back more than the cell. It took a few minutes to charge the battery enough to turn it on. When she did, she texted David on the cell she'd lent him.

AM HERE. WILL KEEP U POSTED.

She scrutinized the house again. It was a lovely four-bedroom Colonial-style house, painted light steel blue. There was a grassy slope that partly hid the rear if you came up a quiet side street, like the one Kate was parked on at the time. From the white picket fence that lined the street to the back door, it was about twenty yards. She swiftly worked out how long it would take to run that far downhill. About four seconds. Four seconds in which she would be exposed to whoever might be watching the house. Not the cameras. If her plan worked, she could zero in unseen but wouldn't have much time.

In Secret Service planning meetings, they assigned a failure rate to riskier options in a scenario, known colloquially as the snafu rate. Any snafu rate above 15 percent was immediately ruled out. Given how little she knew about Julia's kidnappers, her plan's snafu rate was at least 60 percent, which was looking on the bright side.

She gave the steering wheel an angry thump. Every hour that went by lengthened the odds on finding Julia by the deadline. She had to get into that house. There was nothing for it but to gallop ahead with her plan.

All around her, automatic sensors were switching on houses' outdoor illumination to shed pockets of light amid the pale indigo dusk. Kate looked at the time. It would be dark in a few minutes, so it was best to wait.

She couldn't help plucking from her wallet a small photo, which she had swiped the day before from her mom's album. It had been taken after a lacrosse game when they were both at high school. As ever, Rachel's uniform was immaculate, while her sister's was a mess of grass and sweat stains. Rachel's smile looked to have been painted by the delicate brushstrokes of an Italian old master; Kate's was a wild animal snarl. Little sis leaned on her stick with her right hand, with her left arm protectively draped over Rachel's shoulder and holding her crosse.

It was ever thus. Born January 4, 1978, Rachel was fated to be the daughter Aura Robson had always wanted. But Jim wanted a son and heir to take after him. So in December that same year a second baby came along, but one born without the longed-for piece of flesh between its legs.

The girl kicked up a storm from the word go, even when she was in her mother's belly. Complications during labor forced the doctors to give Aura a hysterectomy. When he heard what gender his daughter was and that there would never be a Jimmy Boy Robson, the stern Virginian didn't even wait for them to discharge the baby from Maternity. He drove off and drank the night away in a roadhouse. He didn't get to see his daughter until some friends took him home two days later.

Kate swigged some water from a bottle which had been in the door panel for a couple of days. It had an aftertaste of unwashed laundry and a musty smell that reminded her of the scant affection her father showed her.

Jim, in his way, had come to love the girl they showed him when he was done with his binge. But there was always something holding him back. She would always be the one who had deprived her mother of the energy and life force she should have passed down to their long-awaited son.

Kids, contrary to what grown-ups tend to think, are not dimwits. They have the capacity to grasp complex feelings from early on, and the rift of disappointment as wide as the one Kate's love needed to span, to get through to her father, would be no exception.

How do you compete with a human being who never came into the world, with a notion or a yearning? The obvious answer is: you can't. Despite everything, Kate had grown up determined to be the Robson boy. Her unruliness was a constant pain in the neck for everybody, but it stuck out most in her relationship with Rachel. They had grown up together, as close to each other as two sisters can be. Nevertheless they were complete opposites. Rachel was as calm and quietly beautiful as a mountain lake, while Kate was a fireball. They started school in the same class and little sis became big sis's protector.

It was Kate who swallowed a centipede when Rachel lost a silly childish "dare," then chickened out. It was Kate who snuck into Mr. Eckmann's room to retake the math test Rachel had flunked. Kate was the one who had stood up for her sister when they were caught playing hooky in sixth grade.

At night they would tell each other secrets from opposite sides of the bedroom they shared, until they fell asleep. Rachel had talked to her about parties, boys and tunes. About how when they both grew up they would live under the same roof and have a pair of adoring husbands. The room smelled of bubblegum, erasers and Mom's cheap moisturizing cream. And one night, when Rachel cried her eyes out and whispered to her sister that Randall Jackson had overstepped the mark while they smooched under the back stairs, Kate didn't think twice. She leaped out of bed, pulled on some boots, sat on her bike in her pajamas and rode around to the Jacksons' house. She threw pebbles at Randall's window and when the groper came out to the porch, she punched out two of his teeth.

Randy's father took Kate home and talked with her parents. There were stern words but Kate sat with her arms crossed on the sofa and kept silent over what had led her to smash in the football team captain's face. Things didn't cool down until a panic-stricken Rachel sloped downstairs in her nightie and spilled the beans.

"I regret my son's behavior and I beg your pardon, Jim. You can bet he'll be duly punished," Mr. Jackson had said, wringing his hat in shame.

Jim had watched him leave from the doorway without a word. When the sound of the car engine faded into the night, he had turned to Kate and showed her the bike's chain lock she had wrapped around her knuckles before she punched Randy.

"Was there any need for that?"

"He's got twenty-five pounds on me," Kate had answered with a shrug.

Jim kept his smiles to himself, but Kate knew she'd been right. Now, many years later, as she was about to do the craziest thing ever, her opinion on the matter hadn't changed one bit.

Sure there was a need.

To protect your family you do whatever it takes.

Kate took a deep breath and opened the car door.

18

"When was this?"

"Couple of hours ago."

Dr. Wong avoided my eyes so I knew right away there was more to it.

"What's up, boss?"

"What do you mean, 'what's up'?" Meyer interrupted with a guffaw like a rusty old saw cutting wood. "Do you really need to ask? Look, Dr. Evans, we take you in here, we give you a berth at St. Clement's and the chance to prove you can be a top doctor. All that despite your, um, record."

"What the hell do you mean?"

Meyer opened a drawer and flung a red file down on his desk, one of the ones they cooked up in Human Resources to run the hospital. I didn't need to look at the name on the edge to know it was mine. He was just the kind of rat to dredge up the subject at such a time.

"Ah, 'record.' That's executive lingo for 'past events I can rake over and use against you.' I guess you're not about to refer to my success rate in surgery."

Meyer blinked several times, amazed.

"I know about the problems you had in Johns Hopkins with the head of neurosurgery, but—"

"No you don't."

Meyer's blinks became a sickly grin, a pair of monkeys deftly pulling at the corners of his mouth. He was rarely interrupted and could not brook outright contradiction.

"Excuse me?"

"I don't know what you've got on paper, but believe me, it won't even come close to the truth. I had no problem with Dr. Hockstetter; he has a problem with humankind. In any case, I don't see what that's got to do with anything."

The manager paused and then started again. He's one of those who, if you butt in, repeats his whole argument from the top, in case you might have forgotten what he said six seconds before.

"I'm up to speed on the problems you had at Johns Hopkins with the neurosurgery chief, but my predecessor chose to overlook them. Normally, that sort of disaster would have put your career back a couple of years, had you fixing up cow punchers' heads in North Dakota or someplace. Instead, St. Clement's gave you a break. We let you start over. My predecessor could see you had potential, sure. But potential counts for nothing without proper supervision and a guiding hand."

"Are you insinuating it's my fault we missed our shot to operate on the Patient, Meyer?"

"It is, though, isn't it? We've had no trouble in all the time since they first came to us. Then today up you pounce, go missing for hours to see him, and lo and behold, we get a call from the White House to tell us St. Clement's is no longer the hospital of choice. You're the only one who's been in contact with them, so you're the only one who could have dropped the ball."

I could not believe this. Was he jealous?

"Is that what's eating you? That you didn't get to see the president? You didn't miss much."

"Potential is nothing without teamwork. And you are not a team player, Evans. You squander hospital resources, you find any old loophole to take the patients' side. Most especially if they don't have a dime. Like that gangbanger the paramedics dumped on the emergency room yesterday."

Stephanie glanced at me then and raised her almost invisible eyebrows,.her way of saying "Told you so." The hospital's star patient of the decade had slipped away, a one-off chance to get in the history books. Now that that had gone south, they needed a scapegoat. It mattered little that it was because of me the president had approached them in the first place. What mattered was who put him off.

Meyer despised me in his cold and trite way, but for him such sentiments could take a backseat as long as he got what he wanted. He would have to explain this away to the hospital board, and now he had the excuse and someone to point the finger at: the spendthrift doctor. Any stick would do to beat me with, and the nearest one he had was the Jamaal Carter case.

"I treated a human being, Meyer."

"At high cost. I don't run a charity, and this foolishness does not pay your salary."

"No, my salary comes out of the six-figure bills you hit the clients with—after I've saved their lives, that is."

Meyer leaned forward, his face livid with anger.

"You think you're the only talented doctor on the block? There's hordes of brats out there who can crimp an aneurysm as well as you and who know which side their bread's buttered on! You cost this hospital good money, Evans, and you know it! We've put up with your fooling around these past months because, after all, you've lost your wife and . . ."

I couldn't hold myself back when I heard that. I burned up inside with rage, which overcame my natural shyness and willingness to talk things over, a flamethrower burning down a paper wall. I put both hands on his desk and brought my face to within inches of his.

"You listen to me, Meyer. If you mix my wife up in this again, I swear to God I'll make you swallow your teeth."

"David, back off!" Stephanie shouted, getting up.

"He threatened me! You heard him, right? You're a witness!"

"And I'll do it again. He mentions my wife once more, I don't care if I end up prescribing Tylenol in Alaska. I'll break his face."

Meyer would not back down to start with. His mind was working full speed; I could almost hear him think. After a few moments he swallowed, sat back and raised his hands in a sign of appeasement.

"All right, all right. No need to fly off the handle. We can talk this over like civilized people."

I nodded my head and took my hands away from the table but did not believe him for one second. We had both gone too far, and things would not stop there, no way. The consequences for me would be harsh as soon as I stepped away and Meyer no longer feared for his skin. But right then I couldn't have cared less about my future at St. Clement's, at least not as long as it lasted until nine o'clock Friday morning.

I had to toss him a bone. Something he could gnaw on to buy me time. For all that Meyer made me sick, I needed to avoid a show-down with him and to put off payback time for a few days.

"I know exactly what you want, Meyer."

"I want the best for this hospital."

"No. You want to be on TV. You want your press conference Friday afternoon. You want to break the news to America. You want your fifteen seconds of prime time."

He looked at me, speechless. I'd hit the nail on the head, and we both knew it, although he'd never say so out loud. For the drab, second-rate pen pusher he was, a junior who had never earned his stripes, that would be a dream come true. A TV appearance was the Holy Grail for nonentities.

"I can fix it," I added. "I don't know what went on this afternoon, but I can get back the Patient's trust."

"It was the White House chief of medical staff who called. Name of Hastings. I spoke to him," Dr. Wong said.

"Hastings wanted me to operate at Bethesda. I refused," I said with a withering look at Meyer, to see what he thought now of my lack of team spirit. He said nothing. It was no use; he had made his mind up about me, and to be fair he was not far off the mark. But I could still make him think I gave a damn. "The First Lady took it up with her husband and everything was fine. She's the key."

"Can you go over Hastings's head and get through to the president?"

"I think so."

Meyer pressed his hands together under his chin and smiled. He must have been pondering what suit he'd wear for the press conference.

"Fix it. Get him operated on in my hospital and we'll be square, Evans. But if you don't come up with the goods, I'm afraid you'll be up before the board."

I felt like quitting there and then so the operation would never go ahead at St. Clement's. Or better still, like jumping across Meyer's desk and knocking that smug look off his face, but I couldn't afford to do that.

He'd given me what I was after, so I nodded and walked away.

"Evans, wait!"

Dr. Wong ran out along the corridor after me. I didn't stop, although it was hard to leave my boss behind, even as pissed off as I was.

"That asshole flayed me alive in there, and I can't say you stuck up for me."

"He's right, Evans. I told you the board had complained about your approach to pro bono ops. You could have eased off the gas a little. You can't always shoot from the hip."

She was right. They'd warned me several times, but that didn't mean Meyer wasn't a greedy, soulless shit. Sure, I hadn't helped matters. I normally made quite free with resources, but I had really gone overboard since Rachel's death. My guilt complex was a huge lodestone skewing my moral compass.

"I dropped my guard once, and look what happened."

"Saving a few poor suckers won't bring back your wife, Evans.

There's no wrongs to right. We all saw her, strolling along the corridors without a care, no sign she was sick. I was in a few ops with her myself right before she was diagnosed, hour after hour on foot, but she was as focused and sharp as ever. Nobody could have seen it coming."

She may truly have thought that, but her words rang hollow, a bid to make it up to me after she'd let me down before the manager. Also, if St. Clement's took the operation back, she would get in on the act. With me in the theater, of course. And giving interviews all evening.

All at once, everybody wanted a piece of the Patient. They had scented blood in the water, and were circling around and baring their teeth. I think until then I hadn't quite appreciated the First Lady's concern over picking the right surgeon for the job. She had wanted to avoid exactly such antics, which made her decision to pull me out at that stage of the game even more baffling.

"Thank you, Dr. Wong," I said without a backward look. "You can go back to practicing your smile in the mirror with Meyer. They say blue looks best on TV."

I reached the elevator and rapped the button three or four times until the doors opened. I couldn't wait to get well clear of the executive suite.

"Evans, I've got you pegged," she said behind me as the elevator doors closed. "You're an awesome doctor but naive and headstrong. Don't blow it now that you're so close. Think of your daughter when you make that call."

If only you knew.

Kate

Night had fallen over Silver Spring. A light drizzle sprayed droplets on Kate's back while she searched through the trunk for a canvas bag the size of a vanity case.

She put it under her jacket, where she had also secreted the holster for her SIG Sauer P229. She crossed the street and calmly strolled along the sidewalk like the girl next door coming home after a long day. She lolloped past the house, discreetly checked nobody was around and hopped over the white picket fence.

Heading for the little backyard shed, she ran down the slope until she reached the wall at the bottom. The grass was drenched with rain, and she nearly slipped on the last stretch. She came to a halt with her shoulder pummeled against the plastic framework. The outdoor lights had not come on, because the Evanses were environmentally friendly. They used no timers or sensors, but turned them on manually when they were home. Even so, Kate cast a dim shadow on the lawn in the faint glow from the neighbors' yard. The house next door was quite far off, and there was little chance they'd seen her trespass on her brother-in-law's property. But they might spot her now and call the cops, who'd send around a patrol car. In which case the kidnappers would think David had called them. That could not happen.

I have to open this right now.

The shed was padlocked, but with some imported crap bought at Home Depot rather than a good old Master Lock. Her father would have had a fit had he seen it. Kate took five seconds flat to pick the lock with the clip off a pen. One advantage of having a hardware salesman for a father.

She closed the door behind her on her way in but didn't turn on the light. Instead, she grabbed a little flashlight to see her way around. She pushed aside a sack of fertilizer and found the automatic irrigation hose. The Evanses had an electric sprinkler, which they plugged into a socket in the shed. She unplugged the sprinkler and took the canvas bag from inside her jacket. She unzipped it and withdrew a small gray device, fitted with three antennas and a variable transformer. It was a standard signal jammer installed in temporary residences or cars when protecting people at risk from car bombings. It blocked any radio frequency signal within a fifty-yard radius. Radios, cell phones, GPS, the works. For the president they used a special SUV packed with sophisticated apparatus that set up a bubble for a two-hundred-yard radius around the presidential motorcade. The only signals that could get through were from authorized personnel's phones and Secret Service comms.

Kate placed the jammer's antennas upright, changed the voltage setting from 120 to 110, plugged it in and eagerly waited for the six LEDs to change from flashing orange to a steady lime green. She looked at her service BlackBerry and the newly bought Nokia phone. Both displayed "NO SERVICE." That blocker was way cruder than the barrage-jammer SUV, but it did the job.

She switched off the flashlight, opened the shed door a crack and looked at the house. Unless her intuition failed her, White's cameras had to be connected to a SIM card to beam images directly. A pro wouldn't hook them up to the victim's own Internet connection, because detecting them would be a piece of cake and the upload speed would depend on the service provider. Kate could easily have checked it out if she had the hidden-device scanner she used at the agency, but hers had broken down the week before and the techs had yet to send her a replacement.

It was double or nothing. The kidnappers would know something was up by now. They would be looking at monitors full of white noise and wondering what had brought that about. And even though they knew David was at the hospital, it was only a matter of time before they sent somebody around.

She would have a few minutes, tops.

"Heigh-ho, let's go!" she whispered, as she always did before going on assignment. The mantra bucked her up and doubled as a spell to ward off bad luck.

She opened the door and ran toward the house. She reached the back wall in a few strides. She crouched by the ivy-covered wall and rooted around in the bougainvillea patch for the false stone, where David had told her he kept the back door key. She couldn't find it in the dark, but before she went any farther, she tried the door handle and it opened first time.

So typical of David, Kate thought. *They'd have had no trouble filling your house with mikes, I bet.*

The back door led to a covered porch with a couple of sofas facing each other on a parquet floor, where the Evanses would play backgammon of an evening while Julia pattered around the yard.

That's where it had happened. The night Rachel had worked late and Kate had one drink too many.

Kate looked away. Merely conjuring up the memory made her feel guilty. He had been a complete gentleman and had never brought it up, but things had never been the same again between them.

She opened the patio door and went into the living room. She couldn't help looking at the mantelpiece. Rachel and David's wedding photo was the same as the one in her folks' sitting room. Kate had been to weddings and seen her fair share of brides. They always insisted on being the MCs and belles of their own ball. But not her sister, who had eyes only for her newly wedded husband.

David had green eyes and blue-black hair. Hair to sing about, Rachel had said. In the last few months his temples had gone gray, and lines wrinkled his strong, gaunt face. David had aged five years overnight when his wife died. On the face of it, she was his only link to happiness.

You loved her, Kate thought, and felt as if she was about to burst into tears. *You truly loved her, which makes it all the harder to forgive you, David. I wish somebody would look at me the way you two looked at each other. If I had someone to love like that, I wouldn't let anything happen to them.*

Next to the wedding pic was a framed photo of David and Julia. They were in a park. She sat on his shoulders while he had his mouth wide open with a silly look on his face, as he pretended to bite her knee. Julia was splitting her sides laughing.

But he's a great father who can give Julia more hugs and kisses in a day than Dad used to give us in a whole year. Absentminded and a bit of a mess, though. True, he could spend more time with his daughter. What father couldn't nowadays? But when they're together there's nothing else in the world. Julia gazes at him in endless wonder. And David tries. He learns the name of each TV character by heart; he tells her stories. All in his clumsy way, but he really tries to bond with her.

She came away from the mantelpiece and wagged her head. Too many conflicting feelings plucked at her heartstrings in all directions at once.

I have to quit feeling this way. Come on, stay focused, Kate. We have to find traces of her. Fallback options, clues.

"I need to know what she was like, David. I need a photo."

"I don't have any," he'd answered. "I took the odd one last week with her in it, while she played with Julia, but I hadn't downloaded it to my computer yet."

"We need to think of some way you can send it to me by phone."

"I wish, but my iPhone's photo gallery has been deleted. It was the first thing I thought to check last night when I still thought she was the one who had snatched Julia."

Kate crossed the living room and the kitchen to come to Svetlana's room. The smell of bleach still floated over every surface. David was not exaggerating when he said they must have scrubbed down the length and breadth of that room. She checked the bed, the chest, took the drawers out of it and looked underneath. She examined the floor in the fitted wardrobe, the desk and the wastepaper basket.

Empty.

Like everything else.

She tried to picture Svetlana in that room: asleep, studying—or pretending to, lying in bed, planning her next move. How to win over a family bereaved by Rachel's death. Had the kidnappers threatened her, or had she done it for money?

Well, Svetlana, you reap what you sow. This is all that's left of you now: a whiff of bleach.

She walked to the hallway, where the basement door was concealed below the staircase that led upward. She carefully aimed the flashlight at the floor to make sure she didn't trip up on her way down the creaky wooden steps but kept the beam away from the windows. She didn't want to turn on any lamps that might alert the kidnappers somebody else was home.

She glanced toward the back wall. The bikes were on the rack rather than blocking the way, and Svetlana's corpse was gone. There was nothing in the place where David said he'd seen the body the night before, apart from the smell of bleach again. She dabbed at the wall with her fingers. The old paintwork looked damp and was peeling away from the spot where they must have propped up the body.

Just then a rectangle of light shone through the narrow basement windows. Kate cocked her head to one side, listened and was immediately on the alert. The car didn't drive by, as a couple had done in the short while she'd been down there. The wheels halted only yards away. Somebody killed the engine and footsteps could be heard on the pavement.

It was them.

19

The cell began to ring before I was back in the office. I picked up the phone as I shut the door and leaned against it.

"I had nothing to do with it."

"Dave, right now I'm having a hard time believing you," White said in a voice as devoid of feeling as an answering machine. It made my skin turn cold. "You've had a one-on-one with the Patient all afternoon and now this happens."

"Listen, you already heard the ruckus with my bosses. I don't know what's at the bottom of it; they've told me nothing. I'm as surprised as you are."

"I don't care. You are now a dud, Dave, and I am an incredibly pragmatic man. So . . ."

He hung up.

As quick, easy and neat as that. That's how thin the dividing line was between Julia and death: a click on a cell.

I was transfixed, unable to move. In a few minutes I had gone from fear to astonishment, from astonishment to rage and from rage back to fear. That emotional white-knuckle ride wreaked havoc with my nerves. I wondered whether it was all part of White's plan to rope me in and entangle even more in his scheming. I was a pinball launched up a slippery slope, in permanent danger of falling. I could score the odd point but had no freedom of movement. That click hammered home the certainty that it didn't matter what I did or how far gone I was in that game: sooner or later, the ball would fall into the drain.

White would never let us out alive.

Pinballs have one built-in property, however: flippers and bumpers won't destroy them. To save my daughter I had to be ready to roll with the punches. As long as the ball stayed in play, Kate would have a chance to find Julia.

He'd hung up, but I knew White was still there, listening.

"Wait, wait, please," I heard myself plead. "I know I can make it work. I can fix it if you help me."

I kept quiet and waited. White took more than a minute to call back, but the cell finally rang again.

"What do you want, Dave?"

"If I call the White House switchboard, it'll take me hours to get through to the chief of medical staff. And he may not want to take the call. I need his direct line."

"And what do I gain?"

"We're tight, White. I'm sure you don't have the time or means to set up another . . . operation, or whatever you call it."

A keyboard clicked in the background. A few seconds later he gave me two numbers, for a landline and a cell.

"Don't call from your handset. Use your office line. Got that?"

There was something in the signal, then, something they could trace if I dialed an official line like the White House. I wondered whether the electronic countermeasures could do more than detect that White had tapped my line. Maybe even detect where the signal led.

"Okay," I answered.

"And another thing, David . . . There wouldn't be anybody at your home, would there?"

Shit. White obviously suspects something is up. What have you done, Kate?

"What? No, of course not."

"Great, then there's nothing to worry about, is there?" he said with fake jollity. "You've got ten minutes to convince Hastings and get your patient back. Otherwise, we're through."

He hung up again.

I dawdled over my next move. Should I try to warn Kate or go ahead with White's orders?

It would be stupid to get in touch with her right away. White will surely be watching, listening, keeping a closer eye on me than ever. I can't let it show I know my house has been broken into, I thought.

I dialed Hastings's cell, but it went to voice mail. I hung up without leaving a message and called his landline. I let it ring until it went through to the switchboard.

It's really late. What if he's gone home for the day, won't be back till tomorrow and turns off his cell until then? No, that's impossible, no doctor would do that. There must be some other reason.

I dialed again. Finally, somebody picked up.

"Medical staff. Hastings speaking."

"Captain Hastings, David Evans here."

"Dr. Evans?" He sounded surprised, and a little guilty. "How did you get this number?"

Good question. From a psycho killer who wants me to whack your boss.

"I Googled it. Tell me, what's the problem?"

"Didn't . . . Didn't your bosses tell you?"

"Yes, they told me I got the chop. The decent thing would have been for you to inform me personally, Captain."

"I'm sorry, Dr. Evans. I didn't think it through."

And into the bargain you avoided the hassle of giving me the bad news yourself.

"Sincerely, I am at a loss. Would you care to explain why?"

"I am not authorized to disclose details of my patient's decision to you, doctor."

"You went to a lot of trouble to get me to the White House

and persuaded me to take on a patient and an operation I wanted nothing to do with. And now they cut me loose with no more than a phone call."

"Doctor, please. You must understand my position. I shouldn't even be taking this call."

"And I shouldn't have been a mile underground this afternoon."

The captain snapped to attention. I could hear him square his shoulders.

"If you mean to reveal such knowledge acquired in the course of professional practice, that would be a breach of ethics. And a dereliction of duty to your country, too, Dr. Evans."

"I'm not about to reveal anything, Captain, I'm not a moron. I'm simply reminding you I've already gone beyond the call. I'm asking you for the same professional courtesy."

Hastings uttered a long sigh.

"Fair's fair. I'll tell you what happened if you promise me a favor. I need the MRI scan you did for the president today. I believe you have it."

"Be right with you."

I had the Patient's scan in a flash drive in my pocket. The request allowed me to sift through my pockets and put Kate's cell in my top desk drawer while I pretended to look for the drive. White might have planted a camera in my office, so I had to take good care. I tried to thumb a message at top speed on the BlackBerry. I had only a few seconds.

"Dr. Evans? Are you there?"

"Yes, yes, one second."

"I have to run, Evans."

WATCH OUT. I THINK THEY KNOW SOMEBODY'S IN MY HOUSE. DAVID.

"Wait, I'm looking for it."

I hit the SEND button, withdrew my hand from the drawer and fought back the urge to sigh in relief. I hoped the message would help put Kate on her guard, although she already knew her presence there would raise suspicion. The thought of what my sister-in-law might be having to endure drove me crazy, but at that juncture, I had Hastings to consider.

"Now I've got it, Captain," I went on, pretending to have found the drive at last. "I'll gladly send it over with the rest of the case notes."

"No need, I sent the surgeon over to pick it up an hour ago, he should be with you shortly. I must ask for your cooperation, Dr. Evans."

"Sure. Just tell me what happened."

"The First Lady changed her mind. She spoke to another doctor who convinced her he was the best bet."

"What do you mean? But she said—"

"You have a daughter, right? What would you do if she were ill?"

"I would do the best I could for her. Whatever it took," I said, after a pause.

"Well, that's what's happened."

"I want to talk to the First Lady," I said, my voice a little too strained.

"The First Lady is at an official reception for the French prime minister. She can't talk."

"But if I could just—"

Hastings cut me short. "Listen here, Dr. Evans. The family has made its choice and there is nothing you can do about it. Take it like a professional."

And without further ado, he hung up.

I could not believe it. They had hung me out to dry, without even giving me a chance to defend myself. I was stunned, but the surprise I felt was nothing compared to what was waiting for me when I read White's next text.

GOOD JOB, DAVE. IT'S ALL GOING ACCORDING TO PLAN.

Kate

When she spied the submachine gun's outline, that settled matters. She realized that until then she hadn't entirely taken David's word for everything. Not because his explanation seemed to come out of left field, for day in, day out, she dealt with potential threats and assassination attempts on the president—more than ten the year before—that the public never got to know about. And not because his tale sounded far-fetched, either. On the contrary, experience had taught her that the simplest and most convincing stories most often turned out to be bull. No, she hadn't quite believed him because she didn't want it to be true.

Be that as it may, the shadow of a stranger showed up in one of the frosted glass panes next to the door. And in his hands, the menacing contours of a gun. There was another guy with him, or at least that's what Kate guessed, for somebody was forcing a key into the lock.

Kate looked on, peeked out of the basement doorway, and for a moment she thought of going upstairs and trying to escape through one of the windows, but she decided that was playing with fire. It would take time to get there and she would have to break through them, as they were very small. The odds that she would give herself away were too high. Nor could she stay in the basement. A few more seconds and she'd be trapped in there, with nowhere to hide.

I can't risk an exit through the basement windows, not without being able to see exactly how many of them are out there waiting.

Instinctively, she climbed the stairs and walked at a crouch into the living room, treading carefully so as not to make any noise. She gently unholstered her gun and held it in combat-ready stance, at forty-five degrees to the ground. She had to do her utmost to avoid a shoot-out with the interlopers and would use it only as a last resort.

They can't see me here. If they don't get back, Julia dies. If they find me, Julia dies.

Behind her she heard the front door open. Kate could feel her breathing calm down and settle. The anxiety and doubts that had assailed her dissipated. Her shoulders straightened, her ears pricked up and her pulse beat more slowly but strongly in her neck, a one-armed drummer playing a funeral march.

The only way out is to retrace my steps and vamoose. Without a single goddamned clue. Shit.

She bridged the three-yard gap to the covered balcony. Maybe it wasn't so bad the kidnappers had shown up. If she got out of there unnoticed, she could follow them or, at worst, scribble down their license plate number.

We'll have Julia back asleep this very night in her bed, instead of in some shithole. All I have to do is make it to my car.

She opened the sliding door, slowly, silently. The rail was very stiff, so Kate had no choice but to lay her gun on the floor and shove the panel with both hands. The prowler's heavy footsteps stomped behind her, in the hallway. She opened the door enough to wriggle out, grabbed the gun and closed it behind her. She managed to get away from the panel just as the other guy came into the living room.

Good. Now for the patio door, then that's it. You're home free.

She stole away from the living room door and squatted as she made her way along, with her back to the outside wall. The patio door was only four yards away, at the other end of the porch, which was enclosed by a waist-high wooden partition and six big glass windows.

Whoever was inside abruptly switched on the living room lamp. An oblong of light lit up the space Kate had vacated only seconds before. A man's face appeared outside, looking in through the window from the other side. He shouted in a foreign language.

Shit!

Kate flattened herself against the wall, with no more cover than the shadow of a metal table. She saw that all that saved her from being spotted was the glow of the living room lamp, which had blinded the man outside and given her some shade. She crawled over to the sofa area, realized her body was nudging the chairs over the parquet and prayed they wouldn't notice.

The man inside was also shouting, although not so loudly and in a much deeper voice. He must have given the guy outside an order, because he shifted and headed for the patio door.

Kate shrank down as best she could and kept tight hold of her gun. She could feel a bead of sweat dribbling down her back and slowed her breathing to a minimum. She was scared but not jumpy. Ensconced between the sofa and the wall, she was at the mercy of two or more foes, and with the odds stacked against her. Despite that, the rushing adrenaline made her feel stronger and more alive than she had been in ages.

The footfalls halted next to Kate, and she felt a chill. The heavy was so close she could have reached out and touched him. He partly turned his back to her as he reached for a pack of cigarettes. She plainly heard the cellophane crackle as he opened it, the rustle of his fingertips on the top, loosening a cigarette, and the striking of a match. She smelled the match, the first puff of tobacco, the gun oil. She saw the hard-bitten look on his face, his huge, callused paws covered in latex gloves, the unmistakable squat, oval shape under the submachine gun barrel.

PP-19 Bizon. Russian job. Expensive and seldom seen outside their special forces and very grim criminal elements in eastern Europe. Parabellum nine-millimeter ammo. Less of an impact than my MP5 but able to unleash a wall of fire: sixty-four rounds per clip, three times the norm.

If he catches you, that ruffian can rip you in half.

In the same situation on any regular assignment, she would have stood up, jabbed her gun in the suspect's temple before he knew what was happening and arrested him on the spot. But this was not a regular assignment, nor could she do it by the book. She could only pray the snooper kept on toward the living room, without turning toward her precarious hiding place. It would take only a flick of the living room light switch to reveal her.

Please. Walk. Walk.

The man lurched and Kate's heart leaped. He didn't turn around, however, and entered the house.

It's now or never.

Kate set off from the other side of the sofa and crawled over to the patio door. The intruder had left it ajar, so she could slip out without a sound. She cringed when her body made contact with the soaking-wet grass but didn't dare get up. She couldn't run to the street, because she didn't know whether anybody else was out there. And there was something far more urgent: she couldn't go without deactivating the jammer, or they'd be on to her.

She crawled to the shed, closed the door behind her and yanked out the jammer's cord to turn it off. Then she saw a text from David, sent twenty minutes before.

WATCH OUT. I THINK THEY KNOW SOMEBODY'S IN MY HOUSE. DAVID.

No shit, Sherlock.

She dropped down between the recycling bin and the lawn mower, and shivered with cold, her clothes dripping with sweat.

20

I was still trying to make sense of White's text when the person I hate most in the world opened my office door.

In all fairness, my daughter's kidnapper and his minions now held that title. But Dr. Alvin Hockstetter had worn the laurels for so long it was hard to bump him down to second place.

I distinctly recall the first time I saw him, in the lecture theater at Johns Hopkins, the best hospital in Baltimore, the country and probably the world, too. It was my first day as a resident, and I was one more among a score of youngsters eager to see His Eminence, the "Pioneer of the Brain," as *Time* magazine had dubbed him. He was of medium but imposing height, and when he passed me by on his way to the lectern, I felt I was a klutz, all elbows and knees beside what back then I took to be the paragon of elegance.

Alvin Hockstetter had two furled caterpillars for eyebrows, slim fingers at the end of long, sturdy arms, and a belly as prominent as his ego. He bounded up to the dais with an alacrity that belied his plumpness and looked at us from behind an oily smile for a few seconds, until he was sure he had our complete and undivided attention.

He began to speak in a practiced baritone that came from deep inside his chest, and dropped one of the smartest lines I've ever heard.

"You know the difference between God and a neurosurgeon? It's that God knows he isn't a neurosurgeon."

We all fidgeted in our seats and burst into hesitant and awkward laughter. Some of us had grown up in God-fearing small towns in the heartland, and although we might only have been "kinda sorta" devout, the joke still verged on blasphemy. It was also as accurate a description of a neurosurgeon as they come.

"It's funny, but it's no joke. You are in the holy temple of medicine, the Vatican of hospitals. Neurosurgery is its Sistine Chapel. We, my dear novices, are here to fix God's mistakes."

He pressed a key on the remote he had concealed in his hand and the screen behind him changed to display an MRI scan of a healthy patient alongside one of a patient with a brain tumor.

"Would one of you be so good as to remind us what angiogenesis is?"

No one raised their hand. We were still too awestruck by Hockstetter to dare. We were a penguin colony on the edge of an ice floe, each trusting the next guy would take the plunge first to see whether there were any sharks.

"Come on, take a shot. We've just weaned you off school; all that learning is still fresh. You, for heaven's sake, put your hand down. We're not in grade school, even if you still smell like diapers."

"Angiogenesis is the process whereby new blood vessels are formed from preexisting ones," a tremulous colleague said, and put her hand down.

"Exactly. An essential life process. And cancer's top weapon."

He changed the presentation display to focus on the healthy patient, except that it now showed a video of the same MRI. It zoomed in and switched to a 3D projection of the neurons. One was darker than those around it.

"There you are, my novices. Your Creator's biggest mistake. A minute, insignificant, damaged cell. Any other in its place would trigger apoptosis—cell death; it would fragment and dissolve into the organism. Nonetheless, the process has failed, and the cell has decided it won't die off. Not only that, it's begun to replicate itself."

The dark, mutant cell split into two, then four, then eight. The camera zoomed out to show the tumor's exponential growth.

"This process would halt right away but for angiogenesis, my novices. This astrocytoma would grow a scant couple of millimeters before it would be starved of the oxygen it needs to keep eating and breathing. But this purportedly intelligent design is rife with slipups. Numerous things that ought not to go wrong do go wrong."

The cells in the display recruited blood vessels, robbed the host organ of its life energy and grew out of control. The attack did not stop with devouring the host organ but spread through the bloodstream to take over other areas: the greatly feared metastasis. That animation was terrifying, even for our hard-boiled minds, which had learned to internalize such matters. Underneath lurked the gut fear that one day what you saw on the screen could happen to you.

"So these dumb cells that wanted to be immortal wind up killing the organism that supported them. That's it, folks."

Hockstetter tapped another key to end the presentation and the hospital logo was displayed again.

"My dear novices. You have studied for years to grab a pew in this room. So far you've crammed your heads with facts, but your education begins here and now. You will begin to answer the question: what is man?"

There was the odd wary glance, which Hockstetter didn't fail to notice.

"As it's your first day, I'll bow to your unsullied political correctness. Okay, what is a human being?"

"A primate from the hominid family," a guy in the front row said.

"Not bad, my dear novice. You would surely get great grades in zoology. No, I mean what we really are."

No one answered. Hockstetter's sarcastic tone cowed us all.

"We are machines full of tubes, engines and valves. And machines must have a purpose."

"Survival," somebody piped up.

"Right," Hockstetter said, and could not have looked more surprised if a cow had just mooed Beethoven's Fifth. "We are all survival machines. Especially in your case, my dear novices. And now, look around you. What do you see?"

"Competitors," somebody said.

"To paraphrase the great Professor Dawkins, for one survival machine, another unrelated survival machine is mere background, such as a cloud or a rock. All that distinguishes it from the rest is the way each machine reacts, because it has the same innate transcendental mission: to preserve its immortal genes. At any price. Which allows us to charge the insurance companies top dollar and keeps the American public arguing over who should pay rather than why costs are so high."

Laughter filled the room, the energy shared by accomplices who know they have arrived and are wallowing in it.

"Our brain has only one goal: survival at all costs. And to get there it makes up for all the data it lacks with wishful thinking. Like the existence of an afterlife. For our brain, it is more important to tell a consistent story than a true one. Anybody ever have a tiff with the girlfriend?"

More laughter.

"Then you know what I mean. Questions?" he said with a wide sweeping gesture.

"You mean to say heaven is no more than a defense mechanism for the brain?" a guy spoke up, quite put out.

"The obviousness of that question will earn you several more hours on call."

The residents clammed up and bowed their heads. I had listened enraptured to the whole sermon, which struck me as being as provocative as it was offensive. I couldn't help but raise my hand.

"If we are merely machines that allow our genes to copy themselves, if our allergies are no more than chemical reactions, and if life was not created for any purpose, then why go on living?"

"Well, I see we have a novice with more than half a brain. What's your name?"

"Evans," I replied, proud of myself. I didn't know then that he asked my name not to distinguish me but to mark me. He wasn't overly fond of thinkers. All he wanted was obedient, servile cohorts.

"Many find these assertions distasteful. It upsets them if you prod them out of their cocoon of willful ignorance. I think that attitude is wholly mistaken. Only when you have no bounds can you live to the full."

"But then existence is punishment."

"Think of Sisyphus, the mortal condemned by the Greek gods to roll a huge boulder uphill. As soon as he got to the top, the boulder rolled back down again. And so on, forever. But as Camus would say, I can only imagine Sisyphus to be happy. Because within the bounds of his punishment, there were no gods."

Murmurs of approval sounded behind me. The way we let Hock-stetter's dime-store nihilism dupe us in those early days! We were still wet behind the ears and hadn't read widely or really pondered life. For him it all came down to physicality, but I tell you, there is more to be learned about the human condition in twenty minutes in the emergency room than in twenty months' residency in neurosurgery with Dr. Hockstetter.

"Sadly, within the bounds of your punishment," he went on, and pointed at us, "there is a God, and that's me."

"My dear David," Hockstetter trilled from my office door. "How's tricks?"

"Good afternoon, doctor," I replied formally, and didn't bother to answer his question. First, because I am very choosy over who I am on first-name terms with, and second because he didn't give a rat's ass. I even found it unpleasant to say his name. Hockstetter. Sounded like somebody clearing his throat.

I was not surprised to see him there. As soon as they told me somebody had edged me out, I knew he was behind it.

He came over to my desk. We didn't shake hands, nor did I get up to welcome him.

"Great to catch up after all these years. I'm thrilled to see you've settled into your new, um, position," he said, and looked around. "Very commodious. You guys obviously live large. Nice work if you can get it."

Meaning: your office is bigger than mine because yours is an inferior, undemanding hospital. I wasn't about to let such a heavy-handed opening unsettle me.

"Well, it's to you I owe the great good fortune of being here. Don't think I don't appreciate it."

"My dear ex-novice, the sages say rancor is hatred that stretches into eternity. It's an insane way to live. Above all when we bear in mind it was your mistakes with Mrs. Desmond that got you fired."

I smiled, slowly and sadly. Oftentimes I had gone over in my head how I could get him back for what he'd done to me. He and I alone, no consequences. And now that I could, I didn't feel like it, didn't have the energy.

"You know perfectly well what happened to Mrs. Desmond, Dr. Hockstetter. You screwed up, in front of six others. They were all too intimidated to second-guess you."

It had been a lengthy operation on a middle-aged woman with a multiple myeloma on her spine. I had been on the job eight months, and by then the differences between Hockstetter and me were irreconcilable. It wasn't merely that we saw surgery, medicine and even life from diametrically opposed standpoints, but that we simply couldn't stand the sight of each other. Any resident in any field must build character by taking the knocks that come with the job, even humiliation doled out by superiors. But there are limits.

He had tried to throw me off the program three times, but his golden opportunity didn't come knocking until Mrs. Desmond's op. It was I who prepared the area for surgery and exposed the spine, ready to remove the tumor. It was he who overdid it with an inaccurate incision—most unlike him, it must be said—which left the patient hemiplegic. Guess who Hockstetter blamed, amid my colleagues' thunderous silence?

I wanted the whole business to go to court, to force those who were there to tell all, but that asshole Hockstetter persuaded Mrs. Desmond not to sue, because she would destroy an inexperienced young man's career. The poor woman was so grateful her life had been saved that she didn't mind spending the rest of it in a wheelchair. The disciplinary board wasn't so lenient. It wouldn't do to besmirch their star surgeon's fame, so they had my ass in a sling.

Luckily, the former St. Clement's manager was familiar with Hockstetter's wiles and let me finish my residency there. What was set to be a few months' trial became a long-term contract. I didn't come off too badly, all told. Hockstetter was a great surgeon, 99 percent of the time, but when he messed up, he did so in a big way, so it suited him to have throwaway residents at hand. A bunch of others who'd worked with that skunk had been fall guys for his ham-fistedness, but they hadn't landed on their feet. One of my classmates gave up medicine after Hockstetter slapped her with a malpractice suit. She now runs a vacuum cleaner store in a mall on the outskirts of Augusta.

"Poor David. Are you still ridiculously in denial?"

"Someday, one of those kids you use for cannon fodder won't take the fall. You can't fool all of the people all of the time."

Hockstetter smiled, but it wasn't one of those "Look what your dog's doing on my lawn" pouts he used to pull years before. He had now perfected the look and turned it into a poster-boy smile.

"I'm afraid this isn't the occasion for chitchat, my dear ex-novice. I've come out of professional courtesy to take on the transfer of a certain patient's records."

"You've come to rub my nose in it, doctor. Be honest for once. It won't kill you. Probably."

His smile wobbled slightly. Then he leaned his head back to pretend I'd offended him.

"David, I've come to you in good faith, instead of asking you to FedEx me the case history. I would like to smooth things over. Maybe I wasn't the greatest boss in the world, but you've had time to lick your wounds, haven't you?"

I would have liked to hit him with some witty repartee along the lines of "Good thing you didn't treat them," or "Tell Mrs. Desmond that," but at that moment I didn't have the luxury of time to think up one-liners. So I confined myself to slapping the Patient's file down, with the flash drive on top, and crossed my arms. I was itching to ask him how he'd talked the First Lady into switching surgeons but didn't dare show unseemly interest. Nevertheless I needed to know. What was White's plan really? And where did I fit into it all? If he truly wanted Hockstetter to operate on the president, why take Julia? Was White blackmailing him, too? If so, it certainly didn't look that way.

"Here you go. Just tell me one thing. Will you operate at Bethesda?" I finally dared to ask.

Hockstetter shrugged while he leafed through the Patient's case history.

"I would have to be a very capricious or very insecure doctor not to accept the special conditions attached to this kind of case. By the way, what kind of approach were you thinking of for the Broca's area?"

His gall flabbergasted me.

"You wouldn't seriously be asking for my opinion, would you, Hockstetter?"

"No, not really."

He went to the door, but when he had his hand on the knob, he turned to face me.

"You know something, David? You're right about one thing. I really did come to rub your nose in it. As soon as they knew I was willing to operate, they kicked your ass out. Who would want a second-rate surgeon when they could have the head of Neuro at Johns Hopkins?" he said, lifting up the folder and waving it dismissively. "Again, it merely goes to show you have nothing I can't whisk away."

He waltzed off, leaving the door open.

I sat and stared at the cell, which taunted me from the table.

"Well, White. What now?"

The answer wasn't long in coming.

WE NEED TO TALK.

MARBLESTONE 11 P.M.

Kate

The long wait was excruciating.

Kate marked time with her back against the shed wall and her gun aimed at the door, and ran over events, again and again, wondering whether she had been wrong to get caught in a trap like that. Waiting there troubled her all the more. To go uphill to the street without knowing whether anybody else was lying in wait would be madness. She thought of answering David's text but didn't want to take her eye off the ball for a second.

With no warning, there was a rasping noise, a smoker's cough. Then a voice could be heard on the other side of the door, speaking in English this time. Kate stuck her ear to the shed wall and could make out the housebreaker's every word.

"No, couldn't call before. No, cell not work. Yes, understand. Company problem. I tell you, phone is crap."

Silence.

"I tell you we look all over. Dejan and my brother look in neighborhood, no suspicious car, van, nothing."

Silence.

"Yes, yes, understand. Search house all over again. But nobody here. I know because I set blind trap, hair stuck to outside door. Hair fall if door open, but hair still there. See?"

More silence.

"Yes, remember Istanbul. No my fault."

Silence again, longer this time.

"Your money," the intruder said in a very tense voice.

They'll turn the place over again. If they see the open padlock, in they come. I can shoot down the first one, but the others won't be so stupid.

They'll fire through the shed walls, like shooting fish in a barrel. This flimsy plastic wouldn't stop a gnat.

But Kate could do nothing except wait, with her finger on the trigger.

Outside, the drizzle became an all-out downpour. The raindrops crashed onto the shed roof like ball bearings falling into a beach bucket. Kate thought she heard a car start up a couple of times but couldn't be sure.

Nobody entered the shed and no more sounds could be heard in the yard. Time drifted away in the choking darkness, which made her think of Julia and the hell she must be suffering. She waited for two seemingly eternal hours, feeling useless and powerless. She realized that all her training, all the bravado she showed, her stalwart stance—all that depended on how others saw her. She was Secret Service Special Agent Robson. Telling suspects that put the fear of God in them, not solely because she was a strong woman with a gun but because she was the face of the beast. To touch her was like pulling on Superman's cape or spitting into the wind. Nobody messes with the Secret Service.

Even so, acting under cover and out of fear, she was no more than the victim's frightened relative. She began to wonder whether going along with David wasn't crazy.

Finally, she decided the trespassers could not possibly still be in the house. She stood up, her muscles cramped after hours spent on her haunches. She stretched her arms and legs several times before she stepped out. She had to loosen up if she was to hit the street as quickly as possible.

The extent of her failure overwhelmed her. Her plan had been a train wreck. She was about to leave without a thorough search of the house, but to turn on the jammer again and reenter the place was a no-no. That trick wouldn't work twice; it would arouse too much suspicion.

She picked up the gadget and was about to go through the door when an idea came to her and she turned around. The Evanses' recycling bin was in the shed, where they separated aluminum, plastic and paper. The recycling truck came to Silver Spring once a week.

Maybe they've overlooked it. Come on, please. We simply need a little stroke of luck . . .

She opened the top and took out the blue bag from the paper section. It was featherweight.

Not very promising, but better than nothing.

She opened the door, replaced the padlock and ran back to her car under the rain, wondering whether something in that handful of wastepaper would lead to her kidnapped niece.

Marblestone Diner, Silver Spring

Mr. White watched David Evans enter the diner. What he saw gave him a pleasurable sensation of victory. The person only yards away from him was a completely changed man from the one he had confronted the day before. His attitude was transformed; his eyes no longer burned with yesterday's ardor and fury.

David was capable of staying calm in the midst of chaos but ducked confrontations. He never put up a fight if he could help it but hid behind his sense of humor and intellectual superiority. These were obstacles White had steamrollered over in the last few hours.

Human beings are naturally conditioned to help the young of their species because they are born weak, and they feel responsible for offsetting that weakness. That's why babies' crying is so unbearable, especially in enclosed spaces such as airplanes.

David's bond with his daughter had fed his need to collaborate, but intense pressure was still required to break his professional conditioning.

Nevertheless, White still had his doubts. David's reactions were sometimes unexpected. He wondered whether he wasn't mistaken and there were more people like Dr. Evans out there. Men who cast doubt on his current personality types. Maybe together they could make up a new category. The very idea gave him a shiver of anticipation but irritated him at the same time. He didn't like to get things wrong.

He had to think clearly. The main thing now was to get back in control of his tool. White hadn't expected the Hockstetter business, and when he heard Dr. Wong tell David he wouldn't operate, he felt momentarily hemmed in. But on reflection he reckoned that setback could be a good way to strengthen his hold over David. He needed only to make him think it was all part of his plan. With the right lies, the subject's illusion that White was all-powerful would remain unaltered. He had to pull the right levers in his brain.

Bring him back to the tipping point.

It was almost a decade since White had set up his lucrative business. In the first few months he had made a fairly startling discovery: that public knowledge, news and headlines, were not winnowed into truth and lies. Just palatable lies.

At bottom, it made sense. Nobody wants the truth, because it is too knotty and unpleasant. Humans accept as true the most outrageous falsehoods, simply because they came gift-wrapped. Sunflowers don't follow the sun, the Great Wall of China cannot be seen from space, and neither do we use only 10 percent of our brain.

The same could be said for the economic crisis, the Occupy Wall Street movement, Benedict XVI's resignation or the Osama bin Laden hit. The truth behind the official façade was deeply inconvenient. White himself had had a hand in some of those deeds, had moved pieces in the dark that had changed the world stage. Often he'd been hired by the same man who had put out the current contract, a man he'd never met but who had done much to enlighten him. Somebody whose immense power was based on other people's trust, and to whom he owed some of his most worthy creations. That said, never before had White gone after a piece as big and valuable as the one he would take at nine on Friday morning.

White pondered whether the inherent human need to take the part for the whole could work in his favor at that moment. The tool would be more than willing to be put in harm's way if he thought it was part of the plan from the outset.

He would have to play it by ear it for the next few hours until he could sort things out. To see the ante raised filled him with an emotion he hadn't felt before. Total planning made for more certainty but took the fun out of his projects. Using David Evans to assassinate the president had been a risky choice, but doubtless much more stimulating than the other four he had weighed up.

He had to put the surgeon right back at the point of balance. The point that never moves, no matter how the arms swing.

21

"A Hawaiian Punch, please. Lemon Berry Squeeze. And for you, doctor?"

"Black coffee, Juanita. Double, please."

The waitress smiled and went for the drinks.

"I picked this diner for our meetings because they have Hawaiian Punch," White said. "It's not easy to find outside of supermarkets. Nowadays it's all Coke or Pepsi. If only people knew what they pay for each time they drink down one of those brews."

"You wouldn't be turning all conspiranoid on me, now, would you?"

White looked at me, amused.

"Not at all. Conspiracies don't exist."

Juanita's arrival with the tray took the sting out of how ridiculous he had just made me feel.

"Human beings are very simple," White went on, touching his thumb and forefinger to make a circle. "Take the waitress, Dave. She dreams of being Mariah Carey, she longs to meet Simon Cowell. When she gets home she curses her swollen ankles."

Juanita was back behind the counter, watching *American Idol* with rapt attention, mouthing the words to the songs on the show. It was too late to see it live, so she must have DVRed it in the hope of having a quiet night. Like the day before, we had the place to ourselves.

"Maybe she sings like an angel," I answered.

"Maybe she does, Dave. But that's beside the point. The world is full of people with talent who spend their lives hanging on in quiet desperation, trapped in dead-end jobs. Why do some take the subway while others fly Learjets? It's a matter of character. To really want what we wish for."

"Something tells me there's a point to all your talk. I just don't see it."

"I still have a problem, Dave. I still need somebody to eliminate my target."

"But . . . What about Hockstetter?"

"Hockstetter is not an active part of this operation."

My next words were so selfish it shames me even to recall them, but I have sworn to tell my story like it is.

"Listen, Hockstetter's your man. He'll be no loss to the world if he disappears. Lean on him and give me back Julia."

"Negative. There is no entry route or time. You'll have to do it, David. The old-fashioned way. That was the plan from the start."

"The plan . . . What plan? No, hang on . . ."

"Simple, Dave. It was me who told Hockstetter the Patient's identity. And he called the man in the bow tie from Baltimore and told him he wanted to do the op."

I opened my eyes wide and took a few seconds to digest what he'd just told me.

"What? But . . . Why? Why complicate things that way?"

White picked up one of the pink sachets of sweetener from a container on one side of the table and fingered it for a while before he answered me.

"Why did you study neurosurgery, David?"

The politically correct answer to that question would be "Because I'm interested in the brain, science's final frontier." But the sincere answer, the one I'd never admitted to anybody out loud, other than Rachel, was the one White already knew. So I told him.

"Because it's the top-dog specialty."

"And you have so much to make up for, so much to prove." He nodded contentedly. "And now that they've put you up to the definitive challenge with the definitive patient, I make you lose him . . . I don't know, David, something tells me even the motivation to save your daughter may falter at the last minute."

"That's absurd, White. I won't let Julia down," I hastened to say. But my conscience told me I wasn't that certain. Hadn't I let my own wife down because of the job? What was the difference?

White pointed at me, but to humor rather than accuse me.

"I dare you to tell me you haven't tried to think up a way to get me off your back and your daughter returned."

I sized him up quietly. Those calm movements, the suave voice . . . I'd seen it before and it betrayed some poisonous notion bubbling behind his blue eyes. I didn't want to risk riling him up, so I plumped for the truth.

"It's true," I said with a shrug.

"Aha!" he exclaimed in triumph. "The nearer the operation comes, the more doubts you will have. You will beg, connive, try anything. Drop it, Dave. I've thought of everything."

"I know that. Believe me, White, if I had come up with a sure plan to get Julia back and put you behind bars, right now I'd be hugging my daughter and you a bar of soap. But I cannot and will not run that risk."

"Maybe. But I'm still not convinced you're on my side. So I want you to earn that operation."

His words rang true, but deep inside my intuition told me he was bluffing; it twitched like a stiff and cramped muscle. He wasn't as almighty or as all-knowing as he would have had me think, and he didn't have everything worked out. There were variables beyond his control, but his inflated ego declined to own up to it. White would play the part of superior being to the bitter end. Now I could clearly see the cracks in the cage he had locked us both up in. He knew nothing about what Kate was up to and certainly could not have foreseen the Hockstetter deal. Those frailties, small as they were, gave Julia and me a chance I could use against him. But the question was:

"How?"

I realized I'd said the last word out loud, but luckily White thought I meant how would we unseat Hockstetter.

"Use your imagination, Dave. But be quick about it."

"And what about your minions? They clocked up too much overtime this month?"

"That would be too easy. You have to get your hands dirty, David, or the whole exercise will be pointless."

"I don't know if I'm up to it. This isn't like throwing an operation. I have no clue what to do."

"You'll think of something."

That was a blind alley. Maybe White had lied about my swellheaded old boss's involvement being his idea, but he had certainly seized on it to force me to fight for the operation and the chance to save Julia's life. I hadn't seen her for almost twenty-four hours, and the pain of missing her was eating away at my hope. I needed to know she was okay.

"I want to see her."

White shook his head.

"Negative. Maybe as a prize for removing Dr. Hockstetter from the equation."

"I told you I want to see her."

By way of an answer, the psychopath merely stared at me with his shark's eyes. I held his gaze for an instant before I looked at the iPad on the table next to him.

"You're thinking of snatching it from me, aren't you, Dave? It would be so easy, a pushover. You simply have to reach out and it's all yours. You're taller than me, your shoulders are wider. There would be nothing to it."

I could feel the palms of my hands tingle while the device that monitored the pit Julia was in grew in my mind's eye. I made an imperceptible move toward it.

"I'll burst the bubble of your fantasy, Dave. This marvel is protected by three passwords. If you enter just one of them incorrectly, the data will be erased instantly. But not before sending a signal to a place you know. You want me to tell you about the mechanism that signal activates?"

"No, not really," I said in a voice as dry and hoarse as a barrel of nails.

"I'll show you all the same. It'll be instructive and motivational. Also, you did ask to see your daughter, didn't you? Maybe I was a bit unkind to deny you that small mercy."

He lifted the iPad's cover to shield the screen from my sight and keyed in something. When he turned the device around, there was the same interface he'd shown me the day before.

"Watch carefully, David."

He pushed a button. The image went from black to relaying the live video feed from inside the cavity. Julia was in the corner, digging her fingers into the pit wall. Every now and again she turned and dropped something on the floor. It took me a few seconds to realize she was taking the biggest pebbles from the dirt for some kind of game. I was surprised my daughter was up for playing at a time like that. Julia was a very sensitive girl who could get all wound up over nothing.

"The human mind is adaptable, Dave," White said, reading my mind. "When you transport it from a safe context to a baleful one, at first it goes into shock. But in time, it tries to fit in with the new situation; it redefines the new context as safe to minimize the trauma. But naturally, new challenges can always surface to make everything harder."

He pushed another button.

A little whir and then a click sounded in the iPad's speakers. Julia seemed to hear it, too, because she turned to where the sound came from, to the left of where she kneeled, offscreen, and squinted to try to see through the glow of the lights.

All of a sudden there was a gut-wrenching, earsplitting, inhuman sound.

The image lagged behind the sound, and it took me a couple of seconds to realize it was my daughter who had let forth that shriek of sheer terror. She backed up and kept on shrieking.

"What are you doing to her, you son of a bitch?" I said as I jumped up. I clenched my fists, hard. But I didn't get all the way up. A huge mitt pushed my shoulder down. The same cutthroat I had seen that afternoon in the hospital had sneaked up behind me. I hadn't seen him come in. Making sure Juanita couldn't see, he drew a gun and held it against my neck.

"No tricks, eh, doctor?" he said. It wasn't the same guy as the night before. This one had a much thicker accent, and he sounded high-strung, as well as aggressive.

I tried to turn around, but the gun barrel poked my jugular vein even harder. The brawler's hand might have been made of concrete, the way it anchored me to the chair.

"Quiet. Watch video."

Helpless, I could only obey.

On the iPad's screen, Julia had huddled up against the wall. On the floor, in the middle of the pit, was a dark, long shape.

"*Rattus norvegicus*. An interesting animal. Length ten inches, weight one pound five ounces, long and sharp teeth," White said.

The rat was acting strangely. It didn't move, its snout pointed straight at Julia's bare foot. My daughter, her arms stretched out, had stopped shrieking and looked at the repugnant vermin with her eyes wide open.

"They don't usually attack humans. Unless, that is, they have been starved for days and shut up in an acrylic cage with microscopic perforations. Your daughter's smell all this time must have driven it crazy."

The rat scurried across the ground and flung itself at Julia, but she twisted away just in time, turning her back to the camera. The move unbalanced her and the rat ran over to sink its disgusting yellow teeth into my daughter's skin. I tried to wrest myself free again, but the goon merely dug the gun deeper into my throat, squeezing my windpipe.

"Leave her alone, asshole. She's only seven, you son of a bitch."

The ox made me lean over, with my face almost against the tabletop, until the screen filled my eyes. A drop of sweat rolled down my nose and fell onto the iPad's screen, creating a pixelated rainbow.

"Hush, Dave, you'll miss it," White said. "This sure beats the National Geographic Channel.

Julia rolled aside at the last moment, but the rat had meanwhile snagged itself on her pajama leg. Julia shrieked again, stood up and shook her leg, but the rat held tight and would not abandon its prey. With a snarl which sounded even beastlier than the rat that was attacking her, Julia flailed her foot in the air. That tore apart the cotton legging, and the rodent thudded into the wall, fell onto its back and waved its claws in the air. Julia gave it no time to right itself, but stepped forward and stamped her right foot on the dark, verminous body.

Once, twice, three times you're out.

There was a dense and unpleasant silence, and then my daughter turned around and her face came into view. Her eyes were glowing like hot coals under the lights, and she had twisted her mouth into a savage, primeval grimace. She didn't look like my Julia but the offspring of some ancient race, born in a dark age.

Then the spell broke and the poor girl burst into tears. She sobbed and limped off to the other end of the trap, as far as possible from the bloody pulp the rat had turned into.

"Well done! A truly remarkable defense and a most interesting experiment, one I've been wanting to conduct for years," White said, truly overjoyed.

It was sickening.

The tough released my shoulder and took the gun from my neck. I sat up in my seat and wheezed.

"You see that, Dave? Yesterday, she was a terrified little girl, two minutes ago a helpless victim. But when the occasion called for it she was capable of doing the unthinkable. The mind is flexible, I told you. Let that be an example to you."

I didn't answer. I looked again at the iPad, which was now displaying its lock screen. That instrument held control over my little girl's life and death. I couldn't take it from him, no way. I shuddered to recall how Julia had limped back to her corner. The rat had surely sunk its infected teeth into the sole of her foot before it died, or could have punctured her skin when she squashed its chest cavity. If so, the risk of catching hantavirus or rabies was very high. I tried to remember how long the incubation period for those diseases was, but my mind drew a blank. There was room for one thing alone in there, and that was hatred.

Pure, total and unadulterated hatred for the man in front of me.

"If you pull another stunt like that, I'll kill you, White," I whispered. "If it's the last thing I do."

The psychopath shook his head knowingly.

"I have more rats, fifty or so. All as desperate and hungry as that one, Dave. If you dare screw with me, if the cops get me, if you leave your cell behind on your desk again . . . I'll lift the acrylic hatch that keeps them separate from your daughter. And the system will automatically e-mail a video file to her grandparents with the subject line 'Look what a fine mess Daddy got me into.'"

Kate

The first thing she did when she woke up was look at the timer on her cell.

28:06:03.

Twelve wasted hours, and I haven't found out shit.

She thought of her niece, of how every breath she took brought her closer to death, as she used up the oxygen supply to the burrow where they held her. Kate's mind, her conscious mind, took control of her breathing, and for a couple of minutes she could think of nothing else but filling her lungs and expelling air.. When she was a little girl she used to play that trick on Rachel. She would tell her not to think about breathing, or else she might stop and die. Rachel would take fright and breathe faster and faster until she got dizzy, to her mother's annoyance.

All this is my fault.

Kate stirred, trying as much to get her stiff muscles to move again as to shake off that sinking feeling she had. She was naked but for underwear. The rest of her clothes, which stank of sweat and were covered in grass stains, lay jumbled up by the foot of the bed. She had dropped off to sleep for a couple of hours but her body clock had woken her up at almost five in the morning, as it did every day. Her shift started at six, but that day she wasn't going to show up, for the first time in eleven years on the job.

She didn't turn on the lights to go to the kitchen. She liked to walk in the dark and the scant space between her bedroom and the fridge was sparsely furnished. She never cooked, because she figured dirtying pots and pans was too much hassle for one lone diner. Just as well, because the pathetic countertop had barely enough room for a coffeemaker and the contents of the wastepaper basket she had taken from the Evans place. She turned on the coffeemaker and pored over the scraps of paper again, with the dripping sound that heralded caffeine for sole company. Something was hidden in there, she knew. But she had to find it.

I'm the one who started it all.

The apartment was on North Randolph, a flat, undistinguished street with as little personality as the rest of Arlington. Paying $2,500 a month for a bed, sofa and forty-two-inch TV struck Kate as more of a felony than many she'd had to investigate. But the building came with a garage, and it was a godsend not having to find a parking space when she got back from work, or having to get the Metro at five in the morning. She earned close to six figures a year, so she could afford it, but for Kate it wasn't about the money so much as common sense. As she had grown up on a farm, the tiny space choked her like a blouse that was three sizes too small. But, frankly, she'd inherited some of old Jim Robson's selective and manic stinginess, although she wouldn't own up to that, even under torture.

If only she hadn't spoken to the First Lady about David.

She'd broken all the rules by doing so but thought she was doing a good turn. They were on board the presidential limousine, affectionately nicknamed the Beast by the Secret Service, on their way to opening an exhibition at the Smithsonian. The First Lady was talking on the phone in back. Usually she adopted a normal tone of voice in the presence of Secret Service agents, as they all did after a few months. The agents were so reserved their charges tended to treat them like empty vessels. What went in one ear appeared to go out the other.

"I know, Martin. But that's not the point," she had said in a low voice, while Kate kept an eye on the traffic from the passenger seat. It was only the next sentence that made her prick up her ears.

"I don't need a good brain surgeon, I need one I can trust. You'll have to approach them one by one: Colchie, Hockstetter, Evans . . ."

Right then Kate had turned around without meaning to. Not much, only a few inches.

But the movement did not go unheeded by the First Lady, who pushed the button that raised the glass panel separating the driver's compartment from the passengers. Kate cussed herself for being such an oaf but didn't get to do so for long. A few seconds later the car halted outside the museum and Kate had to get out and run the gauntlet of camera flashes and wildly cheering supporters.

That very afternoon, the First Lady had sent for her. She was by the tennis court, watching her daughters play, her arms folded as she gazed into the distance, miles away. Kate discreetly cleared her throat to bring her back to earth.

"Agent Robson," she said earnestly, by way of a greeting.

"Ma'am."

"In the limousine before, you overheard a private conversation."

Kate didn't answer.

"I don't need to remind you that to reveal any inside information would lead to immediate expulsion from the agency, and possibly to criminal charges," her boss added.

"Ma'am, if you still doubt the loyalty of the Secret Service, then you have learned nothing in all these years," Kate said.

Her tone was polite, the words flashing. Decades of full-time politics had taught the First Lady to take such digs in her stride. But that wasn't a regular day, nor was it a regular issue. Her shoulders shuddered, although it was hot.

To comfort her was unthinkable, so Kate pretended not to notice she was crying.

"It's okay. I'm fine," the First Lady said after she managed to pull herself together. "I'm sorry I snapped at you, Kate. I know you're true-blue, and my daughters are nuts about you, you know. You and Onslow are their favorite agents. At night when we have dinner, they always say, 'I got first dibs on Kate, you had her last week, Mom.'"

"They're darling girls," Kate said with a smile.

"Aren't they, though?"

For a couple of minutes only the thwack of the rackets and the balls rebounding on the court could be heard. Kate watched the two girls wistfully, harkening back to the days when she played with Rachel. She used to get hopping mad and quit playing if she thought she couldn't win.

"Actually, I'm glad you listened. I desperately need to talk about it, preferably to a woman. All those in the know are men, and deal with issues like men do. They either duck them or ram them head-on. You're not married, are you?"

As she was tall, strong and obstinately single, Kate had won an unfounded reputation among her colleagues for being a lesbian, not that she cared.

"I've managed to escape so far, ma'am."

"But I think you get my meaning."

"I believe I do, ma'am."

There was silence again.

"The president's sick, Kate, as if we didn't already have enough on our plate, enough ball-breakers. As if it weren't enough to have to smile while we weather every crisis, every intrigue, every futile power struggle. They stand up when we enter, but they're thinking about what's in it for them before they even hear the last note of 'Hail to the Chief.' If they so much as find out he's got . . ."

Kate bit her tongue for a few seconds before answering. She knew it was wrong but nonetheless she did it.

"Ma'am, I'm sorry if I was out of line earlier. It was a knee-jerk reaction because you mentioned my brother-in-law."

"Your brother-in-law's a brain surgeon?"

"Dr. David Evans, at St. Clement's."

"Is he a good doctor?"

"I have no idea, but he's a good person."

If I had kept quiet, Julia would be sleeping soundly at home right now.

That was another "if" to add to the long list she had drawn up in her life.

But if not Julia, they would have kidnapped somebody else's child. Another innocent kid who did not have a federal agent for an aunt to try to save her. Old Jim Robson always said things happened for a reason. Maybe that was why it had happened to Julia. So she could come to the rescue.

Well, God, if you're listening, you know where you can shove your reasons, Kate thought as she took her first sip of piping-hot coffee.

Kate and her Maker hadn't made up since Rachel's death. At that time of the morning and as she had barely slept a wink, things weren't about to change.

I need a clue. A lead. I need to gather string till I can pull on it. It must be in here somewhere, she thought as she scoured the wastepaper over and over.

She swigged a big mouthful of coffee. It hadn't cooled down enough and seared her throat as she swallowed. It wouldn't help her encroaching heartburn, but it would liven her up a little.

She had thrown out packaging and containers, and made three small piles with the rest of the stuff in front of her. One with flyers, another with bills and a third of seemingly unimportant scraps.

Nothing.

She picked up a notebook and jotted down what she knew about Svetlana Nikolić. To begin with, she could bet her bottom dollar that was not her real name. She had logged on to the National Security database from her laptop and found no trace of her as a visitor. She had entered the country either illegally or under another name. If Kate could have taken on the case as a regular antiterrorist inquiry with the requisite means, she would have narrowed the search down to several days before she showed up at David's, and looked through all the airports on the East Coast for a woman matching her description. Even then the data mining would have taken a dozen agents hundreds of working hours, with no guarantee of success.

That line of inquiry would be a wild-goose chase, no more.

Her next clue was a false lead. Kate thought the doctoral adviser Svetlana had given as a reference might help. David obviously didn't remember the man's number, but he had given her the password to his cell phone provider's website and a rough date for the call. It wasn't too hard to track it down in his call history; it was the only number he had called just once in that time frame. The number was out of service. An Internet search showed it belonged to a virtual switchboard, quite probably located in India, which took calls pretending to be whoever the client chose. You could sign up for one of them for ten bucks a month, plus a dollar for every call. To provide cover for the phony nanny would have cost a measly eleven dollars.

How could you be so naive, David?

Another dead end.

It was hopeless. The kidnappers hadn't contented themselves with merely killing Svetlana, they had eliminated every final trace of her, too. Wiped her off the face of the earth. To all practical intents, she had never been born.

Kate's brother-in-law had also mentioned the conversation between Svetlana and Jim Robson, which was what had made him drive over in the small hours. Although she didn't think it would lead anywhere, she was that desperate that she was ready to chase it up to see whether it could shed any light on events. The problem was how to do so without arousing her father's suspicions.

It was still too early to call the old man, but not for another call she had to make in short order.

"McKenna," a fierce voice answered on the second ring.

"I'm sick, boss."

"Oh no you're not."

Kate was so perturbed she almost spilled her cup of coffee all over the floor. Was McKenna onto her?

"I've been vomiting, sir."

"Robson, you've never been sick in your life, damn it. Do you have to go and pick up a bug today, of all days? We have a tactical briefing for tomorrow's business."

"I really am sick. I've got it bad," she said in a normal voice.

She knew the easiest way to catch out people who call in sick when they're faking it is that they nearly all put on a sickly voice.

"You know what kind of shit you're dropping me in, Robson? We have a very special and tricky operation happening tomorrow. I have to detail a very select team, the sortie is classified and besides, all the civilians at Sixteen Hundred have gone ape. I've been in here since two a.m."

"Sorry, sir, but I'm truly in no condition."

"Robson, tell me how many eighty-fours we've had so far this month."

Chapter 84 of the US legal code forbids attempts on the president's life. Whenever possible, assassination attempts on the president are dealt with out of the limelight, with swift action and trials behind closed doors, so as not to encourage copycat crimes. This policy entails using obscure euphemisms for potential slayings, one of which is "eighty-four."

"Three," Kate admitted, getting shakier by the second.

"The last guy got a rifle to within seventy yards of Renegade, Robson. Each time, there's more of them and fewer of us. Tomorrow's the most screwed-up sortie of the year, and you know that. You can't let me down."

"You can take somebody else to the briefing, sir."

"The hell I can, Robson! Renegade specifically ordered me that only twelve people should be aware of tomorrow's sortie, which seemed like a lot to him. And Renaissance told me one of them had to be you. You want me to wake up POTUS and tell him I have to put somebody else in the picture?"

"I'm . . . I'm sorry, sir. I'll try to get better as soon as I can. I'll go in tonight to read the briefing on my own time."

"Tonight my ass. You've got four hours, Robson. Get yourself down to Walgreens, grab a big-ass jar of Pepto-Bismol and be here by ten. You'll have time enough to get sick tomorrow when the job's done. You're in luck, you'll be in a hospital. I'm sure your smart-ass brother-in-law can give you a discount."

"But, sir—"

Her boss hung up before she could say another word.

Kate was stunned, the cell still beside her ear and every inch of her tautened by the dilemma.

A direct order by Special Agent in Charge Eric McKenna was as binding as one God's fiery finger had written in stone. Nobody would dream of quibbling over a call like that. If you're told to come into work when you're running a fever and have diarrhea, you just do it. You have no choice.

If she were a less committed agent, a troublesome and argumentative one, ignoring an order to show up in four hours' time would lead to punishment but wouldn't raise any eyebrows. But considering that David was to operate on the president and the circumstances surrounding the surgery, it was unthinkable. And she was the opposite of troublesome. So many years of selfless devotion to duty were now turned against her. If she stood them up, they would smell a rat. They could go over David with a fine-tooth comb and find out everything.

The frustration and worry that had been simmering inside her for hours now reached the boiling point.

"Shit!" she screamed, and swiped the useless bits of paper off the countertop, along with the coffee cup, which shattered as it hit the floor tiles.

Enraged, Kate bent down to clean up the mess and glimpsed something that made her do a double take. Stuck to a gummed envelope containing a flyer was a folded oblong piece of paper that she'd previously overlooked. Her heart quickened as she unfurled and read it.

At last, there it was, the clue she'd been after.

22

Summary of Wednesday night's activities: I drank myself into a stupor.

I left the Marblestone in a rage, but it soon wore off. What I had seen on that screen had torn off a piece of my soul, a big chunk. I drove home, dragged myself to the sofa and grabbed a bottle of whiskey. To fall asleep was unthinkable. To face up to my thoughts, impossible. I desperately needed the solace of oblivion, to black out for a few hours, so I let Wild Turkey do its thing.

The sunlight awoke me at nearly eight o'clock.

I was on the carpet, facedown. I blinked a few times and tried to rein in the migraine that was gnawing at my brain. My right arm was smarting. I rolled up my sleeve and found three red lines, almost straight, each about a handbreadth long. They were fresh and very deep scratch marks.

How the hell did I do that to myself?

It had to have happened the night before. There were dried bloodstains on my shirt. But there was a total gap in my memory after I'd hit the bottle.

In the morning light, the rest of the night's events came back a little. The booze and the hangover made them a bit hazy, like a secondhand nightmare. But White's text message made reality abruptly sink its teeth in.

RISE & SHINE DAVE
HOW'S YOUR FLEXIBILITY TODAY?
The cell was by my head, leaning against the wall so I could see it clearly . . . and White could see me. The battery was charged up.

Whoever had done that, it wasn't me.

They broke in and were snooping around while I was out for the count. Did you laugh, you bastards, when you got a load of me stretched out on the floor like a rag doll? Get a kick out of it?

I gave the cell the finger before I picked it up. Then I noticed something on the edge of the sofa. It was a stain left by some grape juice, Rachel's favorite. I remembered the day, almost a year ago, when my wife had spilled a little, and the ever-helpful Julia rushed to wipe it up with a kitchen towel and turned a neat droplet into a purple blotch. We never did get around to cleaning it properly.

As I was driving to the hospital and trying to concoct a plan to get Hockstetter out of the way and myself back in the game, that stain hijacked my thoughts. A meaningless spot that a bit of spray could have cleaned away had stayed the course longer than the love of my life.

It has outlived my wife.

It will not outlive my daughter.

I showered and shaved in St. Clement's, away from White's prying cameras. While I was getting dressed, I glanced at the TV that was always switched on in the locker room. The Patient was on CNN, shaking the hand of the NSA director, General What's-His-Name. Both their faces were frozen into smiles. It seemed they had both attended an event at the White House where the president had mooted possible changes for the agency, "aimed at a freer future for the American people." The president slipped up in one of the sound bites broadcast from the speech, and in another he said the word "people" twice in a row. The newscasters wondered why.

Only I knew what was going on: the president's tumor was getting worse and worse.

I finished dressing in a hurry. I wanted to look the part when I did my rounds with the patients at nine thirty. They were all doing nicely, which briefly relieved my anxiety, but not for long.

Until I read the last name on the list they had given me.

"Is Jamaal Carter still here?" I asked Sandra at the nurses' station.

"They can't admit him to MedStar until tomorrow, so I asked Dr. Wong for permission. She said she'd dock it from your paycheck, Dr. Evans."

"They don't make scissors that small."

"On my pay you could give him a couple of aspirins."

But not too many. St. Clement's charges patients $1.50 for every painkiller supplied, plus taxes. The hospital dispensary buys them for less than a penny each, so you tell me whether they couldn't afford to keep the kid in another night without making too much fuss.

What's more, Jamaal's name had just given me a brain wave. It might work if I could get him to myself. But for that I had to surmount a huge obstacle.

Mama Carter.

I've come across a few religious nuts in my time. Here on death row there's one who sings a hymn at 2:34 a.m. A different one every day. He has a sweet, almost ladylike voice. I have only seen him on his way past my cell, because they don't let us mingle.

But every day we take turns for a half hour in the six-foot-square "exercise yard" surrounded by massive concrete walls. If you crane your neck somewhat, you can see a piece of blue sky up there somewhere.

When they let us out for our exercise, we all take a good look at each other. We want to see what somebody looks like when they're about to die. The hymn singer is a frail boy, with pale, skinny arms riven by blue veins.

It's hard to believe he strangled nine old ladies with his bare hands. He said he wanted to send them to heaven as soon as possible.

Mama Carter hadn't killed anybody, that I knew, but what had happened to Jamaal had turned her already towering faith into something tangible and solid. When I walked into his room I found her on her knees, praying at Jamaal's bedside. I cleared my throat to let her know I was there.

"Do you believe in God, Dr. Evans?" she asked as she stood up.

This time there were no kisses or hallelujahs.

"I believe in doing my best without expecting any reward," I replied.

"Yesterday you told me you prayed."

"I do. Normally when I have a problem. But I don't know if it gets me anywhere."

"I prayed for the longest time for Him to protect my li'l Jamaal. And my prayers have been answered."

Li'l Jamaal tossed and turned his six-foot frame in his cot, making his cuffs ring out against the bedstead he was shackled to.

"Hey, doc, think they can get this thing off of me? It makes my arm sore."

"I'm afraid you'll be up before the judge first, bud," I said, then remembered the gangbanger who'd been knifed. "Say, how's T-Bone?"

"He gonna live. They take him to another hospital. Dunno where."

I looked out of the corner of my eye at Mama Carter. I wanted to talk to Jamaal alone, but for that I needed to get his grandmother out from under our feet.

"Mrs. Carter."

"Call me Mama, please, Dr. Evans."

"I must ask you to step outside for a minute."

She stared at me and pressed her mouth into a straight, sharp slit.

"I'm sorry, but I ain't going no place."

"Pardon me?"

"It was the same with my boy Leon, Jamaal's father. The cops got me away from him, so they could have a quick word. That detective, he asked me to step out for a minute too. Leon's been inside for sixteen years, so I'm staying right here."

"Ma'am, can't you see?" I said, tugging at the lapels on my white coat. "I'm no cop."

"You could be wired."

"Mrs. . . . Mama Carter. I need to talk to Jamaal alone. Believe me, it's not him we're going to talk about."

"I believe you, doctor. You seem a decent man. There's a lot of sadness in your eyes, but also the light of our sweet Lord Jesus."

"Will you leave us alone, then?"

"No way. They could have wired the room."

I suppressed an exasperated cackle.

"Okay, Mama, have it your way. Jamaal, I need a gun."

"What the . . . !?" the kid said as he straightened up a bit and opened his eyes very wide.

Luckily, watching *The Wire* and *Breaking Bad* had improved my word power.

"A nine, a burner, a piece," I said, trying to sound tough. "Whatever the hell you want to call it."

"What this got to do with me, doc?"

"I want you to tell me where I can find one."

"No way, bro, you wigged out," he said, shaking his head.

"Look, kid, do I have to remind you that if you can walk it's thanks to me?"

The grandmother stood between us with her arms stretched out wide.

"Don't you even think of answering, Jamaal."

"Mama, I need your grandson's help."

"I knew you wanted to entrap him. You're trying to catch him out."

"I'm not, Mama, I promise."

"I don't believe you. What would somebody like you want a gun for?"

"I can't tell you."

"That makes it worse. Because you'll break the law."

"I won't mix Jamaal up in it."

"Well, you say that."

"Mama . . ."

"Get out of here before I call that cop who's sitting by the door. Ask him for a gun, not some black kid from Southeast."

I gently held Mrs. Carter by the shoulders and looked her in the eyes.

"Listen, Mama. I won't harm your boy. But I do need a gun."

"He who lives by the sword, dies by the sword. So says the Lord," she said, looking away from me.

"I am not going to kill anyone. I just need it to right a wrong, I can't tell you any more. I need you to believe me, Mama. Before you said there was kindness in my eyes. I need you to look in them and believe me."

Mama finally looked up and met my eyes. Up close, her face showed all the ravages of age. Hardship and poverty had furrowed her brow, but not her soul or her dignity. The whites of her eyes were yellow and bloodshot, and her cheeks were puffy. She was pushing seventy, so she knew only too well what it was to ride at the back of the bus, to use blacks-only bathrooms and fight for her rights. She had lived an unsettled life in which certainty was the most elusive of prizes, and I was asking for her trust on a plate. For her it would be a monumental act of heroism to take a rich white guy's word for it.

"The Almighty moves in mysterious ways," she said after a while, clamping her lips between words. "I'll ponder them while I sit on that chair and not listen to a word that is said in this room."

I nodded in admiration and gratitude, and turned to Jamaal.

"Dude, talk to me."

Kate

Kate checked the address one more time before she got out of the car. There it was: the corner of Twenty-Fifth and Greenmount, in Baltimore.

She had known that scrap of paper was meaningful as soon as she took hold of it. It was a crumpled, garden-variety gas station receipt. But the time stamp and location told her she was onto something. Dave could not possibly have been in Baltimore at one p.m. on a weekday, when he was supposed to be in the hospital. She would have liked to call or text him to make sure and avoid another false lead, but it was too risky. And she had nothing else to go on, either.

The receipt was for $24.71, or about seven gallons of gas. Who-ever it was had paid in cash, so Kate couldn't be sure. But her intu-ition told her that that receipt had belonged to Svetlana.

She shivered with cold as she stepped out. The leather jacket did little to keep out the chill early morning wind. She raised the collar, although that didn't help much.

The yellowish first light of dawn cast her distorted and lengthy shadow along the cracked sidewalk. She had parked two blocks away from the gas station so as to stretch her legs a bit and reconnoiter the place. It didn't tell her a great deal she didn't already know about Greenmount. It was one of the scariest neighborhoods in the country. Derelict buildings were thick on the ground, and most had become crack houses or shelters for bums. There was nobody about, merely silence slicing between the empty shells on the wings of an icy wind.

The local stores were going under owing to the lack of patron-age. The odds of falling victim to a violent crime if you went out at night hereabouts were one in nine. Things were a tad quieter by day, but it sure was no neighborhood to hang around in for the heck of it.

What made you come here, Svetlana? Kate wondered, looking around her.

A shy twig of a girl, who looked unassuming and harmless, according to Dave. One who turned out to be a plant for the worst type of psycho killer: the kind that nobody even knows exists.

Even so, this was no place for her. Were you on your way someplace else?

If that were the case, Kate had nothing. She fought off the urge to run the last few yards to settle her doubts once and for all.

To tease information out of potential witnesses, you must never look desperate. If they are hostile, they'll turn the tables on you. If they are law-abiding, then they'll be so keen to help out they'll probably make up half of what they tell you, without even knowing.

When she laid eyes on Rajesh Vajnuli, Kate discerned the gas station attendant would belong to the second category. He was so helpful and efficient, he seemed capable of being in two places at once. His talents must have been wasted in that desolate backwater, with no customers to bend over backwards for. When she showed him her shield and it became clear she wasn't a client, his enthusiasm didn't dim one iota. The traditional mistrust recent immigrants have of law enforcers was conspicuously absent.

"Are you really a Secret Service agent?" Vajnuli said in a raucous voice and an accent that hissed the S's, like a kid sleighing through freshly driven snow. "Like in that show, you know, the one with Jack Bauer?"

"No, that was the CTU. A make-believe agency."

Kate fielded similar questions at all times of the day and night. When a public appearance was announced ahead of time, an agent could spend hours face-to-face with the crowds waiting for the president. People got bored, and the biggest show in town was the agent standing firm a few yards away. Since she had been on the First

Lady's detail, they no longer picked her for such assignments. So she didn't have to reply so often to questions over vagaries such as Area 51 or the JFK assassination.

"The CTU doesn't exist?" the attendant asked, quite disheartened.

"Afraid not."

"You're kidding me! What if someone wants to blow up a nuclear power plant? Who's to protect us from terrorist plots?"

"The FBI, the CIA, the NSA and thirty-three other agencies. Look, Mr. Vajnuli—"

"Call me Rajesh."

"Mr. Vajnuli, I need you to listen carefully. Look at this receipt," she said, holding it out to him. "Your name is printed on it. Did you serve this customer?"

"Yes, that's what's down there, see? But I can't be sure who it was . . ."

"A young woman, twenty-four years old. Thin, high cheekbones, Eastern European accent."

"Oh yes. That was a few days ago. She was here, I served her."

"Do you know her name? Had you seen her before?"

"No, ma'am, I'm sorry."

"I'd like to see your security cam recordings."

Vajnuli leaned over in a confidential mood.

"Look, don't tell anyone, but the security cam recording system is very expensive. So we can only go back twenty-four hours. Enough for the cops to see who has held us up."

Sure you don't keep them. Because that would have made things too easy, Kate thought, massaging the bridge of her nose.

"I see, and that day you weren't held up, right?"

"No, we're on a roll. We haven't had a robbery for more than a month now. Almost like my hometown, Mumbai."

"And I guess you wouldn't remember her."

"Quite the contrary, Agent Robson, I have total recall, especially for hot chicks," he said, raising his eyebrows twice. Or at least trying to, as they barely rose above the frame of his Coke-bottle glasses.

Kate raised her eyebrows in turn—not in response to Vajnuli's flirting, but in surprise at the attendant's description.

"You'd say she was cute?"

"Oh, most definitely. She was short and very slim, but she wore a soft cotton dress and it showed her to advantage in all the right places, know what I mean? And she was dolled up. That's why she struck me, because that's not usual around here."

"Neither is paying in cash, is it?"

"That's where you're wrong, ma'am. Many of my customers call in for gas every day. They come with a couple of bucks or a five spot and eke things out that way. The odd one has to pawn his TV midweek to pay for gas or food."

"Can't you tell me anything else?"

"What's she done? Robbed a bank or something?"

"I am not authorized to reveal that information," Kate said with a vague wave of her hand, an old trick she had learned in her days on the fraud squad. It could mean any old thing—the sole idea was to momentarily satisfy the witness's curiosity and keep him talking.

Vajnuli sucked his teeth several times before he went on.

"Well, she was very polite. That I do remember."

"When she paid?"

"Not only that, but she also asked for permission to park her car in the lot here. It's reserved for the car wash clients, but what the heck . . . It's been broken for a year and I don't think the company wants to spend money on fixing it. I figure it won't be long before they close us down."

Kate looked out the window. From the counter there was a great view of the space set aside for the lot, merely a couple of stripes painted on the blacktop.

"She asked me to keep an eye on it," the attendant added. "I said yes, be my guest. Although if they'd stolen it, the most I could have done would have been to tell her how many people there were. In my country we have a saying, 'Never get between a bear and his honey pot.' "

"Wise words. Know how long the girl was gone?"

"Oh, I don't know. Half an hour, an hour maybe. I'm busy, you know?" he said, lifting up a book thicker than Kate's arm entitled *Advanced Quantum Mechanics.* "I have to get my doctoral thesis approved."

"So I see. Thanks for your help."

"Aren't you going to give me a card with your number? You know, in case I remember something and have to get in touch with you in a hurry?" he suggested, raising his eyebrows again.

"That won't be necessary, sir. Have a good day."

Kate walked out of the store. The sound of the automatic door closing spared her the good-byes from a very disappointed Vajnuli. Outside, the bracing dawn breeze was laced with the acrid smell of gasoline.

A soft cotton dress.

Dolled up.

It had taken Kate fifty minutes to get to Baltimore. If Svetlana had been there by one, she must have left home at noon. David always took Julia to school on his way to the hospital. Svetlana would have fixed breakfast for them, and then the coast would have been clear for her to get ready.

Why would an ostensibly reserved student who always wore casual clothes dress up and drive forty miles midweek? Did she go for a job interview behind David's back? Then what was she really up to in the house? Could it be she wasn't part of the plot?

No way, José. Because she gave Dave her supervisor's number. A sham number. She must have known.

What truly unnerved Kate was that description of Svetlana. The gas station attendant was a lonely young guy ready to hit on anyone in a skirt who made the door go ding-dong.

Kate was a good-looking woman in her own way. Her lean, wiry frame gave off a special vibe, but she was a severe judge of herself. When she looked in her bedroom mirror she couldn't see past her pointy elbows and the flab that was beginning to gather under her butt cheeks, which no amount of daily jogging could burn off.

You would have to be desperate to pick up a Secret Service agent, she thought.

The attendant was probably no more than a horny youngster who got the hots for anyone. But even so, David's description of Svetlana didn't remotely tally with his.

Could he really have been blind to the nanny?

A healthy, straight man who takes no notice of a twentysomething chick with a nice rack living in his own home?

Although he was in mourning, Kate had been around enough men to know that was not possible.

Unless we're talking about David, right? The man who only had eyes for Rachel from the moment he saw her.

It was the Spring Block Party in Georgetown, the legendary event they held every year right outside the campus. It was Kate's first, and she was raring to go. It was the second time around for her sister, who wasn't much into crowded festivities. She had said no, but Kate didn't know the meaning of the word. She had shown up at her dorm with a huge sign saying "I NEED TO PARTY."

"You will not drag me down there," Rachel insisted, rolling her eyes and turning back to her desk.

"You can't do this to me, Rae. We'll have a ball!"

"No we won't. It'll be all booze and guys trying to get into our pants."

"Sounds cool! Come on, what's with you? I've been working my ass off all winter to get ready for my midterms. Look, it's even chair shaped," she said, shaking it under her sister's nose, while Rachel vainly tried to study an anatomy book. "Doesn't it look flat to you?"

"You get your butt out of my face," Rachel said, tittering. "I said we're not going, and that's final."

So they went. They danced, they drank, and when it was Kate's turn to get more drinks, she bumped into a tall, dark-haired guy with green eyes. They jabbered about nothing in particular, small talk. Kate could remember the conversation verbatim, but that didn't matter. Because the only line that truly counted in their chat (uttered solely because Rachel wouldn't stop pinching her arm to say she wanted to get away) was:

"David, this is my sister."

And the rest was history. His head spun toward her so quickly the girl in *The Exorcist* would have been green with envy. When a half hour later Rachel told her that David ("Guess what? Turns out he's in med school, like me") had invited her to have a drink somewhere quiet, and asked whether she minded. Kate's smile quavered a little, but she said no, no sweat. She would repent at leisure over the years for that hasty lie, wondering what might have happened had she said what she really felt. That she had seen him first, that Rachel wouldn't even have been there were it not for her, that it just wasn't fair . . . but nothing could have taken away that spinning head or the twinkle in his eyes when he saw her sister for the first time.

No, David would have taken no notice of Svetlana, at least not in that way. Nonetheless the attendant's comment hinted at something, something important.

She had dressed up for somebody.

She was on a date, with a guy she couldn't see on weekends, because she had told David she didn't have a boyfriend. David said she used to spend the weekends shut up in her room, with her nose stuck in some books.

But there was someone. A boyfriend. And if there was a boyfriend, there was a lead. Some string to pull on.

Or there would be if I knew where she went from here. A coffee shop, or maybe—

The cell's ringtone disrupted her train of thought. She picked it up instantly on seeing it was her boss.

"What the hell's going on, Robson?" McKenna's voice came through thick and angry.

"I don't know what you mean, sir."

"I've been up all freakin' night prepping for the St. Clement's se-curity op. And before the briefing starts, in comes the chief of med-ical staff and says there's a change of plan, that we're off to Bethesda. The surgeon won't be your bro-in-law, but some Baltimore prick who hasn't had a single goddamned security check, no clearance, nothing. He could be a clean-shaven Osama for all we know."

Rachel was struck dumb.

"Still there, Robson, or has that diarrhea been the death of you?"

"Osama's dead, sir," was all she could find to say.

"So Renegade says. I say show me the evidence. Anyway, you'd better haul your ass over here right now or you'll be sorry."

He hung up.

Kate stared at the phone. She didn't get it. Exactly what was all that about? Who had made that call? Because if it had been the White House, that left David in a real fix and turned Julia into excess baggage.

She yelled out of rage and impotence, because David was incom-municado and she couldn't find out what the hell was happening. They had agreed that he alone would get in touch. That any other option was too dangerous.

Hell's bells, what more can go wrong?

A huge truck went by and blocked out the sun for a few seconds. When it came back, the rays dazzled her and she had to shield her eyes with her hand.

And then she looked straight ahead and saw where Svetlana had gone.

23

The first thing any Washingtonian tells you when you move to the nation's capital is, "Never, never go to Anacostia." They stress the second never. When I entered the address in my GPS navigator, the gadget dithered while it loaded the data. Perhaps it was giving me time to have second thoughts.

I crossed the river and drove into Barry Farm. The neighborhood was composed of little rows of houses, all in desperate need of a good coat of paint. As I looked at the house fronts, I guessed fear loomed over those people's lives. All the downstairs windows (and some upstairs ones) were covered in bars. Many were boarded up on the inside. The boldest residents had curtains for their sole protection upstairs.

I did not see a single open window.

The Lexus created a stir as it went along. Kids of ten or eleven began to chase me when I turned a corner. It was Thursday before noon.

You should all be in school, I thought. *Don't give up. Hang in there.*

I felt like stopping to tell them I'd had it tough, too. That I'd had an awful childhood but had kept going, despite everything. That I'd made it. But I doubt they would have believed me, and I couldn't hang around. After three blocks the kids got tired and faded from view in my mirror.

At last the navigator told me I'd reached my destination. I stopped the Lexus at the corner of a blind alley. Jamaal had told me to look out for a tall tree. Sure enough, a few yards up there was a leafy chestnut tree. I got out of the car and checked the urge to press the lock button on the remote. I felt such a move could smack of fear on my part.

I plodded up to the spreading chestnut tree. The branches cast a wide shadow under which a few folding chairs had been set up alongside a ghetto blaster that was booming out grungy shrieking noises. I love music but hate rap with a passion. If all the rappers in the world were to be struck down this minute by acute voice loss, yours truly would not shed too many tears.

I decided to keep my opinions to myself, because the guys chilling in the chairs seemed to really dig the song. Or at least until a couple of seconds before I came into view. Now they divided their looks of astonishment between the car and me.

"Christmas come early this year, brothers," said one of them, who looked to be the leader. He sat in the middle, next to the boom box.

"Hey, man, yuh wanna score some weed?"

"What is you up to, white boy? This sure ain't your hood."

I walked up to them real slow, with my hands very visible. They wore brash clothes; a lot of bling, some gold; and baseball caps. They also seemed completely devoid of hope. Those young men were teenagers, but in physical years only. Their doleful eyes showed not a hint of naivety or innocence.

"Good morning, gentlemen—"

"What kinda shit is that?" one of them cut in. I tried again.

"Howzit hangin', yoose all?"

"What you say?"

"Shut the fuck up, Shorty. I wanna hear what this dude's game is."

"Jamaal Carter sent me," I said.

"Who he?"

"We don't know no Jamaal Carter round here, dude."

"That's right, beat it."

"I'm a doctor at the hospital where he's been admitted." They didn't stop scowling and muttering while I spoke, but I wasn't going to let that stop me. "I asked him a favor, and he gave me this address."

"Doctor, huh? Got any prescriptions, man? You come to hustle Vicodin?"

"He don't look like no fiend, DeShaun."

"More like a faggot."

"He ain't no fiend. See the wheels he got?"

"Guys, please, will you listen up a minute . . . ," I pleaded, holding up my hands.

"What kinda favor you after?" the chief said, and silence descended in an instant. Gone was the smokescreen his sidekicks' chattering had provided.

"I need a gun."

I didn't try any more wisecracks in tough-guy speak. In that neighborhood, even in daylight, I felt I was on another planet, a very different one from mine. It was just a fifteen-minute drive from the sedate, high-society streets of Kalorama to that glorified war zone. Wisecracks didn't go down well in this neck of the woods.

"You got the dough for that, doc?"

The six faces in front of me gazed my way, devoid of expression, and I could see that the situation was getting out of hand. One of the gangbangers sat up slightly in his chair, while another laid the bag of chips he was eating on the ground.

I also realized that I hadn't had word from Kate for hours. The last text I got from her the night before told me she was home and pursuing an angle. I couldn't risk White's finding out I had another cell, so I had left it in my briefcase and sent no more messages. Nor had I told her the White House had canned me for the following day. I hadn't told her about the details of how I planned to get myself out of this dilemma. But right then, as the gangbangers edged out of their seats and encircled me, I wished I had told her. It had been a big mistake. If anything happened to me . . .

"I want to see the gun first," I said, forcing myself to look at the chief and trying to ignore his followers, who were hemming me in.

He shook his head in derision and leaned it to one side.

"That ain't what I'm askin' you. You cross the river to the brothers' turf, now you play by the brothers' rules. We wanna see some green."

"I'm afraid the deal's off, then."

"For you, mebbe, not for us."

I couldn't help but look around and measure the distance between me and the car. The two gangsters behind me came closer. When I moved again, so did they. The chief dug his hand into his sweatshirt pocket and pulled out a switchblade. He quietly popped it open.

"Shove him this way. So he ain't be on camera."

It was then I finally grasped why they were sitting in the shade on a cold day. A few yards up the street from the Lexus, on top of a telephone pole, there was a white box with a blue shield on it. Underneath it the unmistakable semicircular outline of a surveillance camera, watching over the street and those house fronts, day and night. It wasn't just the neighbors the closed curtains and boarded-up windows were meant to keep out.

That was why those kids hung out under the tree's branches, which they used as an improvised shelter from the PD's watchful eyes. How little the gang knew that the cops were the last people I wanted to deal with.

"Hey, cool it, guys, okay? We can work this out. Just name the price for what I came for."

"Name a price my ass, white boy. You gonna give us everything you got, like the keys to that ride I'm jonesin' for."

Somebody's hand pushed me forward, while another held me by the jacket. I elbowed back, trying to turn around, but it was no use. They closed in on me and jostled me under the shade of the tree, to make sure they could do exactly as they pleased. More arms wrapped themselves around me, holding fast to my chest, wrists and clothes.

"Look at what we got here. Hold him good, homeboys."

"We empty his pockets, DeShaun?"

DeShaun was the one with the switchblade. He gave me a disparaging look and licked his lips a couple of times.

"Hell no. He gonna do that all by himself."

He lifted the steel edge up to my face. The blade glided over my cheek so the point came to rest right below my lower right eyelid. I stood very still. The slightest move and he would gouge my eye right out.

"You gonna play ball, right, whitey?"

I was desperate. There was no way out and all I wanted to do was make myself scarce as soon as I could, and think up a Plan B. I was on the point of saying yes when a voice made itself heard behind DeShaun.

"What the fuck goin' on here? What you all hassle the doc for?"

The tension around me eased a little. A kid sauntered out of the house in front of me, and I remembered him instantly. It was the guy who told me the day before that T-Bone had been stabbed. He was doing up the fly buttons on his jeans.

"Shit, can't a guy take a good dump without you all fucking up?"

The hands let me loose; the gangbangers stepped back. The geometry and balance of power in the group underwent a seismic shift with the newcomer on the scene. Every head turned to face him; a couple of them pulled their caps on or unwittingly fidgeted with their sweatshirt sleeves. Now this guy was the leader, not DeShaun. Nonetheless, the latter Alpha male did not change his stance.

"You know this mope, Marcus?"

Marcus didn't so much as look at DeShaun, and he took scant notice of the switchblade. I could see there and then a silent pissing match was under way between him and his lieutenant. No words, no gestures, no looks. No visible sign to be picked up by the underlings. The one on the throne couldn't take on the challenge without making something of it, and it was obvious Marcus wasn't in the mood. Instead, he came over to me and gave me a friendly slap on the back.

"Sure I know him. He the man, saved T-Bone yesterday. Wassup, doc?"

That friendly move did the trick. DeShaun didn't dare carry on the standoff, so he whisked the blade away from my face.

"You got lucky, white bread."

But he was looking at his boss, not me. There was murder in his eyes, and I didn't doubt they'd end up killing each other one of these days. But that wasn't my problem.

"I want to talk to you, Marcus. Jamaal sent me."

"Something wrong with him?"

I told him Jamaal was recovering nicely and what I had come for. For some reason, Marcus burst out laughing at the thought of me with a gun.

"You gonna rob a bank, doc? You short on dough?"

The rest laughed along with him, and the atmosphere relaxed. That is, everyone except DeShaun, who had sloped away and was leaning against a wall, smoking a cigarette.

"If I wanted money, I wouldn't rob a bank, I'd open one."

"Right on. Give a man a gun and he can rob a bank. Give a man a bank and he can rob the world."

I stared at him, surprised by the quote. There was much more to this kid than met the eye.

"Have you read William Black?"

"No way. I get that off of Tumblr."

Or maybe there wasn't.

"Okay, you tell me how much you want for the gun."

"Can't do that."

Marcus slowly took the measure of me. He wore a thick, black hoodie and his long, tapered fingers fiddled with the heavy-duty drawstrings.

"So, what you say if they arrest you with it? Where you say you get it?"

"Nowhere, Your Honor. I just found it dumped in an alleyway."

"That'll do, yessir. Wait here, doc."

He went inside and closed the door. The rest of the gang sat down on the garden chairs, acting as if I weren't there but never taking their eyes off me. I stayed there in the middle of them, shifting my weight from one foot to the other, feeling stupid and watched.

Marcus took a long time getting back. When he did return, his hand was inside his hoodie.

"You got the paper, doc?"

"How much."

"A G."

"You've got to be kidding me. What kind of gun is it?"

"One that's available, no license, no questions asked. Take it or leave it."

Actually, I didn't care. I merely haggled over the price so he wouldn't hike it at the last minute. I had precisely $1,200 on me, my daily ATM allowance.

I dug into my jacket pocket for my billfold. I could see the look of a frustrated predator on DeShaun, who had to accept that the hunk of meat he had hoped to feed on had landed at the feet of the leader of the pack. I shrugged my shoulders and smiled at him. His expression stayed the same.

"Here you are, Marcus, a thousand bucks," I said, counting out ten bills. Then I peeled off another one and folded it around the others. "And here's a Franklin on me for a few beers and so you forget you saw my face."

"Fuckin' A! We all blind round here. That right, homies?"

He turned around and made sure they all nodded. When he was satisfied, he pulled his left hand out from under his sweatshirt and handed me a grubby, crumpled brown paper bag. I stepped over to grab it and felt a heavy, hard shape inside. I was going to open the bag, but Marcus waved to stop me.

"You crazy? Wait till you in the car. And best when you a long ways away."

I put the package under my arm.

"Is it loaded?"

"Eleven slugs. The clip take four more, but that down to you."

"In the Walmart in Alexandria, they got a box of fifty for twenty-nine bucks," one of the gangbangers said while he struggled to roll a sad-looking joint.

"Shut it, Shorty. The doc know he can't buy bullets in gun stores or joints with cameras. Go to a supermarket, and pay cash."

"Thanks, Marcus."

I turned around to go, but the gang leader's voice stopped me, and what he said weighed me down with even more to worry about.

"Hey, doc. I don't know what the fuck you gonna do with that piece, and I don't give a shit, man. But sure thing, that gun ain't clean. They find you with it, you might go down for more than you bargained for. You better watch your ass."

Kate

There it had been all along, blotted out by the sun's slanting rays, on the sidewalk opposite. A hulking great sign with white letters on a blue and red background.

THE BALKAN GRILL
The best in Serbian cooking

Kate dashed across the street, so quickly a car almost ran her over. The horn's dwindling echoes startled her all the more. She shrugged it off, just as she dispelled all thought of what she ached to yell at Dave, for not telling her about the change of plan. She was completely cut off from the intel, but she couldn't afford to let up now.

Easy does it, Kate. Now's the time to stay cool and take stock of the situation. You have to go in there and talk to them. They're only witnesses, no more, she thought. But she tucked her right hand inside her jacket and unfastened her gun, to make it easier to draw it from her shoulder holster.

The front entrance had a roll-up door that was locked down, so she couldn't see inside. It was covered by a morass of stickers and graffiti, but the lock was solid and well oiled. The place seemed to be in business, but it was way before opening hours. She knocked a few times on the door, which rattled like scrap iron, but there was no response.

There must be another way in, she thought.

She went around to the back of the restaurant building. It was a small place, joined on the north side to the business next door, a closed-down Korean Laundromat. The south side, the one with the main entrance, was at right angles to Twenty-Fifth Street. On the east side was a short, narrow alleyway, carpeted with cigarette butts. At the end of it, a rat scurried between the trash cans. A broken-down brown van blocked the opening to the alleyway.

I have to get into that alleyway and knock on the door, she thought. But it didn't seem to be the best option. Without a buddy for backup, going in alone was risky. If she could have called HQ and told them about her movements, she wouldn't have thought twice about it. But thanks to White, all outside help had been ruled out.

What the hell . . . Your niece could be in there. It's a no-brainer, you dork.

Cussing at herself had always done the trick, enabling her to get up the nerve to do something. Against all expectations, it had been Rachel who had found that out, the summer when they were respectively five and four. Kate had gotten herself stuck fifteen feet up in a tree and didn't dare come down. The branch she was leaning on for support was giving way with a hoarse and steady creaking noise. Her sister was worried it would snap through at any second and hollered all kinds of stuff until she got her to clamber down. Kate couldn't remember the rest of the insults, but the word *dork* stuck. That was the one that had made her overcome her fear of heights and poke about with her bare feet for a foothold lower down. As they hugged on the ground, still getting over their fright, the branch had fallen right next to them and brought down a few others in its wake. They had stood, their eyes like saucers, and sworn never to tell anybody what had happened. Since then, *dork* had become a talisman for Kate, her own code word, one she had never shared.

She went into the alley. She had to squeeze herself between the van and the wall, and scraped the back of her leather jacket against the concrete. Then she ducked under a ventilation pipe, which back in the day had been white, but had since been eaten away by rust. When she got through, her nose curled up at the thick, biting smell of the trash cans.

225

There was a steel door, ajar. It was dark inside, and Kate paused for a moment before stepping in.

"Hey, anybody in there?"

She groped her way around what appeared to be a back kitchen. Her hand guided her over greasy stovetops, and nooks and crannies which opened up into a passageway, then into the restaurant's main dining room. There were about twenty tables, also in darkness. Only the bar was lit up. Behind it an old man who would never see seventy again was drinking coffee and reading a newspaper with glasses perched on a hooked and veiny nose.

"Come in, officer. Sit down."

Kate took a seat on one of the stools. It was too low for her, and she had to reach up to the bar to rest her elbows on it.

"How do you know I'm a cop?"

"Your eyes scoped the room when you came in and you walk like you've got three arms."

She nodded. For now it suited her for the old man to think she was a cop. The less official she could make things, the better.

"Jackets are made to measure, but they can never hide the bump."

"Not only that, officer. Or is it detective?"

"Officer's fine."

The man also nodded, pursing his lips, to make it clear technicalities didn't float his boat, either. He took a cup out from behind the counter and set it down in front of Kate. He poured her a thick, black coffee and refilled his own cup while he was at it.

"The bump doesn't show, less so in low light and with my bum eyesight. No, it's the way you walk. I learned a thing or two when I was younger."

"Where are you from, Mr. . . . . ?"

The thick Balkan accent got thicker.

"My name is Ivo, and I was born in Loznica, although I have been living in this country for eighteen years. I came when the war ended. Looking for something I never found."

"Peace?"

"No, money. The things you say, officer."

The man laughed with a grating and humorless snicker. Kate squirmed uneasily on the bar stool.

"Is business that bad?"

"I'm about to turn eighty and I still have to work. But things could be worse. After I came here I busted my ass to open this restaurant. Now we try to stay afloat. Still, we've had our moments. Once that swimmer guy came here, the one with all the medals. Momir went crazy."

"Momir?"

"I'm his son," a voice said from the darkness to Kate's left. She leaped in her seat and cursed herself for her stupidity and weakness. She could distinguish the shape of a man sitting at one of the tables, but one whose age and face she couldn't make out. He lit a cigarette, and for a moment his gnarled and cruel features shone in the lighter flame.

"We'll pretend I haven't seen you light up in a restaurant."

"We're closed."

"Even so, it's against the law."

"But I bet you won't do anything about it," the shadow said.

She wondered how often Momir and his father had tried to put the frighteners on their visitors. They were more than just a restaurant owner and his son. There was something shifty and mean about both of them. If human souls were tuning forks, most would ring with the harmonious and predictable sound of mediocrity. But some souls in particular gave off a different sound, one that unsettled Kate and awoke in her the instinct of a hunter. And those two had that sound by the ton-load. She wished, not for the last time, she had fallback security to rely on.

"I don't care what you get up to, or not, in your business. I've come about one of your customers. Svetlana Nikolić."

The old man traded a glance with his son, then shrugged his shoulders.

"Never heard of her."

"She had lunch here with somebody nine days ago. A young woman from Belgrade, slim, attractive. She wore a cotton dress."

Ivo pretended to cast his mind back. He looked up to the right, a sure sign he was lying.

"No, doesn't ring a bell, officer."

Kate couldn't take it anymore. She moved up and grabbed hold of the old man's shirt. When he saw that, Momir rushed to his father's aid with his head down and his fists held high. That played into her hands. But he was stocky and broad shouldered. If he found a way to hit her, it would be no contest.

She couldn't let him get to her.

Using the old man's body as a counterweight, Kate put her insole against one of the heavy stools and sent it flying toward Momir. The metal edge hit him on the leg, making him stumble. He fell facedown at Kate's feet but was far from beaten. He grabbed her by the legs and tried to force her down, while the old man fumbled about for something under the counter.

A gun. Shit, he's got a gun.

She shook her leg free from Momir's clutches. Then she lifted her boot, stamped her heel on his back, and heard the air issue from his lungs with a stifled gasp.

"Let him go, *kurva*. Damned bitch."

Kate turned her head and found the muzzle of a revolver jammed into her chin.

"Listen to me, Ivo. I don't give a holy crap about you or your son. But in case you didn't know, you get life for killing a federal agent."

Ivo narrowed his eyes and stared at her in disbelief. They were so close his breathing mingled with hers. The old man's breath smelled of coffee and bitter onions.

"She's no federal agent, she's a bag man for Captain Zallman. He wants more than we've got. But this well's run dry."

"Who the hell's Zallman?"

"What did you say?"

"I'm telling you I don't know this Zallman."

On the floor, Momir writhed in anger.

"Take no notice, Father. She's lying."

"Look, I'm going to reach into the back pocket of my pants for my ID," Kate said, letting go of the old man's shirt. "Don't pull the trigger, okay?"

Ivo didn't answer and Kate took that to mean her brains weren't about to be turned into goulash. Very slowly and with just two fingers, she pulled out her ID and held it up in his face. When he saw it, Ivo looked disconcerted, pulled away his pistol and put it back under the counter.

"I . . . I'm sorry, ma'am. We thought—"

"Father—"

"Shut up, damn it! *U picku materinu!*" Ivo shouted, and unleashed a stream of invective in their language. "And don't move! Can you tell us why you didn't identify yourself as a federal agent, ma'am?"

"That's none of your business. I'm here on a matter of national security which must be handled with the utmost discretion."

"I'm sorry to have pulled the gun. We've had some run-ins with the local cops, which are nobody's business, either. As we say in my country, *sto vise znas, vise patis.* 'The more you know, the more you suffer.'"

Kate nodded. She'd heard rumors that some rogue Baltimore cops had set up a protection racket, which basically consisted in shaking down lowlife criminals. Ivo and his son were surely dealing drugs or fencing stolen goods, for which the restaurant was a front. But she couldn't have cared less about that. As soon as she found out what she needed to know, she would leave the pair of them to sort things out as best they could.

"So why then would I come asking about Svetlana Nikolić?"

"I don't know. We thought it was a trick. There's been a lot of questions about that girl recently."

Kate leaned forward, mouth open and heart pounding.

"Who's been asking?"

"People."

"What kind of people?"

"The wrong kind. People who scare even us, ma'am. And you'd better believe my son and I have come across the biggest collection of sons of bitches to have walked this earth, *svartno*. Really."

"When did they come and what did they want to know?"

"Yesterday evening. There were two of them, and one put his arm on the counter, right where you are. He rolled up his sleeve and showed me a tattoo of a black hand surrounded by barbed wire. He asked me if I knew what that meant, and I said yes."

"What does it mean?"

"*Crna ruka*. Black Hand, the death squads that killed thousands in Kosovo. Bloodthirsty, crazy guys. I'm a tough old man, not a coward, but believe me, I was real scared to see that tattoo."

Ivo turned back to the bar, grabbed a bottle of *rakia* with trembling hands and poured himself a stiff drink. Kate patiently waited for him to finish it before she carried on.

"What did they want?"

"They asked about Svetlana's boyfriend."

"Was that who she ate with a few days back?"

"His name is Vlatko, he waits tables in a bar in Mount Vernon. I don't know what they want him for, but God help him."

"The guy's a friend of yours?"

"No, but we spoke a little. He dropped by now and again for my *podvarak*. He said I make it just like his mother."

"Did he come alone, or with the girl?"

"Sometimes alone, sometimes with the girl."

"Did they meet here?"

"No, from what I heard they met before, in the old country. They'd been childhood friends, or some such. The last time they came, he was very angry. They spoke in whispers, their heads close to each other. She cried and ran out halfway through the second course. I never saw them again. That's it."

"I see. And how can I reach Vlatko?"

"I don't know."

Kate gave an exasperated sigh.

"Listen, Ivo. You're lying, and we both know it. I could threaten you with sending over a bunch of men in black, but I won't, because I don't think you're the kind to give in to threats, right?"

The old man didn't answer. He confined himself to pouring another shot.

"I think you like that boy and that's good. Because he's got very bad people on his trail, and I'm Vlatko's only chance to keep breathing."

Ivo sighed in turn, but it was a sigh of resignation. He went to the till and opened it with a resounding *cling,* and lifted up the front compartment. He ruffled a handful of papers until he found a corner torn off a page of the Baltimore *Sun.* He held it out to Kate.

"He gave me this number in case I ever needed a waiter. I don't even know if it works."

24

I put the paper bag and its deadly contents under the seat, started the car and headed north again. And here my plan had a big hole in it, which I wouldn't be able to plug unaided.

I looked at the phone and held it in front of me while I drove.

"Where?" I asked it.

There was no reply. The blank screen merely showed my own reflection. One block, two blocks. The Eleventh Street Bridge was drawing near.

"Listen, White, I'm playing by your rules and I'll win my place in tomorrow's op. I can do it. But I can't do it alone. So tell me, where?"

The Lexus's wheels exchanged the smooth hum of the highway for fitful juddering as they rolled over the bridge's expansion joints. A worker in orange overalls stepped out and held up a sign saying STOP. Men were at work on the bridge, and I heard jackhammers ripping into the concrete.

The cell phone was deathly quiet.

I bit the inside of my cheeks, thinking things through. The engine was ticking over, with 345 horsepower chomping at the bit, and the steering wheel shook in my hands with a restless rumble.

Finally, the message landed.

LAZ PARKING NEXT THE MAYFLOWER, SPACE 347.
YOU HAVE TEN MINUTES, OR YOU MISS HIM.

Five miles in rush hour. That's not possible.

The workman in the orange overalls finally stood aside and I put my foot down.

I don't know how I did it. I avoided three intersections normally jammed with traffic. I went through two red lights and grazed a messenger's bike with my rear bumper when I turned a corner. The guy landed on the hood of a parked car. My heart stopped for a second, but I did not slow down.

I can't, buddy, I'm sorry.

In my rearview mirror, I saw him get back on his feet, holding up a buckled bike wheel in his hand. Judging by the lively way he used his other hand to give me the finger, I guessed he hadn't broken anything.

Eight minutes and nine seconds after receiving White's text, I drove into the LAZ lot next to the Mayflower. No attendant came to meet me, so I figured it was unmanned. A machine made me pick up a ticket before it raised the barrier.

I went past rows of cars, looking for space 347. It was on the second floor, although I had to work out the number from the two adjacent spots. The one I was looking for was covered by the tail end of a huge and very badly parked maroon Porsche Cayenne.

I had no doubts that outlandish object was Hockstetter's. It was sadly like him to drive a $150,000 SUV but park it in a commercial lot rather than the hotel one to save nickels and dimes. Once I saw him stiff a waitress out of a two-buck tip in the Johns Hopkins canteen, for crying out loud.

That was his car, but he was nowhere to be found. The garage was full, but at that time of day all the owners would be busy at their desks. There wasn't a living soul in sight.

I didn't understand why White had given me that location, but it was perfect. I just had to find an escape route afterward. I parked on the floor above and sat on the backseat, where I had left a sports bag. I stripped off double quick and changed out of my suit into a sweat suit, tennis shoes and ski mask I had bought before I crossed the river. I put the ski mask on my head like a cap, with the bottom rolled up, and went back to the driver's seat.

I groped around underneath and pulled out the paper bag.

It seemed to weigh much more than before. Gingerly I put my hand inside it, as if it were full of scorpions. I withdrew the contents very slowly.

There it was. A Glock nine-millimeter. At least that's what it said on the side. Personally, I don't know one end of a gun from the other, just that you point the hole the way you want the bullet to go. That big lump of metal smelled of oil and something else besides, something filthy and wicked.

I wrapped my hand around the handle but didn't dare put my finger on the trigger. Guns are reputed to endow the owner with bravery and a false sense of security. To make you feel more powerful and invincible when you hold them.

I was just shitting myself even more.

I struggled with folds of cloth, attempting to put the gun down the back of my pants. The elastic waistband stretched a lot and I was scared of dropping the gun on the floor. I pulled on the drawstrings at the front and felt the cold steel dig a little deeper into my skin, but at least the pistol held steady.

I got out of the car.

I left the door ajar and the keys in the ignition. If all went well, I wouldn't have a second to lose after I rushed back. Nor could I risk dropping them. As they were part of a personalized electronic locking system, the cops would track me down within hours.

I glanced at the cameras in the corners. I could do nothing about them. I could console myself with the thought that the place was poorly lit. I wished I had remembered to take off the Lexus's license plates before leaving the hospital, but it was too late now. When the cops went over the recordings they would be onto me; that was obvious. I could only hope they wouldn't have time before the operation.

I walked down the ramp that led from the top floor to minimize the risk of meeting somebody on the stairs. As I went along, the soles of my brand-new shoes made a squeaky sound on the concrete.

HE'S COMING DOWN.

GET READY.

The text made me jump. I was wondering where in hell I could lie in wait for him without his seeing me. I had expected to have a few seconds more, but it was not to be.

Hockstetter's Porsche was next to a pillar that partially blocked the car's right side. It was painted crimson, rust-stained and covered in metal pipes. The space between it and the wall lay in shadow, making it a great place to hide. But in that case the car would be in my way. To attack Hockstetter I would have to traipse around the beast and he would hear me coming, which would give him time to get in the car or run off.

On the other side was a black Lincoln Navigator and very little space to hide in. The stairs were down at the end of the floor, on the side of the pillar, so I would have to choose one spot or the other.

In the distance I could hear a ping, telling me the elevator had arrived.

I ruled out the pillar. Too risky. I kneeled behind the Lincoln and realized too late that the ghastly fluorescent light behind me cast a shadow on the floor.

I set my teeth and prayed Hockstetter would not notice. I could hear his steps approaching. He dragged one of his feet and the sound of his soles on the concrete got louder and louder. I wanted to sneak a look but knew that would give me away, for sure. My heart beat faster and I panted. I lowered my ski mask to cover my face. The wool trapped my hot breath and burned my skin.

His footsteps rang out loud and clear, until they stopped dead. He was next to his car.

Now, Dave. Up and at him.

I went to stand up but couldn't do it.

My feet refused to move. I was rooted to the spot. Thus far I had done nothing irreparable, but this was too big for me. I had come to the point of no return.

I tried again, as I heard him fiddle with the keys at the trunk. But I couldn't do it. I was mortified.

He turned off the car alarm with a beep and the door locks clicked open. He was going to get away. I was about to miss him, and with that the chance to save my daughter.

Help me, Rachel. Help me.

And so she did. She sent me a memory.

I remembered that dinner.

While I was making the macaroni, I told myself, over and over again, that I had to talk to Julia. To give her comfort and affection. When I was my daughter's age, I got next to none of that, so I always made a point of kissing and hugging Julia as much as I could. I particularly liked lifting her up and carrying her all over the house while she hung on to my chest with her arms and legs like Velcro straps.

"Stowaway on board!"

The journey always ended up with the intruder thrown overboard and onto a soft landing—bed or sofa—by the swift expedient of squeezing the soft flesh on her tummy with both thumbs at once. She would have an attack of the giggles, loosen her grip and fall. That moment of weightlessness, eyes wide open, smiling from ear to ear; that was happiness.

But after Rachel died, there was no horseplay or tickling, simply whispers laced with sadness. My wife had not left behind a gap; she had rent a yawning hole in our lives, and it was an especially hard one to fill. Julia didn't quite get it yet. She had come to her mother's funeral and kept hold of her grandmother's hand the whole while. But when the reception was over, when the distant relatives had departed, when the neighbors were done snooping under the guise of offering food and condolences, when we were alone at last, Julia asked:

"Will Mommy be home for dinner?"

I left the dishes and went up to my little girl. A week had gone by since Rachel had passed away, and Julia hadn't asked after her mother once. Now she was squatting on the living room floor, with a handful of dolls perfectly lined up in front of her.

"Julia, sweetie, Mommy can't be with us anymore."

She didn't look up from the dolls.

"Because she's dead," she said, using the word for the very first time. A drop of cold sweat rolled down my spine.

"Yes, baby," I forced myself to say.

"You're a very good doctor. Mommy told me so, she said you're one of the best. Can't you make her live again?"

"No, Julia. I would love to. If there was the slightest way I could help her, I'd do it, but I can't. Death cannot be undone."

She was quiet for a bit. She rearranged a couple of dolls and sank her head into her shoulders.

"And will I die?"

I had the entire range of aphorisms possible for such a question on the tip of my tongue, begging to be spoken out loud. Easy answers to complex questions. *God only takes away good people. Mommy's in a better place. Everything will be fine.*

"Yes, Julia. We all have to. But you're little, and many, many years will go by before you die. You'll be much older than Grandma."

"And what happens when we die?"

"I don't know, darling. Nobody knows. That mystery is part of life."

"You'll die, too."

"That'll also be a long time coming."

"You don't know that. You might choke on an Oreo, or have a *corony*."

I didn't know what to answer, so I just kept quiet and put my hand on her shoulder. She raised her head, at last, and when I looked her in the eyes I could see she already knew the answers to all of those questions, that she had merely been preparing the ground for what was really eating her up inside. In a smart girl, that didn't surprise me. But I was terrified at what could be so awful as to make her beat about the bush.

"Daddy, did Mommy love us?"

"More than anything in the world, Julia."

She hesitated a second.

"The Blacks' daughter says she gave in. That she went down without a fight. That if she loved us she'd have faced up to cancer."

The Blacks' daughter, who lived two blocks away, was nine. She would have picked those words up from her parents at the dinner table. They were head lice in the mind she had brought to our house and infected Julia with. Maybe the hardest thing was to realize she had already thought it all out. As a neurosurgeon I had seen patients react in myriad ways after receiving a hopeless diagnosis. The vast majority turned to their nearest and dearest and made the most of every second they had left with them. In no time, those who had always been ornaments in the background took a front-row seat, ushered there by the final curtain. And strange to say, many were happier in those weeks they spent with their family than they had been their whole life.

Rachel knew all that as well as I did. But she had also seen the other side. She knew about the blurred vision, the sickness, the maddening migraines, the personality disorders, the dementia. She had seen glioblastoma patients talking normally one second, then three seconds later tearing their clothes off in the middle of a crowded corridor and rolling in their own feces. In front of a family who would never forget it.

"Julia Evans," I said, raising my voice a little. "Your mother was an incredible woman. Full of life and wisdom. She became an anesthesiologist so others wouldn't feel pain. She could put you to sleep in a second so the worst was over as quickly as possible. And then she would watch over you while you slept on the operating table, so everything was okay. She didn't go without a fight, she simply fought in another way."

I realized I was crying. Julia hugged me and tried to comfort me by patting me on the back. I was kneeling on the floor, the roles reversed, me being consoled by a little girl.

"Oh, Julia. I love you so much."

"It's okay, Daddy. We'll fight for Mommy."

And I'll fight for you, Julia, baby.

I took three deep breaths, like a swimmer about to plunge in the deep end, then gripped the pistol and stood up.

Kate

A phone number written down on a scrap of paper. Ten digits in scrawl as thin and tight as a spider's legs.

Kate memorized them before she shoved the paper into her pants pocket. She drove the whole way back with her hand in her pocket, guarding that bit of pulp that was her only operable lead.

The question was, what to do with it.

She drove south until she found an acceptable coffee shop near the Inner Harbor, and ordered the biggest, strongest and hottest coffee on the menu. A triple espresso, the first sip of which made her hands tremble slightly but did little to wake her up. She decided to take a walk along the waterfront to stretch her legs and try to think up the best way forward. The fresh, salty breeze brought her to her senses.

I can't call the suspect cold. With no more details than his name and with no face time, all he would do is hole up and never come out again.

She had to track him down first, but that was the hard part. Vlatko would need to have his cell switched on, and the necessary tools were in Washington HQ. To complicate matters further, she would need authorization from a superior before conducting a search—and in theory, a judge's warrant, although the Secret Service always skipped that formality if there was a serious threat to the president's life.

She couldn't go to DC to do it herself. She ran the risk of bumping into McKenna or one of those chosen for tomorrow's detail, which would mean she'd have to drop the search for Julia immediately and join the assignment. There was only one option, and that was to seek outside help. She had to trust somebody else, even if that meant going out on a limb.

Finally she decided to call headquarters. She tried to remember who was on duty that Thursday, someone who wasn't a dick or by-the-book flunky. There was a techie named Barbara Hill who owed her a favor. No big deal; Kate had done no more than slap around a couple of wretches who sprayed graffiti on her parents' storefront at night. It was a small favor to call in compared to what she was about to ask, but it would have to do.

She punched in her department's number and waited for them to put her through.

"Hill."

"Hi, Barbara, Robson here. I need you to triangulate a device for me."

"Okey-doke. What's the case number?"

Kate cleared her throat.

"There is no case number."

"Well, you're going to need one before I activate the system. If you like, I can put you through to the supervisor and—"

"No, Barbara. I don't want this on record."

On the other end of the line, her colleague could be heard shifting about.

"What the hell are you mixed up in, Kate?" she said, lowering her voice.

"Nothing that'll get you into hot water. But I just have to find this person."

"Kate, I could get into trouble simply for discussing this with you. The bosses don't give a goddamn if a search isn't clean as long as it's part of an active investigation. Talk to Soutine, he always cuts us some slack . . ."

"Barbara, this isn't—" She interrupted herself to clear her throat again. "This isn't about work. It's personal."

"Now I'm sure you're out of your mind. You can't use the department's resources to find out if your boyfriend's playing around, Kate."

"Barbara, I wouldn't ask you if it weren't important. I swear. I need help."

The other woman tut-tutted.

"Damn it, Kate. All searches are recorded. An alert will pop up on the boss's monitor."

"Then assign it an old number from a cold case. Please . . ."

"Tell me more."

"What do you mean?"

"Tell me why my ass is on the line. If I get caught, they throw me out, so the least I want to know is what sad story's at the back of this."

Kate waited, pretending to mull it over. She wondered whether Barbara could hear the seagulls squawking in the background.

"Swear you won't tell anyone?"

"Girl, my lips are sealed. Remember the guy from ID Theft who knocked up someone in Accounts? I knew before everyone else and said nothing. Not a word."

In her eagerness, her voice seemed to have gone up an octave. Not for one second did Kate imagine Barbara would keep her secret. She could just see her, eyes wide open and twirling her fingers around the telephone cord, thinking how to get the most mileage out of this gossip by the water cooler. Dishing up other people's dirt, bit by bit, spicing it up with her shamefaced jokes and trying to feel better about her own humdrum life. There is no more valuable merchandise in the Secret Service corridors than gossip about colleagues, and better still if it's to do with body parts below the belt. Kate only hoped she'd keep her trap shut for a few more hours.

"I met a guy a while back. He's with the Company, in Langley. Recently we've been an item, but he goofs off for days at a time. He blames it on the job, but I think there's someone else. I need to know where he's at."

"Is he cute?"

"Tall, slim, sad green eyes. Sensitive and smart," Kate rattled off, before she was aware, with a shudder, that she had just described David Evans.

"Wow, girl, I want to meet one of those, too. He got any brothers?"

"He's an only child."

"What a drag. At least tell me he's got an ass you can crack nuts with."

"His ass is okay."

"Way to go! And are you really sweet on him? You hear, like, wedding bells?"

This time Kate didn't have to fake her hesitation.

"Yes, I'm in deep. I've been smitten ever since I first saw him."

There, you've admitted it.

Barbara squeaked a quick titter like a happy rodent with a lump of cheese.

"Say no more, I'll come through for you. But next week we must do dinner and drinks," she warned, in her element. "Your treat, I get to choose where. And you owe me, big-time."

"Sounds like a plan. You won't regret it."

"Give me the number. And be patient, I'll have to wait until the coast is clear before I can track him down."

25

Our brain is an amazing machine. It processes eleven million bits of information per second, of which fifty are on a conscious level.

In the exact same second in which I leaped out from behind the car, I could discern the nine bits that counted, as clearly as when somebody presses PAUSE on an HD television.

I saw Hockstetter thumbing a text message on his cell. I could tell it was an iPhone by the colors on the screen. He was obviously so absorbed that he wouldn't have heard me even if I'd come from behind the pillar. I could see every detail of the intricate arabesque pattern on his impeccably pressed and knotted tie. His glasses straddled the bridge of his nose. His eyes opened in surprise and fear when he saw the gun barrel aimed at his head. He was clean shaven, although there was a smidgen of foam under his left ear.

"What the hell is this?"

"A stickup, asshole," I answered, straining my voice to speak from the throat. It sounds easy when you hear Christian Bale do it, but my words came out all puny and laughable, like somebody was tightening a rope around my windpipe. I tried to sound fearsome but came across as pathetic.

I took another two steps toward him. He was standing right next to the driver's door. I saw him glance at the handle, but he had the cell phone in one hand and his briefcase in the other. I could not allow him to open the door and get in.

"What do you want? You won't take my car, right?"

I took one more step and noticed the front fender next to my right leg.

"Do I look like your bitch? I have the gun, you obey."

Hockstetter took a step back and held his hands up.

"Cool it, cool it. I'll give you my wallet."

I moved around the front of the Porsche, keeping the gun aimed at him.

"You'll give me what I want. Turn around."

"Yes, yes. Whatever you say. But don't shoot."

Two more steps. I was homing in. It was now or never.

"I said—"

I didn't get to finish the sentence. Hockstetter leaned to one side and hit me with the briefcase, using it like a mallet. The brass-reinforced edge hit me in the arm and made me drop the gun.

"Like hell you're going to take my car, you lousy punk!"

He swung his arm back and hit me with the briefcase again. I dodged it by a hair and aimed a kick at him which went very wide. My foot connected with the edge of the door and dented the bodywork.

"My Cayenne!" Hockstetter wailed.

He tried to swipe at me once more, but I managed to duck and the briefcase went over my head. The metal dials on the combination lock drew sparks as they grazed the pillar and the briefcase clicked open, scattering the contents in a whirl of papers and X-rays. I recognized them in a beat. The leader of the free world's medical file now blanketed the floor of a grungy parking lot, but at that moment neither of us cared overmuch.

Now that he'd lost his blunt instrument, Hockstetter was defenseless. We both had the same idea at the same time: there was a nine-millimeter on the floor. We dived into the shadow cast by the pillar and scrabbled around where it had fallen, all arms and legs as we growled and panted. He got a hand on the handle and I on the barrel. We struggled for a few seconds. Although I was taller and ten years younger, the fat pig was strong, and he was furious. He elbowed me square in the ribs, which made me gasp. The blow buffeted the gun and it went off with a deafening bang.

Luckily, the shot went well clear of us.

My former boss tried to bite my wrist, but I leaned on his throat with my forearm to keep his pearly whites at bay. His face was flushed with the effort while I could barely breathe under my mask. Whoever came out on top in that tussle would win the day.

And I, against all odds, was losing.

My fingers relaxed their grip and slid over his sweaty skin. And the Glock's muzzle was turning inexorably toward my face. Hock-stetter cackled in triumph. He was within inches of blowing my head off. For a split second, I thought how cruelly ironic it would be that I, who had removed so many bullets from brains, would wind up with one pancaking mine.

No.

I snatched away the forearm with which I was squashing his neck. Hockstetter was suddenly let loose and his momentum carried him forward. He was momentarily stunned and I took advantage of that to elbow him in the throat. He abruptly dropped the gun and grabbed his neck with both hands, fighting for breath. I got tight hold of the gun and rolled out of range of his feet, with which he was trying to kick me.

I got up and aimed the Glock at him. What a genius I turned out to be, what a well-laid plan. I had thought the gun would make that arrogant bastard cower and quickly put him in his place. Evidently, the pistol had turned out not to be the magic wand we see in the movies, making people your slaves the instant you wave it at them. And Hockstetter had shown tremendous guts. The credit wasn't all his, of course. In cases of extreme stress, our reptilian brain—the deepest and most primitive part of our gray matter—reacts with a fight-or-flight reflex. Fittingly, the guy had turned into the survival machine he liked to crow about.

I tried to get my breath back. The Cayenne was lopsided now. The bullet had punctured a front tire. Hockstetter lay on the floor and filled his lungs eagerly and noisily, so at least my elbow hadn't broken his windpipe. I did not want to become a murderer.

But that is precisely why you're here, isn't it? So you can kill somebody tomorrow, a voice said inside my head.

For my daughter. I'm doing all this for Julia, I answered back.

"On your feet, loser. Gimme the fucking wallet. Gimme the cash."

Hockstetter made a deep-throated sound and tried to crawl away to the car. I came up behind him and he planted a kick right on my shin. I shook my leg a few times to stop myself from crying out.

If I had been an honest-to-God mugger, I'd have shot him. Hell, I was tempted to shoot him anyway.

I'll teach you, asshole.

He already had one hand on a door handle. He was on his knees, trying to stand up, with his legs apart and his back to me. I swung my leg back, as I did when I was about to kick Julia's soccer ball. Just like the kick-arounds we used to have in the backyard, until it was too dark to see the ball and Rachel would call out for the third time that dinner was ready.

I took the kick.

At times it's so cool to be a neurosurgeon. To know in wondrous detail the effect a blow to the testicles has on the central nervous system, to know the pain is equivalent to having twenty bones broken at once, and to look forward to the violent reactions to the trauma . . . but that's mere data. Except when you apply it to a poor excuse for a human being such as Hockstetter.

My former boss hung on to the door handle and instinctively— or inadvertently—he managed to open the door. Then time stopped as the pain washing over him flowed and ebbed, then gave him back control over his motor system. He slumped against the side of the Porsche and tried to shout, but all that sallied from his lips was a bleat:

"Help."

"You don't get it, do you, dumbass? I own you and I want your dough. Just hand it the fuck over."

I crouched down and probed inside his jacket until I felt a familiar lump on the right. I grabbed his wallet and put it in my pocket.

"See? How hard was that?"

He didn't answer, too busy grabbing his groin, with his eyes and teeth shut so tight you'd think he wanted them to meet halfway.

"You've got what you were after, now leave me alone," he groaned.

But I hadn't gone there to take his wallet. The whole performance had been no more than a cover for what I really meant to do.

"No. You need to be taught a lesson and I'm going to give you one, asswipe."

I aimed the gun at his head. His determination must have been in shreds after the kick, because this time he just opened his eyes wide and turned to crawl inside the open door. He leaned on the door sill and tried to get up.

That's the ticket.

At that exact moment I placed my heel in the middle of the Porsche's door and shoved it with all my might.

Hockstetter's loud scream didn't quite drown out the crunching sound the fingers on his right hand made as they were broken. I stopped pushing at the door and let him loose. He raised his hand to his face, with a look of complete terror and disbelief. His index, middle and ring fingers were at an odd angle to his palm, and stuck out in the opposite of the direction they were supposed to.

I took one look at the state he was in, then ran off, his yells following me, echoing off the ramp as I left the crime scene. I tore off the ski mask when I reached the floor above, where I had left the Lexus. I saw a car about to leave and for a second feared its driver might have heard the shot or the scream, and called the cops.

Shit. The phone.

I had been so stupid that I hadn't taken Hockstetter's cell off him, and he'd lose no time in calling 911, if he wasn't doing so already. Gasping for breath, I reached my car and sat behind the wheel.

I took off the sweat suit top and changed into my shirt. I gave myself just enough time to do up a couple of buttons and started up the engine. When I got to the booth by the exit, I tried not to look at the attendant, but he was riveted by something in front of him, a newspaper or magazine, and there were headphones stuck over his ears. On my way in I had paid for the whole day up front, with unlimited access, so I simply put my ticket in the machine. The barrier rose right away.

"Just a minute, sir. You can't leave."

The attendant waved at me. I looked out, at the ramp and the sunny street. I could not stay there a second longer. I was about to ignore him and hit the gas, but he came out of the booth and tapped the window a couple of times with one of his knuckles. He had thick, strong fingers and the folds of his skin were flabby.

"Could you unlock the doors, please?"

I wondered whether he'd noticed I was wearing sweat suit bottoms and not suit pants. Whether he would remember my face, whether he would note down the Lexus's license plate number.

"What's the matter?" I said, as I pressed the central locking button.

The attendant opened the back door on my side. Astonished and terror stricken, I turned around, but I couldn't see what he was doing. He closed it again right away.

"There you go. Your jacket was caught up in the door, sir."

I thanked him and took off up the ramp and out to freedom.

When I reached street level, I could hear the police sirens wailing.

SOMEWHERE IN COLUMBIA HEIGHTS

Mr. White leaned back in his chair, exhilarated. He'd had very little trouble hacking into the server at the security company that monitored the cameras in the parking lot. Nonetheless, stopping it from reconnecting them had taken several minutes of frantic and exhausting typing. He had scarcely been able to pay attention to David, busy as he was preventing the monitors in the attendant's booth from showing him what was really happening on level three.

Although he was an expert hacker, White's skill had its limits. The system had detected his break-in and had tried to bump him out, a loose end the Secret Service might uncover and which would doubtless spark their curiosity. Luckily his employer had provided him with not only the technology to monitor David's cell phone but access to the most powerful software in the world. White clicked on an icon on the screen, which opened to reveal a window with two more icons. The first showed a bald eagle spreading its wings above a globe. In the other, a polygon sheathed a block of glass with refracted light passing through it.

ENTER USERNAME AND PASSWORD TO LOG IN TO PRISM

White entered the combination, then the system requested another authentication code. He unlocked a drawer, reached inside for a token with a liquid crystal display and then keyed in the number it showed, one which changed every few minutes.

He pressed ENTER *and the program started up.*

A couple of seconds later, a drop-down menu appeared on the screen. He selected REMOTE ACCESS *and entered the name of the security company. Within a couple of minutes he had the security codes to breach its defenses and access its servers. The owner had noted them down in a text file, which he had sent himself and which was lying in an e-mail folder.*

"You should be more careful, buster. Or somebody might just do something like this."

A few more keystrokes and White had remotely deleted the system data. Not only from that afternoon in DC but from every place the company guarded up and down the country, in order to cover his tracks. It would look like a system failure and set them back millions of dollars.

"We've saved your ass again, doc," he said, switching his attention back to the monitor relaying images from the hidden camera in Dave's car's dashboard. The doctor's eyes looked startled on the screen, and his jaw was clenched as he drove back to the hospital.

He was not responding as predicted, which truly perturbed White. In the last few hours, his much-vaunted self-confidence had taken a severe knock. There were big bags under his eyes and his skin was ashen and dull.

Thanks to PRISM, finding Hockstetter's whereabouts and setting up a window for David to act in had been kid's stuff, but until the last second there was uncertainty hanging over the outcome, given that unforeseen twist. If they caught his puppet, his plan was all washed up. White would miss out on a fat fee for doing away with the president—$25 million, no less. But he wouldn't lose any sleep over that.

If he didn't kill the president, White would have failed for the first time in his life. And that was simply not possible.

It had nearly happened once before, in Turkey, months ago. A chain of unintended consequences had led the subject, an attaché at the Russian embassy, to jump from the fifty-first floor of the İşbank Tower eight minutes ahead of schedule. White himself had had to remove the docu-

ments the client had requested, which had truly bothered him. He liked to keep a close eye on things, not take part.

But there had never been so much at stake as in this present operation, and never had he lost so much control.

Now that the brain surgeon had gotten away from the garage and no longer needed him, White could allow himself a quick breather. Although he had not let the garage attendant's screens display what was happening, the cameras had been recording it. White had projected a ten-second loop of clean footage on the screens, while he stored the real sequence on his own hard drive.

He now played it back on his own screen and studied David's moves. There was no sound, but that was not necessary. The brain surgeon, with his mask on, had been transformed into something more. Bungling and amateurish, but determined and violent.

Brutal, even.

White congratulated himself and smiled. He would have given anything to have seen things for himself, in place of that blurred, tiny video.

He sent the file to a remote server, with carefully programmed instructions on what to do with it the day after. His concerns had withered away as if by magic. The little hiccup in his plan had merely confirmed that the subject was ideal for the mission and had furnished him with valuable research material, which would help him to perfect his behavioral model for the doctor's rare personality.

It was also the definitive tool for destroying David Evans.

The phone interrupted his musings. He'd been expecting this call. His employer monitored his every access to PRISM and must have seen something was up.

"No sweat," White said when he answered.

"I saw what happened. You were on the verge of fucking the whole thing up," a steely voice retorted.

"Have I ever let you down, sir?"

There was silence on the other end of the line.

"This time it's different," the other man finally replied.

"Isn't the free world's salvation at stake? The home of the brave in peril?"

"What's at stake is this country's power. I won't let that asshole in a tie endanger what it's taken so many years to set up."

"Consider him dead."

"He'd better be. Else I'd say the same for you."

White snorted in disdain. "If you can find me, that is."

"Yeah, yeah. Your firewalls, your security measures, your expendable middlemen. All that ain't worth a flying fuck, son. We know where you are. We know how many bottles you drink of that shit you've got in the fridge. We even know you're scratching your cheek right now."

White drew his hand away from his face and looked around.

"That's right," the voice on the other end said. "Not so much fun now that the boot's on the other foot, eh, son? Now you just concentrate on getting that stumbling block out of my way."

"Yes, sir, General, sir," White replied with a strained smile.

26

I didn't begin to simmer down until I was holed up in my office again. My pulse had slowed from jackhammer to frantic drum rate. I flopped into my chair and finished buttoning up the shirt that I had hastily put on in the car. I suddenly thought it would be best to ditch that suit—too many people had seen it that day. I had a spare one in my locker, in a different color, so I went down to get changed and on the way I stealthily picked up a few biohazard waste bags. I put on my scrubs and white coat, and into the bags I stuffed the sweat pants and top, my suit and shirt. I put the wallet I'd stolen off Hockstetter into another one and didn't even open it to see what was inside. I threw it all into one of our red containers, sealed it and wrote on the label in thick, block letters:

DANGER

HIV RISK

I told a porter to take it all away. No one in their right mind would open those bags, and in a couple of hours they would be reduced to ashes.

As I watched them go away, the adrenaline began to wear off and relief kicked in, making me buckle at the knees, so I had to lean against the wall. Somebody had taken his hand out of the ventriloquist's dummy I had turned into.

I also realized I was aching all over. I shut myself up in the first empty consulting room I found and raided the supply trolley. My elbows and knees were covered in cuts and grazes from wrestling with Hockstetter on the concrete floor. I lathered them good and proper in chlorhexidine and could feel a sharp pain on the left side of my chest as I leaned over. I breathed deeply a couple of times, which turned the dull ache into a bewildering, stabbing pain that filled my whole thoracic cavity.

Just great. Goddamned asshole has broken one of my ribs.

Fine action hero I'd turned out to be. Tooled up and I couldn't even overpower a fat fifty-year-old without getting a broken rib in the process. I must have made the injury worse by bending over to disinfect my grazes.

I couldn't go to Radiology and ask them to do me a couple of X-rays to see whether I ran the risk of a punctured lung, so I had to prod with my fingers to check it out. The bone seemed to be in the right place, so it must only have been cracked. It wasn't much to worry about and wouldn't kill me, but it hurt like hell. I would have to stuff myself with painkillers and struggle on as best I could.

I went back to my consulting room. Several patients who would need surgery in the medium term were waiting outside.

I treated them mechanically, getting their names mixed up a couple of times, something that had never happened to me before. I pay careful attention to my patients; their lives and their selves matter to me. But by that stage I had one eye on the door, in case the police burst in to arrest me for assault and battery. The other I had on the phone, expecting Meyer to call any second to tell me events surrounding the president's operation had taken a surprising turn. But nobody came to the door, nor did anybody call.

I did what I could with the patients. I scheduled the most urgent cases for the following week, although unbeknownst to me I'd be in jail by then.

Seconds after the last patient was out the door, while I was doubled up in pain and wondering what the damage to my liver would be if I took a couple more painkillers, my cell phone rang.

"What the hell is it now, White?"

"Dr. Evans?"

I froze on the spot. It was the First Lady's voice. Only then did I notice the display showed the caller ID was blocked, rather than merely blank, as it was when White called.

"Forgive me, ma'am," I answered. "I thought you were somebody else. I wasn't expecting you."

"Honestly, Dr. Evans, I just wanted to apologize."

"To apologize?" I repeatedly dumbly.

I had not imagined her calling me up, in any way, shape or form. I thought she would get Captain Hastings or the man in the bow tie to call the hospital director. I was not prepared for what came next.

"The way in which we decided . . . in which the decision was made to change the neurosurgeon for the president's operation was not very appropriate. I should have called before now."

"It would have been more polite, yes," I said before I could stop myself.

What am I getting at?

"I'm sorry. I want you to understand it was not my doing," she said defensively. "The cabinet met; a lot of people heard for the first time that my husband was ill. The meeting went on for hours and there was a lot of pressure over where to operate."

"I understand, ma'am. Everybody insists the president is more than just another patient. Unfortunately, I don't. For me he's just a person. If I treated him otherwise, I would expose him to unnecessary risks."

She stayed silent for a while. I could hear her breathing on the other end of the line and I wondered where she was. Maybe in the Oval Office, with her husband nearby, looking at her expectantly. No, that was impossible. She'd be in her room, alone, trying to keep her emotions under control.

"That is very commendable, doctor. It is rare to find people with such unshakable convictions today. As a wife, I thank you for it."

"But the decision was not yours. I understand that, too. I'm sure Dr. Hockstetter will do a great job tomorrow."

"Dr. Evans, actually . . . something's come up."

"What is it? Is the president okay?"

"The president's fine. Sadly, Dr. Hockstetter has broken one of his hands."

She said it casually, trying to sound calm and collected. Without going into details. And she wasn't offering me the operation either.

Then it occurred to me that maybe this was some kind of test. She was playing politics with me, although I didn't really know to what end. Did she suspect that Hockstetter's mugging had been a dirty trick? If so, why was she calling me? Or was her reticence just sheer pride?

Be that as it may, my fate and Julia's depended to a large extent on what I said next. Should I clam up and wait for her to make the request I so wanted to hear, in order to avoid suspicion? Or should I massage her ego and show that I was at her beck and call?

I had only a few seconds to make up my mind. I decided to act the innocent over Hockstetter's injury.

"Why are you telling me all this, ma'am?"

She cleared her throat.

"I suppose you can guess."

"I can guess, but you have yet to ask me."

"Actually, Dr. Evans, I was hoping first to persuade you to take back your original condition, so you can operate at Bethesda."

"Ma'am . . . In the cabinet they can ponder the scenarios and political fallout all they like. But the one with the scalpel a hairbreadth from the area controlling your husband's speech will be me. So the answer is no."

"Dr. Evans—"

"Tell me something, ma'am," I interrupted. "Tell me how much the columns in the *Post*, the polls and the ratings, will matter to you on Saturday morning, when your husband can see his daughters and say their names without getting them wrong."

The silence that descended seemed everlasting. I could feel anxiety gripping my shoulders, making them as heavy as lead. I had gone for broke, and stuck to my guns in order to clear myself of suspicion, but had left everything in the hands of a gut decision made by her. I had to dig my fingernails into my hand so as not to shout out, "*I'll do it wherever, just give me the operation, I must be the one who does it.*" Because to do that would have revealed me to be the opposite of what she wanted—somebody who was not dying to operate, who didn't desperately need it. She had made that very clear to me when we first met.

Talk. Say something, damn it.

"You win, doctor. You can have it your way."

My body tingled all over with relief, from head to toe. I tried to make my voice sound as cool as possible when I answered.

"This is no competition, ma'am. Your husband alone has to come out on top here." The words spilled out as crisp and clear as a mountain spring. But I felt like a fraud.

"I'll get Hastings to make the arrangements. And, Dr. Evans . . . Thank you. Anybody else in your situation would have made a big deal of the whole business. May I say it's an honor to know somebody as levelheaded and professional as you."

I muttered an unintelligible reply, but she hung up before I had finished. I dropped into my chair, weary and disgusted with myself. I just wanted to go home as soon as possible and sleep for a full day. But that day's emotional roller-coaster ride was far from over.

27

I had to go see Meyer in his office to tell him, of course. The meeting was brief and embarrassing. While I was on my way up he'd been given the news and he was happy as a clam again, although he didn't thank me this time, either, for getting the Patient back. He dismissed me with a wave and mouthed the words "Don't screw up again" before he got bogged down in another call with Hastings about the details. I had no more desire to stay in his office than to have splinters shoved under my fingernails, but even so I found his peevishness and, above all, his parting words insulting.

I went back to Neurosurgery, much the worse for wear and in a foul mood. Meyer had ordered me to stay on a couple of hours for a briefing on security protocols for the day ahead, and I had no option but to go along. I had hoped to hide away in my office, lie down behind my desk and get some sleep while I could, but inevitably that was also to be denied me. When I walked past the nurses' station, one of them beckoned me.

"Dr. Evans! Somebody's been asking for you, named Jim Robson."

I blinked in amazement. That was the last thing I'd expected. My father-in-law had never been to see me at work. In fact, I'd have bet a case of Bud he didn't even know the name of the hospital where I practiced. By the looks of things, I'd have lost.

"I'm not in the mood for monkey business. For God's sake, get rid of him. Tell him I'm not here."

The nurse swiveled her eyes and pursed her lips. I got her meaning a second before I heard a voice behind me.

"It's too late for that, David."

I wanted the ground to swallow me up, or to jump over the counter and hide among the half-open boxes of rubber gloves. But I had no alternative other than to turn around, shamefaced.

"Hello, Jim."

There he was, with the creases on his pants straight as knife edges and his stare every bit as sharp. He said nothing, although I would have preferred him to shout and call me everything under the sun.

"I . . . I'm sorry," I went on. "I didn't mean to insult you. It's just that I'm tied up right now."

"For a change. I don't want to waste your time. Is there any place we can talk?"

We went to the snack bar in a typical Robson silence, as impalpable as smoke but as solid as a brick wall. Rachel used to take her time getting mad, but when she did she was exactly like her father, much as it would annoy her for me to say that. She would sink into a baleful sulk, at which I would throw everything I had, from jokes to hugs. It was useless; the best thing to do was ride it out.

We both ordered some of the god-awful coffee they serve there and went over to a table by the window. When I sat down I felt a shooting pain in my ribs that made me jump. Jim looked at me askance but said nothing. I guess he was working himself up to speak and I didn't want to sway him.

"Thing is," he said after he cleared his throat, "I've come to beg your pardon."

That I did not expect at all, and it put me even more on my guard. Jim had never asked my forgiveness for anything, and, as far as I knew, Rachel took after her father when it came to apologies. And I had sampled many of my wife's. Rachel belonged to the *sorry but* species. The group of people who never simply apologize. If after an argument you manage to corner them and make them face facts, they apologize, only to counterattack with an explanation that shows you were actually to blame. "Sorry I was late, but I wouldn't have been if you'd remembered to buy the bread."

That had stoked many an argument in my first few years with Rachel, until I ended up accepting that that was the way she was and she wouldn't change. She would never acknowledge her mistakes in words, but in more subtle and tangible deeds. For example, by making juice and bringing it to me in bed for breakfast. Buying me a novel on her lunch break. Putting on the stupid show about pawn-shops that I loved and she hated. And at the same time I realized that those gestures were better than the five-letter word most of us say far too easily.

"Why do you want to beg my pardon?" I said carefully.

"For the way I behaved the other night, but I thought you deserved a dressing-down . . ."

I used the coffee cup as a shield so Jim wouldn't see me smile at the *sorry but*.

". . . and even so I went about it the wrong way. You were in my home and I behaved like a punk. That isn't the Virginia way, David."

I had personal experience of Jim's Virginia ways, so I did no more than give a nod, without committing myself.

Jim couldn't look me in the eye but stared into space while the twilight cast half his face in shadow.

He clearly wanted to keep talking, but our shared history had been a very rocky road. We had never talked, not really talked. At most a couple of noncommittal pleasantries—nearly always pathetic attempts on my part—before Jim got tired and turned up the volume on the TV. The nearest thing we had ever had to a heart-to-heart was that Tuesday night.

"I need to ask you something, Dave."

"Go ahead."

"Did you ever cut a deal with God? You know, talk to Him, ask

Him to bring Rachel back. I have, many times. It makes me feel so stupid and so childish."

His frankness disarmed me. Like many guys who've been the man about the house for decades, Jim was used to having others interpret his feelings for him. It must have been a painstaking effort for him to say those words. I thought maybe I'd been too hard on him.

"No, Jim. I have not. But I would have, had I thought it was any use. I'd have done anything. You may believe I didn't do enough, that she died because I didn't notice she was ill. You know what? I don't care. You can't think anything I haven't thought already."

My father-in-law shook his head.

"I haven't come to blame you, even if I do, damn it. I'll blame you as long as I live, because I've got nothing better to do. I spend the whole day stuck at home moping over old photos and brooding. Photos in which just three people are having a good time and which I don't recall taking. Photos of birthdays, special occasions, a heap of good memories which a stranger captured on film because I was too busy breaking my back to support my family."

He paused to take a sip of coffee. Mine had been finished for some time.

"All those years I thought it was enough to put bread on the table. That someday there would be time to relax and enjoy life with my daughters. But there never was. And when I was at home, when we had a little time together, I was too busy setting an example of the damned rectitude I wanted to instill in them. I was strict, too hard. I was a shitty father, Dave."

A tear trickled down his cheek and splashed on the table. He either didn't notice or didn't care.

"If I had a second chance, if I could have my time over again . . . this time it'd be different. I'd get it right. If I had a girl again, I wouldn't talk to her about the importance of hard work, or hellfire, and never, ever would I spank her. If I had a girl, I wouldn't force any rules or values on her. I'd tell her to go after whatever it took to make her happy, because before you know it you're dead and can't make amends, nothing can be undone, there's no . . ."

His voice was full of broken glass and he couldn't finish the sentence.

"No turning the clock back." I finished it for him.

We remained silent for a few minutes. Back there in the kitchen somebody dropped a tray of cutlery on the floor. They were getting ready for suppertime. The place would soon be full of weary relatives and companions who would chew their soggy spaghetti out of sheer boredom.

"I know how you feel," I said after a while. "That's how I felt the first time I killed somebody."

He looked at me distrustfully.

"A neurosurgeon is not a dentist. If I cut something, it stays cut. And at times, above all while you're learning, you cut where you shouldn't. It's that simple."

"I don't know if I want to hear this, David."

"No patient does, and we don't like talking about it, either. It isn't great PR. We all have our own private cemetery. And the one you most remember is the first."

Jim hesitated for a second but in the end curiosity got the better of him.

"What happened?"

"Her name was Vivian Santana. She was a fifty-year-old teacher who loved crackers. She ate tons of them, so the upshot was mammoth blood pressure and an aneurysm. She was one of the first ops I did on my own. Supposedly, all I had to do was clamp the clip in the right place. I'd already done it a dozen times under supervision. But this time, there was only me and my fingers, nobody else. The aneurysm burst and she went without blood supply for a few minutes. By the time I got another neurosurgeon's help, it was too late. She died two days later."

My father-in-law stared at me long and hard. He said nothing, but I believe there was a flash of understanding between us. He understood I was a bit more than a smart-assed know-it-all with a degree in medicine, and that it takes guts to do what we do.

"After you deal with the relatives and your bosses as coolly as you can, you have a guilt trip. You get depressed, you think of chucking it all to become an attorney or an insurance salesman. If you're lucky, a buddy helps when you're down in the dumps, although that almost never happens. And sooner or later you realize somebody had to do the op. Somebody had to hold the scalpel. And the only way to get anywhere is by doing it."

"So you hear me."

"I hear you. There may be no way back, but you did the best you could, which is all anybody can ask for."

Jim leaned over toward me. There was a weird glint in his eyes.

"But I want to try again. I can do it better than last time around. That's why I asked you to let Julia come live with us."

I hardened my expression.

"I thought I'd made myself clear, Jim. That will never happen."

"I know, I know. I won't insist," he said, raising his hands. "But you could let us spoil her a bit now and again. I could swing by your place now and take her away for a long weekend. There's a fair in the next town. We'd drop her off on Monday, with a bellyful of cotton candy and a bunch of teddy bears."

For a second I froze, not knowing what to say. I could not believe this was happening.

"She's got school tomorrow," I spluttered.

"At her age a day off school won't make any difference. I'm not asking just for my sake. It would also perk Aura up a bit. Every night, when we turn out the light, she sobs away in silence for hours. She thinks I don't notice, but I do. And it breaks my heart."

"Can't be done."

Jim's face darkened, and he contorted his lips into a crooked smile.

"Why, David?"

I don't know whether it was the heat in there, the sunlight, the tension, the fatigue or dehydration, but I began to feel lightheaded. It was an effort to look straight ahead and pain hammered at my temples.

"Next weekend," I said when I could find a reply.

"There won't be a fair next weekend. We always used to take Rachel to the fair, you know? But her mother and I never let her go on too many of the rides."

I felt faint again. I tried to ward it off by massaging my temples. For a second I thought I would collapse onto the table, but I held myself upright.

"I'm sorry. It's simply impossible."

"It has to be possible."

"Enough, Jim," I said, raising my voice almost to a shout. I just wanted him to shut up and leave me in peace. I had no credible excuse to offer, no explanation to satisfy him.

There was a sudden change in the look on his face when reality forced its way through to his brain and smashed the props for his phony smile to smithereens. It was like watching a building being demolished by explosives, leaving behind a pile of twisted girders and rubble.

"I know what's going on here," he said. "Own up."

I was befuddled by the dizziness and a dawning migraine. I heard that sentence clearly and I gauged it inside my head until it acquired monumental proportions. I was so scared somebody would find me out that I began to stammer.

"Wha . . .What are you talking about?"

"What's up with Julia. You think I don't know what's going on?"

"I . . . How long have you known for?"

"Since you came over. Then I knew it. When were you going to tell me?"

"I was going to leave it as long as possible. I hoped you wouldn't find out."

"For God's sake, Dave. What do you take me for? These things are obvious, and if you want my opinion, it's too damn soon."

I was totally at a loss. He had blindsided me. *How could it be too soon to kidnap my daughter?*

"What did you say?"

"Don't act dumb with me. It's normal for you to want to find another woman, but it's still too soon. It's only been a few months. Show a bit of respect, Dave. Take it like a man."

"I haven't got another woman . . . How could you even think that?"

"Don't you lie to me! I knew you were hiding something as soon as you walked through the door. You're a terrible liar, David."

"You're barking up the wrong tree."

"Julia's very young. This could do her great harm. I'm afraid another woman will make her forget us. Her grandmother and I want to spend more time with her so that doesn't happen."

I had thought of nothing other than losing Rachel in the long and painful months that had gone by since she had passed away. There had been only a void, a void and memories. For that reason, Jim's words hurt and humiliated me as much as if he had spat in my face.

I got to my feet, vaguely aware people were stealing surreptitious glances at us. Jim huffed and puffed, and his face was livid. If I didn't end that conversation we would come to blows, and I could not afford to make a spectacle of myself.

"Jim, your granddaughter will spend next weekend with you. This weekend is out. I'm sorry, I have to leave."

I stormed off and tried not to run, while Jim shouted behind me and underlined each sentence by slamming the table.

"She's my flesh and blood, damn it! My flesh and blood! You can't keep her away from me!"

Kate

Kate went back to her car and drove to the outskirts until she found a quiet spot in a parking lot by a carpet store. Huge "FOR SALE" and "CLOSING DOWN" notices covered the storefront. Another of the many businesses the economic slump had put paid to. The loud but faded letters matched her feelings.

She had gotten an enormous weight off her chest with the words she had just spoken over the phone to Barbara, and massive relief had been left in its place. But those words were out there now, and there was no getting away from them.

I've been smitten ever since I first saw him.

For many years she had been incapable of admitting to herself that she was in love with her sister's husband. Now she had let the cat out of the bag, just like that.

She cried for a good while.

She didn't feel sorry for herself. She never had, and despised those who did. She cried because it was so unfair, because she wasn't strong enough, and out of exhaustion. She was physically and mentally tired out with all that was going on. She turned up the ringer volume on her cell and moved to the backseat. She needed to rest her eyes, for a few minutes only, to recover after being up almost all night.

She cried there for a while longer and let the long salty tears comfort her, until she fell asleep.

The cell woke her up.

Her mouth felt like the bottom of a birdcage and her neck muscles were as taut as piano wire. She blinked in astonishment at the low light. Night was falling, so she must have been out for hours.

Shit, she thought when she saw the caller ID.

"Hi, boss," she said.

"You're not coming in," McKenna replied. It was not a question.

"I'm afraid I'm still sick."

"Robson, guess what? Suddenly tomorrow's venue is your brother-in-law's goddamn hospital after all. Those cabinet guys are making a lot of very stupid decisions in a very short time. I have to set up briefings again tonight and do a shitload of overtime. And everybody is on edge. Especially me, because I'm wondering why the agent who gathered all the intel from the simulator isn't here to lend a hand."

Way back when, Secret Service agents prepared for important missions using maps and cardboard models made to scale by specialists. Now it was all done by computer. The parameters were entered into a program which perfectly simulated the surroundings the agents would operate in, so they could run over multiple scenarios, as well as plan access and escape routes, without drawing attention to themselves. Kate didn't usually do fieldwork, but she had stepped forward on this occasion. The week before she had been to St. Clement's a couple of times. Both incognito, both without David's noticing, both without admitting he was the real reason she had volunteered to go there. She had pulled together an impeccable scenario, so McKenna didn't make a fuss. But it was her obligation to be beside her boss to give the briefing.

"Sorry, sir."

"If I had a nickel for every one of your excuses, I could buy myself the *Post*. Something's cooking here, Robson. I don't know what it is, but I can smell it. I've asked Renaissance to cancel tomorrow's gig, to postpone it."

No. That cannot be. If the operation doesn't take place . . .

McKenna waited for her answer.

"You don't say? That's big news," Kate lied, her voice faking relief. "If we can put it off until Monday everything'll be so much easier. At least I could take part in the preparatory briefing. I hope to fin—"

"She said no."

Kate felt her heart falling back into place.

"Pardon me?"

"Everybody's gone plumb loco over this, and no wonder. For now, only the cabinet and those of us on duty tomorrow know about it. The agents have no clue what kind of op Renegade's having, just that it's a bigger secret than the color of the Pope's underwear. But tomorrow they'll have to activate protocols, there'll be more people in on it and there could be setbacks during transfer. Somebody will see him, somebody will tweet it, or whatever. And before lunch everyone and their dog will know Renegade is in St. Clement's. This is Grade A explosive shit. There's no way to keep it under wraps. And that's what I told Renaissance."

"Let me guess. She didn't take the least bit of notice."

"Like talking to the wall. A half hour going over all the cons of the operation, the pros of going to Bethesda exactly as they'd told me they would do this very morning, damn it. And when I finished, she says, 'Thank you for expressing your point of view, but we'll stick to the original plan.' And I got to wondering . . . is your bro-in-law Jesus Christ? Do they work miracles in that place, Robson?"

"I think not, sir."

"Well, neither do I. I met him yesterday, I don't know if he told you."

"Truth is, we're barely on speaking terms, sir."

"Why am I not surprised? You may be family, but he's an unbearable, smart-assed mother."

Takes one to know one.

"I agree."

"Now I'm off to St. Clement's to run over the scenario with my own eyes, and while I'm at it, to talk to your in-law. I'm going to shove a microscope up his ass, and if I find so much as an atom of shit, Renegade will not set foot in that hospital if I have anything to do with it."

"Sounds fine to me, sir."

"This isn't about you. You're out of it."

Those last words hit Kate like a hammer to her head.

"What did you say?"

"You heard. You're off the case and suspended until further notice."

"You can't suspend me just for being ill," Kate protested.

"No, but I can suspend you for staying off work and dragging your ass all over Baltimore."

Kate was dumbstruck.

So Barbara's been telling tales to McKenna. What a bitch, she couldn't even wait five hours.

Kate hadn't expected to be let down so soon, but to a certain extent her friend had done her a favor. McKenna was married to the job. No kids, no partner and the most paranoid kook in the whole agency. He must have had a hunch something was fishy about Kate's story, so he'd be wondering what it was. She couldn't let his anxiety over the next day's operation fuel his suspicions. Luckily, her boss, as well as being paranoid, was an old-school macho pig. He thought all women were capricious.

"Sir, I—"

"Shut up. You once got through an eleven-hour mission running a temperature of more than a hundred. Did you really think you'd get away with that 'I'm sick' baloney? I can forgive your human failings, even for lying to me. But not if you take me for a jackass."

There was no anger in his words, just a leaden, barren and sullen sadness. He was convinced he was right.

And the worst thing, Kate thought, *is that he is.*

"You've disappointed me, Robson," he said, and hung up.

She burst out of the car, leaving the back door open behind her. She loped along to the middle of the deserted lot, its ethereal yellow lamplight her sole company.

She screamed.

It was a shrill, tooth-jarring outburst that emptied her lungs. Blood coursed through her veins as she looked around, but the only echo was the far-off roar of cars on the highway.

How much more? How much more shit must I swallow?

Her cell rang. She took a deep breath and picked up the call.

"Robson."

"Barbara here. I'm sorry."

"Sure you're sorry. I'm suspended."

"What did you expect? I waited until nobody was around and then I triangulated the device. I did what you asked, but I got caught. An alarm tripped in my boss's office; I guess I must have gotten twitchy and didn't plug in the—"

"Take it easy, Barbara."

"They summoned me to McKenna's office. McKenna! He stares at you with those Sphinx eyes of his and you have to talk. He tells you it'll be worse if you don't."

Kate stayed quiet. It was true. It was almost impossible to get away from that stare. She knew because she'd been there, many times.

"Are you mad at me?"

The childlike naivety of the question surprised Kate.

"I won't be if you tell me where my boyfriend is."

"McKenna kept hold of the file. And he revoked my system access for a few hours."

"That's not what I asked you."

"They've forbidden me to tell you."

"Meaning you know."

"Yes, I know. It's registered in the name of V. Papić, 6809 Bellona Avenue, Baltimore."

An address. A surname.

"Last known position?"

"Also a Baltimore address. But I can't tell you. McKenna says three separate federal laws have been broken, which should teach you not to use agency resources just to make a booty call."

"Barbara, I've got no time to lose."

"It may be more than my job's worth."

"It may be. But they've already thrown me to the dogs, which is partly your fault. You owe me."

"I don't owe you zip. You were the one who asked me. It's your own fault you got suspended!"

"And it'll be your fault if it was all for nothing."

Barbara took some time to answer. Kate could hear her thinking on the other end of the line.

"Six fifty-four Whitehead Court. You'd best get moving. The last known position was an hour and a half ago. By the time you get there, he may have skedaddled," she said, and hung up before Kate had time to thank her.

Kate entered the address in the map app on her cell. It wasn't far, a mere ten minutes away. Unfortunately, time was running out for Julia.

She looked at the timer she had set up on her phone.

14:31:21.

She ran to the car. There would be no stopping her now that she was locked on to a target.

28

My pager beeped as I fled from my father-in-law, summoning me to a security briefing. By the time I got to the fourth-floor meeting room, the whole gang was there. Manager Meyer and Dr. Wong were sitting down, as stiff as pokers, opposite four Secret Service agents I did not know.

And seated at the head of the table was the boss, the huge shaven-headed guy I'd had a spat with the day before, in the bunker where they took me blindfolded.

I remembered his name was McKenna and that he was an asshole. He didn't seem ready to forgive and forget, either. There was a glimmer in his eyes when I sloped in and he didn't take them off me.

"Glad you could make it, doctor. Sit down."

I walked past him and across to the first free seat, affecting casualness, but it seemed to take an eternity. I could feel McKenna's gaze boring into me, his eyes hooked into my back. When I turned around, a smile crept across his face.

That was why he'd said the day before that we'd be seeing each other. He obviously had it in for me and would do his utmost to make me feel ill at ease or make my life difficult. I wondered what he was cooking up and how he could harm me. I realized I had better watch out.

And then some.

I scarcely paid attention to the boring security briefing. The president's entry route was decided upon, as were the parts of the hospital that would be off-limits and which staff would operate. I was glad they picked Sharon Kendall to be the anesthesiologist; it was an excellent choice. It was also a good idea nobody should know the Patient's identity until minutes before the operation. That way they wouldn't have time to get stressed out or to let the weight of responsibility hinder their performance. The foreknowledge that you were to operate on the most powerful man on the planet could drill holes in your brain. I knew all about that.

They discussed more important matters, but I was too frazzled and worried to get too involved.

"I personally will assist Dr. Evans in the operation," Stephanie said.

I grunted in agreement. I knew my boss would show me up every which way and make sure everybody knew she was chief medical officer in the post-op press conference. Her specialty was the spinal column, an area in which operations were three times as expensive, that drew three times as many patients and in which a third of them died on you. But the public did not know that, and in the eyes of the world she would get all the credit. I couldn't give a damn. But the next sentence shook me out of my complacency.

"The White House has also asked me to locate three expert advisers who will supervise the operation from the balcony. These specialists have been—"

"You said nothing about experts." I couldn't help jumping in.

"Excuse me . . . do you mind if I speak while you're interrupting?" McKenna protested.

"There was no talk of hand-holding and I'm all grown up now. It strikes me as a staggering lack of trust. At the very least you could have consulted us over this."

I looked at Wong and Meyer. They were as annoyed as I was but remained silent. They weren't going to back me on this one.

McKenna took his time, to make it clear I was on my own here. "There will be no discussion on this point."

"I have already talked this over with the First Lady. And she has made her choice."

"Which has not changed. You are the head surgeon. You'll have extra pairs of eyes watching you, that's all. It's nothing personal. We merely wish to do what's best," McKenna said, joining his hands and leaning over the table.

"Then you ought to do something about your taste in ties while you're at it," I snarled.

The agent lowered his eyes to his boring blue tie, realizing a second too late that he had reacted to my childish jibe with a sign of insecurity. He frowned.

"The expert advisers will be Lowers, Ravensdale and Hockstetter. The first two are flying to Washington as we speak."

His tone of voice hardly wavered. The operative word is *hardly*. There was a sign of something coarse and feral in him, which gave me the shivers. That was when I realized I would have one more flaming hoop to jump through.

I had heard of them. Both Lowers and Ravensdale were first-rate neurosurgeons, one from the West Coast while the other was British. They weren't as expert as Hockstetter or I in removing tumors from the speech area of the brain, but they were highly competent. What really unsettled me was my old boss's name. And the way McKenna had pronounced it.

There was something more than mutual bad blood here. McKenna was clearly suspicious of me, and the timely "accident" Hockstetter had met with in the parking lot.

"I thought Dr. Hockstetter had had an accident."

"He can't operate," McKenna said. "He has broken fingers. Were you aware of that?"

"The First Lady told me."

"Dr. Hockstetter cannot help out in the operating theater. But he will be with us on the balcony. That way we can count on his advice."

And for sure he would rattle my nerves and pour poison into my ears over the intercom when I most needed to be at ease. Circumstances were conspiring to prove the old saying, that success has many parents but failure only one. My name was down as being responsible for the op, although if it turned out well, anybody who had so much as dabbed a swab would take the credit for it.

What really had me spooked was how White's plan would fit in with all that. How the hell did he expect me to kill the president? With so many vital veins nearby and scalpel in hand, it wouldn't be too hard, assuming I had the nerve to do it. But White had insisted it should look like a complication arising from the operation. There could be no overt violence. And under the attentive eyes of three of the best neurosurgeons in the world—one of whom hated my guts—who would be hanging on my every move . . . how was I to carry out White's orders?

"I'm not overjoyed about that, Agent McKenna. Dr. Hockstetter and I do not really get along."

McKenna stood up.

"Ladies and gentlemen, we're done. Thank you, see you all tomorrow."

Everyone followed suit and headed toward the door, myself included. Even so, I knew perfectly well what McKenna would say next:

"Dr. Evans, a moment please."

Stephanie Wong gave me a wary glance before she left. I limited myself to sitting back down again.

"I'm beat, McKenna. Be quick about it."

"Hard day, doc?"

"Aren't they all?"

"Anything especially eventful happen to you today?"

"Same old, same old. Patients, rounds, paperwork."

"Really. And where were you around one this afternoon?"

Danger. Here we go.

"I went out for lunch."

"Did you go with a colleague."

"No. What's the point of all this?"

"You just answer the questions, doctor."

"I don't have to."

McKenna filled his lungs and starved the room of air.

"Actually, you do. The protocol says you should have been through strict security clearance before being in the position you are in. But circumstances got in the way."

"And you think asking me where I had lunch is going to be of any use?"

"I asked if you went with anybody. But now you're getting all—"

"I ate where I usually eat. In the Corner Bistro."

"I see. Is it far?"

"Three blocks."

"And so you always take the car to go three blocks?"

My heart stopped for a split second.

"What did you say?"

He pretended to shuffle some papers he had in a folder in front of him.

"According to the hospital parking lot log, your car left at eleven thirty-eight. Did you know all that stuff is on record? It's because of the access card you use. It's all in there. Modern technology, you know."

I made no reply. That had caught me out. I wondered what else the asshole might have on me.

"Where were you off to at eleven thirty-eight, doc?"

McKenna kept up his stony, unfaltering stare. It was suddenly terribly hot in that room. Beads of sweat began to form on my back and the palms of my hands while I tried to seek a tenable explanation for the two-hour gap in my story. I plumped for sticking as close to the truth as I could.

"I have a patient called Jamaal Carter," I said at last. "He has family in Anacostia and I went to see them."

McKenna raised an eyebrow. Now, that had surprised him.

"Are you trying to tell me a patient in this ritzy joint," he said, making a circle with his index fingers, "has relatives in Anacostia?"

"Not only that; he lives there."

"You're putting me on, doc. You know that lying to a federal agent is obstruction of justice?"

"I'm not putting you on. He's a gangbanger who stopped a bullet in a shoot-out and was rerouted from MedStar because their emergency room was full. I removed a bullet from his spinal column which would almost certainly have left him paralyzed. In doing so I flew in the face of my bosses, who thought it would be enough for me to stabilize him and let somebody else pick up the astronomic tab that'll be more than that kid will earn in his life, and one he'll never pay us back for."

I would never have spoken about myself that way unless I had a Secret Service agent in front of me . . . who rightly suspected I was capable of assaulting a rival surgeon and putting him out of the game. I thought it might help me to win over my interrogator by stressing my humane side.

"Aw, how sweet, doc," he said with a caustic smile. "In my opinion a wheelchair's the best place for that piece of shit, rather than out on the street playing with guns, or in jail, wasting the taxpayers' dime. But who am I to judge the motives of a bleeding heart like yours?"

I thought wrong.

"I don't play God. I'm merely a doctor. But I don't cut corners or sit in judgment. I just heal the sick."

"Really. And does visiting a gangbanger's relatives come under your Hippocratic obligations?"

I lowered my voice in a bid to add a confidential edge to my words.

"Not really. It was a personal favor the patient asked me for, and I thought what the heck. If word were to get out in the hospital, it could spell trouble for me."

"Really. And what did you discuss with the family?"

"That's private. It's covered by doctor–patient confidentiality."

The sly smile widened.

"You just said it was a personal favor. That cannot be covered by confidentiality."

I sighed, trying to gain enough time to think up my next lie.

"The kid's got a girlfriend, see? And I was stupid enough to agree. I feel responsible for him. He's had a screwed-up life and it's not asking too much for somebody to look after him for a change."

McKenna got to his feet. With his dimensions, the only way to describe that is in geological terms. He was a mountain rising in slow motion. He came around the table and sidled over to me. I got up in turn.

"We done here?"

"No, we are not."

McKenna raised a hand and placed it on my shoulder. I'm not exactly a featherweight, but in comparison that paw was as heavy as concrete and the arm attached to it a steel piston rod. He had as little trouble making me sit down as he would a five-year-old.

"What the fuck?"

McKenna rammed the chair with me in it against the table, squashing me against the woodwork. I groaned as the sharp rosewood edge connected with my broken rib. The pain was unbearable. And he did not let up. The agent leaned on me, his bulk cutting off any retreat, while his mouth whispered in my ear.

"I don't like you, doc. I don't like shit about you. I don't know if you're an unbearable jerk who thinks he's God, or whether you're hiding something. I don't give a flying fuck if you're a rock 'n' roll star at what you do; nobody comes close to my guy with a blade unless they're clean as a whistle."

I tried to get my breath back, although I was fainting from the pain in my chest. I needed to talk clearly. If he happened to roll up my coat sleeves, he would see the grazes I had gotten in the fight, and it would be all over for me.

"You picked on the wrong guy," I finally said.

"Where were you at one p.m. today?"

"I've already told you."

"Tell me again."

"I went to see a patient's relatives, I ate something, then came back to my consulting room."

"Oh yeah? Well, it just so happens that at that very time Dr. Hockstetter, who only yesterday was chosen to replace you in the operation, was mugged in a garage. His assailant broke his fingers in a car door."

I could just about turn my head enough to see his face. We were so close we could have kissed. His breath smelled of nicotine gum, his skin of the sweat of a caged animal.

"They told me it was an accident," I said, trusting that the fear he instilled in me—and the pain—would be taken for surprise.

"That's what they said, yes. A fluke. But in my line of work flukes don't exist. And what can I tell you? You stand to gain a lot from this. That's motive. And you were away from the hospital. That's opportunity."

I pressed my feet on the floor and tried to overcome the force leaning against me, to push back a fraction of an inch so I could breathe. My hospital clogs slipped over the carpeted floor. I shook them off and succeeded in backing up a little.

"Did the First Lady tell you I didn't want to operate on him? That she had to ask me as a favor not once but twice? What kind of a half-assed motive is that, McKenna?"

He blinked a couple of times. It was clear he didn't know. That comment seemed to unsettle him briefly, but then he counterattacked with the third element he needed to establish guilt. He had already constituted motive and opportunity. Now he needed the means.

"You have a gun, doctor?"

"What?"

"A gun. Do you have a gun?"

"No, I do not. I hate weapons, you prick. I've never held one in my life."

Except for when I had one in my hand a few hours before. And for sure there would be gunpowder residue left on my skin, even though I had been wearing gloves when I wrestled with Hockstetter and the gun went off. And the gun was underneath the front seat of my car. And my voice was trembling with all the tension and pain in my chest.

I knew he didn't believe me. That he would find out what I'd been up to from the very beginning. And I wouldn't have the chance to beg for help from White, who would be listening in on the whole deal. By the time I had convinced them of what was going on, the rats would have devoured Julia.

Then I was saved by the bell.

His cell phone rang. He lumbered away from me to pick it up, and at last I was able to get my long-suffering rib away from the table's edge.

"Special Agent McKenna."

There followed a series of grunts and acknowledgments. I couldn't hear the other side of the conversation. McKenna had walked over to the window, with his back to me, but the volume on his phone was turned up high enough that I could tell the voice on the other end of the line sounded hot and bothered.

"What? No shit. Who the hell's in Ballistics now?"

There were more explanations and grunts. McKenna's shoulders sank lower and lower the more the caller's words torpedoed his pet theory.

He hung up without a word.

And then I got it.

The shot that had burst the car tire. The techs must have retrieved the bullet and put it in one of those fancy computers. During the trial that brought me to death row, I would learn that the metropolitan PD had checked the bullet against their database. They found that my pistol matched one used in several assaults and two homicides. That is why Marcus had insisted I couldn't be caught with it. Curiously, at the time, the gun's shady record made it a red herring and cleared me.

But right then I knew none of that. And luckily McKenna, as

good as he was, couldn't see the link between my visit to Anacostia and the gun. Don't be too harsh on him, because you have been following events from the start, and in chronological order, but he hadn't been. In the gorilla's favor, it must be said his instinct had turned him against me from the first, and rightly so. But then, in the end, when he had the final piece of the puzzle in his hand, he got muddled and goofed. He was human and fallible, as were all of us who danced to the tune of that particular nightmare.

He didn't turn around. He simply said:

"You can go now, doc."

I couldn't.

I knew what I had done, and I knew the link between Jamaal Carter, the gun and me existed. And that maybe in a short while McKenna would be clearheaded enough to make the same connection. I couldn't afford to let him make it. I had to clip his wings, so he wouldn't dare grill me again.

I put my clogs back on, slowly. I stood up and gritted my teeth in pain, and on my way across to the window I could visualize the couple of Vicodins I would lift from the pharmacy as soon as I could get out of that dreadful meeting room.

"I'm going nowhere."

"Pardon me?"

McKenna turned around, rattled. The adrenaline coursing through his veins during the phone call had put his nerves on edge. Gone was the long arm of the law that had terrified me a couple of minutes ago. Now his skin was sallow, the color had drained from his cheeks and two hammocks hung below his eyes.

Even so, he still posed a big risk. And if he had a cup of coffee or took a half hour's nap, he'd tie up all the loose ends. There was only one way to forestall him.

"I've said I'm going nowhere, you shithead of a bully. I'm going nowhere until you apologize."

McKenna snorted in disbelief. In a more evolved human being, that might have been taken for laughter.

"You've got to be kidding me."

"I could ask you if I look like I'm kidding, but I doubt you could find your ass with both hands, so I don't think you're up to interpreting facial expressions. For some reason you took an instant dislike to me, which frankly I don't give a shit about, because the feeling's mutual. But what you've done is an abuse of authority. There are laws against that."

"You're going to report me? You threatening me, you cocky spoiled brat?"

"Spoiled brat my ass, you Irish potato-head. Listen, I come from the street, from a shit-heap probably just like the one you grew up in. And I've made it to be one of the best neurosurgeons in the world, all by myself, by working my ass off and eating enough shit to drown in. And from the onset of all this business the one and only condition I set was to be allowed to approach him plain and simple, as if he were a regular guy, without his apes or his office getting in the way. That's why I was happy for them to take the case off me, even though it was palmed off onto the biggest ass licker ever to hold a scalpel. And if you don't apologize right now, I'm going to have to explain to the First Lady why the best doctor there is, the one who can make the difference between her husband coming out with his head together or as a vegetable, won't operate because you've slammed him into a table."

McKenna didn't answer. He gaped at me with his eyes wide open. His jaw was clenched and he was clearly dying to punch my head open.

Without looking away or blinking, I put my hand in my pocket, took out my cell, and showed him the display.

"Well? Will you call her, or shall I?"

I didn't have the First Lady's direct line. But he didn't know that. He turned to look at the display and lowered his eyes.

"I apologize."

"I apologize, what?"

McKenna ground his teeth so hard the windowpanes rumbled.

"I apologize, Dr. Evans."

"Thank you. I will interpret your heavy-handedness as excessive zeal. As long as you don't step out of line again, this will go no farther," I said deferentially.

Maybe that was overdoing it, I don't know. And maybe it prompted what came next.

I turned to go and walked toward the door. Slowly, no looking back, and no stopping. But halfway there the agent's voice stopped me in my tracks with a parting shot.

"To prevent you having any mishaps like Hockstetter did, I'll detail a couple of agents to keep watch over you until tomorrow."

The elation I had felt upon browbeating McKenna expired.

Yes, I had escaped by the skin of my teeth. But that same night I had to see White, and with a pair of agents shadowing my behind, that would be impossible.

Kate

It was a sleazy motel north of Catonsville, between a Taco Bell and a pizza parlor which looked like it had closed decades before. The motel had also seen better days. Half the neon lights on its sign had burned out, while the older black plastic lettering promised "BUDG T RO MS," which nonetheless didn't fail to get across the desired message quite plainly.

There were just five cars in the lot. Supposing that one or two belonged to the employees, that meant the motel had three or four guests. There were twenty rooms and they were all in a single-story building. The lights were on in two of them.

I won't go asking around in reception, Kate thought. *It's brightly lit and the counter can be seen from every window. I might as well show up in a patrol car.*

There would probably be a way out at the back of the building, maybe through the bathroom windows. She didn't have the time or the inclination to run across an empty lot in the dark after a potentially armed suspect. But locating Vlatko in one of those twenty rooms was vital. If he was still in the motel, that is, and hadn't merely stopped there to take a leak or get a drink from the soda machine.

She got out of the car, making sure the soles of her shoes made no noise on the concrete. She had parked on the opposite side of the lot from the reception desk, so she wouldn't be lit up the moment she got out. She walked toward the room doors and when she was close to number twenty, she took out her cell and called Vlatko's number.

It was a long shot. His phone might have been switched off or muted. But it was also her best chance to approach him without drawing too much attention to herself. And Kate knew one thing for certain: Vlatko would want to see Svetlana again, so he wouldn't cut off his only communication channel.

She raised it to her ear.

I've got a ringtone. Good.

She lowered it to hear better. No sound came from room twenty, or from nineteen. She walked on and counted down the numbers. The phone kept ringing, but nobody answered.

Seventeen, sixteen, fifteen.

It went to voice mail.

Kate called again. There was light coming from room fourteen, so she stopped outside for a couple of seconds. Nothing.

Thirteen, twelve, eleven.

It went to voice mail again.

She called once more, and this time it didn't ring so much as once. A hasty voice answered in Serbian.

"Svetlana?"

"Vlatko Papić?"

"Koga ste trebali?"

"Vlatko, I'm a friend of Svetlana's. I need to talk to you."

Silence.

"Vlatko?"

"You are lying. Svetlana has no friends."

He hung up.

Kate looked back. All was quiet in room fourteen. In room nine, however, the lights were on. Kate walked toward it decidedly and knocked on the door.

"Vlatko, open up."

Nobody answered. Kate heard the sound of bare feet and something falling on the floor.

"Don't force me to break down the door, Vlatko. I'm from the police."

The noise stopped. Kate thought she could spot the curtains

moving out of the corner of her eye. The door opened slightly, with the chain in place. An eye peered through the gap.

"Show me your shield, or I won't open."

Kate tried not to smile at his innocence. That toy chain wouldn't withstand half a kick, but even so Kate showed him her ID. The eye opened wide in astonishment.

"Secret Service? But—"

"Let me in and I'll explain everything."

The youngster closed the door, unhooked the chain and let Kate through.

She surveyed the room. He must have been living in it for days, judging by the number of take-out food cartons stacked up by the TV. He was not wearing anything apart from a towel wrapped around his waist, his body still covered in drops of water. He was diminutive and thin, with dark skin and sad eyes. Undressed, he looked even younger, almost like a teenager.

"I was in the shower, that's why I didn't hear the phone."

"So I see," Kate answered, spying a puddled trail on the floor.

"And Svetlana? Where is she?"

Kate grabbed a chair, turned it around, sat on it with her legs apart and leaned on the backrest with her forearms.

"Get some clothes on, Vlatko. I'll explain right away."

"But is she okay?"

"She's fine. Go on."

A couple of minutes later the kid appeared in a sweater and jeans. He sat on the edge of the bed and put on a pair of worn tennis shoes before he gave Kate a searching look.

"Svetlana's gotten herself into trouble, Vlatko."

"I knew it. I told her those people couldn't be trusted. That it would all end in tears," he said, fiddling with his wet hair.

"Did you know what was going on?"

"Didn't Svetlana tell you?"

Kate could hear alarm in the boy's voice. Here came the dilemma. She couldn't interrogate him too closely on what he knew, because she was supposed to have Svetlana in safe custody. Nor could she force the guy to go with her. The success of her plan hinged entirely on his going with her voluntarily.

She had to wing it, praying she wouldn't slip up.

"I need you to tell me in your own words."

The kid seemed bright. He spoke grammatically perfect, almost accentless English.

"I've been over here for three years now. Svetlana and I were dating in Belgrade, but she couldn't get a student visa. I thought I could finish off my industrial engineering degree here, but I couldn't get a scholarship and everything in America is so expensive. I'd been doing odd jobs, trying to save up to help Svetlana come over. But she was getting more and more anxious."

"So she decided to take a shortcut."

"Those guys got in touch with her in Belgrade."

"What guys? What do you know about them?"

"She told me they were ex-army and worked here in security now. But I knew that was false. They said they would give her a visa and fifty thousand dollars if she told them about some doctor or other. All she had to do was live in his house for a month. I told her not to do it, that the whole business stank."

"But she didn't listen."

"She said it was precisely what we needed. That at last we could be together. After being five thousand miles apart, to suddenly be only an hour's drive away seemed a heaven-sent opportunity."

Kate nodded her head.

"Well, now she's in big trouble."

"Where is she? Under arrest?"

"I was just getting to that. Now tell me what happened on Tuesday."

"She'd been worried for days. She told me to get ready to leave my apartment immediately if something should happen. I only know it was to be this Tuesday. We had arranged to meet up here as soon as she had the money."

"But she told you to run for it."

"She sent me a text. It simply said, 'Run.' I knew she was in a fix, but what could I do? I didn't know where she was, and if I went to the police I would only land her in trouble."

"You did the right thing, Vlatko. We've been wise to Svetlana and have safeguarded her all along. For all that, she did enter the country illegally."

Vlatko blanched.

"Will you deport her?"

"That depends on her. And you."

"Tell me what I can do. I'll do whatever it takes."

"We've given her a choice. Either she takes the stand against these people, or we put her on the first plane back to Belgrade."

"You can't do that. These people are dangerous! If she testifies, they will kill her. I'll tell her not to do it."

Kate straightened her jacket sleeves with deliberate indifference.

"Tell me something, Vlatko. What do you think will happen to Svetlana as soon as she lands, now that she's failed these dangerous people?"

The boy's jaw sagged. He closed his eyes and wheezed in despair.

"They will make mincemeat of her and throw her in the Danube."

"So, you help us, and we get you both on board the witness protection program. Either that or she goes home on her own, where we can't help her, and it's lose-lose all around."

Vlatko stood up and paced around the room a couple of times.

"What does she say?"

"That she wants to talk it over with you first. I need you to bring her around. So she knows what's good for her."

"Will you protect the two of us?"

Kate kept quiet, pretending to think the answer over. She needed to make it sound as believable as possible.

"Yes. It's not usual, because you're not married, but these people are big fish. It'll be worth it."

Vlatko nodded.

"Okay, then. Will you bring her?"

"She's in a safe house now and will be until we can mobilize enough agents to secure her transfer. You'll see her in the morning."

"Do we wait for her here?"

"This place isn't secure. Tonight you'll go back to your apartment. There's a couple of agents parked on the street outside. In any event, there's nothing to worry about, they don't have your address. You'll be back together in the morning, we'll take you to headquarters and you can talk her into it there."

"Svetlana told me not to go back to my apartment."

Kate shrugged.

"I can take you to HQ tonight, but you'll have to sleep on the floor. Tomorrow you'll be a real mess and your clothes will stink even more than they do already. Is that any way to meet up with your girl?"

Vlatko thought it over for a couple of minutes while Kate stared at the wallpaper.

"Okay, officer. Let's go to my place."

Vlatko took only a couple of minutes to cram his stinking clothing into a backpack. He had flown the coop with little more than he stood up in. Another twenty minutes and Kate's car braked to a halt a half block from the kid's apartment.

"Here we are. Which one's your apartment? Can we see it from here?"

"Yes, it's on the sixth floor. First window on the left," he said, pointing upward.

"You left the light on?"

"I'm afraid so, I left in a real hurry when Svetlana warned me."

"Okay. Out you go."

"Aren't you coming with me?"

"I don't want anybody to see us together. Walk quietly. Although you can't see them, agents are watching you this second."

The youngster gave her a nervous look.

"Will you be watching, Agent Robson?"

"My shift's over. I need to hit the sack."

"I'd feel better if you stayed too."

"You're asking me to keep my ass on this seat all night while you're snug in your bed? In your dreams."

Vlatko hesitated before he got out.

"Oh, for God's sake! Okay, then, I'll stay. Now get out of here."

"Thanks for everything you're doing for us, Agent Robson," he said with a smile.

He got out of the car.

"Vlatko," she called after him through the car window.

The young man turned around to face her. Kate paused for a second. But it was too late now. The die was cast.

"Nothing. Sleep well."

She watched him walk to the door of the apartment building. He cut an ungainly and innocent figure. A nice kid who just wanted to be with his girlfriend, to work and finish his studies. She kept her eyes on the boy's window for a long time, until the light went out.

Don't think. Don't think.

There is nothing harder than making your mind go blank. When you're in an unlit car, on a godforsaken street, watching an innocent young man's doorway and waiting for some of the most murderous and pitiless human beings on earth to appear, the task is practically impossible.

And if at that moment the person your thoughts revolve around should call, your soul can turn inside out.

"David. Where are you? How did you get to call?"

29

I arrived home at about nine p.m. I wasn't alone. Parked on the sidewalk opposite was a sedan with a couple of Secret Service agents inside, exactly as McKenna had promised.

I was beyond tired, although the pain in my chest had subsided by the grace of St. Vicodin. I felt hot and my eyes were swollen and irritated. I needed a big slug of whiskey and twenty hours' sleep. But the second I closed the door behind me, my phone rang.

"Nice escort you've got yourself there," White said.

I backed into the door and let myself slither down until I was sitting on the floor.

"There they go, wasting taxpayers' money again."

"This greatly complicates matters."

"You should thank me for getting McKenna off our back."

"Don't get me wrong, Dave. Your performance today has been brilliant. And the way you showed the supervisor the phone, so that I could see his defeat on camera, that was a stroke of genius. You're a natural. I regret that after tomorrow we won't be working together."

I was too enfeebled to insult him.

"I wish I could say the same."

"Get some rest, and leave all the lights off so the Secret Service think you're asleep and lower their guard a little. At one o'clock sharp, go out through the yard to the next street. Wait for my men there."

"Okay."

"Oh, Dave. Leave the cell at home. I don't think those meatheads will be smart enough to have put a tracker on your signal, but we can't run any risks now. Not when the prize is so close."

He hung up and I complied. For the most part. Because although I left my iPhone behind, I took along the phone Kate had given me. And I left the house two minutes before the appointed time. At last I could get far enough away from the bugged phone to talk to Kate.

I walked up the slope in my yard and sheltered behind a tree. There wasn't a soul on the street, nor any sound other than the distant squawking of the TV in the Salisburys' house. They were a deaf old couple who always fell asleep on the sofa.

My precarious hideaway kept me out of the two heavies' sight, so I punched in the number and Kate answered on the second ring.

"David. Where are you? How did you get to call?"

"On the street. I don't have much time. They're coming to pick me up to go see White."

"And your phone?"

"He's ordered me to leave it behind. You get anywhere?"

"I'm following a lead I'd prefer not to discuss. What've you been up to these past few hours?"

I gave her a quick roundup, including the bit about the rats and how White could act against Julia merely by pushing a button.

"We won't let him do it. Will you be in the operating theater tomorrow?"

"Yes. It's been a real nightmare of a day. There was a change of plan yesterday that almost scrapped the whole ball game."

"Don't give me that 'ball game' crap, David. Speak straight. Call it murder."

"Will that make you feel better? Because it certainly won't do it for me."

"It nearly always hurts to do the right thing, eh, Dave?"

"Do you really want to talk about that now?"

"I can't think of a better time, David. In a few hours I might be dead."

I took some time before answering, while the images of the night it all happened came back to my mind. Julia had gone to bed, and Rachel wouldn't be back for couple of hours. Kate had come over to see her niece on one of her rare days off. The three of us had dinner together, just as we had done many a time. Kate and I drank wine, just as we had done many a time. We chatted for a while on the sofa, just as we had done many a time.

Then, without warning, she kissed me. And that we had never done.

I was too stunned to react. For a decade, only Rachel had kissed me, so Kate's lips pressed on mine felt odd, overwhelming. Somewhere outside of us was the sound of something breaking that would never be fixed again.

I didn't kiss her back, but I did not fend her off either, I don't know whether out of fear or confusion. But Kate understood right away what she'd done, what I didn't feel, so she drew away from me. She was dying of shame, blamed it on the wine and ran off. The day after she called me to say sorry, and I said we should tell Rachel, hard as that might be.

Because it nearly always hurts to do the right thing.

"Kate, I know what you're doing for Julia," I replied. "And I am endlessly grateful."

"No, David. You have no idea. Of what I've done or what I'm about to do."

Her voice broke down at the end of the sentence, into a wounded whimper. I could hear her sobbing quietly, as if choking on emotion.

"It doesn't matter what happens, you and I can never be together, can we, David?"

"All I can offer you, Kate, is the truth."

"Then say it, I need to hear it."

The ensuing silence could not have lasted more than a couple of seconds, but on that cold and lonely street it seemed to take a lifetime and to be as deep as the ocean.

"We can't be together."

"I saw you first," she said in a whisper.

It took me a second to realize she was talking about the day Rachel and I met, at a campus party.

"I know, Kate. But the moment I saw her, there was nobody else for me. She was all I'd ever wanted."

"I hear you. She was a very brave woman, the bravest person I have ever known."

I couldn't help smiling.

"And that's coming from somebody whose job it is to stop bullets meant for someone else?"

Kate laughed, a sweet but heartrending laugh.

"I protect others because I'm incapable of protecting myself. I wish I had her sort of bravery. David . . ."

"What?"

"You never told her? You never told her that I kissed you?"

No, I never did. I didn't want to drive them apart. It would have been ugly, messy and painful. Because I was wrong, and now I know that. When doing the right thing causes harm, maybe you need to find another way.

"I didn't."

"Are you sorry?"

"No. Wherever she may be, she'll know the truth."

I had wanted to tell her. I didn't dare. And then she went away without warning, so now I'd never be able to tell her, or ask for forgiveness.

"Kate, if you want to ask for her forgiveness, find Julia."

I didn't intend to put it so bluntly, but that's how the words came out—harshly, pitilessly. I knew I had broken her heart once and for all before I heard her reply.

"I know that's all you want me for. Consider it done, David," she said icily. And hung up.

Before I could call her back to say sorry, the headlamps on White's henchmen's car appeared at the end of the street.

30

"Have you noticed? There's something about Juanita."

White was drinking coffee when his stooges dropped me off at the Marblestone Diner. As ever, we were alone, with the sole exception of Juanita.

"What about her?"

"The waitress likes us, Dave. She's watching us. Our little *American Idol* contestant is checking us out; she strokes her hair when she looks this way. And she doesn't understand that we would never take notice of someone like her, an uneducated, unskilled cow."

I wasn't going to lower myself to reply to that vile comment.

"Less of the 'we.'"

"Well, well. So now plural pronouns don't agree with you?"

"I know perfectly well what you are. And you are nothing like me. Or anybody else."

White guffawed. The son of a bitch was in a great mood.

"Well now! So the chief mechanic has realized what's wrong? A failure of the limbic system, in my prefrontal lobe? You think I wet the bed and was an arsonist as a child? You think the cats in my apartment building used to disappear, Dave?"

"I don't doubt it for a second."

"You're wrong, Dave. It may be that, by normal standards, I am what you take to be a psychopath. But believe me, I'm not the one with the problem. It's the rest of you who are limited by your boundaries. And tomorrow you are going to cross them."

I decided to have one last try.

"Why don't you wait, White? Even if the operation is a success, he'll be dead soon. I don't think he'll last out his term."

"You just don't get it. I thought you were better than the rest, Dave. People think too much. They always mull over a heap of different scenarios—within ten years, twenty years, heaven, hell, the consequences, blah, blah, blah. Juanita, more coffee, please!"

He smiled and lifted up a fork that was on the table. Its three tines glittered in the lamplight.

"But what is important, what is real, Dave, is the here and now. Choosing the moment. There's nothing else, there's no moment beyond right now. This fork is real, this moment is real. You say he'll be dead soon, without understanding that the client who has contracted me needs him to be dead now. Right now."

Juanita came up to us, armed with a coffeepot and a smile. She leaned over my cup and began to fill it.

"Human beings only reach their full potential when they are capable of giving free rein to instantly satisfying their needs without a moment of doubt," White concluded.

At that very second, he sat up slightly in his seat, grabbed Juanita by her hair ribbon with his left hand and knocked her head against the table. The poor waitress's forehead barely made a sound as it struck the Formica, compared to the clatter made by the cups jumping up from their saucers. With his right hand, the one holding the fork, White stabbed Juanita at the bottom of her skull. The fork sank up to the handle in the soft flesh, reaching the medulla oblongata and killing her instantly. Juanita's legs gave way, her limbs turned to jelly. The pot smashed to pieces as it hit the floor, drowning out the dull thud of Juanita's body as it collapsed in a heap.

As quick and simple as that. One second there had been a

friendly, attentive person beside me. Three seconds later, nothing but a bag of flesh and bones lying in a pool of coffee.

White merely had a few spots of blood on his starched shirt cuffs. He took a napkin from the metal container on top of the table and tried to rub them off, but without much success.

"Well. This will never come out. I'll have to throw it away," he said, genuinely disgruntled.

And me? What did I do during those three seconds in which a human being was rubbed out before my very eyes?

Absolutely nothing.

We might say that it all happened too quickly, that I was over-tired, that I was frozen in horror. It would all be true, but I've thought it over a lot these past months. And what if I had known a couple of minutes beforehand what was about to happen? Would I have done anything? Would I have warned her?

I don't know.

I don't know and that terrifies me, maybe more than anything that had happened before or would happen the day after. Because White had won. He had taken me to the point where the opposing forces of humanity and expediency canceled each other out.

"I know why you did that," I said when I got my wits back together.

White had finished scrubbing the spattered blood on his shirt and scrutinized me.

"Why have I done it, Dave?"

"You've just eliminated the only witness to have seen us together."

"True. I had a need and I satisfied it. Now I feel better."

"And what about me? I've seen your face. I could describe every pore on your disgusting skin. Have you decided how you're going to kill me when this is all over?"

He elegantly tut-tutted, a teacher reprimanding a pupil.

"My dear Dave, it would truly relieve me to end your existence. Believe me, I'm not thrilled that you know who I am and what I do. But we have a bond. Tomorrow afternoon, the whole wide world will know your name. Disposing of you would draw too much attention. It would be too much of a coincidence."

The lie sounded tremendously persuasive, although I didn't buy it for a second. But with just seven hours left until the operation began, my fate didn't come into it.

"How do you want me to do it?"

"I thought you'd never ask."

White put an attaché case that had been beside him on the seat on the table. He opened it and placed the contents in my hand, two metallic pouches with black labeling on them, each the size and shape of a packet of M&M's.

"Now do you understand?"

Of course I understood. The smart bastard had given me the infallible means with which to kill the president in front of a dozen witnesses, without a single one suspecting a thing.

"They're so perfect. How did you manage that?" I asked in amazement.

"That's my little secret. Replicating the pouches exactly was the easy part. The hard part is getting the right pouch to its destination."

What I had in my hand were packets of Gliadel. Each pouch holds four wafers of soluble material the size of a quarter. They cost more than a thousand bucks a pop, because they are capable of doing the magic that finishes off a surgeon's handiwork. Right where we complete incisions, we apply one of those silver bullets packed with a localized chemotherapy dose. For an additional $8,000 (we charged the patients triple that), we could extend the sufferer's life by retarding the reappearance of the glioblastoma.

But of course, those particular patches would not work.

"What do they have in them?"

"A very unusual toxin that acts within a few minutes. For your own sake, it's best you don't know the name."

It made perfect sense. When the president died they would perform an autopsy, although bearing in mind that he would have died on the operating table, it would not be a very thorough autopsy.

Even in a worst-case scenario, to find a toxin in a test you need to know which one to look out for. They don't show up out of the blue. A compound from the list of usual suspects would be virtually undetectable.

"I don't know if I can switch the real bags for these."

"You'd better find a way. Because if you fail me tomorrow, I won't leave her to suffocate, Dave. I won't even press the button to release the rats. That will only happen in the unlikely event of my being unable to dispense some more creative form of justice. What would be appropriate for Julia?"

He paused briefly and tugged at his lower lip, pretending to think up something.

"I know . . . I have a client in the gulf, a sheikh with idiosyncratic tastes. He has an enormous secret chamber in his palace, decorated in bright colors and totally soundproofed. Inside there's a merry-go-round and a cotton candy machine. Your daughter would last him weeks."

The horror of what he had just said stabbed me with an ice-cold knife.

"Listen, White. You can do what you like to me. I know you will, in any case. But if you harm my daughter again, you'd better kill me first. Otherwise, the world won't be big enough for the two of us."

White flashed me a saintly, delicate and condescending smile.

"Go get some sleep, Dave. Tomorrow's your big day. Oh, and mind you don't trip over Juanita's body on your way out."

Kate

David's words echoed around her head, an endless loop of guilt and reproaches.

"If you want to ask for her forgiveness, find Julia."

Did she have any regrets? She had kissed her brother-in-law one night when her defenses were low and her spirits rock-bottom. She had never gone farther, not even in her innermost thoughts. She respected her sister too much for that.

No, she couldn't feel guilty for having fallen in love with David. That would be to betray herself. It had been a horrible move on her part to think of it that way.

If you knew what I'm about to do for you, David, then would you love me? Or would you hold it against me just as I hold it against myself right now?

The night wore on. The moon scarcely lit up the stretch of the street between the apartment blocks. The darkness was made deeper still by little pockets of light cast underneath the few streetlamps that hadn't burned out.

Kate writhed uncomfortably in her seat. Although she had reclined it, after several hours of lying motionless it felt as if it were digging into her on all sides. She had only gotten out for a minute to pee between the parked cars and then headed straight back to her observation post, afraid that somebody might have spotted her. But all was quiet. Not a single car had gone by in the past hour.

That gave Kate all the time in the world to stew in thoughts that spiked through her heart like broken glass.

David's words had hurt her but had also come as an eye-opener.

How long have I been chasing shadows? How many years have I wasted fooling myself, saying it was all because of the job, never really admitting that I didn't want to be with anybody but him?

As painful as those questions were, there was one that lacerated her soul more than the rest put together.

Have I ever truly been happy?

She had taken Vlatko to his home as a shot in the dark, her last chance to locate Julia's kidnappers before dawn came and it was too late. She knew they'd be looking for him, as he was the only thing that linked them to Svetlana. From what she knew of that crowd's modus operandi, they would rely on technology to cover as much ground as they could. So it was reasonable to deduce they had planted devices in Vlatko's apartment. And if they had, the kid's homecoming would set in motion an unstoppable chain of events.

Kate felt for her gun through her clothing. Its normally comforting heft now seemed unbearable. If everything went as she had foreseen, then she would have to confront them. She alone against a trained, pitiless force that played by no rules and outnumbered her.

I've got no chance. Today I die. I'll die without knowing whether I've ever been happy.

And all of a sudden, the answer came to her as blindingly clear as the midday sun. A flash in a clear sky, in the shape of a memory.

She and Julia at the Evanses', two summers back, playing catch. Sun streaming down on the lawn, giggling, the sound of the neighbor's sprinklers. Perspiring skin, the smell of sunscreen, the taste of popcorn and ice cream. Rock music that came out of nowhere, a song as light as air, close enough for them to glory in the moment, but far enough away that they could hear themselves panting as they ran. The two of them fell on the grass and gazed up at the sky, their ears nuzzled together. They whispered secrets, cracked jokes and saw shapes in the clouds.

Then Julia said it.

"I want to be like you when I grow up, Auntie Kate."

That had taken her completely aback. Nobody had ever said

anything remotely like that to her. With that breathtaking, clear-cut certainty.

"Wouldn't you rather be like Mommy? Or somebody real important, I dunno . . . like SpongeBob?"

Julia looked at her as if she were crazy.

"Come on! SpongeBob is as dumb as a rock."

"I thought you liked SpongeBob."

"I think he's funny, but I don't want to be like him."

"Okay, but what about Mommy?"

"Mommy's awesome. She's super-duper. But you're mega-super-duper, Auntie Kate. Mommy always says so."

"Really? What else does Mommy say?"

"She says you're the most amazing person in the world. And I think so too."

Julia raised a hand, sticky with ice cream, and stroked her cheeks with it. Her eyes were electric blue, deep and perfect.

"I really love you, Auntie Kate."

That day. That day I was wholly and unquestionably happy. It was all worthwhile, if only to live that afternoon, that minute.

She leaned her head on the window, grateful for the cool glass against her forehead. Her breath misted up the pane, and Kate drew a smiley on it.

You don't belong in this world, Julia. Yours is a world of games, dolls and safe places, where a sheet can protect you from monsters all night long. And I'll make sure you go right back to it.

The smiley faded as the mist evaporated. Kate sat up to breathe on the glass again but was cut short. The glare of headlamps lit up the smiley's eyes with a ghostly shine before it died away.

Kate shrank down into her seat. The car approached very slowly, the engine purring softly. Observing it in the rearview mirror, Kate judged by the odd shape of the headlights that it must be a foreign car, most likely a Mercedes. When it drew level with hers it was already coasting downhill with the engine and headlights switched off.

It's them. Shit, it's them.

She grabbed the gun and slipped off the safety, while trying to move as little as possible. As the Mercedes glided past she could make out a pair of dark shapes through the windows on the driver's side.

There must be three of them, maybe four. Somebody else would be riding shotgun.

The car went past her and rolled on for another ten or twelve yards. A creaking noise told her the driver had hit the handbrake. A pair of doors clicked open, although Kate couldn't see them from where she was. She could, however, see the dark shadows that came out of nowhere and turned into a couple of men wrapped in black leather jackets as they walked into the light shed by the lamp atop the entrance to Vlatko's apartment building.

Kate put her gun on her lap and forced herself to grab the steering wheel with both hands. Her instinct and training, her whole body, demanded that she jump out of the car and into action. She went over two different tactical approaches from her position to their car, almost without thinking.

She knew she could do it, that she could make it.

And she could also fail. Another one of them could have stepped out of the car along with the two who were now going upstairs. He might be behind those trees, or in the doorway, to cover the other two's escape. Or the driver might have a radio channel open. Or, worse still, nobody might get out of there alive. Or if one were to survive and she caught him, she might not get the truth out of him in time. And White would know if they didn't arrive back.

These were all pointless arguments, because she'd been over them a thousand and five times in her head to while away the long hours she had sat there, as she thought about an untenable position for a lone person with less firepower than those animals. And because despite everything, she had already made up her mind.

David, if you only knew what I'm about to do for you.

Except that he would never know, because she would never allow it. It was a bitter cup she had to drain all by herself, down to the dregs.

She made herself look at Vlatko's window and gripped the wheel so hard her knuckles turned white. When two brief flashes punctuated the darkness in the boy's room, Kate's body shuddered twice in sympathy.

They've used a silencer, she couldn't help thinking.

She closed her eyes and felt tears well up in them and spill down her cheeks, leaving a trail right where Julia's sticky fingers had stroked her when she told her she loved her. She tried to evoke that memory, to remember again what that touch had felt like, to get away from the chasm of darkness that was opening up at her feet and threatening to engulf her forever.

She stifled a sob and struggled to pull herself back together.

There'll be time enough to cry afterward. You can feel sorry later. You can even put a bullet in your goddamned head if you want, but for now you have to concentrate. Concentrate!

She opened her eyes again, in the nick of time, because the hit men were getting back into the Mercedes. The engine was running and they were off before the doors were quite closed.

Kate made sure her headlights were off and started her car when the others were a couple of blocks away. She turned the wheel and began to follow them, drying her tears with the back of her hand as she went.

An hour before the operation

31

The neon light in the pre-op room blinked every eight or nine seconds. It was driving me nuts. I elbowed the switch a couple of times, a trick that usually worked. This time it didn't.

"It's been like that for a week. I've asked the maintenance crew to change it, but they take no notice of me," Sharon Kendall told me without raising her head. She was studying the Patient's medical history intently, while she leaned next to the passageway door.

"He's just a patient," I reminded her. "His weight, height, clinical records, everything you're reading, is real. He has a different name than the one you expected is all."

"Hey, I'm cool," she said, shaking her head.

She wasn't. Her face was rapt, and she was biting her lower lip. She had yet to digest the news I had given her a short while before, she and the rest of the crew. At first they had all thought I was clowning around, that it was yet another bad-taste joke. But when they saw my expression didn't change and realized that it was true, they had all made an effort to act normal. There were a couple of exclamations and one of them scratched his head, but that was it. That's how I knew they were scared. If there is one thing a surgery professional fears, it's VIPs. Whether it's a lawyer specializing in litigation or the boss's sister, if somebody tells you the patient is special and deserves

309

special treatment, then expect trouble. We call it the VIP syndrome, and it massively affects the odds of screwing up.

Nonetheless, they were first-class professionals, a dream team, and that day they proved it. When it was all over, the enormity of the task would sink in, but at that stage the adrenaline had kicked in, ensuring their nerves wouldn't take over. We had done well to put off letting them in on the secret until the last second.

In fact, I was much more nervous than they were. Against all odds, I had grabbed a few hours' sleep the night before, if collapsing from sheer exhaustion can be deemed sleep. I had gotten up at six thirty a.m., taken a quick shower and driven to the hospital. All the while I had turned over whether I was capable of going through with White's plan. And something much more worrying. Kate had sworn to me that if she couldn't unearth Julia by the time the op began, she would call McKenna and give him the goods.

That deadline was less than an hour away, and still no news. My iPhone was in my consulting room, as was the BlackBerry Kate had given me. The ban on cell phones in the operating theater would spare me from White's scrutiny, not that there was anywhere I could hide one, anyway.

I was wearing my best gown and lucky cap. In theory it's just a scrap of cloth to keep hair or sweat from falling off us and into the patient, so any old cap ought to do. But we neurosurgeons are more superstitious than a witch doctor or a baseball player. So I had chosen a personalized surgical cap, made out of black cloth showing a Bengal tiger with its jaws wide open, embroidered in orange right in the middle of the forehead. I have six dozen of the things embroidered in all sorts of designs, from turtles to the Superman logo. This one was Rachel's favorite. It had never failed me.

I absentmindedly touched the embroidery with my fingers, thinking of all the times we had operated together. Of how she would stand on tiptoe to give the tiger a discreet kiss to bring me luck.

How ironic that I should put it on for the one operation that must fail, I thought.

I leaned against the wall and heard the metallic crinkling of the poisoned Gliadel pouches. I startled, thinking Sharon might have heard it, but she was still going over the Patient's case history. I had secreted them behind my back, secured by the elastic in my pants, and was waiting for the right time to switch them with the real ones.

There was movement on the other side of the round glass window in the door that led to the passageway. We both stood up straight. There he was, followed by the Secret Service agents. I went to the door and opened it.

"Just you, sir. They wait outside."

There was a chorus of protest, which the president hushed with a wave of his hand.

"Good morning, Dr. Evans. You'll have to excuse them, they're very worked up. I've made them bring me here in a regular SUV and a motorcade with only three cars in it. For them it's like walking the street naked."

The rest of the hospital had been turned upside down. He had been admitted by elevator through the service area, but the second floor, where all the operating theaters were located, had been completely evacuated three hours before. That morning only one person would be operated on in St. Clement's. Plainclothes agents watched over the elevator and stairways, to prevent anybody from entering. Unauthorized personnel had been sent a memo telling them the operating theaters were being disinfected with toxic products. That would make them stay away and enjoy their day off.

"We must keep the area sterile, sir."

"I understand. They'll wait here."

We gave him a little time in which to get changed behind a screen and don the blue smock we give to all patients. When we went back in, he had sat down on a bench, with his legs crossed, making the gown gape open. It often happens to patients. They are so preoccupied with what is about to happen inside that they forget they aren't wearing any underwear.

"Sir," I told him. "You may want to fold your legs in a less revealing way."

"Oh. Oh, right. I'm sorry, doctor," he said to Sharon.

"Relax, sir. We're doctors. We're used to it."

She kept a straight face, but if I knew Sharon, within a week she'd be boasting to all her girlfriends that she'd seen the presidential pecker.

"You should also put on the blanket we've given you."

"I'm not cold."

"It will be a long operation in a very low-temperature room. You will be losing body heat. Even a small variation in your body temperature may harm your ability to fight infection. Just do it."

"You remind me of my wife. Okay, I'll just do it."

He wrapped himself in the blanket.

"Where is the First Lady?"

"Distracting the press. She'll be making public appearances around town all morning, all smiles while regretting from the bottom of her heart that she can't be here. But that's the way it has to be."

"I guess it must be very tough on her."

"It was her idea. Nobody can know what's going on. We've informed the attorney general and the vice president, who will be acting president while I'm under anesthesia. But we won't say a thing until after the operation. By the way, she has a message for you."

"Which is, sir?"

"She said, and I quote, 'Cure him or I'll kill you.' She said you'd know what it meant."

We all laughed. Me included, attempting to cover up how dirty and treacherous I felt.

I left Sharon to ask him the routine questions and give him his final instructions, while I discreetly went out the other door. Between the pre-op room and the swing doors leading to Operating Theater 2 there was a passageway, opposite which was the scrub-up sink and the side entrance. In theory, nobody was allowed into the surgical suite without scrubbing up, but I had no time to play with. The nurses and the rest of the crew would be along any moment now. I walked past the sink and into the operating theater through the side door.

Theater 2 is the biggest in St. Clement's and one of the world's most advanced. Anybody who enters is instantly astonished. To walk through a nineteenth-century building, with its plate-glass windows and Victorian air, disconcerts you. It brings to mind images of old doctors with bushy eyebrows and long beards, liniment rubs and pots of leeches. And then you clap eyes on Theater 2 and leap forward three centuries into one of Steve Jobs's wet dreams. The walls, the array of instruments, the trolleys, everything in the room is pristine white, with soft, round designs. A huge robotic arm, six feet high and weighing three tons, supports the operating bed and can place the patient in any imaginable position. There are only three like it on the planet.

And at the other end of that theme park straight out of *Star Trek*, a humble instrument trolley. The Gliadel pouches would be in the second drawer down.

I looked up, to the balcony. A couple of people were chatting in the observation room. They were standing side-on to me, so they wouldn't see me if I was quick about it. I walked over to the trolley and turned my back to it when I got there. There were cameras everywhere, and what happened down here would be relayed to monitors upstairs. I couldn't tell whether the cameras were rolling—I know now, of course—but I didn't want to draw anybody's attention. I took the pouches from behind my back with my left hand, while with my right I felt for the edge of the second drawer down. I pulled it open a couple of inches with my fingertips and slipped in my hand, groping for the familiar feel of the bags. There they were. I extricated them using the index and middle fingers of one hand, while sliding in the new ones with my other hand.

"Dr. Evans!"

McKenna's voice was a whiplash of sound over the loudspeakers connecting the operating theater to the balcony.

I jumped out of my skin. I don't suppose I have to describe the scene—the footage was replayed before, during and after the trial. The moment in which the evil doctor made the switch and the courageous chief of the president's security detail interrupted him.

"Turn that down, for God's sake. You want to deafen me?"

But what the cameras did not see was what was going on behind my back. The sudden noise had startled me and I had let go of the real pouches. The others were already in place, so now all four were mixed up in there together.

"Do you have a minute, doctor? Allow me to introduce you to the panel of experts. That way you'll recognize their voices later."

I began to feel skittish; I could feel my pulse racing in my neck and there was a sensation in the pit of my stomach which, if it wasn't panic, was just as good. How the hell was I going to get back the original pouches and take them out of there? I couldn't turn around and let them see me touching the trolley. I had no gloves on and I hadn't sterilized my hands. If anybody suspected the trolley had been contaminated, everything would be held up. And Julia would be running out of air.

"I'll be right with you. I want to check everything is in place."

"Hurry up."

I could feel the rest of the people up there with McKenna looking at me. My head buzzed as it tried to solve the problem. How could I remove the correct pouches?

Got it. Temperature.

I poked my fingers in up to the knuckles and prodded the bags, which was a lot harder to do than it sounds, behind my back, with the palm of my hand twisted around and all eyes on me. I could distinguish the cold packs from those that had been on my back for more than half an hour. I yanked out the cold ones and shoved them into my pants.

"Doctor?"

"Be right up."

On the way to the stairs leading to the observation room, I threw the real pouches into a trash can. I had a slight dizzy spell, the feelings of tension, euphoria and guilt swilling together inside me. If I had been alone, I would have burst into hysterical, manic laughter. Instead the laugh was stuck in my throat, a half-bitten morsel I was gagging on. I had to clear my throat twice before knocking on the balcony door.

McKenna opened the door for me. The balcony was a cramped space, a mere one hundred square feet with a couple of rows of seats, a few monitors and a glass wall at a forty-five-degree angle that commanded a view of the operating theater, almost right over the bed. Four men were in there, although I had eyes only for one.

First was McKenna himself, who steered his bulk aside to let me past.

Second in line was Lowers, with his folksy smile and breezy manners. He looked familiar from a medical magazine.

Third was Hockstetter, with his arm in a sling and giving me a look that could kill.

But the fourth guy wasn't Ravensdale.

The fourth was Mr. White.

Kate

She observed the farm from a hilltop. She had left the car on the other side, well out of sight of the farm's occupants.

To follow them all the way there had been quite an achievement. They had stopped twice on the way, once to fill up with gas and again at a greasy-spoon truck stop by the Virginia state line, where they chowed down for an hour and a half while Kate nibbled on a couple of stale granola bars she had found in the glove box.

That part of the trail hadn't been too hard. The Mercedes had traveled slowly, ten miles per hour below the speed limit. As the men were armed, they obviously didn't want to risk the state troopers stopping them to give them a ticket, then asking them to open the trunk or get out of the car.

Kate had had to step up precautions when they went through Gainesville. They were no longer on a freeway, where trailing somebody was just a matter of keeping your eyes on their rear lights from a half mile away. Now they were on two-way back roads, with a lot less traffic, which went through towns. She couldn't drop back too far, nor could she turn off her headlights. She had to stay out of range of their rearview mirror, or they would notice her. Which meant she might lose them anytime.

As dawn broke, they made their way into Rappahannock County and Kate began to feel uneasy, because there the highways were just ribbons of blacktop, bordered with orange, that crisscrossed the green expanse.

There were very few towns, just a bunch of scattered farms, which got farther apart as they went. Out in the boonies, there was no way to follow them at a safe distance. She would have to rely on sheer instinct to follow them, hoping to catch sight of the Mercedes's side markers from afar as it went around a bend. Her heart sank with each minute that passed without seeing them.

The inevitable happened. She lost them.

It took her more than twenty minutes to realize they were no longer in front of her.

I must have gone past an unmarked turnoff. But where?

Worried to death, she turned the car around and drove back past a couple of regular-looking farms. And beyond that, not far from where she had last seen them, past a dirt track.

She wasn't so clueless as to take it, but carried on until she hit a northbound back road, drove around the hill that the track she'd seen skirted, then walked to the top.

She kneeled down by some poison ivy which had turned a glorious orangey-red color with the fall. At the foot of the hill was a gently sloping dale. In the distance, she could see Shenandoah Mountain through the mist, and heard cardinals warbling on and off to greet it.

Kate knew the lay of the land well, because she and Rachel had grown up an hour's drive away, on a farm not much different from this one. That Arcadian spot was in the Virginia heartland, the last bit of wilderness to have fended off the maw of the excavators. An earthly paradise.

And two hundred yards from her vantage point, far from the main highway, was the spot where the kidnappers were hiding out.

The Mercedes could no longer be seen, but she knew right away that this was the place. There were three buildings. The farmhouse, from whose chimney rose a thin plume of smoke. A stable to the north of it, with fresh tire ruts leading to the doors, which in all likelihood was where they kept the cars. Beside the stable was a gasoline-fired generator. In the gap between the latter and the house there was a mound of dirt several yards high.

And finally there was a barn to the south, which they obviously weren't using to store hay. No barn she had ever seen as a child had the latest satellite communications antenna.

Kate pulled out her cell to confirm there was almost no coverage. Only one of the five bars was showing while the 3G icon was crossed out.

That antenna provides the bandwidth to monitor the girl in the dugout. It's here. They've got her inside.

She looked at her watch. Three minutes before the president's operation was due to begin.

Now she had to choose. She could call McKenna, explain what had happened and tell him to get David out of the operating theater. Then call in a heavily armed SWAT team, who would take a couple of hours to get down there and storm the farm. In the knowledge that by then White would have been forewarned and exacted whatever vengeance he had decided upon by remote control.

Or she could go in, with surprise on her side and trusting that God, luck and training would tip the balance her way in a mission impossible against untold enemies who outgunned her.

She hesitated for a second, wavering, for the umpteenth time in the past forty hours, between the call of duty and her feelings.

Finally, she picked up the cell.

ON THE OBSERVATION DECK, OPERATING THEATER 2

The best part was seeing the look on David's face when he realized he was there.

He had moved forward to shake White's hand, feigning indifference, but his eyes abruptly went glassy and betrayed a whirlwind of emotions. White was flattered to be the only one who held the key to what was going on inside David's head at that moment.

"Hello, Dr. Evans. I don't know if you remember me, we met at a conference in London a couple of years ago," *he said in his best British accent.*

There was a long hiatus while Dave looked at the iPad that White was clutching to his chest.

That's right, take note. I've got my finger on the button. One push and your daughter dies.

"Of course. In the Marblestone, wasn't it?"

"What an excellent memory you have."

That Dave himself had been obliged to corroborate his alias had been the icing on the cake. Not that White needed it. His highly placed employer had tipped him off about Peter Ravensdale some time back. He was second on the list of experts the White House had drawn up.

"Have you come all the way from London?"

"I've just flown in from New York. I rented a car at the airport and got here half an hour ago."

"It's quite a surprise to see you here."

"And an exciting opportunity for me to learn from you. They say you are faultless."

They had gotten in touch with the real Ravensdale on Tuesday, the same day Svetlana died. They sent him an e-mail from the State Department asking what his fees would be to supervise an operation and whether he'd be interested, without mentioning the patient's name. Ravensdale had replied to accept. He said they wouldn't even need to fly him over from London, because he would already be visiting patients in New York.

Eleven hours later he was dead, his corpse in a safe place, while his cell phone, e-mail account and documentation were in White's hands.

The president was right about reining in the NSA. It was so big that not even those it was meant to protect were immune from its prying and conniving. All it had taken to get White into the hospital had been to use PRISM software to tap into the Secret Service database, alter Ravensdale's details on file there to match White's, forge a British passport . . . et voilà, Peter Ravensdale had a new face.

When he showed up on the second floor that morning, a Secret Service agent had done no more than check his ID, frisk him and call McKenna. After all, he was merely an observer who wouldn't even come close to the president, right?

"I try to be," Dave said. "Besides, you will all ensure I don't make any mistakes."

Lowers uttered a pleasantry while Hockstetter mumbled an impudent remark about having to take what you could get. White ignored them. He was savoring the moment.

This was his masterstroke, his secret weapon for wiping away his victims' last remaining scrap of willpower. He was always in at the kill, to make sure they fulfilled his wishes. The face of a neighbor among the crowd, the mailman nobody noticed, the photographer poised behind his camera. The first time had been in Naples, when he had dressed up *as a cop to deliver the head of the elusive writer to the Mafia man who wanted him dead. From then on he couldn't resist seeing with his own eyes how the last domino passed the tipping point and toppled perfectly into place.*

And now the tall green-eyed man who was already on his way out of the observation deck was about to complete his masterpiece, his Sistine Chapel.

"Good luck, Dr. Evans. We'll be here, following your work with great interest."

32

After I quit the observation deck, I went back to my room. My presence wouldn't be required in the operating theater for a couple of hours. Sharon Kendall would take half that time to sedate the Patient. Dr. Wong would use the other hour to perform a craniotomy and lay bare the area on which I would work. She would make an incision around the skull, peel off the scalp and cut into the bone with a circular saw. Nothing you couldn't do yourself with household tools. Except that we do it accurately, so we can then put it all back together again.

I wasn't involved in any of that. Although short and simple, it was a very intense and physically tiring business which neurosurgeons in charge of the delicate parts usually delegated to residents and less experienced staff. It's not because of arrogance. An operating theater is very stressful, a thousand times more so in the exceptional situation we found ourselves in, in Theater 2. The idea was that the experts should be fresh when they got to work.

The very fact that I was sitting comfortably while the medical chief at one of the country's best hospitals was doing the donkey work prior to my operating on the president of the United States had to be the high-water mark of my career.

If my father had been alive, I would have called him that second. I'd have told good ol' Doc Evans the score. For sure he'd have given me some sage, homely and useless piece of advice, which would have warmed the cockles of my heart. If Rachel had still been around, she'd have been in there with me, keeping an eye on the Patient's readings and glancing at me now and again, when she thought I wasn't looking. And if I was alert enough, I could even have discerned a look of pride out of the corner of my eye. I know because she had always betrayed such a look.

They had both seen the kid I once was, and what I had made of myself. I thanked my lucky stars they weren't here now to see what I had become: a weapon in the hands of a murderer, as responsible as him for the heinous crime we were about to commit.

I remembered the day my dad had found me playing with the kitten's guts and initiated me in my career as a doctor. That day he forgave me. Twenty-six years on, as I stared blankly at the wall while a couple of bags of poison lurked in the instrument trolley drawer, I could only imagine him spitting in my face for betraying all that he had taught me.

Then I heard a quiet buzz. I had put Kate's phone in a desk drawer. I doubted White would be observing me now through the camera on my iPhone, but just in case I had stashed it away inside my doctor's bag.

I took out the BlackBerry, and when I read the text my heart derailed and tears filled my eyes. I had to read it again and again to check that my eyes weren't deceiving me.

FOUND HER. I'M GOING IN.

DON'T DO IT, DAVE. TRUST ME.

She's found her. But she doesn't have her yet. Anything might happen.

Then a second text landed.

WHATEVER HAPPENS, I'LL LOVE YOU ALWAYS.

There was knocking at the door. I dried my eyes quickly before I turned around.

It was Wong. She came in with coffee from the vending machine and a tired smile. If she could tell I'd been crying, she didn't say so. She leaned on the door, stirred the unappealing brew and nodded her head at me.

"I've lifted the lid, Evans. Now get in there and strut your stuff."

Kate

She went back to her car, opened the trunk, took off her leather jacket and threw it inside. She pulled a blanket off a lockbox and opened it with a tiny key from her key ring, then locked away her keys, purse, everything she had on her. She wanted to carry nothing that might get in her way or jingle.

She took an MP5 submachine gun out of the case. She had dismantled, cleaned, greased and reassembled it on Wednesday night, so it was combat-ready. The ammo situation was more worrying. She had only three small magazines, forty-five rounds in all, which ruled out continuous fire. She made sure she selected single-fire mode, fitted one of the magazines and clipped the other two to a special belt. She also donned her gun holster and SIG Sauer P229 pistol, then hooked them to the belt, too.

Lastly, she put on her Kevlar vest. It was a light service model, with the letters *SECRET SERVICE* embossed on it in yellow. Her mind went back to the intruders in the Evans house and the shadows of the PP-19 Bizon guns they toted.

Sixty-four shots per magazine, she thought as she patted the vest with her knuckles. *How many could this thing stop, if they hit me dead-on? Two, three?*

Don't think about it. Don't think about it.

She hesitated before she put her jacket back on. The combined weight of her jacket and vest would slow her down, but her white shirtsleeves were too obvious. The black jacket would help her steal across to the barn.

You can take it off when it's showtime. If you get to raise the curtain.

She climbed back up the hill, gripping the machine gun with

both hands. She would have to climb down the other side very carefully, taking advantage of such natural shelter as the vegetation would afford her. She stopped off at a copse halfway down, to rest and to take a last glance at the farm.

They're too confident no one will find this place; there's nobody on watch. Either that or they're too tired after last night's little errand.

There had been at least three of them in the car, so they were most probably resting up in the farmhouse. To take on that part of the farm by herself was impossible. There would be stairs, nooks, blind spots and a million other places for them to hide, and many obstacles for them to throw in her way.

If Julia's in there, we're done for.

But the little girl wasn't in there. She'd be in the barn, where they had their communications center and could watch her.

Okay, here's the plan. In you go, release her from wherever she is being held and run uphill as fast as your heels will carry you. Can't fail.

She couldn't help having a wry chortle at her own stupidity. Julia had been shut away in a tiny space she could not stand up straight in for more than sixty hours. She might be injured or sick, and undoubtedly she'd be in shock. It would be hard enough for her to walk, let alone run. Kate would have to carry her herself.

How much would she weigh—forty-five, fifty pounds? God, this'll be just great.

But she didn't have a better idea.

She came down the slope's last few yards with her heart beating nineteen to the dozen. Her breathing quickened and she could feel a sudden shift in the world around her. The light became brighter, harder, almost solid and unbreakable. Time slowed down and the leaves stopped falling from the trees to hover in midair. By the time she reached the barn door, her senses were as keen as could be, thanks to the adrenaline. She could distinguish every speck, every whorl in the grain and every little mossy shadow on the huge wooden door. She reached out for the rusty handle and could feel under her fingers the wrinkles from dozens of coats of paint applied over the decades. When she turned it, the quiet creaking was a thunderclap to her ears.

She pushed the door open enough for her to slip through. Inside it smelled of dung and rotting straw, a thick, hard stench that stung her nostrils. The place had two floors. The upper one had a window fitted with a pulley, while hay bales lined the walls of the lower one. Somebody had improvised a table by laying a thick, green tarp on one of the bales, which was covered in cell phones, guns, electronics and communications gear. And snoring on a chair behind it all, with his head dangling back, was a tall, bearded man dressed in a white shirt, boots and dungarees. Thousands of specks of dust shimmered in a shaft of daylight, which shone through the first-floor window and hit him in the face.

Something must have caught the man's attention, because in a tick he stopped snoring, blinked a few times and looked toward the door, and Kate.

"Freeze, asshole," she said, aiming at him.

The bearded guy sat up and screwed his eyes into a cruel squint.

"Hands up, real slow, and on your feet."

He complied. Kate could see great big sweat stains under his armpits as he raised his hands. She wondered whether he was one of the ones who had drilled holes into Vlatko Papić's head in Baltimore.

"I'm going to walk over," she said. "When I say so, you will walk toward me and away from the table. Don't even think about looking dow—"

She didn't finish her sentence. A gleam in the man's eye, a slight shrug of his shoulders put Kate on her guard. They weren't alone. There was somebody else, behind her, somebody about to attack. She ducked as a reflex action, dug one knee in the ground and toppled forward.

Not a second too soon. The bearded man jumped aside and threw himself on the hay bales, while a gun barrel took his place and poked into the shaft of light. There was a flash and a bang. A dozen bullets rent the air, right where Kate had been standing a moment before, then tore into the barn door.

In the dazzling light she couldn't see who had taken the shot or where he was. Kate fired at a shadow where the flash had come from, without thinking or aiming. She merely pulled the trigger once, twice, three times. A creak and a thud could be heard.

I got him. I got him.

"Whoa! Easy!" the man with the beard shouted. He cowered on the ground and had both his hands on his head.

She stood upright, with her gun aimed at him all the while, then moved over to where the light no longer dazzled her eyes. It took just one look for her to see the gunman was dead. One of the MP5's bullets had hit him in the eye and ripped off half his face. She turned back to the bearded guy.

"Don't even think about it. Don't even think about it, damn it."

The other guy had raised himself a little and his fingers held the handle of a pistol that had been sitting on top of the tarp. The barrel was aimed at Kate. His whole body was tense. He hadn't yet gotten to his knees, but he needed only to get a good grip on the gun and he'd be in firing position.

"Put your hands down. Now," she said. Her voice trembled in the middle of the *now*, making her sound like a nervous teenager.

Perhaps that was what encouraged the bearded man to give it a try, to close his fist and squeeze the trigger. The shot missed her, a yard overhead. But hers didn't. The first entered his right armpit, slicing through his axillary artery and also blowing his arm clean off. That shot alone would have been enough to make him bleed to death in a minute, but he didn't have time to die that way. The second bullet smashed through his rib cage, opened up a great gash in his flesh and dragged his lungs out through a hole twice as wide as the entry wound. The man tried to scream, but all that issued from his mouth was a gurgle of blood before he tumbled to the ground.

What a fool, Kate thought, *to think he was faster than a speeding bullet.*

She took a couple of paces toward him, to make certain he was no longer a threat. Blood gushed from the man's arm wound and seeped into the black, fertile dirt beneath him.

I have never killed anybody before, Kate said to herself. And then the previous night's events pricked her conscience. *By my own hand, that is.*

Shouts came from outside. The firefight had only lasted a few seconds but had made one hell of a noise. The shots must have been heard all over the valley.

On top of the table, and coming from the bearded man's belt and somewhere below the first gunman's body, there was a click and a commanding voice spoke in an alien tongue.

Here they come.

She slung the MP5 over her shoulder, went across to the bearded man and snatched the pistol from his defunct fingers. She aimed at the laptops and boxes of electronic gear on the table and emptied the clip into them, fanning out the shots. The bullets raked over everything, turning thousands of dollars' worth of equipment into smoking, worthless scrap.

So much for evidence. But maybe this will screw up their comms and buy us some more time.

She looked around anxiously and went back to mapping out the place in her head, as she had been doing before she was rudely interrupted by the shoot-out with the two scumbags. The barn had two big doors, one at each end. In between were the rows of hay bales, with a ten-foot-wide passageway down the middle. A ladder led to the hayloft, and that was it.

Julia. Where are you?

She had no time to look for her. The dead men's comrades would be there in no time to find out what was up. They'd be doubly dangerous with their military experience, albeit more predictable. They would regroup and attack from one of the doors, or from both at the same time.

Up. You must go up.

She dropped the pistol and climbed up the ladder. She ran to the window, which was a couple of yards from the ladder. Mounted on the window frame was the jib of a crane used to hoist the hay bales. She peeked outside and what she saw quickly confirmed her worst fears. There were three of them, at least as far as she could tell, and they were running over to the barn from the farmhouse.

Bad idea, you jerks. You don't all run together when there's a shooter nearby.

She had only a couple of seconds before she would lose her line of sight, but she needed no more. She aimed eighteen inches in front of the last man and fired. White's foot soldier, a thin young man, went down with a splotch of crimson in the middle of his gray sweater. The others were now out of sight, sheltered by the building.

Now they have the upper hand. One will come from each end. They know I'm up here. They have walkie-talkies to get their act together. And even if they don't, they only have to speak Serbian for me not to know what on earth they're up to.

The loft was very narrow and there were inch-wide gaps between the floorboards. There was nothing to shield her, nor was there anywhere to hide. And if she lay down flat she could cover only one of the two doors.

I'm a sitting duck up here. And if I try to go down the ladder, I'll be a sitting duck that can't fire back.

While she tried to decide which door to aim at, she saw the one on the right open a little. She fired twice at it, then rolled over and fired to the left, just to confuse them and make them believe she was not alone. But it was futile. The door planks were very thick and the bullets could not burrow through them. And the attackers had a much more evil plan in mind. There was the sound of breaking glass and columns of flames shot up on either side of the barn, making quick work of the dry hay.

Molotov cocktails. I hadn't thought of that. The cunning sons of bitches.

This scenario wasn't covered in any Secret Service handbook.

There isn't a book in the world that can tell you what to do when you're alone, trapped in a hayloft and surrounded by enemies covering your escape routes with automatic weapons.

Kate could hear squealing. Faint and muffled, but unmistakable. She looked below and amid the smoke she could see a patch in the middle of the barn that was a different color, with a metal ring to one side of it. Then she knew what the mound of dirt was doing outside.

Julia was buried alive down there.

"Julia, baby! Don't worry, it's Auntie Kate!"

"Rats! Rats!"

And there's no book in the world that can tell you how to deal with that situation while rats are eating your niece alive.

33

An operating theater where a craniotomy has just been performed has a particular smell to it. Quite apart from the disinfectant, the chemicals and your own sweat. It's the odor of sawn bones and blood. When you fill your nostrils, you realize you have breathed in part of the patient, who is now part of you. It's a bond that will be with you forever. It may sound sick, even horrific, which is why we surgeons shy away from talking about it. But that doesn't make it any less real.

The president was seated and fully conscious. Once the painful job of removing the skull flap was complete, we had woken him up. Dr. Wong had drilled four holes in his cranium and slotted into them a device known as a Mayfield skull clamp, which would stop the Patient's head from budging so much as a hairbreadth.

I stood in front of him, so he could see me. Although it was hard for him to recognize me, shrouded as I was in a surgical apron, with a mask and glasses fitted with surgical eye loupes. But he certainly recognized the tiger embroidered on my cap.

"Dr. Evans, what a surprise!"

Sedation brings out the comedian in some patients. That makes it much more fun. Normally there are peals of laughter all around, but today there was no such mirth. Everybody was tense, expectant.

"Sir, Dr. Wong has enabled access to the area where your tumor lies. We will now place a monitor in front of you showing pictures and words. It is very important that you read those words aloud and describe the pictures as they appear. That way I can use a stimulator to distinguish between healthy tissue and the tumor."

I had just gotten into position when the operating theater's phone rang. My heart leaped. For a moment, I dreamed it would be Kate, telling me she had found Julia already.

"It was the neuropathologist," said the nurse who had answered. "We sent him tissue samples. He confirms the diagnosis: it's glioblastoma multiforme."

"Right you are," I said, masking my disappointment.

I peered into the president's brain, ready to do battle with my deadliest foe. There it was, half-hidden in the brain tissue. Nobody but an expert could tell the difference. GBM is invisible at first sight, and that's where its strength lies. It is identical to the tissue around it; it's just that it's immortal and the host organism can't stop it.

I prodded a finger into an area that I knew was clean. The brain has the same texture as toothpaste when you've left the cap off the tube for a while. Slightly rubbery, weak but hardy.

"Did you feel that, Mr. President?"

"I can feel nothing. But for some reason I can't stop thinking about a dog I once had," he said in surprise.

"There are no nerve endings in the brain, sir. Nothing I do will hurt you. But manipulating it does lead to unexpected results. I have probably stimulated that memory by applying pressure."

I kept on prodding my way around, using my hands to find out what was what. I wanted to get a feel for the healthy tissue. Then I moved to the problem area and prodded again, very slowly. I could feel the tumor under the rubber of my glove. It had a softer feel and was a slightly different color.

"Nimbus."

The nurse handed me a long, black, two-pronged instrument. That gizmo was used to give tiny electric shocks, to stimulate the patient's brain.

"Start reading, Mr. President."

"Dog. A boy throwing a ball."

"Very good, keep going. Don't stop."

When you locate the tumor, you have to use the right tool for the job.

"Cavitron."

Now the nurse gave me an implement with a steel nozzle, linked by a pipe to a three-foot-high machine. That instrument, with a name that sounded like something straight out of *Transformers*, was my own private machine gun. A device which emits ultrasonic waves, fragments tissue and sucks it away. But the Cavitron can't tell the difference between healthy tissue and tumor. You need a steady hand—and totally accurate hand-eye coordination—in order not to probe one millimeter more than needed and fry the patient's brain in the process. And a blob must not look like a tumor to you when it is in fact brain, because then . . .

"Potato, potato, potato."

. . . then the patient gets stuck with a word that will become the sum total of their vocabulary for the rest of their miserable life.

I drew back the aspirator tip just in time. It had been a close call. The operating lights were very bright, so I was getting hotter and hotter. Sweat began to cloud my vision.

"Well, it's not there. Thanks, sir," I said offhandedly.

I turned to the nurse.

"Turn up the air-con."

"Dave, the patient's temperature . . . ," Sharon Kendall objected.

"Put a few thermal wraps on his chest and legs if need be. But I have to cool down right now."

We carried on for quite a while, with no noise in the theater other than the sucking of the aspirator, the monitor's constant pinging and the president's voice, monotonously reciting the things he saw flitting across the screen.

All of a sudden he stopped.

"I'm bushed."

It always happens. Even though they cannot move, the process upsets the brain's chemical balance and spurs a feeling of terrible fatigue.

"Don't give up, sir. We must go on. Just think that each word you say means one more day to enjoy with your daughters."

From then on, I lost all track of time. I do that whenever I think hard, and never in my life had I thought as hard as I was doing right then. I drew a door inside my head and went through it, leaving all my cares behind. Somewhere Kate was trying to save my daughter's life. When I had finished what I was doing, I would have to give in to White's blackmail, if she should have failed, or even if she hadn't, because I had no way of knowing and didn't want to run any risks. But in the meantime, this was the operation I'd spent my whole life preparing for. And for everything I held sacred, I was going to get it right.

I kept on prodding, questioning, sucking.

"That's it, then, we're done. I can't remove any more. What do you say, Mr. President? Will that do, or should I take some more off?"

The president laughed out loud. A short and tired but genuine laugh.

"There was a barber near the Wrigley Building who always used to say the same thing. What do your colleagues think?"

I took off my glasses with the eye loupes and stepped back. Dr. Wong inspected the work area and mumbled in approval.

"I agree. There's no more tumor tissue to be seen. A bang-up job, Dr. Evans. Do you agree, gentlemen?"

The observers' voices could be heard over the intercom.

"You've been outstanding, Dr. Evans," Lowers said. "I feel honored to have seen the operation for myself. Dr. Hockstetter?"

There was an awkward silence, but in the end even Hockstetter had to concede.

"Good work, Evans," he said grudgingly.

"Marvelous. I can't wait to see the final result," White said.

Of course you can't, I thought.

"Good. Just one more thing before we close up. Nurse, the Gliadel," Wong said.

The nurse went to the second drawer down on the instrument trolley, took out the pouches and gave one to Dr. Wong. She pulled at the corner flap and tore the aluminum packet open. She grabbed some tweezers, picked out one of the patches and handed it to me.

"Here you are, David."

I stared at the poisonous wafer. I had only to put it in place and White's demands would be met, my daughter would be safe. Nobody would ever be the wiser.

I took up the forceps and readied myself to kill the president of the United States of America.

Kate

There wasn't a second to lose. Heading toward the lower floor and the doors meant certain death. If the flames didn't do away with her, then either of the two henchmen loitering outside would. Waiting was agony, not only for her, but for the little girl. She had to get Julia out of that deathtrap before the vermin feasted on her.

She had only one shot left. She turned around, ran to the window and stepped into the void. She gained a foothold on the jib, which groaned under her weight. There was a fifteen-foot drop. If that wasn't enough to break her neck, then the Serbs would finish the job.

Come on. Don't look down.

She put her other foot on top of the jib. Now her whole weight bore down on it. She had to wave her arms about to keep her balance and was in danger of falling off.

I can't. I can't.

Then all of a sudden Rachel was down there, like that time thirty years earlier. They were both little girls again, and Rachel was bawling at the top of her lungs for Kate to get down from that branch before it snapped.

Move, you dork. Move!

She took one step. Another. Then a third.

She got to the end. Never mind her lingering fear of heights, never mind the smoke and flames that began to spill through the window she had just left behind. She could feel the jib wobbling perilously as she crouched, kneeled down, then reached out into the void. At the last second, her fingers got a good grip on the hook that hung from the pulley. Gravity did the rest and she descended at full speed.

She let go of the hook, flexed her knees and rolled over as she hit the ground, but even so that was not enough to absorb the shock from the fall. She heard a crack and felt a flash of pain run up her right leg.

Something's broken. Shit, that hurts.

But now wasn't the time for diagnoses. She struggled to her feet and limped to the barn's north corner. She seized the MP5, changed the magazine and took a peep around the edge. Ten feet away, smoking a cigarette with a smirk on his face and a gun aimed casually at the door, was one of the kidnappers. It was the bald guy who had passed by her on David's porch. Kate gave him no warning, didn't ask him to raise his hands, not this time. She aimed, fired and blew his head off in half a second.

She heard something behind her.

She didn't get to turn around, nor did she know what hit her or hear the shots. She was floored suddenly, and there was blood pumping out of an arm she couldn't move. A bullet had wounded her. She was vaguely aware several more had hit her in the back, but it seemed the vest had done its job and stopped them. Or at least they didn't hurt as much as that big hole in her forearm.

The MP5 was beneath her, rendered useless. All she had left was the pistol. Still in a crouch, she grabbed it with her left hand, drew it, spun around and fired, as she had in thousands of drills over the years.

Her aggressor stared at her in disbelief. The bullet had hit him in the stomach and tunneled its way right through. Kate didn't make the mistake he had and kept firing until she emptied the clip, without missing a shot. The Serb fell to his knees and wobbled before he keeled over to go the way of all flesh.

Maybe I haven't had a life. Perhaps this is what I was waiting for, Kate thought.

She didn't stop. Howling in pain, she stood up, somehow took off her leather jacket, and pulled it over her head before going into the blazing barn. The hay bales were all aflame and had turned the place into an inferno that had reached the rafters. In no time the whole thing would come crashing down on top of the rat hole with Julia in it.

Gasping for air, Kate crawled her way into the middle of the barn. She couldn't see, her eyes were streaming and her limbs were racked with pain. She groped along and probed the floor, now covered in glowing ash from the burning hay bales.

Her fingers stumbled across a metallic object. A round piece of iron, fastened to something belowground.

The ring.

She pulled at it, but it didn't budge. She had to stand up and heave with all her strength. Then the trampled dirt on top of the trapdoor swiftly gave way, throwing Kate onto her back. She got up in time to see a dozen dark shapes scuttling out of the pit.

She peered in and there was Julia. She was covered in blood and there were bite marks on her face and arms. Her hair was tangled, her pajamas in rags, her skin plastered in dirt and sweat. But she was alive.

Julia reached up and Kate lugged her out of the hole, barely noticing her weight. She ran to the door, cradling Julia in her arms, while behind them the flaming rafters began to split and fall. They escaped from the barn just in time, and their limbs intertwined as they rolled on the grass.

There they lay in each other's arms for several minutes, sobbing in silence until they got their breath back. Julia still clutched a long, narrow piece of wood.

"They came after me, Auntie Kate. This is all I had to protect me. I pulled it off the wall."

"You did great, baby."

"Take me to Mommy, Auntie Kate. She'll be worried."

Kate burst into tears again. She kissed Julia's forehead tenderly and, without letting go of her, pulled out her phone and punched in a number."

"It's okay, honeybunch. You'll be home soon."

34

I raised my eyes to the balcony, forceps in hand, and looked for White.

You got what you wanted, I thought. *So gloat, you pig.*

But as I was on the verge of placing the wafer on the area where I'd operated, something made me halt. White was there, third person on the left in the row of seats, but unlike the others, he wasn't looking at me but at his lap. He was checking out his iPad. And when he raised his head again, surprise was writ large on his face. Rage. Fear. Defeat.

I could read it in his eyes as clearly as if I were monitoring his tablet.

Kate's there. Kate's done it.

I lifted my hand to my mask and lowered it. I wanted him to see me smile in defiance over what I was about to do.

Quite simply, I loosened the forceps and dropped the wafer on the floor.

"Dr. Evans?" the nurse said, confused.

On the balcony, White frantically tapped away on his iPad, then stood up. I heard him say something to McKenna and open the door. And then I was starkly aware he could still do a great deal of harm, in ways I couldn't begin to imagine. But I couldn't tell McKenna the truth. At that moment, like the naive idiot I was, I still thought I could worm my way out of trouble.

"Watch it, David. You've just trashed a thousand bucks," Dr. Wong said.

"Well, here goes another three grand," I said, snatching the Gliadel pouch from her hands and upending it.

"That is not funny, David."

I went over to the nurse, grabbed the other pouch, ripped it open and emptied that, too. Everybody looked at me like I was crazy.

"Listen, Stephanie. I have reason to believe these two bags were not operative. Would you be so kind as to order two new ones from Pharmacy and close up the patient for me? I'm exhausted and am going to get some rest."

And leaving everybody openmouthed, I ran out of the theater.

I tore off my apron and gloves and flung them into the toxic-waste container in the theater annex. White had left the observation room before I quit the theater, so he wouldn't know I was after him. That was what I wanted.

He was a few yards ahead of me. I looked out into the corridor and saw him get into the elevator, nodding to the Secret Service men as he went. They had been briefed to stop people from getting in, not to prevent them from getting out, so they didn't move a muscle. I ducked back into the annex, where he couldn't see me, and when the elevator doors were shut, rather than running after him I went to my room, opened the door and reached for my white coat. Kate's cell phone and my car keys were in the pocket. At a brisk pace but acting as if all was well, I went to the elevator and pressed the DOWN button.

I was not going to let him get away. Not merely because of what he could do to us that minute, but because of what he might do in the future. And that was how I made the biggest blunder of my life. To set the record straight a little, I must say that I was unaware of the overall situation, nor did I know that at the time I was getting into the elevator, Kate was lurching along a crane boom, fifteen feet up in the air.

Then again, to be frank, I wanted White for myself, not in McKenna's hands. I wanted to make him pay for Svetlana, for Juanita, for my daughter.

I hit the button for the garage. White had said he'd driven over, so that was where he would head, not the entrance hall. I held off stamping my feet in impatience until the doors were closed and I was out of sight of the stone-faced agents watching the elevator. When they opened again, I ran to my car, I started the engine and with a screech of tires I hurtled toward the exit.

White was putting his ticket in the box that raises the barrier when my car turned the corner, right behind him. I saw him look up and see me in the rearview mirror. He took off and got under the barrier with inches to spare. I lost vital seconds stopping to dig out my employee pass. By the time I got out, he was a couple of blocks away. He was driving a black Lincoln, which were a dime a dozen in this goddamned city, and I nearly lost him when he took the Sixteenth Street turnoff. I headed south on a hunch and spotted him a few blocks later, fifty yards ahead of me. I almost crashed into a bus as I ran a red light to get close to him, but at the next light he pulled away again. He turned onto K Street and I gained some ground at the next light. I had him within a few car lengths of me. When he took the Key Bridge turnoff, I knew my chance had come. He would have no escape from me there. I fought my way past the three cars between us, then overtook him on the left side. I spun the wheel to swerve in front of him and slammed on the brakes at the same time. I could feel the rubber sticking to the surface as the car skidded across the freeway. The Lexus cut off White's Lincoln and nosed it toward the concrete barrier.

White had no option but to hit the brakes.

I reached under the seat, pulled out the Glock I had threatened Hockstetter with, and aimed it at him. The drivers who were now stuck behind him banged on their horns like crazy, until they saw the gun. The nearest got out of their cars and ran pell-mell the other way, scared senseless.

I walked up to White's window.

"Get out. Now."

White opened the door and got out, with his hands in the air. One of them was holding his iPad.

And he was smiling.

"So much for the guy who never fought."

"Don't move, asshole. Tell me where my daughter is."

White ignored me and strode over to the walkway. He leaped over the barrier and approached the steel handrail, then drew back his hand back and hurled his iPad into the Potomac. I saw it arc through the air—with the Louis Vuitton cover flapping, like the world's most expensive bird—and disappear.

I went after him, feeling stupid. Why did everybody ignore me whenever I brandished a pistol?

"I hope whoever you've sent is better than my gang, Dave. I really do. They'll have to get a move on to save your daughter from the rats."

I came closer still, aiming at him constantly. He was calm and collected, and looked over the handrail, toward the White House.

"I was so close. Oh well, I'll get there next time."

"Who was it, White? Who hired you?"

He turned around and looked at me, as if seeing me for the first time. Then he looked at the gun and squinted.

"Well, I could kill you right now, Dave. If I don't, it's because I still have uses for you. I need you to take the rap for everything."

"That won't happen, White. You're going down and they'll throw away the key."

He smiled again.

"You've been a worthy opponent. Maybe someday I'll come back for you. Perhaps by then you'll have learned how to flip the safety catch."

Feeling like an even bigger fool, I bent my arm to look for the safety catch on the side of the gun. A catch that Glocks totally lack, by the way. White had pulled one over on me, again.

When I looked back up, White had climbed onto the handrail. Before I could stop him, he joined his hands and dived into the Potomac.

EPILOGUE

Dr. Evans's Diary

Unless you've been living in a cave for the past five years, you'll know what happened next.

Moments after White jumped, I got a text from Kate. I climbed back into the car, made headway on the bridge and drove over to the Virginia side. The cops were on my tail almost right away and the TV networks were soon airing the chase live. But the Lexus had a full tank and the cops had a long way to go before I had to stop and they could catch me. I was in search of my daughter, with my foot down hard and wearing a grin from ear to ear. All I wanted was to hug her again, and nothing and nobody was going to get in my way. I think the CNN chopper's camera filmed me running from the car like a scalded cat and over to the girls. Kate, wounded as she was, hadn't let go of Julia's hand for a second.

You may also have seen the YouTube video of what happened on the bridge. The guy who filmed it with his cell phone had smoker's hands and was as fidgety as a frightened puppy. He was standing so far off that you can only just see me pointing a gun at somebody hidden by a car. Then something can be seen falling, a noise can be heard, that's all.

That recording was what saved me. Although the prosecutors did all they could to deny it, the truth is that somebody was in the car, and it wasn't Dr. Ravensdale. "Coincidentally" the hard disks in St. Clement's security system all crashed the very moment White ran out of the observation deck. There isn't a single picture of him anywhere.

Nothing.

In White's absence, with no signs of his employer and all his hatchet men killed on the farm, the only one left to carry the can

347

was yours truly, so the press and the attorney's office threw the book at me. Svetlana's body turned up at the farm, and they found bits of my skin and blood under her fingernails. That asshole White must have put them there that Wednesday night. Remember when I told you I had woken up with deep scratches on my forearm that I was at a loss to explain? Well, now we know. It terrifies me to think that while I was sleeping like a log in my living room, the Serbs smuggled the girl's body into my house, scratched my skin with her dead fingernails and put me in the frame for her murder. Fortunately my defense attorney got me off that charge, owing to the timing of those scratches. Many witnesses had seen my bare and injury-free forearms on Wednesday morning, while the forensics proved Svetlana had been dead for longer than that. White had certainly planned to kill me after the operation in some way that would implicate me even more in Svetlana's death. Luckily, it never came to that, but it gives me the creeps just thinking of it.

Our house fire didn't help much, either. All the cameras and surveillance gear behind the walls went up in flames. White must have planted incendiary bombs and fire accelerant, and set them off before he ran out. We cannot tell what commands he tapped into his iPad when he saw me drop the Gliadel wafers on the floor, beyond the one that opened the rat cages. But I bet anything you like one of them was set to burn my house down.

The firefighters said it was the quickest and hottest fire they had ever seen. The house was already a fiery furnace when they got there, and within the hour there were only cinders left. They had their work cut out just to keep the blaze from spreading to the neighbors' houses.

We lost everything. Our home, our belongings, our memories. What hurt me most was losing Rachel's farewell letter and her college sweatshirt. Julia, her cuddly toys and photo with her mom, the same one I had on my phone display and my bedside table. She always looked at it before she went to sleep. It was lucky that I had digital copies of all our photos. We salvaged that much.

My cell phone also caught fire, by the way. Not as dramatically as the house did. A nurse could smell burning in my room and saw smoke coming from inside my doctor's bag. She bravely put it out with an extinguisher, but the cops could find nothing but a puddle of plastic and aluminum.

What did not catch fire was my laptop, which wasn't at home where I'd left it but in my consulting room, buried under case files. Inside the Secret Service found dozens of e-mails—which I'd never written—sent from my account, plotting the assassination in conjunction with far-right groups in eastern Europe.

So they accused me of conspiracy to commit murder, and you all know that the trial by media condemned me from day one. This country never had the chance to try Lee Harvey Oswald, John Hinckley was found to be insane . . . But I was sitting pretty for the media circus to chew me up and spit me out. The affluent, crazy, WASP terrorist brain surgeon. I was the perfect hate figure for a whole nation.

Nobody believed the story I told from the word go, the same one I've just told you.

Many still think Mr. White is a fabrication. They never found his body in the Potomac. They found no fingerprints in the car, only a couple of blond hairs that would make a great DNA sample but will not be much use without any comparative data. But at least I'll know what to look for when I hear of a mysterious death. I'll know he's out there, and so will you.

I hear there are even web forums for amateur investigators who believe every word of my story and are looking for traces of Mr. White everywhere, not only in every news story but in the past, too, even back to November 22, 1963. Back then, White wasn't even a sparkle in his father's eye, so don't sweat it, guys.

Someone who didn't stop sweating it was the US attorney. If White's plans had worked out as he intended, I would have been done for, I'm sure. I never believed for a second that he hadn't planned on putting all the blame on me. Maybe I'm mistaken and all the incriminating proof against me was no more than a diversionary tactic to be used in an emergency, like the ink spread by a panic-stricken octopus. But I don't think so.

Luckily things didn't quite work out for him. If I hadn't been alive to defend myself, if I had wound up dead, the courts would have promptly found me guilty, end of story. My attorney fought tooth and nail, however, and we had Kate and Julia's testimony on our side, so he got most of the charges dropped. Most, but not all. Obstruction of justice, conspiracy to make an attempt on the president's life and some other stuff still stood. You must have seen the trial on TV. When I was sentenced to five years' imprisonment in a supermax, half the public gallery began to whistle while the other half burst into applause.

When I heard the sentence, I was thunderstruck. I could not fathom the unfairness of it all. My family and I had already paid in blood and great pain, and that we did not deserve. They threw me in a cell in the courthouse, where I awaited my final transfer to prison.

And then a massive guy with a red goatee, in a dark suit and shades, came along and handed me a cell phone between the bars. I put it to my ear and was blown away to hear the First Lady's voice.

"Dr. Evans, just answer me one thing, honestly. Can you do that?"

She sounded tense, furious and drained.

"Yes, ma'am."

"Did you want to kill him?"

"No, ma'am."

"You took those bags of poison into the operating theater. You gave in to blackmail. You betrayed my trust and the whole nation's."

"Ma'am, I'm a father. A maniac had my daughter. You, more than anybody, must understand why I did it."

"And you knew full well where your duty lay."

"Yes, ma'am. I had to save your husband. And isn't that exactly what I did?"

She hung up without another word. I gave the phone back to

McKenna, who stared at me with such hatred that I was grateful there were bars between us. A sad amateur like me had trampled his professional pride into the dirt. I almost felt sorry for the guy. Almost.

"You won't last a week in the joint, doc. I've got friends inside who would all love to shank you for a half pack of Camels."

Scrub that. I didn't feel sorry for him at all.

"Hey, McKenna. Does that mean you take back your apology?"

His footfalls as he charged off like a furious elephant were music to my ears.

It turns out that crime doesn't pay, but saving your patient from a tumor does. In the end, they didn't lock me up in Cell Block D at the Leavenworth pen. My attorney informed me that the White House had pulled strings to keep me apart from most of the prison population, a move which earned their approval ratings a couple of points in the blue states but lost them eight in the red states. It is said they weighed up the idea of a pardon, but voters wouldn't stand for it. I'm still the man many Americans love to hate.

I'm lucky they didn't put me in a special wing either, with the pedophiles and rapists. I think that call by the First Lady earned me some brownie points. I've done my time here, on death row. Where I've avoided getting a knife in the guts, but where the mental torture has been much tougher. That's why cons hate solitary.

The weirdest thing is that I've been doing time for longer than he would have lived had I not operated on him. That's gratitude for you, from those on high.

And what's to become of me? I don't know.

It's infinitely harder to start afresh than to let yourself go under. My life, as I knew it, was wrecked within a week by an unscrupulous psychopath. I haven't seen my daughter since the trial, when she hugged me good-bye.

"Thanks, Daddy."

She said no more, and she didn't have to.

We chat on the phone for ten minutes every three days, the

most they'll allow me. Basically, I do the talking; I read her stories and tell her about her mother. She hasn't been very talkative since the goings-on, but Jim and Aura are doing what they can about that with lots of Virginia tomatoes and occasional trips to the fair. They've ended up looking after Julia. I'm glad somebody got what they wanted out of all this mess. And frankly, after what my little girl's been through, my in-laws' plan to spoil her sounds good to me.

With a little help from Kate.

Kate, logically, was busted out of the Secret Service. Her statement of the facts was exhaustive and spared none of the gory details, and from the start she took the blame. The attorney's office didn't file charges, after weighing up her impeccable service record and her heroic action at the Rappahannock farm. But she couldn't avoid getting expelled, or dodge the shaming looks from her colleagues.

I can remember her still, taking the stand, with her left hand on the Bible because her right hand was still in a sling, testifying how she had tracked down Svetlana's boyfriend's address just in time to see some shady individuals leaving, whom she decided to follow. When I think of her driving through the night, facing that gang alone and unmasked, my heart aches in gratitude for the huge sacrifice she made.

The Maryland Board of Physicians revoked my license. Never again will I be able to practice medicine in the United States, but these hands were made for healing. I do not plan to use them for anything other than surgery. So I guess I'll collect the advance royalties for this book, take Julia and go to some other country, warmer climes where I can be of help. Both of us have earned the right to forget and start over.

And before you think of berating me, as many others have done, for accepting an offer from a major publishing house and writing my story to try to retrieve something from all this, may I remind you that it was your curiosity that made you want to buy the book in the first place. Unless you've ripped it off from the Internet. In that case, you owe me for all the hours of entertainment you've had, buddy.

I'm done. The jailers will come shortly for me, to escort me from death row. It's just that I, as opposed to the other inmates here, will walk the other way, out of darkness and into light and freedom. Soon the gates will swing open, I'll be out on the street and Julia will be there, waiting for me. Will she have a smile on her face? Will she run into my arms, or will I have to go and lift her up, hug her and swear up and down that never again will we be parted?

And most importantly, will the years have changed her, or will she still have the same deep, innocent stare and electric-blue eyes she gets from her mother, the love of my life?

I'll leave you now. I can hear them coming.

I'll find out soon enough.

ACKNOWLEDGMENTS

I have so many people to thank.

To Antonia Kerrigan and her team: Lola, Hilde, Victor . . . Thanks for spreading the word.

To Martin Roberts, who has translated this book flawlessly and with consummate skill.

To Rodrigo Pedrosa, a great neurosurgeon and good friend, for setting me straight on medical matters and providing a great deal of help. And Rachel, his lovely wife, an anesthesiologist, for filling me in on suicide methods. Any medical errors there may be in this book are all theirs. Just kidding.

To Manuel Soutiño and Manel Loureiro, for their patience in reading through the manuscript again and again—as ever—to soothe my anxiety while I worked on it. I love you.

To all the dream team at Atria Books: Judith Curr, Johanna Castillo, Ben Lee . . . and all the rest whom I cannot name here but who have done so much for my books.

To my children, whose love has been the inspiration for this novel and to whom I dedicate the book, even if they cannot read it just yet. For you I would kill all the presidents in the world. Twice over.

To Catuxa, the best partner a writer could have. Thanks for being there.

And to you, dear reader, thanks again for making my books a success in forty countries and making this storyteller's dreams come true. Best wishes to you all, and I have one last favor to ask. If you have enjoyed the book, please write and tell me about it:

juan@juangomezjurado.com
twitter.com/juangomezjurado